MORE PRAISE FOR ANN LAWRENCE!

VIRTUAL DESIRE

"*Virtual Desire* is a romantic and sensual tour de force. I give it my highest recommendation."

—*Word Museum*

"*Virtual Desire* tells a wonderful tale of love, friendship, faith, honor and courage. . . . It's pure enjoyment from the first page to the last!"

—*Old Book Barn Gazette*

"P.E.A.R.L. award–winner Ann Lawrence is a natural storyteller. Slow and sweet, hot, spicy, and unpredictable, [her book] is a testament to the power of love."

—*Paranormalromance Reviews*

"Ann Lawrence demonstrates a definite flair for creating characters and stories that leave the reader begging for more!"

—*Bookaholics.com*

VIRTUAL HEAVEN

"Brilliantly done, *Virtual Heaven* is a must for fans of fantasy and recommended for anyone else seeking something new and exciting. 4 ¹/₂ stars!"

—*Romantic Times*

"*Virtual Heaven* is an incomparable debut novel that shatters the soul and touches the heart with passion and high adventure. Brava!"

—Deb Stover, bestselling author of *Another Dawn*

"One stunning story. Ms. Lawrence is without a doubt one writer on the way to the top. Splendid!"

—*Bell, Book and Candle*

"Ann Lawrence's clever and imaginative debut novel establishes her as an exciting new talent. With a modern-day heroine and a hero perfect for any reality, *Virtual Heaven* is a nonstop romantic fantasy."

—Kathleen Nance, bestselling author of *The Warrior*

NOTHING ELSE MATTERED

A hand touched Cristina's bare shoulder. The hand was callused, rough. *His.*

Durand stroked down her arm to her hand and entwined his fingers with hers. "I could not stay away," he whispered at her ear, his breath warm on her bruised cheek.

The heat of his body warmed her, thrilled her, drove all conscience, all shame, away.

In answer, she drew their linked hands to her mouth. She rubbed the back of his fingers against her lips.

Vows no longer mattered.

Nothing mattered but his touch.

Lord Of The Mist

Ann Lawrence

LOVE SPELL   NEW YORK CITY

A LOVE SPELL BOOK®

July 2001

Published by

Dorchester Publishing Co., Inc.
276 Fifth Avenue
New York, NY 10001

ISBN 0-505-52443-0

The name "Love Spell" and its logo are trademarks of Dorchester Publishing Co., Inc.

Printed in the United States of America.

Visit us on the web at www.dorchesterpub.com.

Lord of the Mist is set near my father's birthplace of Portsmouth, England. When I was deciding where to place my hero's castle, I automatically thought of the Porchester ruins. Then I researched historical events that took place at or near Porchester and found just what I was looking for. Still, I felt my hero needed his own castle which I've constructed from some of my favorites of the times. Therefore, I've taken a few liberties with history, but nothing that should make a scholar scream. As usual, there are also anachronistic phrases, words, and objects in my story for clarity.

I thank my parents for the many stories of Portsmouth that started me looking there for a setting. I also thank the folks at CraftyCelts.com for help with torques, and Rachel for help with my nursing questions. For my herbal knowledge, I bow to my daughter's patience as we played with soap and sweet scents.

Last, I thank Jon Paul Ferrara for his art that brings the tale to life.

Lord Of The Mist

"There's nothing worse in the world than
a shameless woman—save some other woman."

—Aristophanes
Thesmophoriazusae (410 B.C.)

Prologue

The forest of Ravenswood Manor, England
Summer 1204

Cristina knelt among the tree roots and gathered some ferns for her nosegays. She worked quickly, for the men who escorted her, three woodcutters, were almost finished with their task.

Little light remained to guide them along the road to the village. Mist enveloped the land; it curled from the nearby stream, entwined low-hanging branches, and obscured the men who bundled twigs nearby.

As she rose, the ground beneath her knees trembled. Her heart in her throat, she stared ahead between the trees, searching for those who must be coming straight toward her.

Horsemen.

"Cristina," one of the woodcutters called. "Beware!"

She stepped deeper into the protective shadows. A

phalanx of horses burst into view, tearing the web of mist by the stream.

The lead horse, huge, towering, black as night, churned the ground a scant five feet before her, its rider oblivious to her presence in the shelter of the trees. The ferns fell from her fingers. The beat of hooves stole her breath.

More horsemen coalesced from the mist behind the leader.

His black mantle flew like two wings from his shoulders. She knew him by the heavy gold torque about his neck, the black and gold caparison on his horse.

Ravenswood's lord—Durand de Marle.

She maintained her place, struck to stone by the massive horses, the wind that tore at her gown.

"Did you see him?" one of the men asked her.

"Who?"

"Why, the king."

"Nay, I did not see him," she whispered.

The horsemen were spirits riding the wind as they burst through the fog. They were close enough to touch, a king among them, but she had seen only *him*.

They thundered past, shaking the earth, filling the air with the scents of horses, men, leather, and steel.

The mist swirled in and he was gone.

Chapter One

Ravenswood Castle, England
May 1205

Durand de Marle stood at the foot of his wife's bier and studied her face. "You are lovely, Marion." He touched her cold hand and rubbed the smooth gold of her ring with his thumb. "As lovely in death as you were in life."

Truly she looked to him as if only asleep, as if she might arise to chastise him for being gone so long. Her woolen gown of soft blue was one he did not recognize. Her jewels were those he had given her on their wedding day—long ropes of pearls from the Holy Land, a girdle of silver and gold disks. "Your sister has done well by you." Idly he rearranged a fold of her skirt.

He circled the small private chapel and examined with close attention a tapestry he had not noticed before. The subject, the martyrdom of Saint Stephen, did not lift his heavy spirit. Finally his steps returned him to the bier.

He glanced down at the embroidered cushions placed for mourners that they might pray in comfort by Lady Marion's side. With a sigh, he sank down on one.

Prayer escaped him.

Forgiveness escaped him.

One of the thick candles on the small marble altar guttered and was extinguished with a sharp scent of wax and smoke. He watched the thin thread of smoke rise to the whitewashed ceiling.

He counted seventeen wax candles. How many hours had they been lighted? How many moments until he was plunged into concealing darkness?

Rising, he again paced the length and breadth of the chamber. "Why can I not pray?" he asked of the martyred Stephen.

Two more candles flickered into oblivion.

"Will I fare better in darkness?" He pinched out two more. Deep shadows filled the corners of the small chapel. Returning to the bier, he knelt and clasped his hands, his gaze on his wife's face. Marion's features, cast now in shadow, looked like those of an innocent girl.

"Forgive the sins of my wife," Durand began. "Forgive the winter cold of my heart."

As if conjured by magic, the fragrance of spring came to him.

Sweet violets, wet leaves, rich earth.

He rose and turned to seek the source of the lush scents. At the rear of the chapel, by an ancient baptismal font, garbed all in white, stood a ghost.

"Forgive me, my lord, for intruding on your prayers," the ghost said softly, then stepped backward, closer to a rank of candles by the chapel entrance.

Not a spirit—a woman.

In her arms, she held a huge basket filled with flowers—the source of the wonderful perfume.

"Nay. Stay." He held up a hand, palm out. "You do not intrude. Come forward."

Despite her heavy burden, the woman walked toward him with a graceful motion that only enhanced his first impression of a ghost. Did her feet touch the floor? Involuntarily, he glanced down at her hem. It was ordinary leather shoes he saw. Sturdy ones, at that.

"I could return at a later hour, my lord." She sank into a respectful curtsy, but her gaze was on the torque about his neck. The air filled with the seductive scents of her basket.

"Nay. Remain. Take what time you need." Durand walked to the fore of the chapel and lit more candles to better see this ethereal creature. She came to his side, set the basket on a wooden bench, and then busied herself filling an oil lamp at the altar.

In the candle's glow, the woman's hair was dark and glossy. It lay in a silky plait entwined with narrow ribbons down her back. Her brows were finely arched, her eyes dark when she glanced up at him now and then.

Each time she raised her eyes, he nodded his acceptance of her presence that she might remain at her task. Moving closer, he attempted to put her at ease. He touched a lacy weave of ferns and ribbons in her basket. "Is this your work?"

The woman nodded and ducked her head. She draped intricate garlands of flowers about his wife. Each touch of the delicate petals of violets brought a renewal of the scents of spring.

"May I, my lord?" The woman held up a beautiful

17

cascade of leaves, trailing vines, and ribbons.

He nodded, not understanding what she intended. She opened his wife's hands, and when she was finished, Marion looked like a bride to a forest deity. "You have made her more beautiful than any of these jewels," he said, sweeping a hand out to encompass the ropes of pearls and links of gold.

A delicate flush crossed the woman's cheeks. "I but wish to honor my lady," she said softly. "She was kind to me." Her gaze met his.

A sudden pounding rose in his throat. A throb echoed in his wrists and temples. "Who are you?" he asked.

She tilted her head to examine him. He felt naked.

"Who am I?" She lifted her empty basket and turned away. He watched the straight column of her back, the sway of her skirts, the dark rope of her plait as she glided away from him. "I am your daughter's wet nurse, my lord."

Durand left the chapel a few moments later and entered the great hall. He strode to the fore, where he sat beside his wife's sister, Oriel Martine. She must act as mistress of Ravenswood Castle now that Marion was dead. He waited until a servant poured him a goblet of wine before speaking.

Oriel smiled up at him with the same soft blue eyes as Marion, from a similar oval face.

"Oriel, have I a wet nurse?"

She rose. "You're impossible, Durand. Your *daughter*, as you well know, must be fed just as a son must be. I'm sure if the babe had been a boy, you would not only know the wet nurse, but would have assigned him a groom for the destrier you would have surely purchased the day he was born!" She swept away, chin in the air.

He sighed. "Badly done, Durand." He looked over

the crowded hall. The many folk who sat at the tables and benches spoke in low tones out of respect for death, which had so recently claimed their mistress. The young woman from the chapel was not to be seen.

A man approached him with hesitation in his step. "My lord?"

Durand nodded. The man was darkly handsome, thin as a hungry hound, as finely dressed and elegantly shod as a courtier in King John's court. "What is it, Master le Gros?"

"Please accept again my deepest sympathy at the loss of our dearest Lady Marion," the merchant said in soft, grave tones.

Durand inclined his head.

"I don't wish to trouble you at such a time, nor do I wish to intrude—"

"Then speak quickly, le Gros."

"Of course, my lord." He cleared his throat. "If you are summoning your sons for Lady Marion's services, have they need of"—le Gros dropped his voice to yet an even more somber whisper—"clothes appropriate to the occasion? I've a very fine wool to garb them."

"Don't trouble yourself. My sons have all they need."

"As you wish, my lord." Simon bowed, but remained in place.

"What is it?" Durand had difficulty keeping the impatience from his voice.

"I cannot find Lord Luke. He was to have . . . ah, hem, ah, settled some accounts."

Durand took a deep breath to prevent himself from loosing his temper on the merchant standing before him. "Leave the accounts with me, and I'll see that my brother attends to them."

Simon opened a leather purse at his belt and withdrew a folded leaf of parchment. He placed it precisely before Durand. "Again, may I offer you my deepest

sympathy. I have added Lady Marion to my prayers.
I will say more prayers each day—"

"Aye. As you wish." Durand sought to forestall more
words.

"My lord." Le Gros bowed several times before re-
treating.

"Is the worm gone?" Penne Martine, Oriel's husband
and his closest friend, slid into the seat beside him.
He so resembled his wife, he was ofttimes mistaken
for her brother.

Durand forced a smile. "Worm? I prefer to think of
le Gros as a standing bog, oozing his elegant speech
across all who cross his path. But . . . I have known
him but two days."

"Then why keep him about?" Penne signaled for
more wine. A few inches shorter than Durand, he had
the same knightly build found in men who had
wielded a sword for years and ridden horseback just
as long. Penne, however, lacked the hardness of Dur-
and's features. Penne looked ready to laugh. Durand
knew his own face looked ready to chastise.

"Why not? You know I trust my brother's judgment
in all these matters. Luke claims Simon le Gros's
prices are fair. And he says the merchant's wife makes
scented lotions unparalleled anywhere in Christendom."

"If Mistress le Gros makes the lotion Oriel is rubbing
on her skin these days, le Gros must be retained at all
cost. Or his wife must be. My Oriel's skin is like swan's
down, and she smells like a summer garden. A seductive summer garden. I simply sniff her neck and want
to—" Penne's cheeks colored. "Forgive me. I should
not be speaking of such things when Marion is—"

"Penne. Cease! I'm sick to death of everyone tiptoe-
ing about me. No one finishes a sentence. No one
meets my eye."

Except the maiden in the chapel. She had looked

him in the eye, and reminded him most painfully of what a woman's glance could inspire.

"Everyone loved Lady Marion," Penne said.

"Aye," Durand said. "*Everyone* loved Lady Marion."

After an uncomfortable moment of silence, Durand cleared his throat. "I've annoyed your Oriel." He filled his goblet again, spilling a few drops on le Gros's accounts when a woman in white entered the hall. Dashing the wine from the parchment, he realized she was not the one who had so beautifully adorned his wife. That woman had been more roundly formed, had walked with greater grace, had announced herself with her scent.

"How so?" Penne accepted the cup of wine Durand held out.

"I asked if I had a wet nurse."

"A simple enough question."

"Then why did Oriel take such offense?"

Penne's gaze slid away from Durand's. "Oriel is always sensitive where babes are concerned." His long fingers played with the stem of the goblet. "Oriel believes you neglect the infant. Have you seen her yet?"

Durand felt a hot flush rush up his cheeks. "I don't need to see the babe. When she's old enough to marry off, I'll look her over."

"If you said such a thing to Oriel, no wonder she took offense. It is just how her father thought. Oriel is ever mindful that she and Marion had no say in whom they wed." Penne shook his head and sliced himself a piece of buttery yellow cheese.

"They did not mind for long—" Durand broke off. The woman from the chapel entered the hall. He knew her in an instant, had no need to be close enough to catch her scent. Her walk alone announced her. She crossed the hall toward the steps leading to the east tower, which housed small chambers for upper servants. And his infant daughter, he supposed.

Just as she reached the steps, she turned and looked at him.

Her step slowed. She stopped. With a small dip of her dark head, she nodded, then disappeared up the tower stairs.

Durand's mouth dried. "Penne. Did you see that woman who just crossed the hall to the north tower?"

"Aye." Penne nodded.

Try as he might, Durand could not quite meet Penne's eyes. "Is she the child's wet nurse?"

Penne nodded. "Aye. She is."

Warmth flooded Durand's body. He felt as ashamed of the sensation here in the hall as he had felt in the chapel. Another sin to add to his burdens—lustful thoughts over his wife's body.

"I pity her," Penne said.

Durand jerked around to face his friend. "Pity her?"

"Oh, aye. She may be your wet nurse, but she is also Simon le Gros's wife."

Cristina le Gros forced herself to move up the stone steps that led to the chamber she now called her own. She felt intensely conscious of the attention of the men in the hall.

Of *his* attention.

Finally, after so many months, Durand de Marle was in residence. Finally she had met the man so many spoke of with respect and, in some cases, fear, had met the man who had come to her in the mist and remained in her nightly dreams.

A warrior lord, he had about him a manner that at once challenged and, at the same time, invited. His skin was sun-darkened and lined from exposure to the harsh conditions of the Holy Land, where she knew, from Lady Marion's gossip, he had served the late King Richard. One of her lotions might smooth the cares from his—

Nay, she must not think such thoughts.

"Thank you, Alice," she said to a serving woman, and took Lord Durand's babe into her arms. Alice assisted her in unlacing her gown that she might put the child to breast.

Alice settled on a low stool by her chair and began to weep. " 'Er ladyship be dead two days now. I cannot believe it, miss. Each time I see the babe, I thinks o' me mistress. Cold in the chapel, soon to be cold in the crypt." Alice wiped at her eyes with her apron. "How many days did my mistress lie in 'er bed, weak and fevered? How many? Fifty? Sixty? And *'e* never came within a league o' 'er."

" 'Twas thirty days. And you know Lady Marion forbade us to summon him. And then . . . when she finally succumbed, he came immediately."

Alice shook her head. "I'll miss 'er terrible. I been wiv 'er since she were a babe 'erself."

Cristina leaned over and gently patted Alice's hand. "I know. My mother is dead now and she was much beloved by myself and all who knew her. Of course, she was but a merchant's wife, but still many mourned her loss. It is right you should think of Lady Marion. Pray for her soul." She looked down at the babe, who kneaded her breast with a tiny fist. "Pray for this one, too."

"Aye, miss, but when I sees the babe, I think o' me mistress. Why could not Lord Durand be content wiv 'is two fine sons?"

"Alice! Don't say such things."

Alice shook her graying head. Her seamed face channeled her tears to drip from the point of her chin. "Ye be new 'ere, miss. I 'ave served de Marles for two score years. 'Tis always the same. De Marle men be ruled by lust. 'Is lordship comes 'ome after months away, plants 'is seed, and then disappears. And 'er ladyship must bear the fruit of that lust. And die of it!" Alice's words were lost in choking sorrow.

Cristina closed off her thoughts from Alice's tirade. She shifted toward the hearth and hummed softly to the babe. She combed her fingers through the silky fair hair that crowned the little head.

"Forgive me, miss." Alice knelt at her side. "I forgot ye lost yer own babe."

"Aye, Alice." Cristina bit her lip. Her own infant had died on the very day this one was born. Only three days had her own daughter lived. So sweet, so healthy, then so quickly sickening and so quickly gone.

"And Lord Durand'll wed ere the year is out, ye'll see. 'Twill be another in my sweet lady's place. 'Twill be as if my lady never lived."

"Why do you think that?" Cristina looked up at Alice.

"Lords marry for power, miss, ye know that. 'E'll sniff about for more land and pluck some innocent off the vine like a ripe plum so she can suffer for 'is lust as well." Alice tossed her head and wiped her tears on her sleeve. " 'Tis a blessing ye were 'ere in the keep to take Lady Marion's babe to yer breast."

"Aye, a blessing. I suppose 'twas God's will."

"Humph. God's will. If God were a female, men would lie in childbed, sufferin' and dyin' fer lust. 'Is lordship 'asna even seen the babe."

"Alice. Could you fetch me a cup of warm milk?"

The serving woman rose and hastened to the task, leaving Cristina in blessed silence. She did not wish to hear one more word of lust and death. She rummaged in a coffer and found soft, clean cloths to change the babe and marveled at the tiny toes and dimpled legs as she had at her own babe's.

A child was all she had ever wished for. Was it not a woman's purpose in life to give birth and nurture? She had failed at the one. At least, for a time, she could do the other. Already, holding and nurturing this child had helped her wounds to heal. She planted kisses on the babe's cheeks.

"I hope you resemble your mother, little one. If you develop your father's stubborn chin and noble nose, you may find yourself without a suitor in all King John's kingdom." She tickled the child's belly and received the wide-eyed squirm of a healthy babe. She wrapped her in clean swaddling.

The door creaked open and Cristina hastily pulled the edges of her gown together. "Alice?" She turned to the door.

"I see you're still in your fine nest, Cristina." Simon le Gros eased the door closed behind him and strode about the chamber. He rubbed his hands before the fire. "Aye. This is better than any scheme I could have devised. You're surely in the lord's good favor here."

"What is it you want, Simon?"

"Why, Cristina, I merely wish to know how you fare." He smiled. "You are so hidden here with the babe, I have scarcely seen you since you brought Lady Marion her pomanders—let me think . . . the day you gave birth."

Once his smile had intrigued her, his words had beguiled her, his handsome face had drawn her. Now she thought only that he had not come to see her but once since the death of their own babe, and yet, according to Alice, had inquired of Lady Marion several times each day as that fine lady lay near death.

He swept his hands out to encompass the chamber. "Had her ladyship survived the child's birth, she would have recommended us to Lord Durand. We might have obtained old Owen's charter now that he's too sick to serve, and made our home here. But as Lady Marion is now dead and that fool Lord Luke—"

"Hush, Simon. Don't let the servants hear you speak in such a manner of Lord Durand's brother. Lord Luke is castellan here. It would not do to offend him or Lord Durand."

"No one can hear me." Simon waved off her objections. "You must ingratiate yourself to Lord Durand on the infant's account. Each time he visits, smile and be agreeable. He has no need of your pomanders or lotions, but there is no other woman here in the keep who can nurture his child."

Cristina did not tell Simon that Lord Durand never visited his child. Of course, he had arrived at Ravenswood Castle to find his wife dead of childbed fever. Mayhap his grief kept him from inquiring after the infant. She would not believe him as heartless as Alice painted him.

Mayhap he blamed the infant for his wife's death.

"Lady Marion's death is a sore trial to us," Simon continued.

"Lady Oriel seems to enjoy my wares as much as her sister."

Simon rubbed his palms together. "Excellent. She'll have influence on Lord Durand." Then Simon frowned. "If 'tis suggested some village woman may nurse the child, can you give the infant some potion to sicken her?"

Cristina gasped and shot to her feet. "Simon! I would never do such a thing! I know nothing of such potions."

Simon strode to where she stood, the child warm and now sleeping against her breast, tiny mouth agape. He skimmed his long fingers over the child's head. "I did not mean you to harm her. But it would suit us all if the babe preferred your milk. You'll do whatever I require of you, will you not? Your presence here deprives me of your services in my bed. You have birthed but two babes, females, by God, and dead before they saw a single summer. We know 'tis through no fault of *mine*."

26

His words were tiny hammers on the anvil of her pain.

"Now, the king will surely come here when he embarks for Normandy. The place will be overrun with ladies who may want your wares."

"Here? The king is coming here again?" She bit her lip. "I thought Lord Durand was to leave in a day or two."

Simon smiled. "The gossips say Lord Durand will remain here to await the king, so we must make our place now. You'll do whatever it takes to secure a position for us here at Ravenswood, will you not?"

Cristina rose. She placed the babe on the narrow bed and quickly laced her gown tightly closed.

Simon pulled her around. "You'll do whatever is required. Kiss Lord Durand's muddy boots if he should want it. Anything."

Cristina looked up at her husband's face. His dark hair curled about his neck, fine as swan's down. "I will do what duty requires," she said softly.

Simon nodded. "That's better, more what I expect of you. Ingratiate yourself and be quick about it. I want to be established with a charter when the king arrives. If another secures it, it will be he who reaps the wealth of John's coffers." He rubbed his palms together. "King John spends freely. Lord Durand will have need to spend just as lavishly to please him. Do what is needed."

Simon swept out of the room.

Cristina sank to the bed beside the babe. She gathered the child into her arms. "Oh, my sweet, how innocent you are. How unknowing of the intrigues of men."

Tears burned her eyes as she thought of her own babes, who lay in their graves, one beneath the lavender fields of home, one here in de Marle land.

"Mistress le Gros?"

Lord Durand stood at the bedchamber door left open by Simon after his departure. "Lord Durand." She moved around the draped bed and sank into a curtsy. "How may I be of service?"

Lord Durand did not move from the doorway. His gaze traveled slowly over her. She had to force herself not to touch her hair or assure herself her gown was properly laced.

"It is I who may be of service to you."

She tipped her head and considered him. "How, my lord?"

Finally he entered the chamber, but only a few feet. He looked fatigued, despite his sun-darkened complexion.

"You nourish the child, you adorn my wife; how may I reward you?"

Cristina smiled. "I seek no reward, my lord. I want for nothing. All is provided before I have need to ask, but I thank you for your concern."

"I'm glad of it. But you must come to me if you find some lack here." He glanced toward a deep alcove off the chamber.

Would that she had not tied back the drape that concealed the sunny space.

"What are you doing?" he asked, and stepped into the alcove.

She followed him to the table that held dried flowers and the other assorted ingredients needed to practice her craft. "I'm preparing a mixture of flowers for Lady Oriel's soap." Would he object to her working here?

One by one, he lifted each small bowl and sniffed it, then extended one to her. "This is lavender, is it not?"

Cristina inclined her head. "English lavender seeds from my father. Far finer than any found in France."

He smiled. "Of course. This soap for Lady Oriel," he said, "what will be in it?"

"Lady Oriel misses the summer flowers of Mirebeau, her former home, I believe. I will endeavor to mix something reminiscent of that place."

His gaze captured hers. "Your work brings more than a sweet smell then. What would you mix for me?"

The scents of mist and forest.

Aloud she said simply, "Whatever most pleases you, my lord." This close, she could see his deep-set eyes were the gray of a winter sea. A white scar at the corner of his mouth was more responsible for his stern look than any fault of temper, she decided. Another scar, a pale delta on one high cheekbone, stood out starkly against his skin.

Conscious she was staring, Cristina busied herself with the child's swaddling. "Your babe will be a fine beauty."

He turned abruptly and went to the chamber door. "Don't hesitate to come to me, mistress, should you have need of anything."

Just as he reached the portal and she thought he might depart, he turned back.

"The babe is most fortunate to have you." He bowed to her as one would a fine lady and left.

Cristina stared at the empty doorway. She hugged the babe to her pounding heart. "Aye, my sweet Felice. You are as fortunate as your name. You have a mighty father, a fine and noble warrior to see to your care. 'Tis blessed you are." The child stretched in her arms. Her huge eyes opened. They were a soft gray-blue. Would they become the stormy hue of Lord Durand's?

Chapter Two

Following the lengthy service for Marion's interment, Durand watched his sons depart for de Warre's castle, northwest of Winchester. He had not seen them in almost six months. Adrian, soon to be fifteen, was growing tall. Robert, at ten and two, had supplied the tears so lacking in himself.

Durand returned to the crypt with Luke and knelt for a last time by his wife. Still, prayers eluded him. He touched the cold stone walls and shuddered. "I want to die on a battlefield and be buried there, not here in darkness and damp."

"You've lingered here long enough," Luke said. "May I offer you some distraction? Could you read over a few accounts? Penne says you might leave on the morrow to join the king. I wish he would stop this infernal scurrying from one end of the kingdom to the other."

Durand walked at Luke's side from the old crypt and

out into the wan sunlight. "I've changed my plans. The thought of the ride to Warwickshire wearies me. I believe I'll await John's arrival here."

"Then forgive my intrusion on your privacy. The accounts can wait." Luke touched his brother's shoulder.

"In fact, I have something for you from le Gros that I neglected to pass on, so we may as well see to your accounts now. In a snarl, are they?"

This time Luke laughed. "Nay, Durand. Penne says 'twas you who suffered Father Leo's tongue-lashings when called upon to figure. My sums were always perfect. As was my Latin."

"*Ignotum per Ignatius.*"

"*Ignotum per ignotius,*" Luke corrected with a grin.

When they reached the chamber that served as the counting room, Luke stretched out on a bench while Durand sat in a carved oak chair behind a long table. Despite Luke's casual demeanor, the table held neatly arranged parchments and tally sticks.

Durand pulled le Gros's accounts from the purse at his belt. He unrolled them and tossed them to Luke. "Why have you not granted le Gros a charter?" he asked. "He's been in the village for nigh on ten months. You said his prices are fair, and old Owen will not likely last until August, if Penne's tales are correct. There'll be no merchant in the village once Owen is gone, so offer le Gros the same terms and be done with it."

Luke tapped the items Durand was examining. "I would, save one reason: there is something about the man I do not like."

Durand examined his younger brother. The only resemblance they bore to each other was in their height and quick tempers—those they had from their father. Luke, ten years his junior, resembled their perfidious mother in outward appearance. He had hair the color

31

of fire—dark gold shot with red. Women adored his slumberous eyes and generous mouth.

However, their mother would have become confused if asked how many eggs made a dozen. Luke had a lightning-quick wit and mind. There was no one more trustworthy than his brother.

"I, too, find le Gros a bit . . . snakelike? But these figures indicate he deals fairly. I cannot abide the baker, but I trust him not to give short weight. You say le Gros's merchandise is of good quality, and Oriel swears she'll not bathe without a soap from Mistress le Gros's hands. Why drag out the matter? Resolve it. Draw a charter and have it signed. If he cheats us, the raven will devour the snake."

"Shall I see old Owen about it?"

Durand rose and added a few sticks to the fire. "Of course consult old Owen, but has he not been hoping for just such relief since his son's death? Why not bring Owen to the keep, make him comfortable in his illness, and allow le Gros to take the house in the village?" He poked the fire. "This room is cold and dank."

"I love it." Luke grinned at him. " 'Tis close to the kitchen . . . wenches."

Durand could not help smiling back.

"What of Mistress le Gros?" Luke rolled up the accounts and secured them with leather thongs. "Should she not remain at the keep until another nurse may be found?"

The fire smoked a bit, and Durand avoided responding for a moment by tending it. "Oriel claims the child thrives under Mistress le Gros's care. Why not have le Gros settle himself and see to his stock? His wife may join him later."

"She allows no liberties," Luke said.

Durand surged to his feet. "Liberties? Have you been trying to get beneath her skirts already?"

Luke touched his heart in feigned indignation. "I

have no interest in married women. I am merely conjecturing. In fact, I'm not sure Mistress le Gros dwells in our world. Mayhap a cloud somewhere is her home. She barely touches the ground as she walks. But have you noticed how enticing is her form?" Luke spread his hands before his chest. "Her breasts are—"

"You're a dog." Durand did not want to admit he, too, had noticed the enticing swell of the woman's breasts and how they pressed against her gown, or how the cold of the chapel this morning had . . . "Have you considered taking a wife, Luke?" he asked hastily.

"Each day I consider taking a wife, but each night as some pleasing pair of warm thighs embraces me, I reconsider."

Durand dropped a heavy fist to his brother's shoulder. "Do not sow too many bastards about the keep."

"Nay, I will not. 'Tis the de Marle women who seem to have difficulty in that respect."

Durand froze. "What are you saying?" The words were shards of ice in his throat. What did Luke suspect? Or know?

Luke arched a brow. "Why, I am speaking of Mother, of course. Have you heard from her lately?"

The tightness in Durand's chest eased. "Nay, but I hear this and that from John's spies. Count Bazin keeps her now—in Paris. Father would gnaw his winding sheet if he knew."

"Aye. Though he could hardly complain, as he set her aside—"

"After tolerating her many affairs."

Luke shook his head. "Is not Bazin an old roué? And paying homage to King Philip?"

Durand nodded. "I imagine John will once again question our loyalty, with Mother so situated."

He separated himself from his brother and went to the stables. Ravenswood Castle had fared well under

Luke's care. He ordered his mare and rode from the bailey.

The lane to the village was shrouded in mist before him. He let the mare amble along. Many of the villagers were still returning from the castle and Marion's service. Their devotion pleased him. The men looked well garbed, not ragged, as they had been under his father's care. Luke was a fine castellan.

Once outside the village, Durand rode hard to the river's edge, from whence he could view Ravenswood. Built on Roman ruins, it had served as a Saxon hill fort at one time.

From Ravenswood's towers he could view the roads to both Portsmouth and Winchester. Until Philip's confiscation of his holdings in Normandy, he had meant to pass Ravenswood to Luke. Now it and a few minor holdings scattered throughout Sussex must go to Adrian and Robert.

The same mist that lay heavy on the road also wreathed the base of the castle walls. The four square towers gleamed with the light of many torches. His banner, the raven pecking out the eye of a serpent, flew from every corner.

His land was not yet suffering from the famine sweeping the rest of England. He was affected in only one respect—the draining of his coffers to support John's efforts on the continent. It would not be long before he felt the pinch.

Two small boys rolled down a hillock, squealing with delight. For a moment he imagined them as his sons. Nay, they would not be rolling about. They would be hard at work polishing armor or bent over sums as he and Luke had done, each in their turn.

They were fine, handsome boys, and would grow to be a credit to the de Marle name. They, at least, were his sons. Here, by the river, away from Luke's too clever eyes, he allowed himself to dwell on Marion's infant. Not his. Nay, not his. He probed the thought as one probes a sore tooth.

"Who was your lover, Marion?" he asked aloud. "Why did you betray me?" But he knew the answer. He had left her too much alone. He was at once mournful, angry, jealous, and vengeful.

The last time Marion had strayed, she had chosen one of the men who tended her garden. He had sent the man to one of his Normandy manors and locked Marion's garden. Who was it this time? Another servant? One of his knights?

Someone close?

Cristina enjoyed the brisk walk through the outer bailey, her first free exploration of Ravenswood's extensive environs. She watched the mews master feed the captive birds that graced Lord Durand's banner. Beside her, Alice complained of the hour, the temperature, the mud, the carts delivering goods for war—barrels of nails for horseshoes and quarrels for crossbows.

In truth, the bailey was as busy as a small town. Cristina shifted the infant Felice in her arms and continued on until she came upon a thick wooden door in the castle wall with a tiny window formed of an iron grille. The hinges and latch were cleverly fashioned to resemble vines. "What's through here, Alice? Surely this is not a postern gate?"

"Nay, 'tis 'er ladyship's garden."

Cristina stood on tiptoe and peered through the grille. Before her was a garden left long untended. Paths of white stone wound in what appeared to be concentric circles. The edges were thick with weeds. Tufts of grass marred the pristine paths. A stone bench, perfectly placed to catch the morning sun, sat in the center of the walkways.

And between . . . between lay heaven. Flower beds,

wild and untended, filled the gaps between each path. She saw roses and broom, hawthorn and violets. She caught the scent of sage and marjoram—and rotting wood. Trellises trailed browning ivy. How she wished for her own garden, her own small patch to grow what she needed. "Why is this garden not tended, Alice?"

"Oh, 'twas often so with Lady Marion. She took it into 'er 'ead to do a thing; then once it were done, she would lose interest. This be an imitation of some queen's garden. Eleanor's? Mathilda's? I cannot remember."

"Did her ladyship bore easily?"

"Aye, miss. She were as changeable as the sunset. One moment laughin', the next in tears. God love 'er."

Cristina looked down at the heavy iron lock. "Can we find a key, Alice?"

"Best ye mind yer own business, miss." Alice nodded to the babe in Cristina's arms. "Don't be putting yer nose where it were like to be cut off. Lord Durand be mighty frightening when 'e's in a temper."

"Why should he care if I walk in this little garden?"

" 'Twas her ladyship's, 'tis why," Alice said.

With great reluctance, Cristina followed Alice to the keep. She found herself gazing back at the small door in the high wall. What other delights were there, out of sight? Ever since leaving home as the wife of an itinerant merchant, she had wished for a garden of her own. Seeing such neglect was like seeing a wound untreated.

They were admitted to the keep by a sentry, and Cristina kept her gaze down as she walked through the hall. There were far too many men about, strangers here to join King John, men who had naught to do but drink and dice. Several lingered on the second-story gallery, watching all those below.

Then she saw him—Lord Durand. He stood before the mammoth hearth with its whitewashed chimney-piece. Floor to ceiling on either side, the walls were painted to depict the seasons. On the right winter changed to spring, and on his left summer faded to autumn. The scenes were as familiar as the daily devotions.

Lord Durand still wore his black tunic from the morning burial services. Fine gold and silver embroidery trimmed it. His belt was heavily chased in silver, his dagger's hilt a raven's head in gold. His dark hair gleamed with hints of the color of summer plums. His gray eyes settled on her.

She felt the rush of blood to her face. He nodded, barely, just a slight movement, almost missed save for the lock of hair that fell over his brow and necessitated his raising his hand to sweep it aside. He wore the heavy gold torque, as he had that day in the forest so many months before.

Not often in her twenty-eight years had she acted on impulse, yet she handed Felice to Alice and found herself approaching him.

Several men were seated in great oak chairs near the hearth. One was Lord Luke de Marle, the castellan and Lord Durand's brother. The other was Lord Penne Martine, Lady Oriel's husband, a landless baron now that Philip had usurped his possessions, a man said to be but half as ruthless as Lord Durand.

Lord Durand nodded to her. "Mistress le Gros."

"My lord." Her voice was barely a whisper. What had possessed her to approach him?

The vision of brown ivy, the scent of rotting wood.

Looking up at him, she saw naught but a stony mask. She read neither pleasure nor displeasure on his countenance.

"I noticed a small garden behind a door just beyond the dovecote, my lord."

"Did you?" Lord Durand frowned and Lord Luke rose.

"Aye. The garden is woefully in need of care."

"Is it?" Lord Durand held her gaze. Luke stepped closer.

She felt as if she were a dove being scrutinized by a raven—nay, two ravens. "I thought I might be able to restore it and cultivate some plants for my work."

Durand frowned. "Nay. The garden will remain locked. 'Twould be a waste of my men's time to restore it."

"I could do the work myself, my lord."

His frown deepened. "I forbid it. You have other duties to occupy your time."

She shivered at the harshness of his tone. "Forgive me, my lord; I intrude." She hurried away, gripping her skirt in her fists. "I am the veriest fool," she said beneath her breath.

The bedchamber was cold. She built up the fire, shook her head at Alice, who already nodded by the child, then went to the alcove and snatched up a pestle. In moments, she had pummeled away the worst of her concerns on hapless lavender seeds.

With a small horn spoon, she measured the lavender and some rosemary and daisy into a scrap of fabric, then tied it with a silk ribbon. She hung it over Felice's cradle. "I'll not speak to him again," she said to the sleeping babe.

That evening, Cristina sat sewing by the brazier in Lady Oriel's chamber, Felice in a basket at her feet. The chamber was small, but luxurious, the bed hangings yellow cloth festooned with birds and flowers picked out in silk thread. The room was warm and scented with summer flowers.

Facing the southern side of the castle, a window made of real glass allowed Lord Durand's good friends a view of the way to Portsmouth. Lady Oriel paced her chamber, restlessly toying with a pomander dangling from her belt, finally kneeling by Felice's basket.

"My sister so wanted a daughter." Cristina watched Lady Oriel stroke the child's head. "I hope she will look like Marion. 'Twould be best."

"She begins already. She has not Lord Durand's coloring—"

"Cristina," Oriel interrupted. "What is it you most want in this vast world?"

"A child." Cristina felt heat in her cheeks at her sudden confession of her inner desire held secret from all, even Simon. She hastened on. "I come from a large family. We were eight at table until my brothers set off to make their own way. I do miss my mother. She died three springs ago."

Oriel sat on the yellow padded bench by Cristina. "You think just as I . . . that is, many women feel as you do."

Cristina plied her needle in silence for a moment before replying. "Children will love you unconditionally. Is that not so? If they're good children, raised with love, they'll bring great joy to your life." *Mayhap the only joy.*

"Whereas husbands have other demands." Oriel cleared her throat. "Cristina, do you know of . . . that is . . . I have a lady friend." She worried the pomander's tassel so that Cristina knew she would need to repair it before the day was out. "This friend," Oriel continued, "she and her husband wish a child."

Oriel leaped up and began again to pace. "Much as you wish a child." She then rushed back to the bench and sank down once more, her ivory skirts crushed beneath her. "My friend is ashamed of her failure, you see. She has not conceived despite many years of marriage, and"—her hands fell still on the shredded tassel—"she fears her husband's desire for her wanes as she fails in her duty."

How Oriel's words echoed Cristina's own circumstances. Each time she had failed to conceive or had lost a child through miscarriage or death, Simon had grown a bit more distant, taken her less often.

"In what way might I help your friend, my lady?" Cristina kept her gaze on her needlework. She feared embarrassing the good lady, for surely it was Lady Oriel of whom they spoke. She found most people covered their secret desires behind some "friend's" need. Too much emotion colored Oriel's words for it to be otherwise.

"Have you some potion that will stimulate . . . that is . . . will help a woman to conceive?" she finished in a rush.

Cristina laid her work aside. She lifted Felice from the basket, held her close, and took in the babe's innocent scent. "Women are forever seeking to please men, are they not? When will men begin to seek to please the women?"

Oriel shot to her feet and gave a laugh tinged, Cristina thought, with bitterness. "Men. They have no need to please a woman. There are plenty of us about should one fall short of the mark. But have you anything? If my friend took it now, it might prevent . . . that is . . . my friend does not yet think her husband has strayed, but his disappointment is deep. Will it not soon send him to another, worthier woman?"

"If a man wants an heir, he needs his wife," Cristina pointed out.

"Aye, but if a man seeks a son and the wife never conceives, the bed becomes a place of . . . duty. Surely that alone will send a man to another?"

Cristina nodded and rose. "I know of several things your friend could try."

"Thank you."

The sudden shine of happiness on Lady Oriel's face saddened Cristina. "No matter what I make, my lady, it is still in God's hands."

Lady Oriel no longer listened; she was gone in a rustle of skirts. Cristina took a moment to pack her needlework into her bag, then lifted Felice onto her shoulder. The sweet pillows she was stitching could wait. The husband-luring potion could not.

As she left Oriel's chamber of peace and beauty, she cast a last look at the draped opulence of Oriel's bed and thought of how she had taken many potions herself and still had no living child. Yet she had given the concoctions to others and watched them work their magic. "Mayhap," she whispered, "my lady shall lie in her golden bed and be lucky."

Cristina leaned her palms flat on her worktable and sighed. She did not have what she needed for Lady Oriel's love potion. She could not ask Simon to secure the ingredients. He would question her endlessly as to their purpose, then scoff at her belief in such potions.

Barren women had only themselves to blame for their failure, he had so often said. Cristina tiptoed to where Felice lay nestled in her basket. "Felice, we'll need to spend the day gathering." She glanced at the open window. The morning sun shone brightly. " 'Tis best we make use of the fine weather."

A few moments later, garbed in a dun mantle, Felice in a sling across her chest, Cristina knocked lightly on Lord Luke's counting room. The door opened immediately, but only a few inches. Lord Luke's bold grin greeted her. His hair was mussed and his tunic rumpled. Cristina heard a feminine giggle.

"Forgive me, my lord, for disturbing you. I wished only to obtain permission to leave the keep and gather a few plants."

"You're not a prisoner here; you may leave when the spirit moves you." He leaned in the opening, his grin settling into a kind smile.

Ann Lawrence

She dipped into a curtsy. "Thank you, my lord, but I'll need several strong men to accompany me. I would like to have some plants dug and potted for my use. I've no authority to command even a groom to lead my horse."

With a wistful look over his shoulder, Luke left the chamber, shutting the door firmly behind him. "Come. I'll see to it for you. There are many lazy louts about who have need of such occupation."

Durand, accompanied by Penne, rode into the village. He inspected the baker's ovens, the mill, the village well, and finally arrived at the house that would soon be home to his new merchant. The long stone building stood at the edge of the village on the road leading to Portsmouth.

Pilfered stone from an ancient Roman temple formed a decorative face to the door. Ducking his head to enter, Durand smiled. It had always been thus—a profusion of goods tumbled in happy disorder from shelves and coffers. The myriad scents of old Owen's stock filled the front room that served to house his shop.

The living quarters were overhead. The ladder to the second floor was no longer negotiable by the old man, who now lay on a pallet near the hearth. There Durand found him with Simon le Gros.

"Shall I see to your horse, my lord?" Simon inquired. Durand nodded.

"I have no liking for illness," Penne said quietly, and followed the merchant out.

Durand wandered the crowded room and noticed the many spiderwebs and the dirt that indicated the extent of old Owen's illness. The man had once been as fastidious as a vestal virgin. "What may I do for you, Owen? Is there aught you would like to see taken to the keep for your comfort?"

"There is naught I need, save me bed," Owen said in a low rasp that deteriorated into a hacking cough.

Durand poured ale from a pitcher and supported the man's shoulders as he drank. "I'll see there's a strict accounting of all that remains here, and my brother will dispose of it to your satisfaction."

Owen curled his gnarled fingers in Durand's tunic. "I've some'at as needs saying. S-s—" A paroxysm of coughs shook his body. ". . . betray you."

"Betray me? What are you saying?" Durand helped the old man lie back. Did Owen know something of Marion's perfidy?

Simon and Penne entered the cottage.

"At the keep, my lord," the old man said. "At the keep. I'll tell ye there."

Durand nodded, concerned for the old man, whose color was gray, the whites of his eyes yellow. "Simon, would you see Owen to Ravenswood?"

"As you wish, my lord." Simon nodded. "I shall remain here until Owen feels fit enough to ride, then convey him to the keep."

Durand spoke a moment longer to the old man of their arrangements; then, with Penne at his side, he left. As they mounted their horses, Durand considered the long, low building. "I remember sneaking down here as a small boy. Owen was a god to me. He would allow me to sit by his fire for half a day sometimes. The tales he told! I knew which wives ground flour behind the miller's back, which man would move a field marker. Now"—he looked off into the distance—"I know the number of men King Philip might muster, but not how many men plow my fields."

"Marion complained often of your many absences."

"Aye, she had much of which to complain."

"You were not free to do as you pleased. I know 'tis wrong to speak ill of the dead, but she was petty and childish to expect you to drop the king's business to tend her needs."

Durand urged his horse to a canter. He followed an old deer track into the woods, which bordered a lazy stream. "Do not let Oriel hear your opinion of Marion."

"Oriel would agree. You'd be an earl now if Richard had lived. Your absences suited Marion as long as she could see an earl's belt at the end of it. She complained only when all knew you must prove yourself again to John. 'Tis simple spite on the king's behalf."

"All men must prove their loyalty."

Penne drew his horse even with Durand's as the beaten path widened. The horses slowed to pick their way over the ruts left by heavy carts. "Oriel and Marion argued often about John and Richard."

"And Philip's confiscation of our holdings in Normandy—" Durand stopped and lifted a gloved hand to silence Penne, and pointed to a small clearing near the stream bank.

Penne followed the direction of his hand and raised his dark eyebrows. Together they halted their horses and stared.

Cristina le Gros danced in the clearing—a woodland sprite come to life. She danced to some fairy music only she could hear over the flow of the water and the sough of the wind in the trees. Heat rushed through Durand's body.

She swayed and skimmed over the soft green grass, turned and twirled. Her drab mantle formed a bell about her legs. In her arms she cradled a babe. Marion's.

Slowly Durand urged his horse toward her, Penne behind him. They were upon her before she noticed them.

"Oh, my lord." Her cheeks colored as she fell still. Her plait, half undone, straggled over one shoulder.

The hem of her mantle was spotted with mud. Her pattens were thick with it.

"Mistress le Gros, what the devil are you doing here in these woods?" He swept a hand out to indicate the dense forest about them. Penne's horse whickered a protest at his sharp words.

"Gathering, my lord. These men protect me." She swept a hand out as he had.

"I see no men." Durand dismounted. She stood her ground, although her color rose even higher the closer he approached.

"They were here a moment ago. I but stepped away to this seat to feed the babe." She pointed. A smudge of dirt marred one of her soft cheeks.

"Seat?" He expected to see an elfin throne. Instead he saw only a smooth stump. "You defy sense. And what is that bundle you carry?" He pointed to her middle.

"Your daughter."

"So I assumed. What the devil is an infant doing in the woods? What of fever? What of brigands?"

"I assure you, my lord, I do not endanger your daughter. She is warm and snug here." As if to protect the child—or herself—from his wrath, she wrapped her arms about the babe.

"Where are your men?" he asked.

"Here, Durand." Luke stepped into the clearing. Incongruously, he held an ax. "Your wet nurse is quite well protected. In fact, she's a Tartar. Even I have bowed to her wishes. Have you ever chopped a tree? It is damned hard work." Luke took Cristina's elfin throne. "I would rather fight the heartiest of warriors than dig plants and chop branches for Mistress le Gros. Nettles she wants, and hawthorn! Naught but thorns and rashes."

"I have need of many plants, my lord," Cristina said hastily, lest they suspect she made a love potion. "I thought to bring a few back to the castle."

Somehow the grin on Luke's face only nourished Durand's anger. Three men stepped into the clearing, their arms filled with potted plants, their fingers black with the rich loam of the forest. Able men. Two more appeared, Luke's men. Seven more stepped from the shadows. An ample guard.

He felt the fool. "Get yourself back to the keep. Now." He spoke only to Mistress le Gros. He mounted and wheeled his horse, and clots of mud flew in all directions as he galloped into the trees.

Cristina immediately headed for the horses, a cold chill filling her, despite Lord Luke's assurance that his brother was not so very piqued. "I cannot think what he must be like when truly angry then, my lord," she said.

"Oh, 'tis a sight to behold. Fire streams from his nostrils, steam issues from his ears. He sprouts claws and—"

"Enough!" Cristina burst into laughter. Felice protested, setting up a howl. She patted the baby's back until she quieted. "I still don't have the plants I require."

Luke threw up his hands. "Nay. I'll not dig another moment."

She smiled. "You did not dig at all. And you lied to Lord Durand. You chopped nothing. I believe you used the ax to shape a better seat on that stump."

"Aye. For the sake of my rump." Then he bowed. "Forgive my levity. What is it you're asking, Mistress le Gros? For I can tell you want something," he said.

"Lady Oriel and Father Odo have placed several orders with me. I cannot fill them with the plants I have at hand. I need more than violets and primroses."

"I am castellan here and give you my consent to gather what you will. Do as you wish. Who else will care?" Lord Luke made an impatient gesture toward the trees about them.

"Lord Durand, I imagine."

"Ah. You imagine."

She met Lord Luke's gaze. His sardonic expression shamed her somehow. Could he read her thoughts, know how Lord Durand haunted her every thought, crept into her musings? Nay, he could not. And lustful dreams they were, to her shame. Her thoughts should be of Simon, no matter his neglect of her. "I thank you, Lord Luke, but my husband will be most displeased if his orders are not filled promptly. He depends upon me to see to the needs of the ladies of the keep."

They reached their carts and horses. Without thought, she handed Felice to Lord Luke and accepted a groom's aide to mount a small palfrey.

"Tell me how I may help." Luke handed up the child in her sling.

She looked down at Lord Luke's handsome face. She saw little of the hard features of Lord Durand. Luke left her unmoved. Lord Durand churned her insides. "The walled garden in the outer bailey would suit me most admirably. Much of what I need is likely there in abundance, but Lord Durand has forbidden it."

"He'll come around. I've found he always says nay when first you ask him anything, but upon later reflection, he ofttimes sees the other side. I think the garden would be perfect for you. 'Tis quite extensive, you know. One side is a small grove of fruit trees. It was lovely, I remember, in flower. And there is no need to sit on stumps. There are benches aplenty.

"When we return, I'll take you into the garden. I cannot give you permission to *use* the garden, but I can show you around it. I have the key."

Durand climbed the ladder leading to the roof of the south tower. Damaged by fire in his father's day, it had never been adequately repaired. It had been on an inspection to figure the cost of the repairs that he had realized one could see into a tiny corner of Marion's garden.

Now, elbows propped on the edge of the tower parapet, he stared down at that small corner of lush greenery. Once it had been tame; now it ran wild. The marble bench was overgrown with vines. Then it had held two lovers, his wife one of them.

His anger had known no bounds, but his pride had kept the knowledge silent in his breast until that night. Then he had unleashed it. The next day Marion had joined him on a trip to Winchester, and the gardener had been sent to one of his manors in Normandy.

He watched Mistress le Gros cross the bailey, Marion's daughter in her arms.

Cristina. He enjoyed the sound of her name, the feel of the syllables on his tongue. It was a name to whisper in a lover's ear. Lovers reminded him of Marion's betrayal.

"Nay. I must be honest with myself," he said as he watched the merchant's wife. "I care less of Marion's betrayal than of the man's. What treachery do I harbor when I now most need loyalty?" Then all thoughts of Marion and her possible lovers fled from his mind. Luke appeared at the garden door, unlocked it, and held it open to Cristina.

"*Jesu,*" he said softly. He straightened, a fierce pulse rising in his temples and throat. The torque at his neck felt as tight as a noose.

Only one tiny corner of the garden was visible to the world outside the garden walls, so Cristina and Luke disappeared from view once inside the gate. But not for long.

Cristina very quickly found the little corner in the late-day sun. Where she had placed the child he did not know, but she busily jerked away the vines to expose the marble bench.

"Ah, Mistress le Gros," he said bitterly. "You see a charming seat, one where you might bask in the sun on a cool day or enjoy a sheltered spot on a hot one. Or do you, too, see it as a place to woo a lover?"

She moved out of view, then returned with the child. He wished in that instant to be the raven of his banner, that he might swoop down and perch on the pear tree whose branches hung so close by, for she sat so quietly, face to the sun, rocking the child.

The child. Not his.

And yet, even this far above, he felt a stirring of something unfamiliar as he watched the merchant's wife.

Luke joined her. In moments Durand was down the ladder, through the tower, and across the bailey. He strode through the open garden gate and across the weed-choked paths in the direction of the marble bench in the far corner.

Luke's laughter filled the air. Durand took a deep breath when Cristina's joined in, each note thrilling down his spine. He ducked under the low branch of the pear tree and halted.

There, within but a few feet, sat Luke next to Cristina, head bent in conspiracy toward his avid listener. Both were oblivious to his presence. Luke, Lord of Skirts, was charming yet another female.

What am I doing here?

Slowly, lest they look up and see him, Durand backed into the trees. Once out of sight, he turned and strode away. No woman would make a fool of him. Ever again.

Chapter Three

Durand crossed the bailey with Father Odo on his way from the chapel. It took a conscious effort not to look at the securely locked garden gate. He had not yet confronted his brother about his defiance in opening it to Cristina the day before.

By the stables, his mare's bridle in his hand, Simon le Gros stood talking to his wife. He called out, "Ah, Lord Durand and Father Odo. I've settled Owen in the keep."

"How do you find the cottage?" Father Odo asked.

"The house is magnificent, quite dry and sturdy. Old Owen had some interesting wares, but I'll soon clean them out. In fact"—he turned to Durand—"I've a saddle arriving soon that you must inspect." He gestured in the general direction of the great gate that guarded the castle entrance. "I imagine it would make a most fit gift for our sire when he arrives."

"Send me word when you have it in hand." Durand

looked from husband to wife. The sweetly gentle manner of Mistress le Gros had disappeared. Her back was as stiff as old Owen's knees on a winter night.

"I wonder if I might ask your indulgence, my lord?" Simon gave his reins to a groom. "My wife makes a most sweet-scented lotion much treasured by ladies—Lady Oriel in particular. But to make it, she must—"

"Is this another plea to allow wandering about in the forest?" Durand looked from husband to wife. "Are you so dependent upon a few lotions that you cannot do without the flowers?"

Simon bowed. "I did not wish to disappoint the ladies, my lord. But Cristina is quite imaginative; she will find another flower, will you not, Cristina?"

Cristina le Gros looked at Durand, not her husband. She met his gaze quite squarely. "If that is what his lordship wishes, I will endeavor to comply."

Durand felt as if his heart were being squeezed. The sight of her dancing in the clearing suddenly came to his mind and startled him. Nay, the vision aroused him. *Damn all ladies and their vanities.* He turned and strode away to find a place of peace.

An hour later, a tentative knock on Luke's counting room door disturbed Durand's reading. "Another wench looking for Luke," he muttered. "Come," he called.

Cristina le Gros entered, a familiar basket over her arm. "Oh, my lord. I did not expect to find you here." She dropped into a deep curtsy and began to back away.

He rose from his bench, marking his place in the book with his finger. "My brother has gone to the village, but he should return at any moment. May I help you?"

She lifted her basket. "I have come to scatter some rosemary in the rushes."

With a shrug, Durand indicated she should do as she wished. He straddled the bench and opened his book in a futile attempt to ignore her, the herbs she strewed about the room, and her own scent, which drifted to him along with the other. With a glance in her direction, he caught her looking at him. Nay. Lower. At his dagger with its gold raven's head? His lap?

"Forgive me, my lord," she said when her basket was empty. "What do you read?"

He almost laughed. So much for her contemplation of his body or dagger. "Aristophanes." He put the book into her hands.

"Nay, my lord. 'Tis too valuable." She thrust it out at him as it were a snake he offered, but he pressed it into her palms.

"Valuable, aye, but not for its leather and parchment. 'Tis the words that are of value. Take it."

She sank to the edge of the bench, scant inches from his knees. Several strands of her hair defied her plait and curled against her neck. He regretted his sharp words in the bailey, but didn't know how to retract them.

"Who is Aristophanes?" she asked, lifting her eyes to his.

He thought of the dark, peat-stained waters of the northern lands that stood ice-cold, gleaming in winter sunlight. There was nothing cold in her expression. "A Greek. He wrote over a thousand years ago. I much admire his work."

"A thousand years," she said softly. She smoothed her delicate fingers over the book as reverently as she might God's word, then opened it and read, " 'There's nothing worse in the world than shameless woman— save some other woman.' "

As color ran over her cheeks, he felt heat flush his. He cleared his throat. "Who taught you to read?"

"My father. He wanted his children to be as educated as a lord's, and our priest much appreciated the oils my mother made for his altar in exchange for the lessons." Gently she closed the book and handed it back. "It is lovely. Thank you."

Before he could think of something else to say, or locate some line of Aristophanes less damning of womankind, she was gone.

"*Jesu.*" He rose, wrapped the book in linen, then put it into Luke's coffer with a few other minor manuscripts, manor records, and books he liked to have at hand. Those of greater value were locked and guarded in the west tower. He drew out the tally sticks from the winter harvest. "Mayhap I shall find some peace in counting oats and barley."

Luke wandered through the great hall, stopping repeatedly to speak to those who had gathered to break their fast. Finally he flung himself into the chair at Durand's side.

"It has begun," Luke said at his ear.

"What?" Durand speared a slice of heron with his dagger.

"Lady Sabina is to arrive before dusk. Be sure John will bring a few marriage proposals for you to consider as well."

Durand shrugged. "Sabina comes in vain. She needs a far better alliance than I can offer her. Her father may be a close friend of King John's, but he has little to show for it. As to other proposals, if the offer is worthy, I'll consider it. I must. Should we fail to regain what we've lost in France—"

"Your sons will still have Ravenswood."

"I want you to have Ravenswood."

Luke shrugged. "I'll find my way," he said, but his eyes scanned the hall, and he bit his lip.

"Luke, I'll regain what I've lost and more; I vow it.

Ravenswood should be yours. If a wife is the swiftest way to that end, then I'll wed."

But Luke was no longer listening. "I was in error, Durand." He pointed with his dagger. "Mistress le Gros is not floating about on a cloud."

Cristina le Gros drifted across the hall then settled at a far table.

"What is that supposed to mean?"

"Nay. She is not a cloud-dwelling spirit. She's a forest sprite. Can you not see her, deep in a forest glade somewhere, hair loose over those luscious breasts, kneeling naked—"

"Enough! You could make a priest rue his vows. Aye, he thought, I can imagine it.

Luke left, laughter on his lips. Durand could summon no laughter. He strode to the steps leading to the south tower and his bedchamber. Once there, he tore off the fine blue surcoat he wore but left on the ancient torque each ruling de Marle had worn to remind all of his right to power. As with his ancestors, he never took the torque off.

In moments he was garbed for battle. Returning to the hall, he bellowed a challenge to his men to gear themselves and meet him in the bailey.

Three hours later, sweat-soaked and aching with fatigue, he again climbed to his chamber. Rain soaked his garments, but the demons of his wife's betrayal were exorcised, as well as the images of Mistress le Gros darting naked amid tree trunks.

He threw open his chamber door and the images swept in again. His chamber smelled like the very forest glades he wished to banish. The room tilted a moment.

A tub steamed before the hearth. This, then, was the source of the wonderful fragrance. He trailed a finger through the water before submitting to his squire's attendance.

Finally he sank into the depths of the steaming water and leaned back in the silky water that caressed him with each breath he took. His squire handed him a scrap of linen and a block of soap, then bustled about gathering up wet clothes.

Lathering the cloth, Durand breathed deeply of the scented soap. His mind conjured rain-swept trees and ferns curling from dark loam. The soap was a beautifully formed block, stamped with the image of a raven. "See to your growling stomach, Joseph."

"Can I not make order here first, my lord?" Joseph asked.

"I like everything just as it is. I can lay my hand on whatever I need, when I need it."

"As you wish," Joseph said, and sighed deeply as he departed.

Durand slid down until his chin touched the water. Every muscle in his body ached, but as he soaked, the heady scents soothed him. He allowed himself to revel in the texture of the water, the satiny feel of the soap.

His arousal was intense. "I need a woman," he muttered.

Cristina le Gros.

Had he said her name aloud? He held up the block of soap. Had she made it? For him?

His door opened, sending a cold draft through the room. "What is it?" Durand asked of Penne, who entered.

Penne grinned. "How are you enjoying your bath? Oriel sent the soap."

"Oriel?"

"Don't sound so disappointed. Who else would care how you smell? Certainly not I. And this habit you've picked up from our king, this constant bathing, is dangerous."

Penne draped himself in one of the two chairs flanking Durand's hearth. "Oriel wishes to know if we may have music this evening. Is it too soon?"

"Nay. Marion loved music. She would not have wanted the hall silent."

When Durand rose and dried himself with a length of linen, blood streaked the cloth. He frowned at a long graze on his forearm.

"You've wounded yourself?" Penne offered Durand a small cloth, which he folded into a bandage.

"Aye. It seems so." He dabbed at the cut.

Penne took the bloody cloth. "How could you not feel this?"

"*Mon Dieu.* I have much on my mind. I'm bedeviled by King John. My wife is dead—"

"Interesting the order in which you place your wife and your king."

Durand ignored Penne and continued to dry himself, donning a long linen shirt and braies. He rolled his sleeve to prevent marring it with blood. "*Jesu.* Can you fetch some strips of cloth? Mayhap a salve?"

"Do I look like your squire?" Penne left with a smile on his face. It had always been so between them. There was no better friend than Penne. Not even Luke was as close to him as Penne.

Oriel rushed into the chamber, Penne entering with a rueful smile behind her. She swished her scarlet wool skirts aside and took his arm.

"This is nasty. How did you do it?" She replaced the bloody cloth he had pressed on the graze.

He shrugged. He could not say his mind was occupied with Mistress le Gros. "I noticed it only whilst I was dressing."

Oriel bit her lower lip as Marion would have had she been there to tend the wound. "It has no need of stitching, but still, it should be tended. The leech is in the village. Shall I call Mistress le Gros instead? Surely she knows much of plants. Mayhap she has some salve to put on it." Oriel headed for the door without awaiting an answer. She looked back. "Your legs are quite beautiful, Durand, but I suggest you finish garbing yourself ere Mistress le Gros arrives."

Durand did as bidden, casting aside two tunics before settling on one of forest green. It matched the scents of his chamber and seemed perfect for greeting a woodland sprite. Ignoring Penne, he moved quickly to right the chamber, heaving his weapons into his coffer, sweeping parchments in haphazardly after them.

"Queen Isabelle is not visiting," Penne said from his seat at the hearth.

"Have you something to say?" Durand said in a growl. He held the cloth to his wound and looked about for somewhere to place his dicing cups. He upended a bowl over them.

"I'm sure Mistress le Gros has seen dice before."

"Remind me to have Oriel stitch your lips closed."

"If Mistress le Gros thinks you a slovenly, gambling wretch, who is to care?"

"Her husband is merchant here now. I don't need her gossiping on my ability to lose my coin in games of chance, else he might hang me out for more silver with every purchase I make."

"Ah. I see. You wish to appear to be scraping by on a pittance?" Penne laughed, then swallowed it as Oriel entered with Cristina le Gros.

Durand held out his arm like a simpleton.

Her fingers were gentle. "It's not very serious, my lord."

"Have you a salve?" Oriel asked, going to her husband's side. She touched Penne's shoulder and he reached up and entwined his fingers with hers.

Durand felt a stab of jealousy.

Mistress le Gros nodded. "I'm not a healer, my lady, my lords, but I have this—a salve with a little betony and comfrey." She held up a small wooden pot. "It should serve you well."

She turned over the basin on his table. Penne chuckled as Cristina carefully placed his dice and cups aside and filled the bowl with water. Durand shot Penne a quelling look, then smoothed his countenance when she indicated that he should join her at the table.

"I've just bathed," he said.

"If it pleases you, my lord, I like to see to the cleansing of a wound myself." She gracefully swept her plain blue wool skirts aside and sat down.

"As you wish." He settled across from her and stretched out his bloody arm. Pungent forest scents rose from the cloth she lathered. "Did you make the soap?" he asked.

"Aye. Is it pleasing to you, my lord?" She inspected his wound again. A tiny frown knitted her brow.

"Very much."

When she raised her gaze to his, Penne and Oriel had disappeared. Only she remained.

She wiped away a fresh welling of blood. "How did you come by the wound?" she asked.

"Carelessness," he said simply.

"Sometimes it helps to know what caused the wound. Some fester more readily than others." Gently she probed the edges of the cut. "It may scar."

"I have others."

She looked up, and he felt the flick of her glance across his face as if she had touched his mouth lightly with her fingertips. "Aye. All warriors are so marked."

Cloth in hand, she bent to her task. "I have a preparation that prevents scars. You might wish to use it when this is well knitted."

A shudder ran through him as she gently bathed his arm, tracing the edges of the wound and skimming the rope of veins on his forearm. His blood pounded visibly at his wrist. Surely she must see the telltale throb.

He cleared his throat. "I have several books, not just the Aristophanes. Would you like to read them?"

Her already high color rose. "Would I like . . . I could not, my lord."

"Why not? You can read. I have books."

Twice more she dipped her cloth in warm water and bathed his wound without remark. Twice more she skimmed heat along his inner arm before laying aside the cloth.

"You've not answered me," he said when she patted the wound dry and dipped her fingertips into the salve she had brought. He jerked back when she touched the wound.

A hint of a smile touched her lips. "Hold still, my lord," she said softly, then bound his arm with clean strips of cloth and tied them snugly. She had finished, but did not rise. "I'm not sure it would be proper for me to read your books. My husband would not approve of such idleness." Her warm hands lingered on the bandage. "Would you like me to look at the wound in the morning?"

He had a leech to see to such matters, but no leech had hands so gentle or so soothing. This close, he saw that her cheeks were downy, her lips full and lushly red. Her breath was sweetly scented with mint. Underlying some simple flowery scent was her own womanly fragrance. It seduced.

"Aye. On the morrow. Come see to it."

He wanted her. To his shame, within days of having laid Marion to rest in the family crypt, he wanted another man's wife.

Badly.

Chapter Four

After the evening meal, when Felice was settled, Cristina sought Lady Oriel in an alcove off the hall, where she sat with several ladies chatting and stitching. The instant Lady Oriel saw her, she rose and, with a quick jerk of her head, indicated they should walk out. Cristina followed Lady Oriel to the deserted chapel.

"My friend would be shamed if anyone knew what she was about, Cristina. You don't mind that we meet here?"

With a smile, Cristina offered Oriel a linen-wrapped vial. "What better place?" Before Cristina turned away, she paused, a hand on Oriel's sleeve. "I believe, my lady, what your friend needs is one sweet moment, one moment of total love, a giving without thought for one's own pleasure, a giving that stands only as a token of the passion in her heart. That will best serve your friend. How could a child made in such a moment not be loving and giving?"

Oriel smoothed the contours of the bottle. "Think you such a moment exists?"

There had been no such moments in Cristina's life. "You could offer a prayer to God for your friend."

Cristina was then struck with a thought. "My lady, mayhap God has chosen your friend to care for some orphaned child, just as I am sure you must be a mother to Felice."

Oriel bowed her head. "My time with her will be but little, for I'm sure Durand will marry again."

"Lord Durand . . . wed?" The thought raised an unaccountable flutter in Cristina's middle.

"Aye, and soon—if he wishes to restore what he has lost through King Philip's dastardly usurpation! Aye, he must, and a new wife will dictate Felice's future."

A lump formed in her throat, and not just at the thought that her time with Felice was limited.

Oriel opened the layers of cloth to reveal the vial stoppered with wood. "What should I—my friend—do?"

"Your friend should stir a small spoonful of the powder into her wine each evening. If this does not work, I have others, some that must go in the husband's wine, not often an easy task to perform without his consent."

Oriel nodded. "Aye." She then wrapped her arms about Cristina. "Thank you, sweet Cristina. My friend will be most grateful." Oriel tucked the potion into her purse and shoved something into Cristina's hands along with a coin. "Oh, and this tassel you made me has come undone. Do what you can with it."

Cristina watched Oriel flit from the chapel after offering a lengthy silent prayer at the altar, hands folded with white knuckles, the prayer far too long for simply aiding a friend.

When she was alone, Cristina went forward and checked on the reserves of oil in the lamps there. Her fingers lingered on the altar cloth. She no longer prayed for a child. She no longer prayed for Simon to come to their bed. Soon, though, she knew she must again do her duty. *Duty.* For men it was a pleasure as well. For women such as herself and Oriel, who could not give their husbands what they most wanted, it truly was a chore.

Simon would soon ask when she could perform her wifely duties. She sighed with an ache in her throat and chest. If there was to be a child in her life, someone to love, who would love her in return, care for her in her old age, then she must be a wife—a good and dutiful wife.

Back in the hall, as Cristina crossed to the east tower stairs, she looked about for Lady Oriel and Lord Penne. The lady was not in evidence, but Lord Penne was playing at dice with three other men.

He was a handsome man, strong, filled with laughter. Cristina admired his fair hair and startling dark brows that somehow beautifully framed his fine blue eyes. Surely the glances he gave his wife did not indicate a waning interest. Nay, Lord Penne took every opportunity to touch his wife. He did not keep his hands tucked up in his sleeves as Simon did. Nay, Lord Penne ofttimes linked fingers with Lady Oriel, lifted them to his lips in affection. Mayhap Oriel asked on behalf of another lady after all. There were several in the keep accompanied by their lords and knights now the king's visit was assured.

Oriel used a silver spoon to measure the potion into her wine.

"What's in it?" Penne encircled her waist, leaned close to watch, and perched his chin on her shoulder.

"I've not the least idea," Oriel said. She frowned. "I said a prayer over it."

Penne turned her around. He clamped a hand on

hers as she lifted the goblet of wine to her lips. "You don't need to drink this . . . this love potion. You do understand that? I care not if you conceive. I love you as you are."

Oriel fought the burn of tears against her eyelids, the throb of her pulse in her throat. He said it often, how much he loved her despite their childless state, but she knew better.

Marion had told her of Penne's confession one night of his desire for strong sons like Durand's, of how his desire was even stronger now that he had lost his holdings in Normandy. He had said to Marion that he had nothing now. Nothing. Somewhere deep inside resided a dull pain that Penne had not counted her when toting up his assets.

It was she who had nothing without a child.

Marion had not scoffed at her fears; she had pointed out that Penne laughed quite heartily with the serving wenches. Marion had warned her that it was but one step from laughing words on the lips to a hand beneath a skirt.

"I know you love me, Penne." She raised the goblet and drank deeply, a false smile on her face. The wine was sweet, with a bitter aftertaste. "I love you, too, but surely 'tis worth the trying? There are potions for men as well, you know." She set the goblet on the table and swept back the bed curtains. A flush of heat swept through her body. Her skin tingled.

Penne stood behind her and slowly removed her gown, trailing kisses in the wake of his hands. Was it the potion that set her skin afire as he ran his fingers down her naked spine?

He turned her and held her tightly against his body. "I love everything about you, Oriel," he whispered. "Especially this little freckle on your breast." He bent and touched the tiny mark with the tip of his tongue.

Was it the potion that urged her to boldly entice

him by lying back and opening her thighs like some alehouse wench?

What of the urge to touch him in places no woman should?

"Sweet Oriel," he said with a moan, moving strongly within her. As he loved her, she silently recited an ancient chant learned from the old midwife who had tended Marion. She said it three times, then crossed the fingers of her left hand, the canopy over her head blurring through her tears.

Cristina removed the bandages from Lord Durand's arm for the third and final time. It was as difficult to touch him without a flutter of sensation coursing through her middle as it had been the first time.

He had his own unique scent. Mist and forest. Those were the only words she could think of to describe it. In her world, ruled by the smells of nature, his scent was one she could not catch without thinking of the day she had first seen him.

He held a power over her that went beyond that of the highborn over the low, a power to make a king and dozens of other men invisible as they rode through the mist.

Was a man born with such power? Or was it drilled into him along with his training at swordplay? "There's no need to cover this again." She folded the cloth neatly and rose. "It's quite nicely healed."

Lord Durand stood as well. He stared down at his arm and frowned.

"It won't scar, my lord. There will be little to see in a few days. Rub this on it twice a day to be sure." She set a pot of oily salve on the table.

"I was not concerned on that score." He smiled at her. "It is just that I now have no excuse to argue about Aristophanes with you."

She felt the heat rush to her cheeks and dropped

her gaze from his face to her feet. Each time she had come to tend his arm, he had been engrossed in the little book. Each time, he had read aloud some favorite passage. "Forgive me, my lord, if I offered my opinion too strongly."

"I'm used to women with strong opinions, Mistress le Gros. It is women without an opinion I find of little use."

"Then if I may venture a parting opinion, I wish I could appreciate this humor you find in Aristophanes."

He grinned. "Then take the play and read it for yourself. My poor recitation is obviously lacking."

"Oh, I could not." She put her hands behind her again as if tempted by the offer and determined to resist it.

"As you wish. But come again and let me read one of his plays to you from start to finish."

"Mayhap one day," she said, but she knew she could not.

As she reached the door, she rested her hand on the latch and looked back at him. He still smiled. Sun from the window beside him lit his torque with a golden gleam. "I have but one final thought, my lord, on Aristophanes, lest you think me of little use. He must have lacked the caring of a loving wife to write such bitter words about women."

Lord Durand stiffened. At the same moment, a cloud covered the sun. The sudden shadow on his face made him look carved in stone. She sensed she had taken too much liberty this time.

"Is that what you think? A man is bitter if he has not a woman to love him?"

"Nay, my lord. There are not enough good women about that every man should have one to love him, nor enough good men . . . I am getting in a muddle. I meant to say only that Aristophanes did not have someone to love him, else he would not say such things. 'Let each man exercise the art he knows.' Good day, my lord."

She lifted the latch and departed. It was better to escape before saying something more to anger him. She sighed as she skipped down the stairs. Certainly Lord Durand had never wanted for love. Marion had been beautiful and kind. Surely her lady's heart had brimmed with love for her husband. She had spoken often of love and reveled in the touch of fine cloth and musky scents and wanted to know their properties in bringing a man to bed. In fact, Marion had oft embarrassed her with talk of love play.

Now, to Cristina's dismay, she knew a little of the man whom Lady Marion had treated to her favors.

And she coveted him in a most shameful way.

To banish intimate thoughts of Lady Marion's husband, Cristina spent the afternoon stitching a small gown for Felice, each rosebud in three shades of pink, each leaf in two shades of green, all done in utter concentration until it was time to feed the babe. She had no sooner set the child to rest in her cradle than there was a knock at her chamber door.

To her amazement, Lord Durand stood in the portal. "Forgive the intrusion, Mistress le Gros."

Cristina curtsied and stepped back. He did not enter.

"I have merely come to offer you something to read over which we could never argue."

His gaze held only humor. She could not help smiling as she took the cloth-wrapped bundle from his hands.

She moved to the alcove and her worktable. The cloth, a bit musty when opened, revealed an old book. The wooden cover and leather binding were dirty with mold. She tentatively wiped away a few smudges before opening it.

"My lord!" She turned to him, hand on her heart. "This is . . . I cannot believe . . . surely . . ."

Lord Durand came to her side and propped his hip on her worktable. He took up the book and reverently turned the leaves. "Aye. 'Tis a copy of Aelfric's *Nominum Herbarum*. I remember my father traded King Richard a fine horse for it." When he looked up, his smile was transformed into a wide grin. "Although I think my father lied a bit about the horse's lineage."

"B-b-bartered a h-h-horse? K-king Richard? I cannot touch it, my lord." She edged away, hands behind her back. " 'Tis worth a sultan's treasure."

Durand frowned. He had planned to please her, not frighten her. "Of course you can touch it. 'Tis almost falling to pieces and is useless to me. Why not look it over? You'll find a use for it, I wager. I believe whoever copied it had a canny knack for capturing the likeness of each plant, did he not?"

He held it out. A page slipped from the open book and fluttered to the floor. It lay in the rushes, tempting her. He read it on her face and in the way her body leaned toward the delicate page.

Had he brought the book to tempt her?

When she picked up the ragged leaf of parchment, she sighed. How he wished she would look upon him with such admiration. The thought made him smile anew. "Well? What is it?" he asked.

"Oh, 'tis a wonderful rendering of the simple plum. See, my lord, even so aged, so spotted with damp, the fruit looks as real as the one in the cook's garden."

He moved to her side. In truth, it was not the drawing that drew him close; it was the look of gentle happiness on her face. When had he ever given such pleasure to another with something so simple?

She turned the page to the other side and another plant. "See, my lord, how the poppies just leap off the page? And here . . ." She skimmed a fingertip over the words. "So simple a thing. So beautiful."

Aye, beautiful, he thought. She was beautiful. Not as lovely as Marion, with her fine bones and flaxen hair, but still, a woman who drew a man's eyes.

"My lord?" Cristina held out the leaf. "One who knows his business should clean the book for you."

"Clean it for yourself, Mistress le Gros, and have it with my blessing. I have no need of it. Herbs are of little interest to me. Now if 'twas a list of weapons, I'd peruse it for hours."

He wandered back to her worktable. The mixture of scents in her chamber filled his head. "Which is responsible for the great improvement in the odor of my hall and solar?" Picking up a stick, he poked a dish of seeds.

She snatched the stick from him and covered the dish with a cloth. "Oh, I just mixed up a few things, sage and rosemary, but, my lord, I cannot take this book—"

"I order it so."

They stood in silence a moment—a silence heated with the abruptness of his words.

"As you wish, my lord, but I cannot read it."

"You don't read Latin?" He damned himself for not guessing. "Only French?"

"French and English. The languages of my father's business."

The disputed book was wrapped in its cloth and set upon the table. Her words separated them as surely as her father's business. "I shall come back then and read it to you," he said.

"That is most kind, but—"

He hurried over her embarrassed words. "You'll show me the book when 'tis clean? I'd be most interested to see it. Then I shall share it with you."

She nodded, but did not look his way.

"How fares the child?" He glanced around for the babe and saw a simple wooden cradle more suited to a child of Cristina's than of Marion's. His sons had lain in gilded beds carved with ravens, to remind them of their duty as they slept.

"Felice is quite well. She's the sweetest-tempered—"

"Felice? Did the priest baptize her thusly? I thought she was to be called Elizabeth Margaret Iona, after my grandmother."

"Lady Marion changed her mind, my lord. Lady Oriel was quite angry with the good father over it, but he would adhere to our lady's wishes. But truly, in the confusion of our lady's collapse, no one wished to argue such a thing—"

"It matters not what the babe is called." The child in the cradle was but a tiny tuft of fair hair above the swaddling.

It was a blessing the child took after Marion—or was it a curse? Would that her hair or eye color cried out her father's name. Nay, it would also cry him a cuckold. He clenched his fist.

Had Marion decided it would be playing the hypocrite to name the child for *his* grandmother?

Cristina knelt by the cradle's edge and stroked her fingers through the downy hair. "I confess, my lord, the name suits her. Felice means good fortune, and surely she is most fortunate in having so many to love and care for her."

Cristina raised her large, dark eyes to him. Could she possibly see inside his heart to know how little he cared what the child was called? "She has good fortune in your care of her."

He watched Cristina's face light with a smile. The simple look sent a shaft of sensation arrowing through him. With a physical struggle, he forced himself to leave the chamber.

"Ah, Durand," Luke called to him from the foot of the stairs. "Why have you been hiding from me? Dare I suppose you fear another session with the castle accounts?"

"I fear nothing, brother." Durand clapped his brother on the shoulder.

Nay, he lied. He feared many things: learning which man had betrayed him just at this time when loyalty meant everything; watching Marion's daughter grow to resemble someone he trusted; showing how much he wanted the merchant's wife.

Thoughts of Cristina le Gros sent Durand's reflections to Simon, and from him to old Owen and his words about betrayal. But when he sought the elderly merchant, he found Father Odo instead.

Old Owen had died.

Chapter Five

At Owen's grave side, just after dawn, the priest spoke at length of Owen's virtues. Durand cursed himself. Why had he not sought Owen out earlier? Too much occupied his mind. Now it was too late.

When the folk of the keep gathered to watch the old man laid to rest in the chapel yard, Durand thought about what Owen had said.

Who would betray him?

Someone already had, he thought, looking over at Felice in Cristina le Gros's arms. Had Owen known Marion's lover? The old man had known so much of what went on twixt village and castle. Now he had taken it to his grave.

"You should have come to Owen's burial," Cristina said to Simon as he wandered about her little alcove, touching dried flower petals and sniffing effusions. "He deserved your respect."

"I cannot see every old man buried," Simon snapped. "What have you here, Cristina?" Motes of dust danced in the morning sunlight behind Simon as he whirled about.

With guilty heat in her cheeks, she hurried to where he stood at her worktable. But it was not the potion she was preparing that drew him.

" 'Tis Aelfric's *Nominum Herbarum*." She discreetly covered the bowl of mallows with a linen cloth.

"*Mon Dieu!* How do you have such a treasure?" He skewered her with a sharp look.

"Lord Durand gave it to me to clean." Why was she reluctant to say his lordship had given her the herbal to keep? Nay, Simon would make something of it— something worthy of chastisement.

"With such embellishments, 'twould fetch a goodly sum." Simon treated the book as reverently as she, turning the leaves carefully, examining the binding, stroking the cover bosses. "To the ignorant, fifty pounds. To an abbey, possibly a thousand."

A thousand pounds? "We'll not be the beneficiaries of its sale." She took the book and placed it squarely on the table. "I shall return it to Lord Durand when 'tis clean."

Simon wandered to her bed, the book forgotten. He stretched out and patted the coverlet next to him. "Come. Lie at my side."

Her legs felt liquid, her chest tight. "I cannot. Felice will wake soon."

He glanced at the cradle. "She's dead to the world. Come."

It was said in a tone that brooked no disobedience. She sat beside him. He cupped her breast. "You must give me a son."

A noise at the door sent her flying from the bed, her heart pounding. "Alice. How kind!" Cristina rushed to the door and took the tray from the serving woman's hands. The smell of roasted partridge filled the room.

"What ye doin' wiv yer boots on the bed?" Alice jammed her fists on her hips and glared at Simon.

He rolled onto his side and propped his head on his hand. "You've a tart tongue."

"I say what needs sayin'. Lord Durand will not be best pleased to find ye lollin' about ere the sun has set."

Simon rose slowly, straightening his tunic. "Lord Durand will not be best pleased to find a serving woman is interfering with a man's pleasure."

"Ye're all the same," Alice said as Simon went to the door. "Rutting pigs. 'Is lordship included. Tell 'im what ye will."

Simon's face was suffused with a deep red; he raised a hand.

"Alice!" Cristina darted between her husband and the servant. "There's no need for acrimony." Behind her, Felice woke and burst into a frantic wail. "Just go, Simon; 'tis not a good time, as you can see."

He relaxed. He placed his fingers beneath her chin and lifted her face to his. "We shall continue this when *she* is not about."

"Please, Simon. 'Tis unseemly to come to me here."

"Unseemly? Then hie yourself home to the village. Bring the child if need be; then return when we've finished our business."

He made of it a chore. "I cannot take—"

Felice's wail became a frantic, hiccuping tirade.

Simon's fingers tightened on her chin. "You'll come when it pleases *me*."

Alice scooped Felice from the cradle and stomped to where they stood. " 'Is lordship'll 'ave some'at to say about that." She thrust the child into Cristina's arms, effectively separating them. "Ye cannot be takin' the babe into the evil air of night."

"Evil air! Shut your mouth, hag." Simon bowed at her. "After vespers, Cristina."

"Rutting bastard," Alice muttered.

Cristina frowned. This was a battle sure to become a war. "It would not do to—"

"—anger 'is lordship, mistress. Remain in the keep, else 'e will 'ave yer 'ead and another'll be found to feed that babe."

"Is there another in the keep who's able to nurse her?" Dread filled her.

"Nay. I know of none, but babes are born every day, and babes die. There be three 'ores in the village what be nursin' now, but 'is lordship wouldna allow such as they to feed his sweetling." Alice bustled about the chamber, shifting a bench, adding wood to the fire. "I be thinkin' ye'll not mind so much if'n Lord Durand sends that one packin'." Alice jerked her thumb at the door.

"Nonsense," she said, rocking and kissing Felice until she quieted and fell asleep. She placed her back in her cradle.

"Oh, aye. Nonsense, is it?" Alice settled on a bench and in moments was snoring.

With a glance at the sleeping woman, Cristina drew the cloth from the mallows she'd been mashing when Simon had interrupted her. She dripped eight and twenty drops of morning dew into the mixture, one drop for each year of her life. Next she lit a candle, newly made with strawberry and cobwebs from the chapel.

Last, she set the dew mixture to heat over the special candle. When the aroma told her it was ready, she lifted the bowl, stood in the morning sun, and drank. As the heated drops slid over her tongue, she closed her eyes tightly and fixed her mind's eye on Lord Durand. She conjured every line on his face, every shade of gray in his eyes, the small scar by his mouth.

"May I resist him," she whispered.

"Lord Durand, I insist you do something. Alice is a menace."

Durand crossed his feet at his ankles. He examined his toes. The hall stretched nearly empty behind the merchant, save for servants. It would fill again that evening. Oriel had planned music and song for Lady Sabina, who had arrived within the hour. He yawned. "Surely, Simon, *menace* is a bit strong?"

"A menace? A witch!"

"I cannot send Alice away. She was my wife's favorite nurse. There was some deathbed promise made." Durand hoped God was busy listening in on someone else's conversation. Yet the lie did not trouble him overmuch.

"But my lord! She keeps me from my wife."

"Hmmm. Still, she cannot be moved."

The merchant paced before his chair. It gave Durand ample opportunity to examine him. The man was certainly handsome. He was as finely garbed as a courtier, but his wife wore mended gowns. Durand's irritation edged toward ire.

"I'm sure I need not tell you that a wife has duties!" Simon drew to a halt before him.

Durand rose. He was as tall as Simon; they stood eye-to-eye. "I understand that your wife is Felice's wet nurse. Those are the *only* duties I concern myself with."

For an instant Durand thought Simon might protest. "Of course, my lord. Forgive me for implying your daughter's needs come after mine, but—"

"But?" Durand lifted one brow and crossed his arms on his chest.

Simon's gaze dropped to the torque about his neck. "But nothing, my lord."

"Is there aught else I may do for you?"

"Nay, nay. All is well. That saddle has arrived, if you wish to see it."

"I'll ride over on the morrow." Durand lifted one hand in dismissal. Simon bowed deeply and strode away.

"Goodness, brother, what was that all about?" Luke asked.

"Must you sneak up on me?" Durand felt the heat in his face. How much had Luke heard?

"One hears no gossip if one stomps about like a shod horse!"

"*Jesu.* What possible gossip was there to be had from le Gros?"

"He feels some need to have you think his wick needs dipping at the hands of the ethereal Cristina." Luke gave Durand a toothy smile. "I happen to know he has it regularly trimmed at the Raven's Head. But one must pity the man the loss of the fair Cristina's favors. I wager she handles the wick most gently."

Durand's lifeblood pooled in his groin. He dropped into his chair behind the table.

"Care you for a ride to the village?" Durand ventured.

But Luke did not answer. He had hooked a serving wench about the waist and was whispering in her ear, Simon and Cristina forgotten.

Durand could not so easily forget. His thoughts turned to *her*, just a few rounds up the stairs, conjuring some seductive soap or lotion. How much longer could he resist her?

Musicians strolled the hall, strumming and singing as servants dodged them with trenchers of roasted swan and partridge.

Cristina approached the hearth, where the ladies sat stitching. Several men, Lord Durand prominent among them, stood nearby. She took a seat far to one side.

"Mistress le Gros. Why do you perch like a sparrow in the shadows here?" It was Lord Luke who approached her.

"Would you return this herbal to Lord Durand?" She handed Luke the newly cleaned Aelfric, an ache in her middle that she had had but two days to peruse it. Yet she could not keep such a gift. If Simon knew its worth, surely Lord Durand did as well. The implications of the gift frightened her. Did not a man want something in return for such value?

She had naught to give.

"Most certainly," Luke said. "Come along with me, if you have the time, as I find I have need of your services."

Luke led her to his counting room, where he placed the herbal in a coffer filled with rolls of parchment and other books. She longed to see them, but the lid fell shut on the treasures.

"Sit." He indicated a stool by his fire. "I've a friend who has come to me." Luke cleared his throat. "Ah. It seems, that is . . . *Mon Dieu*, this is difficult."

"Take your time, my lord." Cristina tucked her skirts about her knees and tried to ignore her aching breasts. Felice had nursed little and then fallen deeply asleep as if she had feasted on the stuffed swan from the high table.

"I've a friend who is most distressed that he's unable to . . . that is, he feels himself not quite adequate. . . . *Mon Dieu!*" Luke began to pace. He finally halted at the fire, his back to her. "This friend feels himself inadequate in the bedchamber. There, I have said it!"

He turned around. His face was as red as the streaks in his golden hair.

Cristina swallowed. "I see. Why are you telling me this?" She knew Lord Luke's reputation. Lord of Skirts, they called him. Was it not true? She didn't believe in the friend of Lord Luke any more than she had believed in the friend of Lady Oriel.

"I'd hoped you could conjure up a salve or something."

She almost giggled at the thought of where Lord Luke would need to rub it. "I see." She cleared her throat. "I'm not a healer, my lord."

"This is not something for the leech, mistress." Luke raked his fingers through his hair. "He'd have it about the castle in the time it took me to spit twice."

"Mayhap I can mix something for your friend. But . . ." She swallowed her mirth and gulped. How to ask this next question? Her own face heated. "But in what manner does the man feel—"

Luke frantically waved his hands. "Nay, nay, say no more. He is, shall we just say, distressed he has no children."

No children? Whatever did Lord Luke want with a child? Mayhap he did have a friend in need. Then she thought of Oriel, who also wanted a potion to conceive. "I understand. Your friend wishes something to aid conception."

Luke smiled. "You understand. Make it something strong. Very strong. He's most anxious for an heir."

Cristina rose. Her breasts were as hard as millstones. She ached to rub them. "Shall I leave the potion here, my lord?"

"You're an angel."

Cristina returned to Felice's chamber. Within the curtained alcove, a spare, gray-haired man sniffed at the bowls on her worktable. The leech. His dusty embroidered robes dragged about his ankles as he clucked and mewed over her hanging bunches of drying flowers.

"May I help you, Master Aldwin?" she asked.

The leech turned to her and blew a long breath from

his fleshy lips. "I'll not abide your trespass, Mistress le Gros."

She went to the cradle. The babe lay on her back, hands in tiny fists, and made small puffing noises— sound asleep. With a sigh, Cristina tried to ignore her discomfort and the whine in Master Aldwin's voice. "I intend no trespass, sir."

"What need have you of betony or dock?"

"I keep some herbs for my own use, sir, as does any wife. Surely you cannot object to that? I trade only in pretty scents."

"Hmph. You prepared an herbal drink for Lady Marion, did you not?"

"Nay, 'twas honey in warm milk. It had no healing properties. 'Twas what any cook would prepare if asked!"

Master Aldwin sniffed. "I'll complain to his lordship if I find you are *healing*, Mistress le Gros." He swung about to her table and swept out an arm. In moments, her bowls and oils crashed to the floor.

She could not stifle a strangled cry of dismay.

Aldwin pressed his hands to his cheeks. "Ah, me. Forgive me, mistress. How clumsy of me!"

From the corner came a sudden shriek. Felice pawed the air and wailed. Aldwin turned to where the babe lay and pointed a quivering finger. "Tend to your work and I'll tend to mine, else Lord Durand shall put you out!"

Weeks of gathering lay in ruins, purchased spices mingling with lowly mint. She scooped Felice up and held her close. The babe rooted at her breast; Cristina's eyes burned. She would not weep! She had vowed years ago never to weep, and had broken that vow only to mourn her daughters. She would not break it now.

Ground cinnamon, so little left, so costly to obtain, all lost in the rushes. Lavender mingled with comfrey.

79

She concentrated on the child and forced herself to put the disaster from her mind. Thank God Aldwin had not seen the Aelfric volume lying open on the table but an hour ago. Surely that would be evidence to him that she intended to set herself to healing.

When Felice slumbered, sated, mouth agape, Cristina placed her on the bed. How simple life was for Felice. Eat and sleep.

Alice found her on her hands and knees an hour later, her bowls in a circle around her. "Mistress! What ails ye?"

Cristina poured tainted oil into a large basin and sniffed to see if it could be salvaged. "I'm quite well, Alice. I had an accident."

"Oh, 'tis an ill omen! All yer precious things!" Alice dropped to her knees and began to sweep seeds into a small pile with her hand.

"Alice, the sun is on the wane. Why do you not take a turn in the cook's garden? 'Tis likely to rain on the morrow."

Alice sat back on her heels. "Ye do not fool me, miss. I'm mixing them up, am I not?"

With a quick bob of her head, Cristina acknowledged the truth. Hearing the baby wake, she patted Alice's hand. "Take Felice and sit in the sun."

"Aye, I will, and on the morrow I'll beg some space for ye from the cook to grow yer flowers. 'E owes me a favor or two."

"Oh, Alice, what that would mean to me!"

Alice winked and rose with a groan. "I'll see to it. Me knees are too old for this work." She departed.

Cristina worked for several more hours, sifting seeds and herbs into their bowls. Costly spices were tainted with common herbs, some hopelessly soaked in oils. She tried to imagine new uses for them.

Alice returned Felice for her next feeding. As the

babe nursed, Cristina's mind drifted to thoughts of the kitchen garden and how long it would take to harvest anything useful. Just a few rows was all she needed—actually, many rows, but she would settle for a few to start.

The many scents that mingled without purpose offended her. She contemplated the enemy she had made in Master Aldwin.

Would Lord Durand turn her out at Aldwin's word?

She put Felice in her sling and went in search of Lord Luke. But he sat at Lord Durand's side amidst a group of lords and knights and their ladies, making approach impossible.

The women were draped in gowns the colors of the flowers of the fields; gold circlets studded with gems adorned their brows. Each woman was tended by her servant, each lord and knight by his men. Then she saw a portly man, surely a bishop, with several cassocked men at his side. What illustrious company had gathered for King John's visit. This was what she had missed when last the king had visited Ravenswood. Then she had lived at the alehouse and come to the keep not at all.

Lord Durand looked the finest of the men. He wore a tunic of deep forest green. About his waist he wore a belt of leather, studded with silver and amber. About his neck gleamed the golden torque. She had seen it close now, the twists of metal old and worn, the terminals that embraced the hollow of his throat ravens' heads.

She thought of how the old gold must feel, smooth where it lay against his skin, warm from the throb of his pulse. Why was she having such thoughts? Quickly she ran through the ingredients of the resisting potion. Had she made a mistake? Forgotten something? There was no one to consult. The potion had come from her mother's mother.

A lady rose and went to Lord Durand's side. As Cristina watched, the woman slipped her hand along the back of his neck. She toyed with the hair at his nape, then leaned down to whisper something in his ear that caused him to smile.

Just then, Lady Oriel rose with elegant grace. "Cristina. Come. Join us."

With a quick shake of her head, she took a step back, but Lady Oriel touched Lord Durand on the arm. "Command her here, Durand. Lady Sabina, you'd like to see Marion's babe, would you not?"

The woman draped over Lord Durand's shoulder straightened and turned to where Cristina stood. "Aye. Bring the child."

Cristina walked slowly to the table, aware of many eyes on her. The ladies gathered about. The Lady Sabina had flawless skin, gray-green eyes, and thick lashes as black as her hair. Unkindly, Cristina also noted her sharp nose and thin lips.

"Durand, she is a sweetling. She has the de Marle look. My father will surely want her for my brother. What say you?" Lady Sabina asked over her shoulder.

Lord Durand shook his head and rose. "Nay. I'll settle only for a prince."

Lady Sabina laughed. "Mayhap King John will know of a little princeling who's dangling for a bride. Shall I ask him when he arrives?"

How easily they spoke of princes, Cristina thought. Did she nurture a future queen? She thought of King John coming to Ravenswood Castle, planning a marriage for Felice, sporting with these men and women just as he had this past summer. How long until they all left for Normandy and war? Some of the men in this hall would die. A shiver of fear, a sudden foreboding, filled her.

"Please yourself, Sabina." Durand swept her a bow. "What brings you here, mistress?" He did not approach, but the look he directed at her would melt metal. Had Master Aldwin already complained of her?

"I had need of a word with Lord Luke."

A nearby knight made a remark aside to his lady. The lady snickered. So did the bishop.

Cristina lifted her chin.

"Luke?" Durand turned to his brother.

"Ah, mistress, have you brought me some of your fine soap?"

"Nay, my lord. I have found my stores seriously depleted, and I am unable to make your soap. Mayhap another time." She curtsied deeply and left the company. She did not belong here among these fine folk, and the talk of soap merely informed the company at large where she stood among them.

Behind her several men laughed. They thought nothing of embarrassing a stranger with their laughter. She held them in contempt. At the first opportunity she left the hall.

Durand attended with great concentration to the sauced partridges and fine wines that evening, but by the time the poached pears were set before him, he could no longer contain himself. "Soap?" he demanded of his brother. "What need have you for scented soap?"

Luke grinned and shrugged. "Fine ladies enjoy such trifles."

"So 'tis just to speed the shedding of a gown?" His relief was unaccountable.

"Aye. I'll play at sport in a warm tub—but not alone."

The idea fascinated Durand. "Damn you, Luke."

Luke wagged his eyebrows. "I can have a tub drawn for you, brother. Mistress le Gros will supply the soaps; Lady Sabina will scrub your back. What say you?"

"I've already said it. Damn you." He speared a sliver of pear, poached in the last of the wine from his wife's estates. Sourly he sucked the morsel of fruit off the tip of his blade.

Luke excused himself. "I believe I'll find out why Mistress le Gros lacks what she needs to make my soap. When I visited her this morn, her worktable groaned with smelly things." He headed for the tower stairs and took them two at a time.

Durand watched him go. *Visited her this morn?* He sat for but a moment before rising and going after his brother.

Lady Sabina intercepted him. "Come, my lord. You promised to look at my palfrey." She hooked his arm, and he knew it would be the worst of insults to set her aside.

"Mistress le Gros?" Luke knocked at her chamber door and pushed it open. He followed her into the alcove where she did her work. "What happened here?" He set his fists on his hips and surveyed her nearly bare table.

"Master Aldwin got the notion I was poaching on his domain."

"He didn't discover you were making me a love potion, did he?" He turned an alarmed face to her.

"Nay. He discovered that I'd mixed Lady Marion a drink. Not a medicinal one, but still, it seemed so to him." She sighed when she contemplated the few bowls left unscathed on her worktable.

"Can you gather again what you need? My friend will pay you well to do so."

Cristina shrugged. "I know what I need. Savory and onion I have"—she lifted a bowl—"but the rest is costly."

Luke grinned and tossed her a heavy purse. "Pray, do not consider the cost."

Chapter Six

After chapel the next morn, Cristina and Alice rode quite comfortably to the village in one of Lord Durand's carts. Moisture sparkled on the leaves and grass, and puddles lay in the rutted roadbed, attesting to the previous night's storm.

" 'Ave ye seen the cottage since old Owen died?" Alice asked.

"Nay, but I know just what I shall find. Everything shall march in orderly rows, each item set out to best advantage. It was always so with our cart. No matter how long it took, each time we moved from a village, the cart must be put to perfect order again. I hated moving from place to place."

"Humph. I prefer Owen's jumble."

So did I, Cristina thought traitorously. Her few forays into Owen's cottage had delighted the senses and involved many moments of happy exploration after treasures. "Old Owen seemed a kindly man."

"Aye. We'll miss 'im. Beggin' yer pardon, but what possessed ye to wed wiv Simon?"

" 'Tis an easy question to answer. He is—"

"Pleasin' to the eye. Flattered ye, too, and yer father, I wager."

"Aye. 'Twas just as you say."

They drew up before Simon's cottage. Cristina clambered from the wagon and thanked Lovell, one of Lord Durand's grooms, for his kind attentions to their needs. He nodded and joined Alice in the cart. Felice sat in Alice's lap, sucking on her own tiny fingers.

The long cottage was built of dressed stone, the front entrance decorated with tiles pilfered from some ancient Roman edifice. The wide wooden door gave entrance into the room used to house and sell the merchant's wares. On the right stood a ladder that led to the upper story, where she would reside once her time with Felice was done—or until Simon demanded she give up the chore and come to her new home.

How would it feel to leave the babe? It was what must be if she were to have a child—Simon's child.

She looked about and saw her husband, oblivious to her presence, head bent over a roll of parchment at an old battered table. As he did not see her, she took a moment to walk about.

She frowned. Simon must have laid out a sizable sum to have such stock. Had he been borrowing again? He had once gotten into difficulty with such folly, but her father had set it right.

All about her were the usual goods any villager might need, but there were finer goods more suited to the manor as well: silk thread on small cards, silver needles, citron for a lord's table.

Beyond a marvelous selection of linen and wool sat a leather saddle. This must be the one destined for the king. She ran her hand over the smooth, fragrant leather; the deeply incised patterns of mounted men with couched lances and brandished swords that graced the skirt reminded her of what was to come.

Simon looked up from his ledger. "Cristina! Is something the matter? Why are you here?" He did not rise.

"Lord Luke gave me a purse to purchase a few necessaries," she said, abandoning the saddle and confronting her husband. She held out the purse, but Simon did not take it.

His eyes narrowed. He yelped and leaped to his feet. He shoved past her to push open a shutter and lean out. "Hag! What are you doing here?"

"Simon, she accompanies me."

Her husband drew back into the room and pointed at the door. "If she sets foot in here, I shall take a stick to you. That woman is a plague on me. She told two men in Guy Wallingford's service I—" His face flared red. "Never mind what she said. 'Tis enough to know she is a slandering hag!"

"What did she say, Simon? You've gone too far to retreat; you slander *her* if you cannot put evidence to your complaints."

Cristina drew her mantle close about her middle. What lie would he concoct? For she saw on his stony face that she would not have the truth. "Think you I'll not ask Alice myself when we are away from here?"

"A man need not give his wife an account of himself." With an attitude of great importance, Simon hastened to his desk and took up his quill. "Now, you disturb my work. Lord Durand's man is due to collect the king's saddle, and I've not yet written the charge. I repeat, what is it you want?"

Not for the first time, and certainly not for the last, she found she did not care what he had done. She dropped the purse with a thump on the table by Simon's elbow, along with the list to make not only Luke's potency elixir, but also Lady Oriel's sweet pillows and a wrinkle cream for Guy Wallingford's lady.

"Cinnamon? Ginger?" Simon murmured as he read the list. He looked up, one brow raised. "This is a sizable purchase. What became of the ginger I gave you last week?"

"Master Aldwin used it." That was certainly not a lie.

"Hmmm. If Master Aldwin needs to replenish his stores, he should pay for them. Do not allow it to happen again."

He handed back the list and, with a wave of his hand indicating she should search out the items herself, went back to his accounting.

Old Owen's cottage was still a delight to her, despite the loss of its haphazard nature. She poked in every box and barrel and bin and put aside thoughts of the debts incurred to stock it so. She breathed deeply of the ginger and added some fennel seeds to her heap of purchases for a wrinkle cream for Lord Guy's wife. She placed them in the back of her cart. Felice now lay sleeping in Lovell's lap. He shrugged with a sheepish grin. "I'll be but a moment more," she told him.

But a well-trimmed goose quill tempted her, and she thought of the months of work it must have taken to make the Aelfric herbal. The sound of a party of horses arriving in the lane distracted her from her contemplation. On tiptoe, she peered out the front window. It was Lord Durand himself, with the Lady Sabina and several other men—come for the saddle, she heard Lord Durand say to Simon, who was gushing a welcome to the lady.

Cristina's heart banged in her chest. She put a frantic hand to her head. Her headcovering was askew, her hair straggling from its confines. Hastily she tucked in the errant strands and tugged her gown straight.

Lord Durand entered the cottage, bringing with him the scent of leather and horses, accompanied by Lady Sabina and Lord Penne. Cristina curtsied, but it was to *him* she looked.

His wintry eyes looked as pale as silver pennies in the sunlit cottage; his dark hair was swept back from his brow. He drew his gloves off and tucked them in his belt, but remained at the door while the others spread out to examine Simon's wares. His gaze ran over her in a lazy perusal that felt like a flame licking over her skin.

She nodded to him and he inclined his head.

"Cristina, serve Lady Sabina." Simon called her to the far end of the cottage. She went and, with clumsy hands—clumsy for *he* had come to stand at their side—showed the lady several lengths of fine linen dyed the color of the sea.

He stood within a foot of her, leaned his arm on a tall shelf, and listened to her description of the cloth, its tight weave, the likelihood it would fray when washed, as if he were going to stitch up a gown himself. The thought of him, so large, so male, needle in hand, his men and hounds about him at the hearth, made her nearly choke on a giggle.

"Purchase it for me, Durand, will you? I have naught in my purse save dust," Lady Sabina said, placing a proprietary hand on his arm. "And trim, if it's to be had." She led him away. "Where have I seen the merchant's wife before? I cannot remember, yet she is very familiar." Lady Sabina made her query without lowering her voice.

Cristina folded the cloth and selected several ribbons for trim. They had met but the night before.

"In my hall, Sabina. She brought Marion's babe to you."

"Oh, aye. I remember. She has the sweetest face."

Lord Durand's words, a low murmur, brought a

loud cry of amusement from Lady Sabina. "Nay, Durand, I meant the babe! She will be as lovely as Marion one day."

Heat filled Cristina's body. Lord Durand's answer was lost to her as Penne called out to him to hurry, for they wasted the best part of the day.

The linen in her hands was glossy, fine, finer than any she would use to make up a gown for herself. But she was happy in her old wool. It was soft and sturdy and suited to her work. She could not mix a salve for dry hands in such a linen, nor could it take a washing to remove a stain from mother's milk.

She turned around. Lord Durand stood before her, a wall blocking her way. A turmoil of sensation roiled through her.

"You returned the Aelfric to my brother. Why?"

She could not go around him. Did not wish to. "Forgive me, but Simon apprised me of its value and I could not keep it."

His dark, straight brows drew together in a frown. "Is not its true value the use made of it?"

"Aye, some would say so. Mayhap it would better serve Master Aldwin." Her throat felt tight. What if Master Aldwin had complained of her?

"Aldwin! You may not be able to read Latin, but he cannot read at all. He cares only to bleed a man's blood into his little bowls and mumble over it later. For all I know he drinks it after 'tis bled.

"If you have no interest in the herbal, then say so and the matter is done, but if you can find in it even one page to aid you, then you must have it." He reached out and skimmed his thumb across her cheek. "Have you been head-down in a barrel? You've smudges on your nose and—"

"My lord!" Lady Sabina called from the doorway. He jerked his hand back.

The same color that must be on her cheeks rushed

into his. His frown altered to a flat, cold stare. With a shrug he took a step back. "Say what you will, mistress. Can you find even one page in the herbal of use to you?"

Cristina became aware that the cottage was empty. They stood alone in a pool of shadow behind a cask of salted herring.

When he had briefly touched her, she had frozen in place as if a statue, words caught in her throat, words of begging to have the book, and to have him read it for her. But his cold countenance, the flat sound of his offer now—now that he had been recalled by his friend—stirred her resolve.

"Nay, my lord, there's naught in the book I can use." The lie lay on her tongue like salt on a wound. She blessed the resistance potion that surely aided her now.

He gave her a stiff bow and swung away. She hastily wrapped Lady Sabina's linen and rushed out in time to hand it up to a maid who waited for it. The others, Lord Durand at the fore, cantered away up the lane.

Simon rubbed his hands together. "Did you see? Lord Durand was using the saddle himself! He'll find it so easy a ride, he will order another for himself when the king is gone. Come. Take what it is you came for and be gone. I want to get along to the Raven's Head and see if someone there is willing to go to Winchester and fetch another saddle." He shook Luke's purse.

Two days later, Cristina delivered the elixir for Lord Luke, still warm from the pot. She placed the stone bottle on his table, anchoring a scrap of vellum lying there. The words on it drew her eyes.

12 chapel S

The writing was that of a fine lady, each letter beautifully formed, the *S* larger than the others and finished off with a sweeping curlicue.

So Lord Luke would be wooing Lady Sabina in the chapel this night, for she could not think of any other Lady S.

Of course, it could be that twelve chapel stones needed repair. Then a dreadful thought flitted through her mind: Lord Durand used this chamber. She had found him reading here. Mayhap the missive was from Sabina to him, and they met in secrecy because of Lady Marion's recent death. Her hand went to her cheek, where he had touched her. With a frown, she set the bottle of hope on the scrap of vellum.

Before leaving the chamber, Cristina went to the coffer where Lord Luke had placed the herbal and lifted the lid. The Aelfric was not on top, and she had not the courage to rummage through the rolls and other books. How she wished to have the Aelfric. It was a finer treasure to her than any sum of gold. "If I had ink and paper, I would make my own *Nominum Herbarum*," she said aloud.

When the door opened, she just had time to whirl away from the coffer and snatch up her basket before Lord Penne entered. He glanced at the table. "Forgive my intrusion."

"Nay," she said. "Forgive mine." She left quickly.

Was it Lord Penne who intrigued with Lady Sabina? The thought grieved her. If the Lady Oriel sought her potion for herself, she was wrong that her husband did not yet stray.

The lords and ladies returned from a day of hunting in high spirits, the scent of the outdoors on their clothes. There would be a high demand for her lotions tomorrow, if the red cheeks of the ladies were any indication. Cristina listened from her bench with half an ear as Lord Luke and several men argued about the hunt.

"They shall all be put to shame when King John arrives with his hawks," Luke said, ending the discussion.

"His wagons come on the morrow," Durand said. "His party will eat us out of our winter stores in less than a fortnight. We'll need every penny in our coffers to replenish them."

Lady Sabina leaned over the back of his chair and whispered something in his ear.

Who would meet with Lady Sabina at the hour of twelve? Lord Penne? Or did he but collect the message for another? Lord Luke? Lord Durand? Or had Penne only wanted the love potion?

Cristina ate quickly and returned to the babe, who fretted and refused to nurse. With the child in her arms, she paced the small alcove, past her worktable. There was nothing to do there. The mixture of freckle cream, if stirred, lost its effectiveness. The rose oil was perfect, ready to add to small pots of skin lotion.

She boosted the babe up to the window. "Look, Felice. The clouds seem to touch the towers, they're so low. It shall rain before morning." But Felice would not be amused, nor soothed.

"Walk 'er about, miss," Alice said. "So an old body can rest."

Cristina smiled. "I'll take her for a stroll about the bailey, if it pleases you."

The old woman grinned, revealing she had lost another front tooth, and draped a mantle about her. Cristina tucked the squalling infant into her sling with a kiss.

"Good night to ye. Find a corner when she settles and put her to breast. Ye'll save me ears if'n ye do."

*   *   *

Durand turned over on his back and looked up at the glowering sky through his open shutters. Why could he not sleep? A lump in his mattress felt as large as a millstone. He shifted his shoulders, but failed to get comfortable. He sat up and pounded the lump into submission. As he lay back he heard the wail of an infant. Only one babe dwelled in the castle—or one he had noticed—but the child and her nurse resided in the east tower. Mayhap there were dozens of infants about. There were so many guests now, he could not keep them and their retainers straight.

He rose and went to the window, propped his arms on the wide stone sill, and looked out. Cool air washed over his bare skin. The bailey was filled with folk as if it were daylight. Men worked through the night to see everything was in readiness for the king's invasion of Normandy. He could see the glow of the forge and hear the ring of the hammer on the anvil. Thunder rumbled over the distant hills as if God, too, readied for war.

Cristina le Gros crossed the bailey.

"What the devil is she about?" He drew on his clothing and thrust his dagger into his belt. Within moments he stood in the bailey. He saw her by the stable, no purpose in her manner. Indeed, she wandered, swinging her skirts side to side in what Luke would surely call a fairy dance. He decided it was her way of soothing the infant.

"What the devil am *I* doing here?" he asked himself as he strode to the stables. His steps slowed when she sat on a bench, nearly invisible in her dark mantle among the shadows cast by torches on the stable wall. He propped his shoulder by his destrier's stall in his own pool of darkness. As he watched, Cristina unlaced her gown—slowly, as a woman might to entice her lover—and bared her breast. He held his breath at the alabaster gleam of her skin, the full roundness of her flesh, the dark point of her nipple, which she offered to the child.

Marion's child.

His groin throbbed with desire for Cristina. More confused emotions filled him for the child. Those he set aside.

"I'm as much a dog as Luke," he said softly. "I've been too long without a female if the mere sight of a nursing woman raises my lust."

But flesh was flesh, and she had abundant and beautiful breasts. He could almost feel them in his hands. Yet if she were but a bountifully made woman, he could resist her. Certainly he resisted Lady Sabina's sweet tits when faced with them each day. Nay, he had lost himself to Mistress le Gros's soothing touch and misguided arguments about Aristophanes.

His horse poked its head from the stable door and whickered a greeting. Durand stroked the horse's velvety nose. "I am seduced by philosophy, my fine fellow." But, if he were truthful, he was equally drawn to Cristina by those breasts that would cushion a man's troubled head in heavenly softness.

She murmured something to the babe and shifted the child from one breast to the other. Her hair was loose, in a fall of waves to her waist.

"Ah, Marauder, I am lost," he whispered at the horse's ear.

The chapel bells rang the hour. Twelve. He stroked the horse's head and nourished his parched soul. When she finished the feeding, he'd go. Until then, he could no more move his gaze from her bent head or creamy skin, exposed further as her gown slipped off her shoulder, than a starving man could move from a table laden with food.

Cristina tucked Felice into her sling. "You greedy little pig. Why could you not eat so in our chamber?" She rose and, giving in to curiosity at the peal of the bells, walked not toward the east tower, but to the west.

Several men hurried by on some business, heads together, their voices unnaturally loud in the darkness. A gust of wind lifted her hem and snapped the fabric against her calves.

Two more men passed her: Lord Penne and Lord Luke.

"Bother. They go together! Now I'll never know." But the men parted company, Lord Luke heading for the chapel, Lord Penne turning aside to the great hall.

Mystery solved. Lord Luke met Lady Sabina. Penne must have been fetching the love potion. She did not need to see the assignation, and so, satisfied that Lady Oriel was to sleep in her husband's arms, she turned and collided with Lord Durand and tumbled to the cobbles.

"Felice!" she cried. She pulled back the swaddling and found the babe still asleep. Lord Durand's strong hands swept her back onto her feet.

"Are you hurt?" he asked, raking her hair back from her face.

"Nay. Aye. I don't know." She shook her head. Her bottom smarted most painfully, but she could not tell him that!

The sky opened. Rain pelted her head and shoulders. She yelped and bent over to shelter Felice from the onslaught. Lord Durand grabbed her arm and dragged her the few steps into the shelter of the chapel. It was as cold and damp as a crypt.

Her altar oil filled the chapel with the scent of sage. No priest said mass, no penitents knelt at prayers. No Lady Sabina embraced Lord Luke. They were alone. Where had Lord Luke gone?

Lord Durand laughed as he shook the rain from his head. "We're trapped."

The rain fell in a solid wall of water, formed a curtain across the chapel entrance, and gushed in rivers across the bailey stones. She stared out at the night, black, cold. Private.

"How fares the child?" he asked.

"Blissfully asleep. I came out because she's been fretting all night. Now, when she should by rights be frightened silly, she's completely at peace."

"Why should she be frightened?"

Cristina looked up at him. His hair was wet, his gray eyes dark shadows in his face. Water beaded his skin. "I-I don't know. The rain. Our fall." Her every sense was on fire in his presence. His scent filled her head, negated the powerful altar oils, drew her as if she had never drunk the resistance potion.

"But she's not injured? *You're* not injured?" He lifted her chin.

Simon had done so but a day before. Simon's touch left her cold; this man's enthralled her. He was naught but a tale one told in old age. A tale of a lord who spoke to her as an equal, aroused her senses, made her wish to be a fine lady. It was a sin to think of him at all . . . a greater sin to think of the hard line of his jaw, his scent, here in God's chapel.

"Where?" he asked softly.

"Where?" she whispered. His fingers were warm on her chin.

"Where are you injured?"

"Oh." She stepped away, breaking the contact. "I'm not injured."

"Nonsense. You took quite a spill—"

The soft scrape of a shoe on stone interrupted him. Turning, Lord Durand used one hand to shift her behind him.

Cristina felt the pressure of Lord Durand's hand and she heeded it, backing into the wall of water, and out into the night.

Her heart raced. She ran, mantle close about the

child, to the hall. As she hurried through the vast space, filled with sleeping men and women on pallets, she moaned. Her spine and bottom ached miserably. Her head throbbed on each step up to her chamber. Her heart thudded like a hammer on an anvil.

Had the person in the chapel seen her—seen Lord Durand touching her? Was it Lord Luke? He'd surely say naught, but what if Lady Sabina had arrived and witnessed their exchange? Cristina cringed when she thought of that lady's tart tongue.

She tiptoed about for a moment, then took less care, for Alice snored heavily on a pallet in the corner, a cloud of ale fumes issuing forth with every breath. Felice slipped her fingers into her mouth when placed on her back in her cradle and made her own puffing sounds of deep sleep. "You imp. *Now* you sleep."

Sodden garments clung to Cristina's legs and back. She stripped them and laid them out over a bench by the fire. After donning a clean shift, she knelt there to dry her hair.

The thread of her thoughts wound from Lord Penne, to Luke, to Lord Durand.

A lady's note. An assignation.

All was suddenly clear. *Lord Durand* met the Lady Sabina in the chapel.

"You're a fool, Cristina," she whispered to the crackling flames. "Lord Penne must have retrieved the note for Lord Durand so he'd not be seen to receive it, and Lord Luke merely cleared the chapel for his brother. They work in concert to aid their master." A tangle snagged her fingers. "Of course his friends would see that their lord was not disturbed. Of course 'tis Lord Durand who meets with Lady Sabina. Lady Marion is not long enough dead to allow him to openly court her." She rose hastily to her feet. "Oh, this wretched hair. Ugly as old wool!"

Cristina tossed back the lid of a small box that contained all she owned: precious sewing needles, a length of ribbon from Lady Marion, a horn comb that she plucked up and yanked through her snarled tresses. "What concern of mine is it that Lord Durand makes love in the chapel?"

She threw the comb on the table, where it landed in the rose oil. The dish tipped, spilling the oil across the table. "Oh, a plague on fine ladies," she muttered. Tears pricked at her eyes. "Look what I've done! Hours of work wasted! The oil's ruined!" She dropped a length of linen on the mess to prevent it from dripping off the table.

Her hair still damp and tangled, she threw herself on her bed. The canopy overhead had a rent, chewed by a mouse, she imagined. She rolled to her side, punched her pillow, sat up, climbed out of bed. In two steps she was at her table and had retrieved the comb and wiped it clean. With painstaking care, she mopped up the oil and tidied the worktable. She scrubbed the top, then folded the rose oil–soaked cloth and placed it exactly in the center of the table.

With her agitation's abatement, the wind outside died. The sudden silence drew her to the window. She flung open the shutters and stared down into the bailey; she saw naught but shrouds of mist. At last, she stretched out on her bed atop the coverlet, the damp air stirring across the chamber and over her heated skin.

"Get to sleep, Cristina. *You* shall be gathering roses tomorrow at dawn whilst finer ladies rest from a surfeit of lovemaking."

Chapter Seven

Durand crossed his arms over his chest and tried to ignore the water dripping down his neck. "How do you come to be here, Simon? Were you somehow occupied that you did not heed the closing of the gates?"

"Ah, my lord." Simon licked his lips. "I did not expect to meet you here. I'm to . . . that is, I'm to meet . . ." Simon dipped his head and thrust his hands up into his capacious sleeves.

"You may as well say whom you're to meet, as I'll know in but a moment."

"Then I must confess I'm to meet a woman."

"A woman? When you've a wife as pleasing as yours, you're seeking after another?" Durand took a quick glance behind him to be sure Cristina was gone. He heard nothing to indicate she lingered, and he hoped she'd not heard Simon's words.

Simon glanced about. "My lord, we're both men who have traveled much. You must know that 'tis ofttimes necessary to seek some solace with another. After all, my Cristina is quite occupied with your daughter."

"If her duties are a burden to you, I shall release her."

"Nay! Please. We strive only to serve you. Don't be hasty! Cristina would be heartbroken to be set aside as nurse!"

"Is not the setting aside by a husband—" Durand broke off. Lady Sabina stood in the chapel entrance. He knew her by the embroidered mantle she wore. Rain glistened off the scarlet hood in the meager light of the chapel candles.

"Forgive my intrusion," Durand said. He stepped past Lady Sabina and strode out into the rain. It poured in icy discomfort down his shoulders. He made a search of the bailey, but Mistress le Gros was long gone.

He headed for her tower to see if she was injured from her fall, then hesitated. Would she read the knowledge on his face that her husband strayed?

What ailed le Gros? And what had he to offer Sabina?

"I am a hypocrite," he whispered with a glance up at the light that gleamed through Cristina's shutters. "I'd have done more than touch Mistress le Gros if her husband had not come upon the scene." He could feel the smoothness of her skin, catch her scent on the wind—imagination, he knew. If the truth were known, he would have taken her there in the chapel even if he was to be damned for all eternity.

In his chamber, Durand paced from corner to corner. Every step on the rushes reminded him of Cristina. The scented soap in a silver bowl, stamped with the raven, filled his head, made him ache to call for a bath even as midnight drifted toward dawn.

He fell into a chair. "Ah, Marion, who am I to condemn you for your lovers? Surely I'm as dishonorable to your memory and to Simon's vows as you were to ours. If Cristina put out her hand, I would take it up."

Several hours later, he still stared into the hearth fire, desire rampant. "*Jesu.*" He rose and threw open the door. With a brisk nod, he passed the sentry at the foot of his stairs and then walked quietly through the hall to the east tower. He would see if the child was injured from the fall in the bailey. At Cristina's door, he hesitated but a moment before he opened it.

The act took him past some boundary heretofore never violated.

The scent of roses filled the air.

He felt as if he'd stepped into a rose garden. And in the center of the bower lay Cristina, curled on her bed, one hand beneath her cheek, childlike, her lips slightly parted. Innocent. What would he make of her if he persuaded her to his bed?

An adulteress.

Would she come if he asked? He sensed something between them, like the perfume when she passed that lingered in his head, an intangible thing not seen, but felt low in his belly.

The shift she wore gleamed white in the chamber lit only by the lingering embers of a banked fire. He roamed her chamber, skimming his fingers over her mantle draped on a bench, still wet from their dash across the bailey. The cradle lay in deep darkness, the babe indistinguishable from the shadow. Alice snored noisily on a corner pallet, blankets about her head.

Durand returned to the bed. His body ached for the woman lying there, her hair tangled across her pillow—hair that would flow through his hands like silk. What would it be like to bury his face in that hair?

The blood of desire filled his body.

His breath caught in his throat as she moaned softly and shifted, rolling to her back, her breasts now straining the cloth, dark nipples thrust against the linen.

Against all sense, all the crying fears of discovery that webbed the night, he moved to the head of the bed.

In his dreams, in the days to come, he would touch her cheek. She would open her eyes, lift her arms, and welcome him to the warmth of her bed . . . and her body.

In this, the cold hour before dawn, he retreated to his chamber, where he watched the morning sun rise over the land, cool air washing his face. Glass had once filled his window until Marion had thrown a dish at his head. Thrown it because he had locked her garden and banished her lover.

Tossing open his coffer, he dug to the bottom, to a painted box carved with ravens. A box of keys. He immediately saw what he wanted—a large iron key, rusty with disuse.

He found Cristina later that morning near the castle wall in the cook's garden, the edge of her hem damp with dew, gathering wild roses in a basket. Her skirt swayed with her walk as she bent and cut the blooms. He watched her lift each flower to her face, then skim it across her cheek before placing it carefully in the basket.

Her profile was serene, her cheeks tinted with the same color as the flowers she held.

"Mistress le Gros?" He waited for her to look up.

She turned. "My lord." She dropped into a deep obeisance but kept her gaze on her basket of flowers.

Two kitchen boys ran past, chasing one another. The scent of baking bread filled the air, and yet he thought he could smell the roses in her hands. He sensed a disquiet in her that told him she was not resistant to him or his touch of the night before in the chapel.

Several knights, strangers, cut across the kitchen garden paths on their way to the stable. He waited silently until the men had passed, then cleared his throat. "The cook has little of use to you, as I now see."

" 'Tis enough, my lord," she answered.

"Nay, I believe I've been hasty in denying you the castle garden. It is quite overgrown, but should you succeed in making something of it, you'll have my admiration."

He held out the key. She stared at it, but made no move to take it from his palm.

"What changed your mind, my lord?" She bit her lip. Her hair no longer curled enticingly about her temples or lay loose on her shoulders. Instead, its glory was hidden beneath her headcovering. "My lord?" she prodded.

He shrugged, unable to give her an answer that did not shout his desire. He'd tried to think of something to say should she or others ask just this question, and still after hours of thought had nothing logical, nor any quote from Aristophanes to offer. And because he had no answer, he said nothing.

Finally she reached out and touched the cold metal.

"Take it," he said softly.

She raised her dark eyes to his face.

"Do what you will," he continued, the words a harsh rasp in his throat.

Her fingers were warm as she drew the key across his palm. He shivered. Was it his imagination that her fingertips lingered a moment on his skin? Nay, he made what he wanted—nay, *needed*—of the encounter.

He strode away.

* * *

Lady Sabina lay in wait for him in an alcove off the great hall. He gritted his teeth as she stepped before him, blocking his way to his bedchamber. Exhaustion filled him with ire.

"Ah, my lord, how pleased I am to find you alone. These barons, they occupy you to my disadvantage. Must you all jabber so on your lost holdings, the king?" She hooked her arm through his and with a gentle tug maneuvered him into the alcove. With difficulty, he concealed his impatience.

"Is it not time we came to an agreement, Durand?"

"An agreement?" He gently moved her hand lower on his thigh.

"Aye. One of mutual benefit. I could oversee the keep for you whilst King John is in attendance. You must admit it is a demanding occupation, mistress of a castle overrun with courtiers."

"I have Lady Oriel to act for me," Durand pointed out while parrying busy fingers that crept up his arm.

"Lady Oriel has expressed her concerns that she's not able to see to the task. She's never feted a king, whilst I have traveled with him on numerous occasions. He's quite demanding, you know."

"Then, pray, help her." Durand crossed his arms on his chest.

Lady Sabina burst into laughter. "I've no intention of practicing good deeds, my lord. Whatever *help* I offer, 'twould be foolish to give it without some reward."

"What reward would you require?" Her hand flattened on his thigh. He clamped his on hers.

"It has been overly long since I've been under the care of a man such as you."

"There are many in the keep—or John's court, for that matter—who would be pleased to offer you protection. I cannot do so."

"Cannot? Or will not?" She rose and paced before

him. "We're well suited; your properties would enhance mine."

He knew her father's holdings suffered badly from the poor harvests of late. "I've little without my French properties—"

She waved the truth away with a sharp gesture. "You will soon regain it all. We have no husband or wife to say us nay. You've a cock that wants to crow and I wake at dawn. What holds you back?"

Durand rose quickly. "Is there not a merchant cock you already possess?"

"Merchant?" She knitted her brows. "Who wants a merchant when a lord is about?"

"Indeed." He pushed past her.

Penne rolled from bed. He hid the stone bottle Luke had given him. It would not do for servants to ask about it.

"Penne?" Oriel murmured. "Where are you?"

She rubbed her hand across the bedding, and he imagined her hand on him. In a trice he was in her embrace.

He kissed her breathless. She sat up and pushed him away. "Come, sir, I'm exhausted. Whatever was in the potion Luke obtained for you has made you more randy than Cook's goat." But she planted a kiss on his nose.

"Do you feel different after you drink your love potion?" he asked.

Oriel shook her hair from her shoulders. She took his hand and placed it on her belly. "Nay. You know, Mistress le Gros said I would do better to depend upon one sweet moment—"

"How would you know one sweet moment from another?" he asked, unable to keep the bitterness from his voice. "Are not all our moments sweet?" He pulled his hand away and rose. "If what we do does not please you—"

Oriel leaped from the bed. She caught hold of the tunic he was about to pull over his head. "Nay, my love. I did not mean it that way!"

"What way did you mean it? You said you'd do better to depend upon one sweet moment. If they're not all sweet then say so."

Her lip trembled. Tears flooded her eyes.

"Oh, my love." He pulled her into his arms. "Forgive me. I'm not thinking on my words."

"Nor I on mine," she whispered at his ear. "Every moment we have is sweet. Pray, forget what I said. Come back to bed."

He kissed her forehead, but made an excuse and dressed rather than return to bed, and she knew he would not forget.

Durand lasted only one day before entering the castle garden. At first glance it appeared as overgrown as always. But if one looked, one could see that certain plants stood clear of weeds, the earth loose about their bases, some trimmed or pruned.

As he tried to appear to be just wandering, he noted those beds tended, the clove pinks, primrose—plants useful to Cristina's business. If he inquired, he imagined he would find that Cristina commanded several of his men to do the work. If he came upon them, he'd offer his blessing to their tasks.

He heard her before he saw her. She sang some tuneless air to the babe, he supposed. Ducking under a vine-tangled tree branch, he came to a patch of soft, scythed grass. The overhanging branches cast everything in a watery green. Cristina knelt by a flower bed, digging with a pointed stick.

She did not look up. "Ah, you've finally arrived, Alice. I began to despair of you. Look, this lavender can be saved. 'Tis as I thought. Bring the babe; my breasts ache, she sleeps so long!"

Durand grinned. He crouched down over the basket holding Felice and, with great awkwardness, lifted the sleeping child. Holding the babe as if she would bite— not sure she would not—he walked across to where Cristina knelt. She was jerking open her laces. Hastily, as the child squirmed and began to bubble with noise, and before Cristina bared herself too far, he held out the child and spoke. "Mistress le Gros."

"My lord!" Cristina scrambled to her feet, pulling her gown together at the throat. "I-I thought you were Alice."

He grinned. "The babe is heavier than I expected," he said as she took the child from him.

Cristina returned his smile. "She is, in fact, rather small, my lord." The child rooted at her breast, and Cristina turned slightly away from him and sank to the grass.

He walked to the lavender bed and went down on one knee to inspect it. "Hmm. I expected a babe would weigh about as much as a rather fat capon."

Her answering laughter delighted him.

"A capon, my lord? A fat pup, mayhap."

The child quieted and he assumed she fed, though he resisted the urge to see for himself.

"Did you come to inspect my work, my lord?"

"Inspect? Nay, I came to see if there was aught salvageable."

"Oh, there is a great deal of worth, my lord. 'Tis overgrown, to be sure, but see—there before you is lavender, thyme, sage."

"Enough." He held up his hand and turned to where she sat on the grass, the child discreetly at her breast. "I am pleased with your progress." This time she drew the edges of her gown about the child. This time the small patch of creamy skin did not arouse the hammering lust he had felt the night before by the stable; this time he felt a different ache.

"I never held my sons," he said.

"Never?"

He sat at her side on the grass. "Nay. I was at Richard's side when they were born. I first saw Adrian when he was"—he bent his head back and considered the blue sky overhead—"about three years. Robert, younger. About a year old or so. It is something I regret, not knowing my sons as I should."

"You were at the king's command."

"Aye, I have served both Richard and John as a justice and have traveled much."

"It must be a great honor to do so."

"There are costs to all honors." He watched her move the child from one breast to the other. "I must make a match for her."

"Already?" Cristina tucked her gown about the child.

Durand sensed alarm in her voice. " 'Tis necessary. She'll draw high, for the king needs to curry the favor of his barons now and may not feel so a year from now—or two years. And I must look to what may soon be lost."

"I don't understand."

Durand rose and went to one of the paths. He scooped up a handful of white stone. Dropping back down at her side, he scattered a few of the smaller stones in the grass. "These represent my holdings here in England. Save for Ravenswood, they are small, scattered."

"Scattered?" She touched one stone after the other as they lay near her.

"From the time of William, kings have scattered lands, so that no one baron may become too powerful in one place." He tossed the larger stones in his hand with a quick flick of his wrist a few feet away. "There are my holdings in Normandy, from my marriage."

"They're in King Philip's hands, are they not? Is this why there will be war?"

"Aye and nay. I owe fealty to Philip for my properties in Normandy and to John for those here, but 'tis tradition that I fight at the side of the king who holds the majority of my honors."

She looked from one scattering of stones to the other. "Then 'tis Philip for whom you fight? How can this be?"

"I'm one of John's justices. Therein lies the problem. I'm here, he expects my loyalty, and I have in the past fought at Richard's side, on crusade. I've never fought with Philip, but always paid him due homage for that which came to me through Marion." He rose and paced the swath of grass. "I'm caught in a coil. If John fails, my sons lose all you see here." With his toe, he nudged the larger set of stones. "If John wins, I'll have it all, of course."

"You worry for your sons. They'll suffer if you lose their mother's properties. It must be as if you are pulled by each arm, in two directions."

He sank to her side on the grass. "You understand." Marion had not understood the problems in serving two masters. She only wanted the earl's belt denied him when Richard died. "Penne wants a swift fight to take back what is ours, but if we war on Philip, we deny the homage we owe him."

"And how does your brother feel?"

"Luke believes I should council the king to a peaceful settlement—offer myself, if need be, to go to Philip and try to negotiate a peace if the great William Marshall should fail."

"Did not one of King John's envoys have his eyes put out?"

"Nay, you are thinking of Philip's treatment of prisoners during his war against Richard."

"How can men be so cruel?"

Her own dark eyes watched him. Should he tell her Richard acted in kind, putting out the eyes of his prisoners when Philip began the practice? Or how John's councilors had urged him to blind his rival for the throne and castrate him so no heir could threaten in the future? "Life is cruel."

She shook her head and held the child closer. "I suppose I cannot understand. One can only be in one room at a time."

"One may collect rents from many properties at a time. I have many mouths to feed."

The sky overhead was azure blue. Soft was the warm breeze on his skin. How easy it was to sit here in this peaceful place with her and forget the world beyond. But John's packhorses and carts had arrived, and with them all peace must end. Even deep in the garden, he could hear a commotion in the bailey, the cries of men at their work unloading King John's household goods.

"In truth, I'm a justice here, and it is John that I'll serve, hoping he will act boldly, as he did when he rescued Queen Eleanor. Then mayhap all will be well." He took a deep breath. "But John has no trust, and I'm vulnerable to persuasion from both kings."

She gently laid the child in her lap and closed her gown. This time he did not avert his gaze. "How are you vulnerable? I don't understand. If you've decided, why are you still at risk?"

"Kings take hostages. My sons are at de Warre's castle under John's control, my mother in Paris under Philip's."

"So King Philip could use your mother to bring you to his side against John." She idly twisted the ends of the lacing of her gown as she contemplated the stones. When she looked up, her soft expression was gone. "You must protect your children and your

111

mother. It is a coil, but you will know what to do and you will do it."

There was no hint of doubt in her words. How young she was, how unspoiled.

She was so close, just inches away. He reached out and put his fingers under her chin. She did not resist the pull of his hand nor move when he bent his head to hers. Her lips were warm, soft, yielding. He brushed his lips across hers, once, twice, three times, tasting her.

She sought his kiss, turned as he grazed his lips across hers, following, her breath warm against his skin. A low sound, almost a moan, escaped her throat. He caressed her cheek, so smooth beneath his fingertips, stroked down to the rapid flutter of her pulse. Her hand came up to cover his. He took it, turned it, bent his head and kissed her palm.

"Cristina!" a voice called.

He pulled away, saw the dazed look upon her face, and was recalled to where they were.

"Alice has arrived." He stated the obvious. He would not be ashamed of the kiss, nor hide his presence. Cristina ducked her head.

She looked up, a look not of shame but of confusion on her face. "My lord?" Her voice trembled slightly.

Alice burst through the rough foliage. "Ah, Cristina, milord." She dropped into a hasty curtsy. " 'Tis a glorious smell, is it not?" She swept a hand out to the lavender bed. " 'As she not made a good job o' it, milord?"

"Excellent. I'll expect to reap the benefits of all Mistress le Gros has done here."

Cristina's head jerked up. Her ale-dark eyes impaled him with questions. She stood up. "His lordship has never held a babe, Alice." She placed Felice in his arms.

The child was tiny, warm, with a gleam of milk on

her lips. She squirmed a bit. "She's wet!" He thrust her back at Cristina.

.But she merely turned away to adjust her gown. "Babes are frequently wet. Another experience you've missed, my lord."

"I greatly value this tunic," he said.

Alice grinned a gap-toothed smile and took the child. "I shall see to her, milord."

As Alice began to unwrap the babe's swaddling, he turned. Cristina turned at the same time. They walked side by side along the weedy path. "Luke wants a final festivity before we leave with the king and is making up a hunting party to Turnbull Hill. You'll join the party." He made it an order.

"As you wish, my lord." They stopped at the gates. There was a frown on her face. "At your manors in Normandy, a kiss is considered adultery. I'm under no illusions as to my status here. Please don't interpret my indulgence—"

"You were indulging me?"

"Nay . . . that is, please, my lord, do not interpret my *lapse* to be more than that. I'll not be made a mistress."

He leaned on the garden wall to feign a relaxed attitude he did not feel. Every muscle in his body ached to take her into his arms. He sensed she was at sea as to how to respond—much as he was. If she needed to retreat, so be it. "Who says I wish you for a mistress?"

Her eyes widened, her cheeks flooding with color. He held his breath. She was magnificent when angry. He saw her only in the best of moods. This fiery manner beguiled him. The heave of her breast enticed him.

A sudden clatter of men and horses told him too many walked about the bailey, just inches away behind the closed garden gate, for such intimate discussion. She whirled away, her shoes smacking down against the stones, her skirts twitching from side to side. Only a few steps away she stopped. In moments she was before him again.

"I don't know what it is you want, my lord, but I thought you sought the hand of Lady Sabina, so there can be no other reason for your attentions to me save to make me your mistress."

"Lady Sabina?" He frowned. "I—"

"I know one thing of you, one thing every man and woman of Ravenswood would swear to: you are a man of honor. And I trust you will deal so with both the good lady and me."

She chastised him! Then her words cut him.

A man of honor.

Where had his honor gone?

"I had no intention of dishonoring you or myself," he said softly.

"Then let us forget this moment, my lord." She made a deep obeisance and walked away.

"I want you, Mistress le Gros," he said softly when she had disappeared from view into the depths of the garden. He lifted his face to the sun and watched a pair of the castle ravens course the sky. "But I forgot for a moment that you belong to another. And that I have sons to see settled in this world."

Chapter Eight

Cristina rode in a cart decorated with greens to Turnbull Hill at the edge of the forest. Luke had organized a motley crew of men, women, and children. She saw both fine ladies and kitchen servants. Despite the threat of war, the party was festive.

Bishop Dominic and his men did not linger for the hunt. They sampled the sweetmeats and wines set out by servants, then mounted their horses and set off for home.

Children ran about the pavilions raised to shelter the ladies. Cristina wandered, amusing the children with plaited crowns of daisies. She found herself unable to tolerate the gossip that their capricious king had already bored of his young wife and taken—and discarded—several lovers. Her mind shied from talk of men and mistresses.

She had little to do once Felice was fed, as the female children were captivated by the babe and had taken on the care of her, pretending they were little mothers.

Amid the pastoral scene, disquiet filled Cristina. She had not slept the night before. Did her unease stem from the knowledge that she had several lotions and dishes of scent to prepare, yet sat here in idleness?

Nay, she must not pretend. *He* caused her disquiet, her sleepless night. She stroked her lips for mayhap the thousandth time—touched where his mouth had touched hers. She closed her eyes and could see his head bent over her hand, see the many fine colors in his hair, from almost black to deepest red. Worst, she felt the shiver of desire over and over as it coursed from his fingertips and warm mouth to her heart.

Her heart. It ached to know the man beneath the warrior lord. *Impossible. Impossible.*

Simon would set her aside if he knew how she had strayed; in truth, he might beat her for such errant thoughts of Lord Durand.

Yet she would never forget the moment or the taste of a kiss other than Simon's.

A lick of desire moved from her breast to her groin.

She must gather morning dew, make new candles . . . double the strength of the resistance potion.

Her fate lay with Simon.

She looked over at the hunting men, seeking only one man, but her eyes rested on another. Her husband rode along the perimeter of those who raised their birds, the deep blue of his surcoat a dot of bright color against the green of the hills.

Alice had told her with a sly glance of his presence at the Raven's Head each night. She must force herself to care.

Was her attraction to Lord Durand mere loneliness? Merely that of a woman who knew little of the passions of the body—or heart?

There must be no more kisses stolen in a garden. Surely for that alone God might punish her?

And surely next time she would grant Lord Durand everything he wished. *Everything*.

Simon rode close and dismounted. He sat at her side, full of the hunt, his face sunburned, his dark hair windblown. He had never looked more handsome.

"Simon, I have a request." She knotted her fingers tightly together.

"What is it?" He smiled warmly.

"I want to come home. Mayhap you could speak to Lord Durand. It is not uncommon for a nurse to take a child into her home—"

The smile froze on his lips. "Hush!" he said harshly. "What ails you? You are not coming home, do you hear me? You will do your duty there, at the castle. The king will be here in but a few days, and he will bring Queen Isabelle and her many, many ladies. You must be at hand to please them. Lady Oriel will recommend you, and what use will you be if you are in the village?"

"I see how it is. You want to attach yourself to the court."

His handsome face fell into a harsh frown. He plucked up a nosegay she was working on. "And what is wrong with bettering ourselves? Ravenswood is a fine place, but there are better. If Normandy is lost to the king, de Marle will have little save this one manor. He will be hard-pressed to feed his knights, let alone purchase soap for women!"

He leaned forward. She smelled the rich scent of Lord Durand's wine on his breath. "Do you wish to spend your life making dainties for spoiled women? Well, I do not wish to spend mine selling fine saddles when I could be riding on them!"

"You promised we would settle. A king's court is not settled." She recoiled from his anger.

"I promised if you gave me a son."

His words silenced her. He rose and threw down the nosegay. With an agile leap, he gained his saddle and cantered back to the hunting party.

She could not condemn him. He wanted what other men had—a son, a fertile wife.

Penne nudged his mount closer to Durand's and lifted a dark brow. "I see Simon speaking with his wife. They appear to be in some disagreement."

Durand glanced toward the pavilions and scattered parties on the grass. He had no need to search about for Cristina le Gros. Without any intention to do so, he had kept track of her since first they had arrived on the hill. He saw Simon mount up and canter away from his wife. Her dark head was bowed.

"Gossip says he sees far too much of the inn-keeper's daughter."

"Agnes?" Durand asked with a frown.

"Aye. Think you Oriel should drop a hint to Cristina? Joseph says Agnes has the pox." Penne let his horse wander beside Durand's. They watched a hawk rise and strike with majestic accuracy.

Durand shook his head. "Nay. I will tend to it." He thought of how many of his men frequented the Raven's Head. "Yet another matter for my attention. I cannot have my men soaking their cocks when I need them in the saddle."

Unable to find any pleasure in the hawking, he hooded his bird and handed her off to his squire, along with the heavy glove he wore to protect his hand from the wickedly sharp talons.

Penne did the same. "I suppose you have no need of Agnes with Sabina about," Penne said.

"Sabina?" Durand jerked his reins and turned his horse away from the hawking party lest they hear

Penne's words. He saw Cristina tuck a wreath of daisies about a child's head.

"Come. Sabina is after a new husband, is she not? She must be easy prey. Surely you'll be trying her?" Penne waggled his eyebrows.

"Not even with your cock," Durand said with a smile. He allowed his mare to crop the sweet grasses. Children hovered about Cristina like bees about a hive.

"Why not?" Penne asked. "Sabina is lovely. As long as she thinks you might wed her, she's ripe for the plucking."

Cristina suddenly rose and began to run in his direction. She pointed off to the forest.

He caught the acrid scent of burning. Where Cristina pointed a thin thread of black smoke rose over the treetops. Trust her canny nose to scent the danger ere any other.

"Penne, the road. Gather the men," he called, then wheeled his mare and kicked her into a gallop.

Few women paid any heed to the change in the men's direction or their sudden disappearance into the forest. They continued to stitch in the sunlight or the shade of the pavilions, nibble at sweetmeats, and tease each other with gossip.

But when a lone rider, Lord Penne, whipping his horse to a lather, raced from the grove of trees, they all rose as one. Lady Oriel rushed forward, but he passed her by and skidded to a halt before Cristina.

"Come." Lord Penne held out a hand. She did not hesitate, but put her hand in his and was swept onto the horse.

A wide path wound through the trees, and Cristina remembered following it when first she and Simon had come from Winchester to Ravenswood. "Bishop Dominic's party has been attacked by brigands," Lord

Penne said over his shoulder. There was time for little more. The acrid smell thickened, filling Cristina's throat as they rounded a small curve in the road.

Carnage met her eyes. One of the wagons was on fire, the source of the pungent scent and smoke. Several men were sprawled, bloody on the ground. Horses, likewise slain, lay in their blood beside their masters.

Lord Durand pulled her from Penne's horse. "Come, you are the closest we have to a healer." He stepped in front of her. "I am sorry you must be subjected to this. Try not to look—"

"Please, my lord, if there is one living who needs aid, we waste time."

He nodded, but kept his arm firmly about her so she had but a limited view of the dead. She tried to force her face to the calmness her words implied, but her heart pounded and her stomach heaved as they hastened past a disemboweled horse.

"Here. The bishop." Durand knelt at the side of the corpulent man who so recently had dined at the high table with the other barons. Beneath Lord Durand's mantle, the bishop's bare feet pointed vulnerably to the heavens. The man could have been either a bishop or a thief. He was naked.

Cristina touched the bishop's throat. His pulse beat but weakly beneath her fingertips; blood smeared his pale skin and face. Quickly she examined him.

"My lord, this blood is not his. He may have been felled with a blow to the head, but he has no pressing wounds to treat." She raised her gaze to Lord Durand's anxious one. "I can do nothing. He's in God's hands."

Durand nodded, then called to his brother, who organized several servants to put out the burning cart. "Luke, fetch transport to the castle for the bishop and the two others who still live."

He took her arm again and led her to two other men who lay side by side, one garbed in a plain wool cassock, the other in guard's mail.

She knew the cart would be carrying two, not three. "I'm sorry, my lord; this one man is dead"—she indicated the man in the cassock—"but this other one may yet survive."

"He's but a boy," Durand said, reaching out to touch the youth's cheek. "Word has spread of John's arrival. It attracts birds of prey." He rose and put out a hand to her. As he did, a wild cry tore the air.

A scream in her throat, Cristina froze. Dozens of men burst from the forest, swords and axes raised, hacking without order at the hunting party.

Lord Durand drew his sword. He leaped across the bishop. Cristina gagged as, with a quick thrust, Durand pierced a brigand's throat.

He turned, still between her and the slashing men. She huddled between the living and the dead, unable to move, Lord Durand's boots but inches from her hands, his sword slicing the air before her.

Metal clashed with metal. She could not raise her eyes from the confusion of feet trampling the ground about her.

One brigand wore spurs enameled with blue. They left a terrible wound on a dead man's hand as he heedlessly trampled across the man to escape Durand's relentless sword.

Where was Simon? She searched for him, but saw him not.

Then Cristina could watch only Durand. He moved with economy of motion, each thrust of his sword, each slash, drawing blood. It sprayed across Cristina's lap, her hands, her face.

With a wild yell, the brigands turned, their numbers greatly diminished, and fled.

"After them; they head for our party," Durand

121

shouted, turning to where she knelt. He grabbed her arm, and in a moment she was astride his horse, her arms about his waist. She felt the heat of his body, the tension through his back, as he kicked his horse to a gallop.

She hung on for her very life, her body jarred with every hoofbeat. The horse leaped a deadfall and plunged into the sunlit pleasure ground. The brigands milled about the edge of the field. The women screamed and ran in clumps to one pavilion, the servants taking a stand before them, too few to save them should the brigands descend.

At the sight of Durand and his men, the brigands swerved their horses, taking to the woods again. Durand did not charge the brigands, as she expected. He headed for the pavilion instead, then reached back, his fingers an iron grip on her arm. She was jarred from foot to head as he dropped her to the ground.

"Remain here," he ordered.

Every bone in her body sang with tension. Her heart raced with him across the fields. His men formed up behind him. Within an instant, they had plunged back into the woods.

She never turned from where they had disappeared. Would he be wounded? Killed?

More than half an hour passed. An occasional shout or a blood-chilling cry was heard. The women stood mute, children hidden in their skirts. Lady Sabina paced beside Lady Oriel, their arms entwined, granting each other strength. Lady Oriel paled and trembled with every moment that passed.

Cristina almost cried aloud when a figure appeared in the shadows of the forest. Lord Penne. He moved slowly, but lifted his hand, and even from a distance a grin could be seen on his face. Lady Oriel raised her skirts and flew toward him.

As Cristina watched—and envied—Lord Penne slid

from his horse and caught her up in his arms.

The rest of Lord Durand's party came more quickly, passing the embracing couple. Lord Durand appeared, Simon at his side. They rode straight toward her. Her husband. Her lord.

Traitorous heart, she thought. *You spared little thought for Simon, thought only of* him. She forced her eyes to her husband, locking her gaze there as befitted a wife.

"You are well?" she asked Simon.

He nodded. "Aye. We have lost not a single man, but I have never seen such evil done."

"Mistress?" Lord Durand interrupted Simon. "My men will bring the bishop and his guard. Will you see to them? This time without interruption, I most fervently hope."

Simon answered in a rush, his face pale. "My lord, she will tend all the injured. Have you your pouch, Cristina?"

"Nay. I brought only my stitchery."

"Stupid woman. Then you must do the best you can without."

Lord Durand looked as if he were about to speak, but Luke called his name and he wheeled his horse and rode away.

Tension radiated from Simon. He paced before her, his horse nervously weaving behind him. "You should have seen it. Lord Luke is quick—nay, very quick—but his lordship . . . he was magnificent. I watched him slice a man through from shoulder to groin."

"Simon, please." Cristina tried to stem the flow of Simon's account, but his blood was up.

"You must do what you can for the injured. The bishop, of course, and his guard—so young—do you hear?" He gripped her arm. "Prove yourself of some use!"

She clamped her lips over a retort.

123

"How could you come out without your pouch? You go nowhere without it. Now, when you could impress Lord Durand with your—"

"With my what? Flower garlands? I'm not a healer—"

"You are useless sometimes. Ofttimes! What if those men die?"

Cristina bowed her head. His tirade continued until a cart appeared. "Cease, Simon. I will tend the men as best I can."

She accepted his hand up into the cart, where she knelt by the bishop. His face was gray, his mouth open, and his breath puffed out with a stench of sour wine. As the cart lumbered along the roadbed back to the castle, Lord Durand rode to its side.

"Mistress, you're not injured, are you?" His scowl swept over her where she knelt. "This is not your blood, is it?"

She shook her head and wiped a trickle of sweat from the bishop's brow. "Nay, my lord."

"How fares the bishop?"

"Forgive me, my lord, but I fear he is worsening. I don't think anything from my pouch—"

"Fear not, Cristina. Had I thought we were to encounter such an attack I would have brought the leech myself."

"You don't blame yourself, my lord?" she said. "Surely you are not responsible for what occurred here."

"I am responsible for all that occurs on my land."

Lord Durand fell back. Cristina divided her attention between the bishop and his guard. There was little she could do for either. The youth—for surely he was little more than ten and five—had lost a great deal of blood, but his wounds had ceased to bleed. In truth, the bishop was more likely to die; his color was worsening and his breathing labored.

In the bailey, many came to greet their return, Aldwin among them. He said naught, but the glare he gave Cristina told her he considered her to be once again poaching on his territory. With a few terse commands, Aldwin directed the removal of the bishop and his wounded guard.

Cristina took Felice, sought her chamber, and, after washing her bloody hands and face, attempted to feed the child, who refused to eat. Cristina forced herself to be patient. Her skin itched. She badly wanted to rid herself of her soiled garments. By the time the child had consented to be fed, Cristina was nodding in her chair.

Simon shook her awake. "I have come to tell you the bishop is dead. The leech believes 'twas some neglect on your part."

"Simon!" She shot to her feet. Her entire body quivered in reaction to the day and its horrors. "And you defended me to him, of course?"

He hesitated.

"Well, Simon, I see where your loyalties lie." She clutched the child hard against her breast and forced herself to face her husband. "How is it you did not defend me? Surely a criticism of me is a criticism of you?"

Simon colored. "I could think of nothing to say. He—"

"Cristina?" Lord Luke entered the chamber. "I'll have need of more potion—" He fell silent when he saw Simon; then as if seeing her, too, for the first time, he came forward and clasped his hands on her shoulders. "What is this? Blood?"

"Aye, not mine, though, my lord."

Simon interrupted. "She is wanted in the hall, my lord. Master Aldwin is—"

"Complaining of her," Luke finished, and squeezed her shoulders. She shivered in his hands. "Do not fear,

125

mistress. I shall pluck the old buzzard of his ire. He's jealous, and the bishop's death serves to give him a stage for his grievances."

"I did naught that could have harmed the bishop, my lord."

"She's telling the truth," Simon piped in.

"I've no doubt of her veracity, but still, the man must have his say." Luke turned to the door.

Simon grabbed her arm and said in a hiss close to her ear, "How dare you allow him to touch you so? What if someone had seen you—"

She tried to pull away. "I don't know what you mean."

"Are you coming?" Luke asked, holding the door for them.

"I'm not finished with you," Simon said, and dropped her arm.

With her stomach tied in knots as tangled as her hair, she followed Luke, Simon a few steps behind, her cheeks hot from his foolish accusation.

In moments they stood in the hall before Durand. Aldwin stood at his right hand. Luke took Felice from her.

"This woman takes too much upon herself—" Aldwin began.

"I assure you, my lord—" Simon began.

But Lord Durand raised a hand, instantly silencing both men. "I have listened to you, Aldwin, but I watched Mistress le Gros minister to the fallen. She did what any good wife would, naught more. Now let us all see this wounded boy. Mayhap, Aldwin, you could give Mistress le Gros some advice on caring for the sick should you be unavailable, as you were today."

The leech pursed his lips. "As you wish, my lord." He bowed stiffly and led them all—Simon, Cristina, Durand, and Luke, Felice still in his arms—from the hall. They descended to the cooler levels of the castle storerooms, but heat prickled Cristina's scalp.

After what seemed like ages to Cristina, the leech turned a key and entered a room lit with several torches.

Smoke blackened the ceiling from years of such illumination. The young man lay on a table, pale as death, naked, several leeches on his breast near a long wound shiny from cauterization. The stench of roasted meat filled the air. They ranged themselves about the table.

Simon cried out and fled down the corridor.

"Weakling," Aldwin said, plucking off one leech and placing it in a shallow dish.

Cristina picked up the boy's hand. It was icy, his nails blue. "Should he not be kept warm?" His nakedness offended her. A person should die with dignity, and death, she imagined, was not far off for the youth. Luke and Durand stepped to the foot of the table and considered him.

Her heart ached for the boy's mother, wherever she was. Gently, and in defiance of Aldwin, she draped a blanket over the youth, then moved around the table and tucked the blanket close about his thin body. Aldwin sniffed derisively as she tended the boy.

"Does he not remind you of someone?" she asked the men.

Lord Durand nodded. "Aye. My son Adrian's friends. What can you tell Mistress le Gros about your care of him so far, Aldwin?"

The man bristled, but finally his need to display his abilities outweighed his annoyance with her. "I have a very special paste of goose grease and pitch, cooked just so, stored in a stone crock—not earthenware, mind you. It must be stone." He tapped the boy's chest. "I'll lay it on the wound, just so thick, and no thicker"—he splayed his thumb and index finger to indicate the amount—"then apply leeches to the swelling and pray to God, of course."

With a glance at Lord Durand, she asked a tentative question. "Will you not feed him? Warm his hands and feet?"

"Nay! Food would merely purge itself and foul my herbarium."

The herbarium was already foul, the rushes old and dirty. "What of some sweet water?"

"Water! You know nothing of healing." Aldwin shook his head at her ignorance. With a curtsy, she left the room. The others, save Aldwin, followed her.

Luke shifted Felice from one shoulder to the other when he caught up with her. "Do you think the boy should be fed?"

"Aye, but I'm not the healer," she said, conscious that Lord Durand listened and not sure Aldwin did not eavesdrop at his door.

"Nonsense," Luke said. "Even I know from the battlefield that a weak man is likely to die."

"Then you must make the point to Master Aldwin yourself." She would not be bait between these men.

"Come." Lord Durand took her arm. "I shall see the boy is fed and warmed. You shall bathe."

They reached the hall and Simon met them. His face was white as new milk. "Forgive me, my lord. The smell of burning flesh . . . I am not used to . . . that is . . ."

Durand laid a hand on Simon's shoulder. It quivered like a bowl of jellied eels beneath his hand. "Say no more. You're my merchant, not one of my soldiers. Take your wife and see to her."

When Durand glanced at Cristina, he saw Simon take her arm and lead her in the direction of the tower steps. He thought of what his emotions would be if the blood on her gown were her own.

He would need to kill the man who'd drawn it.

"Luke, find Penne," he said, turning.

"What for?" Luke bent his head and kissed Felice's cheek.

Luke. Lord of Skirts.

He thought of Marion's affection for his brother, a man who laughed, who took pleasure in all things. A man who made love with little thought of the consequences.

An arrow of pain shot through Durand's middle. Was Luke the father of Marion's child?

Chapter Nine

Durand went directly to Luke's counting room. He ignored Oriel there by the fire, stitching a tunic for Penne. He threw open the coffer and began to search.

Outside, it began to rain gently. Not so gentle was the storm within him.

Why did he want to know the child's parentage? *To punish.*

Could he punish his brother?

He tossed a score or more rolls onto the table. They dated back to Luke's first assumption of the position as castellan at Ravenswood. Durand had thought the position beneath his brother, but Luke had begged for it, as he knew Ravenswood was meant to be his one day. Now Durand combed the rolls of parchment for some clue to Luke's assumption of more than just charge of the castle.

"What is it you seek?" Oriel abandoned her mending, sat beside him, and took his hand, turning it over.

He shrugged.

Her fingers were gentle on his. "These blisters may fester. How came they?"

"I fought without gloves."

"Men are fools. I'll call for Mistress le Gros."

"Don't." He jerked his hand from hers.

"Why ever not?" She rose and threw open the door before he could prevent it.

"Oriel—"

"Fetch Mistress le Gros with a salve for Lord Durand's hands," she ordered the sentry who stood there.

"I have no need of—" Durand began, but Oriel overrode him.

"Nonsense. You are just as Marion said. Stubborn." She resumed her seat and picked up the tunic.

"What else did she say?" he asked, flexing his blistered hand, knowing that in moments Cristina would arrive.

"She said you made love like a warrior besieging a castle, and that she imagined my gentle Penne would have suited her better."

Durand stared at her bent, fair head, her quick fingers on her needlework. "Penne would have suited her better?" He wanted to snatch the words back into his mouth.

When Oriel raised her eyes, they were flooded with tears. "We both know Penne wanted to wed Marion, but settled for me. And she wanted someone to fawn on her."

"Oriel. Penne would never fawn on anyone, and he is with me more than away from me."

"Not in this last year. We have been here, thanks to Philip. And you have scarce visited but twice in this last twelvemonth."

Durand swallowed. "Penne is well contented with you. He has nothing of which to complain."

"Save that I am childless. With Marion he would have had sons, a daughter." A tear rolled down her cheek to stain the bodice of her scarlet gown.

A daughter?

Penne. Mon Dieu. Must he suspect his best friend too?

"My lord?" A sentry stood at his door.

"Aye?" Durand threw the roll he held to join its fellows among the rushes. He resisted the urge to pitch the entire pile into the flames.

"Mistress le Gros, my lord." The sentry stepped back and she stood in the doorway.

"Excuse me, Cristina." Oriel bolted through the door.

It was all Durand could do not to run after her and shake out of her whatever suspicions were in her mind. But he could not—ever.

"Enter." He leaped to his feet and glanced about at the castle rolls. "Enter," he repeated when Cristina merely remained in place.

"The sentry said you are wounded, that I was to come."

Durand forced his face to hide his inner turmoil. "Lady Oriel is overly concerned."

"I shall go then," Cristina said, turning to the door.

"Nay. Stay," he said before he could prevent the words. Her dark hair was plaited and wound with ivory ribbons. They matched her undergown. Her overgown was the color of ripe butter, unadorned. He needed her presence, whatever succor she offered— the peace that always surrounded her.

"You wounded your arm again?" Her gaze skimmed from his face to his hand. The glance was as tangible as any touch could be.

"Nay." He held out his left hand, turning it to the light. "It is my hand this time."

She hastened across the room, nodding at the sentry who remained at the door. He could not afford to dismiss the man.

"Blisters can fester, my lord. You should wear gloves." She did not touch him, but glanced again at the guard. "I believe Master Aldwin would better serve your purpose."

"Aldwin tends the wounded boy," he returned.

"I cannot do this, my lord. Master Aldwin closely guards his place at Ravenswood," she said, shaking her head. She placed a pot of salve on the table as if it were a serpent that might strike her. "He resents my every foray into his domain."

"Master Aldwin holds his position at Ravenswood at my pleasure. He has not your touch."

She remained unmoved.

"Sit." He made it an order. When she sat, something tight and coiled loosened in his chest.

He lifted the lid on the small pot. "What's in it, besides mint?" he asked as she dipped her fingers into the pale green goo.

"Dock, almond oil." After only a moment of hesitation, she took his hand. A shiver of desire and molten need coursed through his body as her fingers smoothed the salve across his blistered palm. Her fingers were gentle, barely touching, yet still sending sensations, nearly unbearable, through his body.

I will never wear gloves again, he thought.

Was this what drove Marion? A touch of desire from someone forbidden?

With what he hoped was indifference, he watched the fire, not their hands, but soon turned to the scattered rolls when the fire in his blood matched that of the hearth. The rolls of parchment merely served to remind him of what he sought.

Luke. Penne. He must know who had sired Felice.

One of them might have betrayed him. Could he ride into battle with a man who was a betrayer? Was this what Old Owen had wanted to warn him about?

Cristina clasped his hand more firmly, stroking her thumbs in his palm. All thoughts of Penne, Luke, and Marion fled.

He felt her touch to the soles of his feet. He no longer resisted her, nor thought of betrayal.

Only her touch, her scent, her luminous skin held him. . . . He frowned. "Where did you get the bruise?" he asked.

"Bruise?" she asked. "I-I didn't know I had a bruise."

He raised his free hand and touched her cheek just beneath her eye. "Were you struck by one of the brigands?"

The look on her face told him she was about to lie. Her gaze slid from his, to the torque about his throat. "I must have been, my lord."

"I would kill the man for you if he were not already dead."

Her face paled, but she said nothing. Then she bent her head and set herself to her work. She tortured him, skimming and smoothing the salve on his skin. Each touch seduced.

She would soon stop. He placed his other hand on the table.

Without looking up or saying a word, she dipped her fingers in the salve again and began the same torture on his right hand.

Of course . . . the bruise was the work of Simon. For forgetting her pouch? Or for angering Aldwin? Regardless, Simon would know before the sun set that if he laid a hand on her again, he would rue the day.

But thoughts of Simon also vanished as she drew her fingers down the center of his hand, from wrist to fingertips, gently, slowly. He imagined just such devoted attention to the rest of his body. His manhood filled at the thought, and his heartbeat thundered in his chest.

She neatly rolled his shirt to his elbow. Every turn of the fabric stripped away his composure.

"Your wound healed nicely," she said. Her fingertips wandered along the mark she had tended so recently, lingering on the sensitive new skin. She returned to his hand. There was no longer a need, but still, she again rubbed salve into his palm and fingers. Skimming, soothing, arousing. Every nerve of his body flashed to fire.

"Cristina," he said.

She shot to her feet. Her body quivered.

"Go," he ordered the sentry.

When the door closed behind the guard, her words tumbled out in gasping syllables. "My lord. I beg of you. Order me . . . home."

He rose and shoved the table away so nothing stood between them. "Send you home? I'm not sure I could sleep at night thinking of you in *his* bed."

Her pale face flooded with color. "Please, I beg of you. I have never broken my vows. Do not ask such a thing of me."

"I would never ask such a thing. You misunderstand me," he lied. "I have spent my life abiding by vows I have made—to my liege, my wife, God." This, at least, was perfect truth. "But I do not want you within his reach." He lifted her face to the light. "This is his work, is it not?"

Her eyes met his, but she said nothing.

"Many a husband has struck a wife, but I somehow . . . I will not send you home. I want you here. Felice needs you, and Marion would never have countenanced the child's placement outside the keep." Why had he fallen back on the child as an excuse? Why not speak the truth and damn the consequences?

She kept her intent gaze on his face.

Damn the consequences.

"I want you. But you need never fear I'll ask you to

break your vows," he said, and found he meant it. There was something gentle and sweet about her that guile would destroy.

He turned his hand over and held it out.

She stared down at it. Hers shook when she slipped it into his. "Would you take a vow on it, my lord?"

"Aye. I vow it."

Chapter Ten

Cristina left Lord Durand's chamber and walked slowly to the east tower. She was confused. Her lot lay with Simon, her chance for children and a home. Yet her mind turned again and again to Lord Durand. She had made him vow to her. Could she have so honestly vowed the same in his position?

Alice stopped her in the hall. "Mistress, may I go to the village? The midwife says Rose, in the village, be due ere dawn comes, and I may be needed there."

"Of course you must go. I will pray for Rose." She remembered the midwife who had tended her and Lady Marion—a gentle woman who had wept for her lady.

Alone in her chamber save for the sleeping Felice, Cristina dropped her gown over a bench, then wandered about clad only in her shift. In the alcove, she examined the bundles of flowers drying over the worktable.

The air was warm and damp as it moved lazily through the flowers. She would lose some to rot if the weather did not turn.

She shoved the bed curtains open a bit before lying on the furs. She said her prayers, then closed her eyes as she rolled to her side and drew up her knees. In her mind's eye she saw Lord Durand's hands, palm up on the table. He had not the smooth, tended hands of Simon. Nay, Durand's hands were callused and blistered, in need of care.

Not her care.

Her heart tapped a bit rapidly at the thought of how she had touched him. Too long. Too intimately. She shifted uncomfortably on the soft mattress.

The sound of men carousing came to her through the stout door. Rain pattered on the stone walls in a soothing beat. . . .

Metal scraped on metal as the door latch lifted. Alice must not be needed. Cristina remained still, that Alice might settle on her pallet without engaging her in chatter.

A breeze curled mist through the open shutters. As she watched with eyes half-closed, the mist moved like a spirit toward her. With it came his scent. That indefinable forest scent. The scent that was only his. She breathed deeply.

Someone moved quietly across the chamber. Not Alice.

The mattress behind her sagged as someone settled there. Her heart tapped rapidly.

A hand touched her bare shoulder. The hand was callused, rough. *His.*

He stroked down her arm to her hand and entwined his fingers with hers. "I could not stay away," he whispered at her ear, his breath warm on her bruised cheek.

The heat of his body warmed her, thrilled her, drove all conscience, all shame, away.

In answer, she drew their linked hands to her mouth. She rubbed the backs of his fingers against her lips.

Vows no longer mattered.

Nothing mattered but his touch.

He cupped her face and turned her so she had no choice but to roll to her back. His mouth was hot, his tongue urgent to taste her. She welcomed him, wrapping her arms about his neck and lifting her body to his.

He was naked. Her shift was as negligible as a cobweb between them.

When he swept the shift up her hips and tugged, she lifted that she might feel all of him.

And she did.

His skin was hot, his body aroused.

He tossed her shift to the floor.

A moan escaped her lips, taken into his mouth in that instant as he kissed her. The kiss was gentle.

The kiss ended all doubts.

They lay completely still, his body covering hers. Every touch of his tongue, every brush of his lips, stoked a fire in her body. The fire smoldered, flamed, swept out of her control.

She ran her hands over the hard muscles of his back and cupped his buttocks. He shifted against her, moving his hips to rub the most sensitive parts of her with his own.

Thunder murmured. Rain sluiced down the stone walls outside and within her. Heat ran liquid in her loins.

His mouth journeyed to her throat, her shoulder, the sensitive tip of her swollen breast. He suckled her, lapping up the sweet milk with his tongue as it trickled along her ribs.

"Durand," she cried, filled with an insatiable ache when he moved lower.

His teeth dragged along her arching hip, his fingertips roaming the soft inner skin of her thigh. Each touch, each taste, fueled the flames that licked through her body. She entwined her fingers in his hair, urged him to the ache he raised.

But he heeded her not. He nuzzled her inner thigh, then kissed her knee, and before she could beg for what she knew must be coming, he slid up her body to claim her mouth again.

He tasted forbidden. Earthy. He tasted of hidden places found deep in the forest.

She would know all of him before the night was ended—mayhap for just this once, but still, know him she would. She urged him to his side and explored every inch of his hips, thighs, ribs, and buttocks with her lips and hands.

He was molten hot. So was she.

Her hips arched off the bed as he used his strong hands to spread her legs apart. The rain splashed on the stone sill and she felt the mist envelop them, but it could do naught to cool the fever raging within her. He bent his dark head. She threaded her fingers into his thick hair. When he lifted her hips to his mouth, a luscious, liquid ecstasy cascaded through her. He lapped with his tongue, nipped with his teeth, then nuzzled his lips . . . *there*.

The pleasure coiled, grew, expanded, flooded from where he feasted.

The chamber lit with lightning. He looked up and smiled, his white teeth gleaming in the stark glare.

Simon.

Not *him*.

Lightning streaked across the sky, filling the room.

She screamed, struggling from hands that turned to claws and raked her thighs. With another scream she scrambled from the punishing hands and fell to her knees on the floor.

"Cristina!" Someone shouted her name.

A fist pounded her door.

She gasped for breath.

Felice wailed.

A hand to her breast, she sat back and stared around the chamber and realized she still wore her shift. It was drenched with sweat. The pounding grew urgent.

Felice's mad cry was real.

On hands and knees, she crawled to the cradle and felt for Felice. She swept the babe into her arms and buried her face against the soft blanket in which she was wrapped.

There was no scent of mist and forest in the chamber, only that of rain and wet stone. Her body trembled, icy cold as she knelt on the wooden floor.

"Cristina! Open this door!"

The sentry. She rose on shaky legs and did as bidden, opening the door but the span of three fingers.

The man pressed his face to the narrow opening. "Are you ill? Hurt?"

"Nay," she said, her voice a hoarse croak. "I had a dream." Heat rushed through her. "Nay. A nightmare. Forgive me for disturbing you," she finished.

"Shall I call Aldwin?" he asked.

"Nay. Nay. Go back to your post. I'm well now." Despite the rudeness of the action, she shut the door in his face.

She gripped the latch till it bit into her palm. The pain was real. Felice rooting at her breast was real. The warm trickle as her milk let down was real.

She laid Felice on the bed, then stripped off her sweat-sodden shift. With brisk motions as the child whimpered behind her, she dried herself. In the meager light of the candle, she inspected her thighs. Her skin was smooth and unblemished.

This time, when she curled on her side, she had the child within her embrace. She cocooned them in blankets and a fur as the babe nursed. Every inch of her throbbed. Her pulse beat to the rhythm of the rumbling thunder outside.

How could she have dreamed such things?

Did her vows mean so little that she could tear them to tatters in her dreams but moments after declaring them aloud to *him?*

She slept not at all, even as the castle grew silent and the rain stopped.

Durand slept little. He rose several hours before the dawn, resolved to right one problem, at least. A stable boy, yawning and scratching, chatted happily about Marauder's mighty appetite. Durand could not help smiling as the boy then waxed quite eloquent about the length of Durand's sword, the size of his boots, and the raven's head on his dagger. It was the boy who changed his mood from near murderous to something more manageable.

He did not knock on the merchant's door, but threw it open. After all, every building in the village was his own—rented out, to be sure, but still his.

He climbed the ladder to the second story. It was filled with boxes and stores for the space below. A tallow candle flickered and filled the space with scant light, enough that Durand could see a meager pallet against one wall, a coffer nearby. The space smelled of the stores below and something else—a night of passion spent in close quarters.

With the toe of his boot, he prodded the woman's bare arm, which poked from beneath the coverlet. The innkeeper's daughter sat up. She did not cover her full breasts as she rose and flicked a disheveled blond braid over one shoulder. "My lord," Agnes said with a small smile.

"Out." Her simper vanished. He tossed her gown to her. She stood up, dragging on her gown, grabbing her clogs, and backing toward the ladder.

"Aye, my lord. Aye," she mumbled as her head disappeared from view.

Simon woke with a jerk and scrabbled up on his knees.

Durand drew his dagger. He flipped it sharply, pinning Simon by his linen shirt to the rough wall behind him.

"My lord!" Simon shrieked. He reached back and screamed again as his palm met the razor edge of the blade. "Sweet Mother of Mary!" he cried.

Durand stood over the kneeling man.

"My lord! What's wrong? What have I done?"

"Done?" Durand crouched down on his haunches. He placed one hand on the blade handle, and with his other encircled Simon's throat. "What have you done? Beyond breaking your vows? Beyond abusing your wife? I know of nothing, Simon."

"Please, my lord, please let me explain." He was as still as if confronted by a wild boar. His pulse ran wild beneath Durand's hand. "I can explain, I swear it."

But Durand merely squeezed his throat, cutting off his protests. "Nay, Simon, you have no need to explain. You're merely my merchant, one who has recently signed a lucrative charter, worth a fortune if you deal well with me and mine." Simon nodded vigorously. "Ah, I see you understand. Let me say just this—the innkeeper is my tenant, a man I imagine wishes to remain in my good graces."

Again Simon nodded. He licked his lips.

"Do not touch your wife again. Do you hear me?" He tightened his fingers. " 'Tis said Agnes has the pox. If you have been with Agnes but this one time, you may be lucky. If you are in the habit of playing night games with her, you will soon know the truth of my words. You'll not pass this illness to your wife. She cannot serve the ladies of my keep if she is ill."

Durand jerked the dagger from the wall and stood up. He stroked his thumb across the blade as if in idle contemplation. "Do not abuse what is mine or your charter is void."

Simon remained as if still pinned to the boards. "Aye, my lord, aye, but you have to hear me. Cristina is no virgin angel. She allowed Lord Luke to handle her—"

Durand froze. "Luke?" He thought of how Luke might have charmed Marion. Had he also charmed Cristina?

Never. She held herself aloof.

Simon must have seen something of his thoughts on his face. "Aye, 'tis truth. I could say naught to Lord Luke, for 'tis a woman's place to guard her virtue, is it not, my lord? Nigh on to an embrace it was, before my very eyes, my lord," Simon said as Durand leaped down the ladder to sweeter air.

He did not look back to see if Simon followed, nor did it matter if he heeded the warnings. There would be pleasure in killing him if the man disobeyed, and acceptance if he did as required so that Cristina remained unblemished and unashamed.

Durand avoided the hall, where he might run into Luke or Penne. Instead he headed back to Aldwin's lair. His mind tangled on the prospect of betrayals— Luke's, possibly, but less likely Penne's, and now Simon's.

Numb, he forced himself to think only of the brigands' attack and what they might have been after. Certainly a bishop's fine clothing and jewels were obvious bait.

The boy lay in the same place he had the day before. His head rolled restlessly and he mumbled through dry lips.

"What have you done with the boy's clothes?" he asked of Aldwin.

With a bony finger, the man pointed to the door. "In the empty storeroom with the belongings of the other dead."

"Have Father Odo see to the burials of the other victims." He left the sickening air of the herbarium and walked deeper into the bowels of the castle. Water dripped down the wall of the empty storeroom. There was a large pile of assorted clothing and saddlebags cast against one wall.

He went through each piece, more to occupy his mind than for any real purpose. Anything of worth had been stripped by the brigands from their victims. What remained was mostly the mundane uniforms of the guards and the humble coarse cassocks of the lesser clerks. The saddlebags held little beyond bread and other foodstuffs.

With a thud, an object fell from a tunic. Durand lifted the woolen garment. Beneath it lay a linen-wrapped bundle, stained with blood. The tunic must have belonged to the youth. There was a blood-soaked rent over the heart where a blade had done its near-lethal duty.

Slowly, a throb beginning in his temples, he unwrapped the bundle. There in his hands lay the Aelfric he had given Cristina.

"What have you there?" Penne asked, coming across the storeroom.

"My Aelfric," he said, stunned. He leafed through it. "I know 'tis mine. Look here, where this page is loose." He saw it in his mind's eye floating to the floor in Cristina's chamber. "And here, this small cut in the leather, and here where the gilding is worn off."

145

"What's it doing in here?" Penne asked.

"Come." Durand strode back to where the boy lay. He drew the blanket off the boy's chest to assure himself that the wound was in the same place as the rent in the tunic.

The boy licked his lips and opened his eyes. "Father?"

"I'll fetch him for you in a moment." Durand poured a cup of water and, with Penne's assistance, held it to the boy's lips. The youth sipped it, then fell back, his color gray and his breathing labored.

The blade thrust had missed the heart and lungs, else the boy would be dead. Behind him, Aldwin bustled about with little purpose.

The boy mumbled and rolled his head. "What chance has he?" Durand asked quietly of the leech.

"Eh, he wakes and sleeps, wakes and sleeps." Aldwin shrugged. "His wound festers."

Durand gently tapped his fingers on the boy's cheek. His eyes fluttered open—blue eyes, the whites yellow. He licked his lips. A small smear of blood stained his lips.

"Do you know what this is?" Durand asked, holding the Aelfric before the boy.

His eyes widened. "The bishop . . .'tis the bishop's."

"The bishop's?" Durand looked up at Penne.

The boy shuddered, raised trembling hand to Durand, and began to weep. "He bade me take it to him. He bade me."

Durand took the dry, cold hand in his and thought of Christina's recommendation that the patient should be warmed. The boy's fetid breath bathed his face. "The bishop asked you to take the Aelfric to him?" Durand exchanged a look with Penne. "I don't understand."

The leech gasped, hastened to the table, and looked with avid interest at the book in Durand's hand.

The boy clutched Durand's tunic. He wept with great sobs that shook his thin body. "Nay. My father. He bade me deliver the book . . . to the bishop. Have you a priest? He . . . says I am dying. Can you fetch my father?"

Aldwin sputtered a protest, which Durand silenced with a glance. "Get Father Odo," he ordered. Aldwin scuttled off.

Durand tucked the boy's hand beneath the blanket. "I shall fetch the priest, but you must be sure to cleanse your soul. Tell the good father all."

It did not take long to summon Father Odo. Penne and Durand stood by to discreetly hear the young man's confession.

The young man was not, as they had believed, of the bishop's party, but instead had dressed as one of them in order to deliver the Aelfric volume. The bishop had bought it, the boy sobbed, from his father for three jeweled rings, worth a king's ransom.

"I don't understand," Durand said after the priest anointed the boy. "The bishop bought my Aelfric for three rings from your father?"

The boy's lips were as pale as his skin; his hand trembled. He shivered with fever. "Aye."

Durand leaned over the boy. "Tell me who your father is."

Father Odo said, "You must tell us, for he is a thief to take our lord's fine book."

Durand scowled the priest silent, but it was too late.

The boy's gaze jumped from the priest to Durand. "I-I will not tell you." He began to weep.

With great gentleness, for the boy looked as if he might die in but moments, Durand tucked the blankets close about him as Cristina had done.

The boy rolled his head. His eyes darted wildly about the room. "Bless me, Father, for I have sinned," he chanted.

147

Father Odo made a sign of the cross over the boy's head, and when their gazes met, the priest gave a quick shake of the head.

Penne spoke at his ear. "Does he not look much like our merchant?"

The boy died within the hour. Durand and Penne walked from the herbarium to the counting room.

"Penne, did you not think the brigands too finely garbed for mere men on the hunt for stray travelers?"

Penne nodded. "Aye. Their weapons were very good for men on the road, and their horses were fat."

"I've been thinking they did not idly pick their prey. I'm sorry we didn't capture one of the brigands and question him."

"Was the bishop so influential that he needed to be murdered?"

"This is not a war with the church. It is between John and Philip, although kings at war are always of interest to the church. As with us, the church must choose sides."

His thoughts returned to the book in his hand. He opened the coffer and stared into the neatly arranged parchments, tally sticks, and books. He placed the Aelfric on top and withdrew the Aristophanes. Whoever had taken the herbal knew what it was and knew its worth. For in truth, the gilded cover of the Aristophanes made it look far more valuable.

"You think the boy resembled Simon?" he asked Penne.

"Aye." Penne poured himself a cup of wine from a skin hanging by the hearth. "But mayhap I'm dreaming. He has no children that I know of."

"A bastard, mayhap?" Durand had had enough of bastards. "But how would Simon come into possession of the book or know where to find it?"

"Someone gave it to him."

Cristina.

He thought of her immediately. She knew the book's worth. But she had given it back to Luke.

He straddled the bench and stared into the hearth flames. The thought that she might have contrived to steal his Aelfric pained him as much as thoughts of Luke and Felice.

Durand did nothing to challenge Simon on the identity of the dead youth. Instead, he found himself but moments later on his knees in the hall, accepting the greetings of his king.

"All omens are good," King John said when Durand rose. "The weather is fine for hunting and our ships are almost ready. We but await the arrival of William Marshall to know what offensive we must launch."

The king then turned and held out his hand to a small woman. "But before we inspect our galleys, let me present Lady Nona, Lord Jean de Braisie's eldest daughter, Lord Merlainy's widow."

Durand bowed. *De Braisie's daughter.* Her holdings were immense, dotting England in the south, and France in Aquitaine.

"My lady," he said, lifting her hand and kissing the back. She was slim and young, no more than a score in years. Her skin was rosy pink with good health. Her eyes were as green as peridots, the hair peeking from the edges of her headcovering a soft fawn brown.

"You may go," the king said to the widow, and when she was out of earshot, being led by Oriel to the women's solar, the king gestured that Durand should take a seat. "Accept our condolences on the loss of our dear Marion. We loved her."

Durand inclined his head. The king handed him a ring.

"Give this to your son Adrian." The small circlet of

gold was studded with fine blue stones. John much loved jewels.

"With thanks, sire," Durand said, slipping the ring on his finger. "Is Lady Nona under your protection?"

"Aye, until she is under another's."

So it was as Durand had thought. Lady Nona was a candidate for his hand.

"Ah," cried the king, rising quickly, "one of our favorite little birds!" He held out his hand and Lady Sabina knelt to kiss it. "What brings this nightingale here? Nay, say nothing, child; you are on the hunt for a husband." When Lady Sabina colored and glanced at Durand, he merely arched a brow. The king pulled Sabina to his side, and a servant hastily placed a stool for her by John's side. "You will make a lovely wife, Lady Sabina, but we doubt of this worthy baron here." The king swept out a hand to Durand. "We have other uses for you. Lord Luke is not wed, and he is surely creaking with age to be so unencumbered."

They all laughed with the king.

When finally King John had finished with Sabina, Durand endured a lengthy meal and an evening of song and music by the king's side. The royal musicians were the best in the realm, and Lady Nona's voice sweet, but not quite sweet enough to rival the young Queen Isabelle's.

Durand found himself unable to do more than nod to most of the king's conversation. Too much filled his mind: the dead youth in the herbarium, the theft of the Aelfric, Marion's betrayal, two females vying for his hand, a hammering lust for Cristina le Gros.

Did he see the resemblance in the boy to Simon, as claimed by Penne? In truth, Durand could not say either way. Was there aught else but hair and eye color there?

Would Felice one day betray *her* father's blood by the turn of her cheek or the color of her hair?

His gaze fell on Lady Nona. He nodded to her. He found the possibility of marriage to Lady Nona created a terrible conflict in him. If one counted the wealth of her French and English properties combined, they would more than compensate for all his sons might lose if the king's plans for Normandy failed. But it would also place great power in his hands.

John's choice of bride for him raised myriad questions in Durand's mind. Why choose a woman of such power if he questioned Durand's loyalty? And as long as John withheld the earl's belt, Durand knew he was under suspicion.

Chapter Eleven

Durand was challenged by Penne to a game of dice. He used the pretext to escape the king's notice and discuss the dead boy's resemblance to Simon. But Penne turned his thoughts elsewhere.

"So we have two prospective brides for your hand. You should be flattered. Lady Nona is quite a match."

"Aye. But why? It is as if the king is dangling something before me. No doubt when I reach for it, he will snatch it back."

"Will you reach for it?"

Durand glanced at the king. He was a small man, mean of mouth and surrounded by his bachelors, men not of royal rank, but much within his confidence. "He is as changeable as the wind, but I'm not a fool."

"Nona's a fetching little morsel." Penne rocked the dice cup in a manner imitative of a woman's swaying skirts.

"It matters not if a wife is fetching." Durand frowned

at his friend. What was behind Penne's approval of Lady Nona? The marriage might allow him to offer a bribe and avoid taking up the sword against Philip himself. But did Penne not need him negotiating for the return of their properties? If he remained in England with a well-dowered wife, he could do none of those things for his friend. He hated suspecting every word his friend spoke.

Penne tapped the table to gain his attention. "You could negotiate Mistress le Gros into your marriage contracts, if you are shrewd about it. It has been done before, a wife's agreeing to tolerate a mistress."

Durand frowned. "I beg your pardon?"

"Come. You look at our merchant's wife as if you would devour her. If Marion were alive, she would dismiss the woman the instant she saw you and her in the same chamber. There is heat in your look. Hunger. You would do well to conceal it before Lady Nona." The dice rattled across the tabletop.

Durand's throat dried. Was he as transparent as the glass in Penne's chamber windows? "I've no intention of—"

"Don't lie to me," Penne said, leaning close.

Durand recoiled from his friend. If it was Penne who had betrayed him, what right had he to make sport of Cristina? "I admit only that she is a taking woman to look upon."

"Take her then, for I suspect our Cristina wants you as much as you want her, but see"—he pointed with the dicing cup—"she's sitting with Luke. Do you not think it will be he who charms her into his bed if you do not?"

Durand looked from Penne to Luke. From Luke to Penne. Marion had oft berated him for qualities found in abundance in his brother—and friend—and sadly lacking in himself.

Humor. Patience.

He remembered le Gros's accusation that Luke had handled Cristina. Was there aught between them? She was taking. Any man would think her so. "Think you Luke pursues her?" he asked with studied indifference.

Penne shrugged. "She invites no liberties that I see. The perfect picture of gentle modesty. But she's damned well made, if you ask me, and 'tis sure she finds a cold bed with le Gros. In fact, offer le Gros a few marks for her. He slavers to increase his importance so, I imagine he would probably lift his wife's gown for you and help her into your bed, if asked."

"How can Oriel abide you?"

"How can I do what?" Oriel asked. She plucked the dice from the table and kissed them before giving them back to Penne.

"Abide this man here," Durand said, attempting levity.

"*All* women find him 'abidable,' Durand. 'Tis his lovely blue eyes, I wager. Was I not saying just today that Penne was Marion's first choice?" Oriel perched on Penne's knee. "I believe she envied me. Not to belittle *your* worth, Durand."

Penne smiled. " 'Twas I who had not Durand's worth."

Oriel tugged on Penne's hair in a playful manner, but there was little playful in her tone. "Which, thank God, made you perfect for me, the younger, less important daughter."

"You could never be unimportant," Durand said. "I am blessed to have you here."

"You are kind." Oriel rose and kissed Durand's cheek, then went back to Penne's knee. "But I've always felt a need to watch Penne every moment, else Marion might have stolen him away."

"Or I her." Penne kissed Oriel on the neck. Tension underlay Oriel's bantering tone.

Hastily Durand rose. "Excuse me," he said, almost knocking his chair over in his haste to rise. "I must find where Joseph has placed my pallet."

The next morning the hall filled as everyone clamored to see and hear the king conduct business. He did not, as he had the previous autumn, lie abed with his young wife in neglect of his duties. Nay, he had been first to the hall after Lord Durand, and now, several hours later, he was still there. The long table was filled with barons and other men.

Cristina took her place with the women of lesser importance, stitching diligently and nursing Felice on demand. She should have been well rested, as Felice had blessedly slept through the night, but instead Cristina felt weary to her bones.

She tried—and failed—to ignore the chattering women who surrounded the very pretty, very young queen.

"Mistress?" Luke sat at her feet. "What so occupies you that you must ruin your lovely face with a frown?"

She could not help smiling down at him. "This stitch is difficult."

"I'm not a lady to know needlecraft, but it looks to me like simple mending. Why are you not truthful?"

"Forgive me," she said softly. "I am much concerned about this talk of war."

"Aye. We await the arrival of William Marshall and the king's new galley; then we'll be off."

"So soon?" Her throat felt tight. "You will—" She broke off when one of the queen's ladies came to their side.

"Let me present Lady Nona," Luke said. Cristina rose and made a respectful curtsy. "And Lady Nona, please meet a woman who fills our lives with sweet scents—Cristina le Gros."

"Is this Lord Durand's daughter?" Lady Nona asked,

155

dropping to her knees in a pool of bronze wool skirts.

"Aye, my lady," Cristina said.

"She is a sweetling," Lady Nona said, peering in the basket.

Luke pulled Felice from her swaddling. He set her in Nona's arms. "She's plump as a stoat and pretty as her mother was. Thank God she has naught of Durand!" He paused, then peered closely at Felice. "Is she losing her hair? She's almost bald."

"My lord Luke, you are hard on the poor child." Lady Nona laughed. "In a few years you will wish for such a thatch!"

Luke touched his head and frowned.

Lady Nona took the child and held her close. The lady's cheeks were soft as a summer peach. She wore her golden brown hair held back by a circlet of silver and gold entwined and decorated with small squares of blue enamel. Her bronze gown covered a fine linen undergown of a deep blue. The embroidery was inches thick about the sleeve and hem. Her girdle repeated the richness of her circlet.

"Have you children of your own?" Luke asked, leaning negligently on a nearby table. He crossed his arms over his chest. He had never looked more handsome, his red-gold hair, thick enough to last a score of years, agleam in the sun streaming in the solar window. His brown tunic and heavy leather belt emphasized his slim waist.

"To my great regret, I don't, my lord," Lady Nona said. "May I take this sweet one away whilst I walk about the castle grounds?" She directed her question to Cristina.

What could she say to this companion to the queen? "As it pleases you, my lady." The lady smiled and turned away.

"The king wishes Nona to wed Durand," Luke said, staring after her.

Wed Durand? An impossible ache lodged somewhere near Cristina's heart. What right had she to feel anything?

She stared at the empty basket by her feet. *It is as it should be,* she thought. *Lord Durand's wife-to-be must learn the place and his daughter.* Her throat burned, as did her eyes.

Lord Durand was naught but the substance of dreams.

"Cristina? Have you something for my hair?" Luke asked.

"Your hair?" She forced herself to concentrate on his words and the frown upon his face.

"Aye. Is there something to grow new or prevent its loss—"

"Prevent its loss?" Cristina watched Lady Nona leave the hall. "I believe the lady but teased you."

Nothing could prevent the loss of Felice, she thought as the babe who had come to take the place of her own in her heart left the hall in the arms of Lord Durand's future wife.

"I have noticed some change here." Luke tapped his brow.

She needed to escape this place in which she was so much a servant. "I'll mix you something, but it smells so, 'tis likely you'll need to make a choice twixt your hair and your bed partners."

She left him frowning and rubbing his temples and sought out Alice, who sat with Lady Sabina, sorting the woman's silks.

They remarked not at all when she excused herself, telling Alice she would work in the garden.

But it was not to the peace of Lady Marion's garden she went. That space was not hers either, just as Felice and this life was not hers. She found herself alone on the road to the village save for a boy and his goat. At the fork she stood a moment, contemplating the many directions to be taken: Portsmouth, where the men would go to embark for war; the village and thence to Winchester; or the forest. She turned to the forest.

In moments she had stepped from the work of man to that of God. The deep green, the coolness of the air, embraced her. She felt at home, welcomed. Her breasts told her it would be hours ere Felice needed her, and, heeding a basic need of her own, she hurried through the trees.

A furlong from the road, she came to the clearing where Lord Luke had hewed himself a smooth seat. She sat there and lifted her face to the meager sunlight weaving its way through the boughs overhead. All about was innocent of man's intrusion. Only the rush of the river and God's creatures could be heard.

She pulled off her plain leather circlet and headcovering, then let down her hair, combing it out with her fingers.

Clouds obscured the sun; the wind rose, teasing her skirt hem. It swirled the mist over the riverbank and slowly toward her. She reveled in the peace of the concealing fog, the caress of its intangible fingers on her skin, the deadening of sound.

The jingle of a harness made her turn. Lord Durand sat there atop his terrible black horse, as if a spirit come from the mist.

She rose and faced him. "Are you real?" she asked. "Or have I conjured you?"

He swung his leg over the front of the saddle and slid to the ground, then looped his reins about a low branch. "I'm real, but can I hope you would conjure me if I were not?" he asked.

She sat down, then remembered her hair; but her headcovering was a tightly creased mess and could not be quickly donned.

He walked about the clearing, the fog moving from

his boots as if running away. She watched him in silence. His dark green surcoat made him almost a creature of the forest, blending with shadows, at one with his surroundings.

Then he came to stand before her. "Have you forgotten the danger of brigands?"

"Aye, my lord, I must confess I've other matters on my mind."

"What matters are of such import that you would endanger yourself?"

His cheeks were shadowed with beard, his brows drawn together with concern or anger—she knew not which.

Cristina shifted on the stump and sought to deflect the heavy weight of his scrutiny. "Ones of little interest to a man such as yourself, my lord."

To her astonishment, he let it rest, only stepping closer. He wore a jeweled ring on his left hand, one too fragile for a man such as he. It would make a lovely gift for a new bride.

"I have a difficult question for you, Cristina."

"A question?" She saw a softening in the harsh lines about his mouth. "Ask me whatever you wish."

Her throat felt tight. Would he ask her to be his mistress? Or would he honor the promise made between them? And if he did ask . . . what would she answer?

Praise God, she had taken two doses of the resistance potion that morn and had added crushed thorns of hawthorn to make herself less amiable in temperament as further discouragement. She readied herself to resist.

He didn't speak, but paced the clearing, his steps almost silent on the many layers of pine needles.

Finally he went down on his haunches before her and touched her knee. "Has your husband a son?"

Heat filled her cheeks. "I don't know what you mean.

We have no children." She hated the compassion she saw on his face.

"I didn't mean issue with you, but with another. Has Simon a son?"

Cristina ducked her head to hide from his direct gaze and nodded. "He has a son. He would be ten and four or five now."

"I see." Lightly, he placed his hand over hers. "I believe the youth who died from the brigand's wound is Simon's son."

She looked up and saw a terrible truth in his eyes. "Nay. Nay. 'Tis not possible. He resides in Winchester—"

"Had he not the look of your husband?"

She shook her head. "Nay, my lord."

"You asked if he did not remind us of someone."

"Aye. As you thought he reminded you of your son's friends, so he reminded me of an innocent child. I thought of Felice, no one else, my lord."

His hard expression softened. "Aye. He did have the beardless cheeks of an innocent, but that's not who he resembled. He resembled your husband."

She could not accept what he said. "You're wrong, my lord. It could not be." She twisted the linen cloth in her hands. "Oh, 'tis a misery, if you are right. Simon . . ." She could not finish. The boy had meant so much to Simon. It was the boy Simon held up to her as proof that their childless state was not his fault.

Her heart throbbing in her throat, she stood up, pulling her hand from under his. "I must . . . if I may ask, my lord that is . . . I don't know what to do. . . . Felice needs—"

"We'll see to her," he said. "But first, sit. I have questions to ask you."

She felt a cold chill down her spine. Clutching her headcloth tightly, she sat on the edge of the stump.

Simon's son could not be dead.

Lord Durand's gray eyes were dark, his expression kind but also closed, like a coffer hiding its treasures. He remained on one knee by her, but did not touch her this time.

"What questions, my lord?"

"You knew of Simon's son?"

With a quick nod, she looked down at her hands. "I know he *has* a son."

And Durand knew he must cause her pain, possibly immeasurable pain. He could not ask the most important question, though he had planned to be direct. She was too pale, her fingers crushing the fabric in her hands, plucking at stitches.

"Let us assume for a moment that I'm right, that the boy is Simon's. Do you know how the boy could have come to be with the bishop?"

"Nay, in truth, I've never met Simon's son. His name is Hugh, my lord," she said, her voice dropping to a whisper. "Named for Simon's father. He lived—lives— in Winchester with his mother, although I've never . . . that is . . . Simon kept him separate."

"How did you know of him?" Durand watched her milk-pale skin blotch red.

"Simon told me. After the death of our first daughter. The boy was ten, I believe, at the time. I've been wed to Simon but nine years, so 'twas naught of my business to inquire beyond what Simon—"

"Thought you should know?" Durand asked sharply, rising and striding to the edge of the clearing, his steps tearing the fog.

"Aye, my lord. Do not condemn him. Would you have shared your bastards with Lady Marion?"

He whipped around. "I have no bastards, Mistress le Gros. Now. Do you know how Hugh came to be with the bishop?"

"Was the young man not a guard?" She tipped her head back to stare up at him, and he bit back some of his anger at the blank look upon her face. "That surely proves 'tis not Simon's son. Hugh works for a baker in Winchester, I believe. How could a baker's boy rise to such a position with the bishop?"

"A simple bribe would gain him a place if the boy was not really with the bishop at all."

Cristina rose. Her hair slipped over one shoulder as she hastened to where he stood. "What are you saying?"

"The boy said his father had taken my Aelfric and sold it to the bishop. The boy was delivering it."

"The Aelfric?" She stared at him blankly for a moment, and immense relief swept through Durand. If Simon had stolen the book, she had not aided him.

"Aye." Durand touched her lightly on the shoulder, her hair silk beneath his fingers. "Did Simon know I had a copy?"

"He would not take your Aelfric!" she insisted. "Nay, my lord. Nay. Why would he do such a thing? You're wrong!"

"The sum the Aelfric would fetch might be very tempting. Did Simon know about my Aelfric?"

"He saw it in my chamber," she whispered.

"Should we ask Simon about his son in Winchester?"

Durand chastised himself for not saying what he thought. Why did he dance about the point? Because she was near to fainting. She swayed on her feet, and he clasped her shoulders to keep her upright. Her shoulders were thin beneath his hands. "Come. I'll take you to your husband."

He lifted her onto Marauder's back and climbed up behind her. She felt small within the circle of his arms, not coming against him, not seeking shelter or comfort in his embrace.

With no thought this time of lust, he wrapped one arm about her waist and drew her against his chest.

She shuddered once and then rested, her soft hair grazing his cheek, and he kept his arm around her that she might not fall. He sensed she was not really aware of her surroundings, the trees that plucked at his mantle, the rattle of wood beneath the horse's hooves as they crossed the old bridge near the merchant's cottage.

In the yard he dismounted and then reached up to clasp her about the waist. She clamped her hands on his arms and allowed him to swing her down. She had lost her headcovering somewhere along the way.

For a brief moment they remained that way, his hands on her waist, her hands on his arms.

"I will help you," he said, not sure what he meant, only knowing she needed someone at this moment, for he was about to take her world apart.

In his heart, he knew she would hate him for it on the morrow.

Chapter Twelve

Cristina preceded Durand into Simon's abode. He stood before the hearth talking to a young woman dressed in a simple kirtle and gown of gray wool. Cristina recognized her as the innkeeper's daughter and felt Lord Durand stiffen beside her.

"Ah, my lord," Simon said. He flushed a deep red. "It is good of you to escort my wife." He cleared his throat. "This is Agnes. She'll see to the cooking and scrubbing from now on."

"That's good, Simon," Cristina said, unable to look at Lord Durand, who stood by the door. Tension radiated from his body.

"Agnes, see that a boy tends my horse, and remain in the yard until we call for you," Lord Durand said abruptly, and the girl made a quick curtsy and slipped out the door. "Now that we're alone, le Gros, I've a matter of grave importance to discuss with you." His voice was hard, but when he placed a hand on her shoulder, his touch was gentle. "Would you like to wait outside?"

Cristina stepped away from his touch. "Nay, my lord. I'll not be sent away like a child." Her face felt wretchedly hot, but she would know every word Simon spoke, see his face when Lord Durand asked his questions. Know that Lord Durand was wrong.

"What is this about, my lord?" Simon shoved his hands up into his sleeves.

"Do you know the youth who died under Master Aldwin's care? The boy from the bishop's party?"

There was something of a threat in the way Lord Durand's hand rested on the hilt of his raven's-head dagger.

"I don't know what you mean, my lord. I've never seen the young man before." Simon shook his head.

"Your wife said there was something familiar about the boy, and I agree. I believe he looks like you."

Cristina watched her husband pace before the hearth. His lips were as pale as his face. His hands, thrust up his sleeves, shed no light upon his agitation. He did not meet her gaze.

"I know him not. And if the boy looks like someone of Cristina's acquaintance, then she is wandering beyond *my* knowledge and must answer for it."

"Simon!" She made to go to his side, but Lord Durand held her still with a quick shake of his head.

"Can you deny you were greatly affected by the sight of the wounded boy?" Lord Durand crossed his arms over his chest.

"I'll not deny that, my lord. I've never seen such a wound, nor smelled one. It sickened me. I was moved by pity, my lord, nothing more."

Lord Durand turned to her. "Did you not see something familiar in the youth?"

"Aye. But I thought of Felice, my lord."

She felt Simon's emotion as tangibly as if he had

raised the stick he threatened her with so often and actually struck her.

"Felice! You waste our lord's time with your nonsense! You will shut your mouth and speak only when I bid you do so, wife."

"I beg your indulgence, le Gros." Durand lifted a staying hand. "Penne saw a resemblance as well, though not to the babe your wife nurses. He saw you. Is the dead boy your son Hugh?"

"Hugh's with his mother in Winchester. Cristina has never even seen the boy. She's not his mother and knows nothing of him at all."

Cristina bowed her head. She had heard those words so often—that she knew nothing. But Lord Durand was wrong. The boy could not be Simon's. Simon would never lie about such a thing. When she looked at the two men, Lord Durand met her gaze, his eyes filled with pity. She turned from him to her husband.

He looked away.

Lord Durand shrugged. "It is of little moment, and the question easily answered. Fetch your son from Winchester."

"But my lord," Simon protested, "I have several men coming on the morrow for a millstone—"

"They can wait." Durand strode from the cottage into the yard. "You'll come to the keep with me, mistress. Felice misses you, I'm sure."

In the yard, the boy Simon had hired to tend the old horse was standing with Lord Durand's destrier, patting the great horse's neck. Agnes sat on a bench, her back against the wall beneath the window, likely eavesdropping for what tidbits she could share at the well.

Durand praised the boy's care of his horse, then mounted and put out his hand to her.

When she looked at Simon, he turned away and beckoned the boy, leaving her to be pulled up by Lord

Durand. "Saddle my horse," Simon said to the boy. "I must get to Winchester."

This time she did not ride before Lord Durand on his horse, but behind him, her arms about his waist. She found it almost impossible to bear. How hard and unyielding his body was against hers. Not like that of her dreams.

Fear filled her. This man held such power over her—not just in physical temptation, but in his dealings with Simon.

The instant the horse came to a halt by the keep steps, she slid off and ran up the steps, two at a time, heedless of what Lord Durand might think.

Instead of going to Felice, she darted down to Aldwin's lair. He was stirring something black and noisome.

"Oh, 'tis you. What do you want?" he asked, and went back to his task.

"The bishop's guard. Where is he?"

Aldwin gestured vaguely at the soot-blackened ceiling. "At the chapel, being readied for burial."

"Thank you." She curtsied, then ran back through the keep, out the door, and across the bailey to the chapel. Inside she found Father Odo and the tightly wrapped body of the boy.

It was too late. She could not see those waxen features for herself, could only conjure them in her imagination.

"Mistress le Gros!" Father Odo rose off his knees with a groan. "How may I help you?"

"Oh. That is . . . I came to pray for the boy."

Father Odo took her arm and led her to the bier. How different it all looked from when Lady Marion had lain here, flower-bedecked. "He needs our prayers. There's no one to mourn him, and the others will be buried at the abbey. No one from the abbey claimed him, I'm afraid."

No one from the abbey claimed him. She knelt on a soft cushion and folded her hands. The good father faded away and she tried to pray for the boy's soul, but her mind kept returning to Lord Durand's suspicions. He must be wrong. Simon would fetch his son and prove him wrong.

No one from the abbey claimed him.

Durand offered Joseph a small purse. "Use what you need. The man may try to disappear, and I would be most grievously angered if he succeeds."

"I'll see where he goes. He'll not escape from me, my lord. Ye know me well enough to know that."

"Aye, 'tis why I've chosen you. Take a good horse and stay in the shadows."

Durand walked Joseph to the stable. When his squire was gone to follow Simon le Gros, he wandered about. He had no private space in which to brood. His chamber was now the royal apartment. Other chambers overflowed with barons and their men. He turned to the chapel. He would pray he was wrong, that Simon would appear with his son, that Cristina was not wed to a thief.

Did her pale face and anxious defense of the man bespeak love? She had not spoken of love in the garden, he thought as he entered the chapel.

The boy's body lay on a bier, a fragrant garland of dried flowers draped over it. He recognized Cristina's work. A simple rose lay on the boy's breast.

Was it his imagination that he could catch her scent on the air? Somehow her care of the boy tightened his throat. He put his hand there and his fingers encountered his torque. If Simon ran, or if Simon could not produce his son, Durand knew he would pursue the man for theft of the Aelfric. He had judged other such crimes and enacted heavy penalties.

And if Cristina loved Simon, would she ever forgive him?

Chapter Thirteen

From a bench in the hall, Cristina watched the evening sun slip away. One of the queen's waiting maids was making love to a knight in Felice's chamber, and all assigned a sleeping space there must await their pleasure. In truth, Cristina dreaded sleep. Would her dreams betray her again? And when would Simon return?

Her throat was scratchy; her head pounded. Felice had fussed all evening and finally fallen asleep in her arms. Each time she tried to set her in her basket, she woke and set up a howl. There was naught to do about preparing Luke's hair salve while the child fussed and the waiting maid made love.

She kissed the babe and closed her eyes, listening to the hum of conversation among the ladies surrounding the queen in the hall.

"Who is that magnificent man who just entered?"

Lady Sabina whispered to Oriel. Cristina had not the strength to look up.

"Gilles d'Argent," Oriel said, laying aside her stitching.

"I've heard much of him," Sabina said, smoothing her skirts.

"Aye, Penne and I wagered he would come late. His wife is said to have just birthed their fifth son."

"I'd birth ten sons for such a man."

"He's a hard-looking man," Oriel said. "He frightens me."

As the party of men who had just arrived in the hall approached the king, Cristina saw whom it was they discussed. The baron was tall and black-haired, bearded, hard of face and unrelenting in his manner. Even the king seemed to be honored by his presence. The baron had an entourage of seven knights. One was his son, she heard as the king greeted each man. The son, Nicholas d'Argent, was a handsome man.

Oriel nudged Cristina's side. "Now, the son has none of the harshness of the father. He would appeal much more to me."

"You'll be able to test his appeal," Sabina said. "Your husband brings him."

The ladies rose to greet Lord Penne and the newly arrived Nicholas d'Argent. He bowed over each lady's hand and even Cristina's, which she considered a kindness.

Sabina drew the newly arrived man's attention to her. "You and your father come late to the king, do you not?" Sabina chastised, one hand on d'Argent's arm.

"My father's wife was lying in. You could not peel my father from her side."

"So we understand. The troubadours make much of your father and his *weaver* wife," Sabina said with a bit of a sneer.

170

Cristina stroked Felice's back, but paid more attention to the conversation. Gilles d'Argent had married a weaver? She found the idea ludicrous. Men so high did not marry women so low.

"Aye," Nicholas said with a slight bow. "My father's *weaver* wife is a beautiful, talented woman. He would give his life for her. Other women can only envy his devotion."

Oriel caught Cristina's eye and winked. Lord Nicholas had certainly told Sabina he cared naught for her opinion.

"Have you a wife?" Oriel asked.

Nicholas smiled. "Aye. My wife is a gifted healer and it is only her promise to care for my father's wife that persuaded him to heed the king's command."

"He would defy a king?" Cristina wanted to snatch the words back into her mouth. The ladies and their maids turned in her direction. She saw concern on Oriel's face and contempt on the others', but Nicholas d'Argent merely smiled.

"Oh, aye. 'Tis why I am here. To see he does not have himself cast into a dungeon or say something to start a baronial war. And you are?" he asked.

But Lady Sabina waved a hand. "She is naught but a wet nurse."

Lady Nona joined the group. "This is Cristina le Gros, Nicholas." She linked her arm through Cristina's. "A woman as talented as your own Catherine with herbs, but not in the healing vein. She makes soaps that would have you think you were bathing in a pool in Eden."

Cristina felt her face heat at the compliment.

"Lady Nona!" Nicholas d'Argent did not kiss Lady Nona's hand. He engulfed her in a swift hug and kissed each of her cheeks. "You are lovelier than ever."

"And you flatter well. Come, Nicholas, Oriel, Penne, sit here by me. And Cristina, bring that sweet babe

171

with you." She turned toward an alcove with two cushioned benches. As much as Cristina appreciated the lady's defense of her, she could not abide their banter one moment more.

"Pray, excuse me," Cristina said, and hurried across the hall. The king and the newly arrived men were drinking ale and wine and speaking in hard tones with little levity today.

She had nowhere to go, no place to call her own here in the keep. She could not leave, could not go to Felice's chamber.

Without thought, she found herself at the garden gate. She turned the key and wandered the paths, holding Felice in her arms. This space was not hers either. The garden's design reflected a desire for beauty but no knowledge of what plants needed. Sun-loving blossoms lingered in shady corners; delicate blooms withered in sun. It brought no comfort to wander here. This was where *he* had kissed her and, in doing so, had torn apart her comfort, her ease, so that even her pillow betrayed her.

Stars filled the ink-black sky overhead, but instead of filling her with awe, they reminded her of the gems in Lady Nona's circlet and stitched onto Queen Isabelle's gowns.

Locking Lady Marion's garden, she headed for the stable area, but the arrival of d'Argent had also meant the arrival of many more horses and men. The heat of the forge drew many to stand about and talk of the coming offensive against Philip.

There must be privacy somewhere. She found herself near the postern gate. Cristina knew it was meant to be a secret exit for use in times of seige. Alice's idle tongue had informed her of the gate's location. A man lolled on a bench there, not obviously a guard, but one nonetheless.

Cristina was about to head back to the inner bailey

when the sentry rose, ambled a few steps away, lifted his tunic, and began to relieve himself. She turned with some embarrassment and took a step into the shadows. A hand reached out and grabbed her.

The king's personal guard had said not a word as he dragged her unceremoniously to the bowels of Ravenswood Castle and a damp cell. She had stared at the dish of oil and the smoking wick for more than an hour before she heard footsteps followed by a key turning in the lock.

The Lord Durand who released her was not the Lord Durand who had kissed her. There was no gentleness in his manner as he swung the key on a large iron ring.

"Mistress le Gros. This way." He gestured her out of the cell.

"I cannot," she said, touching Felice, who was greedily nursing at her breast.

His jaw clenched. He turned to the guard. "When Mistress le Gros is able, escort her to me," he said. The door clanged shut behind him.

Cristina heard the angry words Lord Durand directed at the guard once the door was locked behind them. "Are you mad? You imprison a child?"

"I am duty-bound to protect the king," the guard said stiffly.

"Even from babes?" Durand demanded.

The guard sputtered an excuse, but Lord Durand accepted none. "I'll hold you responsible if even one cough issues from the child's lips. Do you understand?" Lord Durand snapped. The men moved off, and in a few moments silence fell.

At least he cared for the babe's welfare.

She took her time with Felice, delaying Lord Durand's wrath. How could she soften it? What ill luck to have been found by the king's man. The Ravenswood

173

guards would most likely have just bantered a few words with her about the weather or the war.

Finally there was not a drop of milk left, and Felice was nodding and kneading her breast, a sure sign of imminent sleep. With dragging footsteps and a heavy heart, Cristina followed an anxious Ravenswood sentry when he opened the cell. She ignored his nagging inquiries after Felice's health.

Lord Durand was in the counting room, a roaring fire at his back. He stood with his hands locked behind him, his legs spread.

"You may leave Mistress le Gros with me," he informed the sentry.

"You were running away," he accused as soon as they were alone.

"Running away? Nay, my lord. Why would I do such a thing? Where would I go?"

"How do you come to know where to find the postern gate?"

"Alice. But I pray, my lord, do not punish her; she gossips from time to time, but I would not have her suffer for it."

"So. You did know you were at the postern gate. Now explain why you were there." His gray eyes were stormy. Even his hair seemed angry.

Cristina looked down at his boots. Mud stained them, as it did the hem of his black surcoat. "I needed solitude, my lord."

"What of your chamber?"

"I have no chamber, my lord," she said, anger rising to color her words.

"Felice's chamber, then, mistress." He bowed slightly in acknowledgment of her assertion.

"Felice's chamber was occupied by lovers."

"The garden?" he countered.

"It is not mine either." She would not say it was

memories of him that had driven her from that green space.

"You were running away to join your husband."

His words struck her silent. An expression flitted across his face. Compassion? Then it disappeared.

"Aye. Running away to your husband," he repeated.

"S-Simon is on his way to Winchester, my lord. What need have I to go there? I don't know what you are saying."

He tossed a scrap of parchment he had been holding behind his back onto the table. "This says differently."

Her hand shook as she took up the much-creased vellum. She scanned the words. "I don't understand. This says Simon took the east road. . . . I don't understand."

"I understand completely. I asked Simon to fetch his son, and since his son lies dead in my chapel he had no choice. He fled."

She sank to a stool. Her heart pounded wildly in her chest. "Nay," she whispered. "Nay."

"He lied. Can there be any other reason for him to take the east road, not the north?"

Cristina examined his face. He looked every inch a warrior lord, someone with the power to crush others in his hands and beneath his muddy boot. "I have no reason to offer for his behavior."

"I've sent my men to collect him." The words seared through her. "What were you doing at the postern gate?"

"I sought some privacy and just wandered in that direction. The guard there started to relieve himself, so I stepped away."

"Or you sought to leave whilst he was occupied."

"Nay. I did not!" She stood up. She wanted to reach out and touch him, but could not bring herself to raise her hand.

"Think you there is but one guard for the gate? The other saw you step to the door."

"I stepped into the *shadows* so the guard would not see me. He was relieving himself."

He said nothing. His face was as hard as one carved in stone. This was not the tender lover of her dreams.

She tried again. "Would you suspect Lady Sabina or Lady Nona of some perfidious act if they had done the same? Would the guard have imprisoned them?"

"They don't have husbands I suspect of theft!"

She ached inside and out. "What would you have me do, my lord?" He would imprison her in the damp cell again, but this time Felice would not be with her. Her throat burned.

"Return to your duties."

"My lord?" she whispered, rising, Felice tight against her chest. But he had turned his broad back on her. She stood a moment looking at him, but he did not acknowledge her.

Without another word, she left. Climbing the tower steps, she tentatively touched the latch to Felice's chamber. This time it was not barred against her. This time she would not be alone. This time no lush dreams would keep her from sleep.

Myriad smells and sounds came to her from the dark. The banked fire cast enough light that she could see her way to an empty pallet, one near the door and offering no warmth at all.

Her hands were shaking as she tucked Felice against her side, not even removing her mantle or shoes. Simon had not gone to Winchester. Lord Durand thought him guilty of theft and—worse—suspected her as well.

She would not weep! But her eyes burned and some moments later she felt tears slip over her cheeks.

*　　*　　*

Luke snorted and tossed the note Cristina had so recently held onto the table. "You think she had a part in this?"

"What am I to think?" Durand said in a snarl, slamming his fist on the table. "She was *leaving*."

"That I cannot deny, but if she witnessed this side of you, then no wonder she fled."

"*Mon Dieu.* What does that mean?" Durand balled up Joseph's note and cast it into the flames.

"I've never seen you so angry. She's a thorn in your palm, and it festers."

He could not deny it. "She was at the postern gate!"

"What did she say again?"

"She said she needed to be alone."

"What of her chamber?"

"It held lovers."

"Did you look into it?"

Durand nodded. "Aye, one of the queen's maids was with a lover, but that does not excuse her! She could have walked in the garden! She had the key on her person."

"Searched her, did you?"

Luke grinned, and something inside Durand snapped.

He reached across the table and snatched his brother by the tunic. "And how many times have you searched her?"

Luke wrenched the fabric away from his grasp. "Durand! Take hold of yourself. You know I never dally with married women. I believe Cristina had no motive beyond what she said." He straightened his tunic.

Durand unclenched his fist.

"I'll speak with Cristina for you, if you wish. Mayhap I'll not frighten her so she cannot think straight."

"Do as you please." Durand shoved past his brother and strode into the hall, a grievous mistake, as the king called to him and there was naught to do but obey.

"Sire?" Durand said, bowing.

"We have spoken to our guards about a woman at the postern gate. Have we need for concern?"

"Nay. 'Twas just a woman seeking privacy."

King John stroked his beard with this thumbs. "Hmm. We would know more of this. We don't need spies among us."

Something hot and heavy settled in Durand's belly. "She's not a spy. Women have moods, sire, as you well know."

The king threw his head back and laughed. "Oh, aye. We know a woman's moods. If you are sure of her, we'll not interfere. Spurned by a lover, having a fit of pique, no doubt."

The men about the king laughed with him. The heavy feeling lifted just a bit. "Come, de Marle," the king commanded. "Tell d'Argent, here, how many men you will give to our noble cause."

Durand could not refuse. He turned to the only man not laughing—Gilles d'Argent. The baron had not the problems he must face. D'Argent's lands were all in England. He had no divided loyalty, and enough wealth that Durand imagined most of d'Argent's conversations with the king were about how much his scutage costs and baronial bribe would be.

Luke nudged Cristina awake with his toe. She looked up his long leg but a moment before rising and following him from the bedchamber.

"Have you been weeping?" He took Felice from her arms and cradled the babe against his shoulder.

"Nay. I never weep," she said, but her eyes felt swollen.

"Come." He walked away, up a set of steps she had never climbed, and opened a door. A sentry greeted him, and they stepped out onto the wall walk. Far below, the bailey was alive with men and women, torches and conversation. In the distance the river was a silver ribbon. "Now, why were you at the postern gate?"

"You don't mince your words." She leaned against the parapet wall. The cold stone soothed her hot cheeks.

"Durand's in a rage. He doesn't need such business at this time."

"I don't know what to say. I needed to find a place of privacy. Felice's chamber—"

"Your chamber—"

"Lord Luke, I have no place here. I nurse Felice. That is my *duty*. It makes me your brother's servant. Servants do not have chambers."

He gave a low whistle. "I stand duly chastised, Mistress le Gros. Why did you not retire to *Felice's* chamber?"

"Lovers, my lord." Why explain? Durand's men would bring Simon here to Ravenswood and he would explain himself. She would wait for his arrival and know the truth about the boy in the chapel.

But if she did not believe in her husband, she had nothing. Nothing. And if Simon lied, she would be cast out by Lord Durand. Set upon the road. And Simon . . . She would not think of his fate—a fate now in Lord Durand's hands.

"There are places aplenty in the keep if you need privacy."

"The jakes?" She rubbed her swollen eyes.

" 'Tis not a time for levity. Marion's garden, then?"

Cristina turned around to face him. Moonlight painted him in a silver gleam—his hair, his skin, his white linen shirt showing at the neck and sleeves of his tunic. He was handsome, but not stupid. "You have said it, my lord. 'Tis Lady Marion's garden."

"I see. Does her shade walk there?" He turned Felice and inspected her tiny face.

"In a manner, aye. I may nurture the plants, but still, 'tis her garden."

"Has my brother made you feel unwelcome there?"

"Nay," she said softly, then looked up at the black velvet sky, studded with stars. "Nay." Instead Lord Durand had beguiled her there, kissed her, made her wish for what could never be—the strength of his arms, the feel of his body against hers. A quiver of fear and want, indistinguishable one from another, ran through her.

Now he thought her perfidious. The thought was a deeper pain than any illness, any stab from a dagger, could be.

Durand woke from a vivid dream. His body was bathed in sweat and ready should a willing woman have lain beside him. But his pallet was in his brother's counting room, and only Luke lay snoring by the fire to disturb his rest.

He sat up, cast off the furs, and clasped his arms about his knees. In his dream he had pursued Cristina through the postern gate, past the village, and into the forest. It was deepest night in his dream, for purple and black shadows filled the clearing. She was clothed only in her hair, and he had wanted to bury his face in the sweetly scented tresses.

The pursued became the pursuer.

She had fetched a bowl of water from the nearby river that seemed to writhe and breathe as if it were a living thing. Without a word he had stretched out on the ground for her as she approached. He, too, was suddenly naked, and she had bathed his skin in scented water as moonlight shone on the shape of her full breasts and womanly thighs.

His body had arched to her gentle caresses, and

just as the pleasure had come, she had lifted the bowl and spilled its silver stream as his body had poured forth its ecstasy.

Awake now, he felt as drained as if he had spent himself, and yet was still as aroused as if he had not.

Why must he dream of her now? Now, when he doubted every word she spoke? Now, when he most wanted to believe she knew naught of Simon's thievery? Yet she had lied about her reasons for seeking the gate. Her face, so innocently expressive, had told all.

His eyes felt as if filled with sand. He rose and poured water into a basin and splashed his face. Near to hand sat a pot of soft soap—his brother's. Its smell was not that of the forest glade of his dreams. He set it aside, unused.

Once in the hall, he ate little of the bounty set before him. The fat congealing at the edges of the trenchers did naught for his appetite. He searched but failed to see Cristina at one of the many tables in the hall.

Given no unforeseen events, brigands or otherwise, Simon would be here before nightfall. As he chewed, he noted the king's arrival in the hall. He rose and bowed, as did everyone else. Thank God John had not the habit of his father of wandering around and ofttimes eating while standing. Durand kissed Queen Isabelle's hand and led her to a chair next to his.

"What is this we hear that you are bringing in a thief?" the king asked.

"It is not determined that the man is a thief. He'll have his say." Durand lifted his goblet, but quickly set it down when Cristina entered the hall. She was garbed in the white gown in which he had first seen her, but no ribbons held her hair looped back. Was it mere imagination that traced shadows under her eyes? She did not look toward him, nor settle at a table. Instead she wrapped a heel of bread in a cloth and returned to the tower.

The king leaned close to Durand and spoke at his ear. "Fetching."

"Sire?" Durand said.

"That woman. A fetching morsel."

Durand licked his lips. "Aye."

"She made our dear queen a most wonderful soap. A talented hand with scents and potions."

"Aye, sire," he said. He did not want to think of Cristina's scent. It filled his dreams and tormented his sleep.

Chapter Fourteen

Cristina feared to walk about the keep, yet could not remain in Felice's chamber. There, she would not know when Simon arrived. She'd left only once to get bread, but had found that every step crossing the lofty hall meant moments of torture before *his* scrutiny.

Eating the bread, feeding Felice, and attempting to make sweet pillows for the queen's waiting maids did naught to assuage her panic. The sentry had moved from his position at the foot of the tower steps to outside her door and served as a reminder that Lord Durand did not trust her.

She tested the hair salve for Lord Luke, judged it cool enough to pot up, and finished it off with a dab of day-old butter just as a light tap came at the chamber door.

Her heart tapped rapidly in her chest. "Enter," she called.

It was Lady Nona who lifted the latch.

"Do I disturb you, Mistress le Gros?" the lady asked. Cristina curtsied and brushed back the loose strands of hair at her brow. It was carelessly tied at her nape. Now, faced with Lady Nona's splendid perfection, she felt slatternly. "Enter, my lady. You do not disturb me."

Lady Nona wore a gown of soft green stitched with pearls and trimmed with ivory ribbon. Her hair was entwined with ribbons, and ropes of pearls looped her neck. "I thought to see the babe," she said in a manner that suggested she would not trespass if Cristina forbade it.

"As you wish, my lady," Cristina said softly, continuing her task, pouring Luke's hair salve into an earthenware pot.

The lady plucked Felice from the cradle and brought her near. "That certainly stinks like the pigsty," she said with a grimace.

"Oh, aye." Cristina pressed a fat cork into the small pot's neck. "But it is not harmful to the child."

Nona peered down at Felice's face. She brushed a fingertip across the rosebud lips. "Nay, I did not think such a thought. But I do think it harmful for you to eat nothing. Lady Oriel says you've not attended meals and took only some milk yestereve."

"I had some bread." But the cloth still holding the bread showed she had but nibbled at the edges.

"Please me, mistress, and eat, else you'll make yourself ill." Lady Nona went to the door and spoke to the sentry as if she had commanded the men of Ravenswood all her life.

While they waited, Nona watched Cristina stuff dried flowers into small pouches of linen and tie them with narrow ribbons. The women did not speak until after a servant had placed a tray on the worktable. It held cheese, roasted partridge, and wine.

Cristina felt no wish to eat. All would taste of ashes in her mouth, she knew, but to please the lady she sat on a stool and sliced some cheese.

"What will you do?" Lady Nona asked. She tickled Felice's stomach, and Cristina could not keep jealousy from filling her as Felice batted her legs and wriggled happily.

"Do?" She crumbled the cheese between her fingertips. "About what, my lady?"

"About your husband. 'Tis all the gossip that he has stolen from Lord Durand."

Cristina clamped her hands on her knees. "My husband is not a thief. He just signed a charter that will yield him much. Why would he steal?" If she said it often enough, it would be the truth.

"Indeed. But can you continue here if he is accused and found guilty?"

She searched the good lady's face for some sign of what she wanted. "I cannot." The words almost caught in her throat.

Lady Nona rose. "If I might be so bold, I'm sure I could find a place for you at my manor in Bordeaux. Of course, we must see if there's another wet nurse about. You would not want Felice to suffer when you depart." Nona rocked Felice in her arms as she headed for the door. In moments Cristina was alone.

"*We* would not want . . ."

Cristina's mouth went dry. How could she have forgotten that this lady was to wed Lord Durand? She jumped up and, ignoring the sentry at the door, dashed down the steps to the hall.

As she rounded the steps, she almost stumbled over Oriel. Her blue gown, trimmed with black stitches, looked crumpled.

"My lady, may I help you?" Cristina placed a hand on Oriel's arm. The sentry backed away.

Oriel licked her lips and wiped away tears. "I'm so

concerned about Penne. He's at odds with the king today. He wants to do the honorable thing, but 'tis difficult with John. The king trusts no one, and Guy Wallingford has urged Penne to desert this effort. 'Twill end in disaster or death for so many."

"His holdings were confiscated by King Philip?" Cristina asked. Her stomach lurched at the thought of the deadly sword wounds of the recent brigand attack. She could not bear to think of Durand in a pool of blood on a battlefield with no one to see to him.

What had fate in store for him? For Felice? For . . . her? She became aware that Oriel had answered her question.

"Aye. Penne's lands were granted to him by King Richard, that the Martine family might serve, with others, mind you, to break up King Philip's power in Normandy. 'Twas one of Richard's reasons for approving Marion's marriage to Durand. But one of the barons reminds Penne daily that if he just went to Philip and swore fealty there, he would very likely get his lands back without risking his life. It must be done before Philip portions them out to another if it is to be done at all."

"So Penne might leave John for Philip?"

"What?" Durand stood before the alcove, a frown on his face.

"Oh, Durand," Oriel said, rising, swaying a moment. He shot out his hand and steadied her. "I didn't see you there."

"So it would seem. What were you saying about Penne leaving John for Philip?"

"I didn't say such a thing. Cristina asked if Penne might leave John. I was just about to assure her that Penne swore to John and will not desert him."

"I see." His doubting tone told her it was not just the king who had no trust.

"If I might, my lord, may I speak to you in private?" Cristina asked.

"Be quick about it, as your husband should arrive at any hour," he said to her.

"He will make all clear, I'm sure," Cristina said.

"All is clear now," he said abruptly.

Oriel touched her arm. "Excuse me; I intrude." With that, Cristina found herself alone with him.

"You are a doubting man," Cristina said, unable to keep a tart tone from her voice.

"Aye. I doubt what I cannot see or hear or touch."

How intense was his gaze, a sharp dagger that stabbed through her composure.

"You need trust." She looked at the raven's head on his dagger and at the ends of the torque at his throat. They were predatory birds and symbols of power. He would soon wield that power for good or ill.

"You trust your husband?" he asked.

"I have no one else," she said, unable to truly answer him.

"If you know something more about this business, you should tell me."

"There are times when silence is best, my lord." How could she tell him that to deny her husband was to deny the life fate and her father had chosen for her?

"Name one."

"Lady Marion told me she had withheld news of Felice from you until this spring, as she felt so ill she feared she might lose the child and disappoint you."

A hard look overspread his face. It was as sudden as if someone had taken a torch and plunged it into water—cold water. "Is that what she told you?" His words were icy.

"Aye, my lord." Cristina dropped a curtsy. "Forgive me, my lord, if I—or she—broke some confidence. Lady Marion was much alone as you traveled with King John, and as I was to have a child at the same time, we spent a great deal of time together and oft talked of babes and—"

"—husbands?" He almost spat the word. He pushed himself away from the wall. He was suddenly taller and broader.

"On occasion. She gained much benefit from a soothing drink I made her, and she would talk to me as she sipped it."

"And what were your opinions of husbands?"

Cristina bowed her head. She had done her best not to complain of Simon, but Marion had been like a bird pecking at seed, picking and picking at her for every detail of their life together. "In truth, my lord, Lady Marion spent more time peering into my life than I into hers. She spoke of you with affection."

"And the babe? What were her thoughts on Felice?"

She raised her gaze to his hard face. The lines about his mouth were etched deeply. He looked to be in some pain.

"Don't blame the child for your lady's death, my lord."

The pained look was replaced with blank surprise. "I don't blame the child. Why would you think such a thing?"

She hurried on. "Lady Marion must have had some glimmer of her fate, for she feared the child's birth. She oft asked Lord Luke if you had sent word of when you would return."

"I don't blame the child for Marion's death. Nay. Never that." He began to pace. "Where's the infant?"

Cristina indicated the hall. "Lady Nona took her, my lord."

"Lady Nona! What business has she to take the child?"

Two men came past the alcove, and he made a quick gesture for her to follow him.

The path he took led to the west tower, a place she

had heretofore never visited. He climbed the steps at a quick pace, then halted by a door similar to those in the east tower, a stout wooden door strapped with iron, guarded by a tall Ravenswood guard. Lord Durand drew a small, ornate iron key from his purse, unlocked the door, and gestured her in.

She gasped. Before her lay a chamber filled with shelves of books and rolls of parchment. "My lord," she whispered.

He entered the chamber and threw open a shutter. "Come. No one will bother us here." He had chosen the room because the guard was above reproach and there was no bed or place of comfort in which to practice seduction or be tempted by it.

Durand watched as Cristina set one toe over the threshold. He thought of a wading bird testing the water, a lovely, gentle bird, easily frightened. "Come," he repeated, all anger with her gone. She was not responsible for Marion's perfidy.

What had possessed him to suspect her? He could not see her stealing anything—save some man's heart.

At last she stood a few inches within the chamber. "How is it no one mentions this room?"

He shrugged. " 'Tis mine, and mine alone. I rarely visit it myself."

Sun gleamed on her hair as she edged along the shelves. He found he liked it loose at her nape rather than tightly plaited.

"Why have you shown me this, my lord?"

"You wished to speak where no ears were able to hear."

She turned from the shelves. "You think me too bold?"

He leaned his shoulder against a shelf. "I think you have something of importance to say and need privacy. This is a private place."

The whisper of her skirt across the rushes reminded him of the first time he had seen her. She moved like a wraith. Mayhap if he looked away she would disappear.

Her soft white woolen gown hugged her ample breasts. The cool air of the chamber tightened her nipples and distracted him from her face a bit, but not enough that he did not see some shadow of the anxiety with which she had approached him.

Would she beg for her husband? And would he, so drawn to her as he was, find a way to release Simon and send them both safely away? How long would his conscience bother him? How long before he ceased to think of her in Simon's bed somewhere?

"Speak, Cristina. My time is not my own."

"I beg you believe me, my lord. I was not leaving by the postern gate."

"Is that what you wished to say?"

"Nay, but if you doubt me . . . that is . . . Lady Nona said you might seek a new nurse for Felice."

She bit her lip. He remembered well the taste of her mouth. "Lady Nona is bold," was the only answer he had for her.

"Lady Oriel claims Lady Nona will soon be your wife. Should she not be bold in such a position?"

Durand pushed away from the shelves and went to the deep window. As far as he could see was the land that should have been Luke's. He turned his back to the window. "So I am wed to her already?"

" 'Tis none of my concern, my lord." Her hands stroked along a shelf, skimming the spines of books, and he wished he could see her face. Her tone was bare of inflection or meaning.

He wanted her to care that he would wed, then realized she had gained a promise from him not to put her vows to any test, and so he could not demand or request such emotion.

"You'd be the wrong nurse for Felice if you didn't have her welfare close to your heart."

"I do, my lord, I do!" She finally faced him, a look of pain or sorrow on her face, but it was quickly chased away when she turned her back. "I'm not deaf to gossip, though, and the lady has indicated that a new nurse must be found if Simon is . . ." Her voice broke.

"If Simon is found to be a thief," he finished for her.

"Nay, he is not," she said, but with less of the heat of her earlier avowals.

"Cristina." He said her name as he might if he were her lover, and she reacted to the tone. She turned to him, her face half in shadow, half in sun. "You will remain here, with Felice, for as long as you wish," he said gently.

"You have judged Simon already."

"I have not."

"You will promise to be fair—to hear his excuses?"

He gave a curt nod. "I am considered very fair, else I would not be one of John's justices."

"Does not the king choose those who will see to *his* wishes, my lord?"

"You are hard to please," he said, pacing the small chamber. He cared almost as little for this talk of justice as he did for the talk of marriage. "I will be fair." *I may even see a thief freed,* he said silently.

"What penalties have you given for men found guilty of—"

"Theft?" He held out his hand as if offering it for punishment. "From branding to hanging."

Her face paled. "Are any found innocent and released?"

"Few." If possible, her face washed even whiter.

Was there any chance Simon was innocent? He might assure her he would allow her to remain as Felice's nurse, but would she want to stay if Simon was proved a thief? There was shame in such an association.

Where would she go? What should he do about Felice in such circumstances? In his mind's eye, he saw Cristina with the child in arms. It was a wicked coil.

Her hand trembled as she raised it and briefly touched her throat. "What of Lady Nona's wishes regarding Felice?"

"She will want what I want."

Cristina shook her head. "She will want, as all good wives do, to direct a daughter. That would include choosing a nurse."

"Felice is content with you."

"And if Lady Nona is not?"

"Is she unkind to you?"

"Oh, nay, my lord. She's very kind."

"Then you have naught to fear." In that moment he realized he was lying. Marion had once sent away a kitchen wench for teasing their son Adrian. Was that what Cristina thought, but would not say? That Nona might be jealous of her? That Nona might sense there was something between them? He knew well what it was to lie in a lover's arms and wonder if it was someone else who filled the lover's mind.

He could treat neither Nona nor Cristina in such a way.

Cristina went to the window where he had stood. Below, the river moved lazily in the sunlight, small sparkles lighting its surface. She breathed in deeply. He wanted to go to her and wrap his arms around her waist and offer her some strength for what was to come. But he stayed where he was.

"You need have no fear for your position here with Felice." He could do nothing about her fears for Simon. They were an ugly truth she must face on her own.

"I do fear for my position—now. Yesterday you did not trust me. Today you do. On the morrow you may not again." She turned from the view and met his gaze as boldly as a man might. "You have posted a sentry outside Felice's chamber."

"The sentry is not to keep you in, but to keep others out."

She paced as he had, her skirts swaying with every step, her hair swinging across her back. "You must trust me."

"How does one trust another?" he asked, his mind leaping to Luke and Penne.

"Trust the history you have with a person."

"And if we have no history?" She moved close to him. Her skin was smooth and downy. He wanted to skim his fingers across her cheek, his thumb across her lips.

Her eyes snapped fire. "Then you must make a leap of faith. You cannot believe me to be leaving by the postern gate one moment, then not the next. You cannot have it both ways, my lord. I am completely confused!"

"Aye," he said softly. "You are right. I cannot have it both ways." He realized that in the moment the king had questioned him about her, in that moment when he had defended her, he had decided to believe her story. "Let us say I've had a few hours to consider your tale and find it more to my liking now. I ask that you trust me as well."

She knotted her fingers together. " 'Tis difficult. I do not know what you are thinking."

"It is better for both of us that you do not."

Chapter Fifteen

Durand locked the room of books and led Cristina back to the hall. Lady Nona sat by King John, Felice on her lap. The child fussed, arching her back and struggling in the lady's arms.

"Mayhap the child would like her nurse," Durand said. Before he could stop himself, he had pulled the babe from Nona's lap.

"Oh, aye. I am useless to a nursing babe," Nona said with a laugh. "She is surely hungry."

The babe fell silent in his arms. He stared down at the soft blue eyes and smooth cheeks. Her gown was stitched with delicate flowers, her wrap likewise embroidered with the bounty of summer. She stared up at him and then lifted a tiny hand. Her fingers explored the torque at his neck, then gripped it with surprising force. She tugged as if to pull the torque into her mouth.

"She will have it off if you let her," Nona said.

The king smiled. "The child knows to reach for the symbols of power. She tried to eat our ring, did she not, Isabelle?"

"Aye, sire," the queen answered indulgently.

Cristina stood silently by. Durand knew he should hand the child away, but somehow he did not wish to set her down. Gently he plucked her fingers from the torque. How small and delicate the bones of her hand felt. Fragile.

"You'll drop her," the queen said, and reached over to settle his hand behind the child's head, showing him how to hold her more securely in the crook of his arm.

Nona and the queen hovered close by, each making small adjustments to Felice's long skirts and her wraps.

"She'll need a worthy alliance," Isabelle said to John.

"The Count of Poitou's nephew would do," Nona said.

"Perfect! We approve," the king said with a grin. "The count's future is as uncertain as any old man's, so she might be a countess before her teeth are in."

Durand stepped away. The Count of Poitou was a very high match, but he knew the nephew. He lacked spirit. "Cristina, what do you think of the match?"

"I don't know the count, my lord," she said. She moved to the end of the table where the king sat. Durand didn't offer her the child; nor did she reach out to take her. "You must do what you believe best for her."

The child reached for his torque again and he shifted her to put his throat out of her reach. She opened her mouth. A high, keening shriek issued forth.

"She wants the gold," declared the queen.

"She's hungry," Cristina said softly so only he could

195

hear. Their fingers skimmed each other as she took the babe from his arms. "May I go, my lord?"

He nodded and forced himself not to watch her progress across the hall to the tower steps.

Nona touched his sleeve. "When you hang her husband she will need to leave," she said gently.

"He's not yet judged, my lady."

Lady Sabina tapped his arm with her fingertip. "Her husband's a thief. One has only to look upon his handsome face to know he's filled with guile. Do you not fear for your daughter's welfare in that woman's care?"

Durand shook his head. King John was paying far too much attention to the conversation. "I would fear for Felice's welfare if Cristina were not seeing to her care."

One of the king's knights, Roger Godshall, who had escorted Sabina to the table, moved closer. He was a dark, stocky man garbed in a fine but careless way.

"What gossip have I missed?" he asked the company in general.

"We discuss the future of Mistress le Gros should her husband be found to be a thief," the queen said.

"She can earn her way on her back," Godshall said, waggling his eyebrows.

"Be civil," Durand said sharply.

"She's not pretty enough for such sport," Sabina said abruptly, hooking Godshall's arm and stroking his hand.

John called for their attention. "Enough of children. Let us attend to the matter at hand. Our men are ready at Dartmouth. We but await William Marshall's attendance and a favorable wind."

"If Marshall is not successful, should we not consider one more attempt to make peace with Philip?" Gilles d'Argent asked. "He has the support of Gervase of Gascony and Ellis of Toulouse. I know both men well and would willingly go in hopes they may be persuaded to peace."

"They will not listen." John's face was suffused with deep red as he confronted the older man.

Roger Godshall rose and jammed his hands on his hips. "You do not go with us, so who are you to speak at all, d'Argent?"

Nicholas d'Argent shot to his feet. "How dare you! Draw your sword, Godshall."

In the instant before blood could be shed, Durand and Gilles stepped between the two men. It was the king, however, who ended the matter.

"D'Argent has no need to go. He is creaking with age, and his kind donation to my cause will yield forty fit men in his place. We know he loves us and will seek to support us in all ways. Be seated, you two whelps."

Nicholas and Roger subsided to their seats, but their hands remained on their dagger hilts. Durand thought it would be best if they could leave and shed some Frenchman's blood, or soon they'd be shedding each other's.

He ventured to further restore some semblance of order to the table. "I'd go with you to speak with Philip or his agents, d'Argent, if you think the scheme would work," Durand said. Gilles and he had made this same suggestion over and over to the king with the same results. John wanted war.

Roger Godshall spoke. "Is not your mother with Bazin in Paris, de Marle?"

Silence fell around the table. Durand had expected this event. The fists on dagger hilts remained in place.

Guy Wallingford, a baron with a son of Adrian's age also fostered with de Warre, spoke up, "What does it matter with whom de Marle's mother aligns herself? She has no retainers, and Bazin's sword rusts from a decade of disuse."

Laughter ran about the table; even John smiled.

Several hands slid from daggers to lift goblets. Durand gave a signal to the serving boy, who quickly rounded the table, filling the cups again.

Durand drank deeply of his wine as if unconcerned. "My mother is concerned with gems and sweetmeats. I doubt she knows what day 'tis."

"Still," King John said, "Bazin supported Philip's father. He may still wield some influence. Can you attest to your mother's loyalty?"

"My mother has never been loyal to anyone."

"But she makes a worthy hostage."

"Aye," Durand said. "And I'm honor-bound to do what I may to protect her, but you may be assured you have my loyalty and that of my men as well. If Philip takes my mother hostage, he will demand a ransom. I'm sure there's a price we can agree upon." He also knew he did not have the coin to pay it.

The conversation turned to swords and who best wielded them. When the discussion deteriorated to lewd comments from the younger men, Durand made an escape to the stable.

There, Joseph sat with William, one of his men-at-arms, pitting Marauder's many fine qualities against that of other warhorses.

"Joseph? You are back rather quickly," Durand said, frowning.

"Aye, my lord," Joseph said, rising.

"Where's our prisoner then?"

"The merchant put up no fight, but his horse went lame and I had to hire a cart. 'Twould have been torture to drag along at that pace. He'll be a few hours yet."

"I have another journey for you." Durand unhooked his purse.

"Nay. My rump is sore tested as it is, my lord." But he took the purse and hefted it readily enough.

"Bring Father Laurentius here from the abbey."

"As you wish," Joseph said. "But what need have we for ecclesiastic lawyers?"

" 'Tis Simon who may feel the need. And William." Durand turned to Joseph's companion. "I have an errand in the village, a bit of quiet searching for you to do."

At dusk, when the party bringing Simon back to Ravenswood had not yet arrived, Durand rode out to meet it. At the fingerpost, he saw a cart and a cavalcade of men about a league off. He allowed his mare to graze as he waited for them.

When the cart drew near, he nudged the horse into a lazy walk and then halted in the center of the roadbed.

Simon sat in the rear of the cart, his hands and feet bound. Never had he looked so disheveled or so arrogantly self-righteous. As the cart drew to a halt, Simon struggled to his knees. "Lord Durand, thank God! I've tried to convince these simpletons they've made a grievous mistake."

Durand patted his horse's neck and then spread his gloved hand on his thigh. "Have they made a mistake?"

"Aye. I shall see them punished, my lord." Simon raised his hands as if Durand might step down and loose his bonds.

"Can you read, Simon?" Durand asked.

"My lord?" Simon cocked his head.

"Can you read? A simple enough question."

Simon sat back on his haunches and dropped his hands to his lap. "Aye. I read. Latin, English, French, a bit of the northern tongues. One needs such skills if one is to trade above the common laborer."

"Ah. I see. Then read that fingerpost." He swept a hand out to the tall wooden pillar at the crossroads.

Red suffused Simon's face. He said nothing.

199

Durand lifted his gloved hand to the cavalcade and led it back to the castle. As they approached, full dark fell. Every arrow slit, every window gleamed with torchlight. The moon hung over the towers, painting them silver. The sounds of revelry floated on the wind: music, song, cries of laughter. Yet Durand felt no desire to take part in any of it.

He wanted only to go to her, take her in his arms, and assure her all would be well. But he could not. He must imprison her husband and on the morrow perhaps condemn him to some punishment that would surely be just as great a punishment to her.

Chapter Sixteen

Durand searched for Cristina as soon as Simon was settled. She perched on a stool in Oriel's chamber, spooning something dried into little pouches. The rich scent of apple wood filled the air. Oriel and Felice lay on the bed, the babe on her back, arms and legs outspread like a fat pup basking in the sun.

"Can you watch the babe?" he asked.

Oriel smiled. "Felice and I shall rest here quite well. Her belly's full, is it not, Cristina?"

Cristina nodded. He noticed that her hands trembled. She knew why he had come.

Before he rose, he lifted Oriel's hand and kissed her fingers. "You are contented here?" he asked. "You will remain if our efforts in Normandy fail?"

"Penne will decide. He says he's young enough to make his fortune again."

"As are we all, I suppose. But you know you are both welcome to live here always?"

201

"Nona will not need another wife lying about, confusing things." Oriel shook her head.

"I am not yet wed," he said, but with little heat. He would wed the lady for his sons. It was the only reason to wed—land and power. The other—what Penne and Oriel shared—it had caused him naught but needless pain. He wanted none of it.

"Go." Oriel shooed him with her hand as if he were a fly annoying her. "Go."

He went to Cristina and held out his hand. "Cristina. Simon has arrived."

She rose but did not take his hand. "Will you take me to him?" she asked. Her voice was barely audible, but her head was high and her gaze did not evade his.

"Aye. Follow me."

The hall was filled with men. Very few women chose to linger there during the evening revelries. The conversation was coarse, the manners coarser. Roger Godshall sang with several men. The ribald ditty painted a blush on Cristina's cheeks.

With a hand at her elbow, he led her through the throng to the steps leading to the storerooms and dungeon below Ravenswood's great hall.

The dank scent of the cell in which Simon sat reminded Cristina all too well of her brief sojourn there. The old man who unlocked Simon's door asked her in whispered tones if she was sure she wanted to visit such a place. She assured him she did, and without further argument or a glance at Lord Durand, she stepped inside. The sound of the key in the lock made her stomach lurch.

"Do you know why I'm here?" Simon's voice trembled.

"There is some question that you took Lord Durand's Aelfric."

"Some question? He accused me of stealing it!"

Simon fell to his knees before her and buried his face in her skirt.

She stood there without touching him for but a moment, then settled her hands on his head. His body shook with sobs, and her own eyes filled. She would not weep.

"Simon, come; you must rise. 'Tis a damp chamber, and you will take ill."

He flung himself away from her. "What matter if I am ill? *He* will hang me! Who cares if a man coughs on his way to his death?"

"You've not been condemned yet, Simon. Take heart."

"*He* will see to it, make no mistake. He will find a way to kill me!"

"Lord Durand will be fair." She paced the small cell, seeing the loss of her husband's fastidious nature in the crumpled blankets tossed on the floor.

"Fair? You jest." Simon grabbed her arm. His fingers bit deeply into her flesh. "He has no interest in fairness. He'll hear what he wants, believe what he wants. He's controlled by his brother."

"Luke?" Shocked, she stared at Simon's face and the contorted anger she saw there.

"Aye, Luke. How easily his name comes to your lips, sweet wife. Think you Lord Durand will care what becomes of me if it frees you for his brother's attentions?"

"What?" She could barely say the word. "Y-you blame me for this?" She jerked from his grasp. "You're mad! *Lord* Luke cares nothing for me. I've sworn this to you already. He was not taking liberties! He but touched me with concern." Involuntarily her hand went to her cheek. "You were in error before and err still!"

"He lusts after you." Simon made a grab for her arm, and she stepped quickly out of reach.

"Let me understand. Because Lord Luke touched me once, you think that Lord Durand and Lord Luke conspired to place you here so Luke might have me? What madness!"

"Who else could take a book from a lord but another lord? You had no access; I had no access. I'm accused because I'm nothing to them and Lord Luke wants you in his bed. You'll be on your back, your legs spread for him within an hour of my death, whether you want it or not!" He fell again to his knees and clutched her skirts. "Save me, please. Save me."

The sudden change from accusing and shouting to begging froze her in place. "I don't know what to say to you! You weave a tale of nonsense."

He imprisoned her about the knees. "I do not. You hide from the truth. A noble took the book. A noble, I tell you."

She sank to her knees before him and cupped his face. "Look at me, Simon." He lifted his grime-stained face, streaked with tears, to hers. "I have never done aught to be ashamed of with Lord Luke. He has never touched me with lust."

Thank the Blessed Mother Simon did not accuse her of wrongdoing with Lord Durand. Her stomach churned.

"I'm afraid," he whispered.

She embraced him. "Aye. So am I. Now tell me the truth. Was the dead boy Hugh?"

"Nay. I don't know that boy."

She leaned forward. "Tell me the truth."

" 'Tis the truth." But his eyes slid away.

"Then answer me this. Why did you not go to Winchester to fetch him?"

Simon covered her hands with his. "They will take my hand, or hang me, brand me." A shudder ran through his body as he turned his face and kissed her palm. "You'll have to care for me like a babe. I cannot bear it! Go to Lord Luke. If he wants you, he'll bargain with you."

"Answer me, Simon." She would not be deflected. "You owe me honesty."

This time it was he who jerked away from her. He stood up, towering over her. "I owe you honesty? You who made this coil for me? You who did not guard your virtue and allowed a man to embrace you before your own husband? You who upset Aldwin with your trespass on his work—"

A flash of anger, so intense it burned through her body, forced her to her feet. "Enough! I'll hear no more." She went to the door. Simon was on her in an instant, his hands on either side of her, pinning her with his body to the stout wooden portal.

"You will listen, wife. You have caused this. You must undo it. Beg your lover to release me, if he be one, or beg your kind Lord Luke to aid you as a friend if he be not."

His warm breath heated her cheek. He held her still.

"You're wrong, Simon, so very, very wrong."

He ran his hands from her shoulders to her hips. "Is he your lover? Does he want me dead?"

She managed to lift a hand to bang the heel of her palm on the door. A call from the guard made Simon move away from her.

"Beseech Lord Luke to release me, Cristina. You must. You are tied to me unto death."

The guard opened the door and she almost fell into his arms. Half-blind with confusion and pain, she stumbled to the upper reaches of the keep. Unsure what to do, where to go, she hastened to Lady Oriel's chamber. She lifted Felice to her shoulder, grabbed her basket, and fled to the garden.

Moonlight washed the paths bright white. Each pebble seemed to sparkle like a gem as she set down the heavy basket. Soundlessly she walked around and around the plants, breathing the soothing scents, listening to the night sounds—not those of the men still at revelry within the bailey, but those of leaves dancing with one another in the breeze.

Her anger over Simon's accusations subsided with the simple act of walking. He feared for his life. He concocted tales to suit what he saw. And Lord Luke had held her shoulders with great familiarity. And her heart *was* traitorous—not with Lord Luke, but with Lord Durand.

Her heart was as traitorous as any adulteress's could be.

Finally she sought a bench and opened her gown. Felice nursed in the slow, lazy way of a child half-asleep. Her time with the babe would be short—a day or two until Simon was punished.

"Did Simon take the book, Felice?" she asked the babe. "I do not know what to believe." She hugged the child and breathed in the sweet, milky scent of her. "He's right that few would have access to the Aelfric unless they were nobles. But what of the many women who visit Lord Luke? Have they not access? Might they not know what lies in the coffers?"

Felice fell asleep, but Cristina continued to talk to her as if she understood. "The boy is Hugh. I know that in my heart, too." Simon had not answered her question but returned to his accusations, and in that moment she had known he avoided the issue because it kept a lie from his lips.

She became aware that the moon no longer filled the garden with light. It had begun to sink beneath the garden wall. Carefully she made her way along the paths to the gate. She locked it securely and knew what she must do.

Once in the keep, she saw it was filled with many of the king's men. She did not see Lord Durand, but did see Lord Luke in the gallery. With quick steps, lest her courage fail her, she went up to him.

Luke leaned against the gallery rail, his arms crossed over his chest. He wore a black tunic trimmed in gold thread. Black did not become him as it did his brother. Nay, black was Durand's color. Black as secret as the night. She shook off the errant thoughts. "Do you know where I might find Lord Durand?"

"Mayhap I do. What need have you for him?" Luke asked with a frown.

She sighed and looked away across the many gathered below. Lord Durand was not there. She could no longer avoid what must be done. "I want to speak to him about Simon." Could she beg Lord Durand for mercy?

Without another word, Luke led her to the counting room, then stepped back. "Are you sure you wish to see him?"

In answer, she shifted the heavy basket to her left arm and tapped lightly on the door.

"Enter," Lord Durand called.

She hesitated at his sharp tone, but Luke gave her a small push as he lifted the latch.

No candle lit the chamber. Only the dying embers of the hearth told her he sat at the long table. His face was in shadow, concealing his expression. She sank into a deep curtsy and tried to stem the thunder of her heart. "My lord. I beg of you a few words." Luke remained behind her.

"Wait." He rose and went to the hearth, where he touched a small stick to the coals and then to the wick of a thick candle.

He wore a long gray tunic trimmed in scarlet over a white linen shirt. Laced high at his throat, the shirt almost concealed his torque, but still she saw the gleam of the gold as he moved. How powerful he looked, forbidding, stern—a judge, not a lover.

"How may I serve you?" His voice was gentle.

She placed the basket on the floor and lifted Felice to her shoulder. With a deep breath, she knelt before him. "I beg of you, my lord. Release my husband. He did not steal the Aelfric. He had no need. I could have given it to him so easily, had he coveted it. I believe the boy stole the book after hearing Simon speak of it. The boy is dead, my lord. What would it serve to punish the father?"

Luke made to speak, but Durand lifted a hand and silenced him. This was between himself and Cristina.

He went to where she knelt. The candle shone on her dark hair. Lightly he touched her head. "Don't beg, Cristina. It ill becomes you." He would hurt her. He knew it as he knew his own name. For her to beg for Simon bespoke an affection he did not understand. The man abused her, yet she defended him. Would Marion have done so much for him?

"I must beg, my lord," she whispered. "He's my husband and I owe him my loyalty."

He let his fingertips wander down her satiny cheek to her chin. He tipped her face up. What a sweet face she had. Gentle, trusting.

"One must never put too deep a trust in another. One is always hurt by blind faith," he said softly. He took her hand and placed in it the bishop's rings. "These were found hidden beneath Simon's pallet, secreted under a loose floorboard. The boy did not steal the book." Gently he folded her fist about the cold metal and waited.

Her hand trembled in his. "Nay," she whispered.

"Aye."

She ripped her hand from his and opened her fingers to stare at the jeweled rings. With a soft moan, she placed them on the floor. Staggering a bit, she rose. He put out a hand to her, but she shook her head. Her lip trembled. She thrust the child into Luke's arms, lifted the latch, and disappeared.

Chapter Seventeen

"Cristina," Durand said, but the door closed with a bang and she was gone. He wanted to go after her, but could not.

Luke placed Felice on her back on his pallet and then took a stool by the table. "That was not so very well done."

Durand stared at the door. "I could not let her beg for him. He's a blight on her life."

"Still, he's her husband and mayhap there is affection there. Could you not treat her more gently?"

With a sigh, Durand sank into his chair. "Luke. I'm about to find a reason to let a thief go."

"What? John sees the theft of the Aelfric as tied to Bishop Dominic's death." Luke leaped to his feet. "If you let Simon le Gros go, John will suspect *you* of God knows what. Treachery? The brigands' attack? Penne said they were far too finely garbed and mounted for mere thieves—"

Durand surged to his feet. "You don't tell me anything I do not already know." He stood over Marion's child. "I cannot let Cristina suffer."

"You can find another nurse!" Luke swept a hand out to where Felice lay.

But Durand shook his head. "Is that what you think this is about? I've been thinking for days on what will become of us all when we go to France. If I die, who will look after this child? You? You'll be lying dead in France with me, I fear."

Or would Luke betray him? Remain behind at the last moment with some plausible excuse?

Luke strode from one corner of the chamber to the other. "Oriel will see to her. And this is nonsense. You survived a crusade, for Christ's sake."

Durand knelt by the child and put out his hand. The babe snatched and held his finger. Her grip was very strong for one so tiny, but yet so easily broken.

Aye, Oriel could guard Felice's interests. But the child must serve as his excuse to aid Cristina. He could not tell Luke that he also much wanted to see Cristina at peace, even if it meant she would be somewhere else with Simon.

The sky was beginning to lighten as Durand walked across the bailey to the chapel.

Cristina knelt beside Father Odo at the fore of the chapel. "Seeking sanctuary, mistress?" he asked.

Felice lay heavily on his shoulder. Now, when she should be eating, she slept. She was as contrary as every other woman he knew. He saw the babe's basket by Cristina and was relieved. Surely the basket meant she intended to take the child from him.

"Mistress le Gros was praying, my lord." The priest patted Cristina's hand. "I will leave you now. God will decide all." He bowed to Durand and left.

Durand settled Felice in Cristina's arms. She sat

back on her heels and unlaced her gown. He paced. Behind him, Cristina whispered to Felice, and when he turned back, the child nursed.

He wished for an itinerant painter to capture this moment for him, the child at Cristina's breast, the chapel candles bathing them both in a golden glow. It took his breath away. "You must face what will be this day."

"What would you do if someone betrayed you?" she asked.

He took a deep breath. "I would run him through."

She nodded. "Men can do that—draw a sword and strike down those who harm them."

Unless it was one you loved. Then you were powerless to lift a hand.

Pale light seeped through the chapel entrance. The bailey stirred as day broke.

She kissed Felice's fingers. "She's a sweet babe, my lord. I've been with Alice, and she and I have thought of a plan for when I must leave."

"You may stay as long as you wish—"

She interrupted him, speaking quickly. "I cannot stay and we both know it. It would be a shame beyond any of my imagining!" She paused to take a deep breath. "Rose, the baker's sister, had a babe yester-eve. She's an honorable woman much in need of a few extra pennies and has twice before taken a child to nurse along with her own. If you'll allow it, my lord, I'll stay with Felice until Rose is ready, mayhap a sennight; then I'll go to my father in Norwich. I've enough pennies put by to make the journey."

"As you wish, but you need not go," he repeated.

Denial came with a quick shake of her bowed head.

She would go, and he would mourn the loss of her as he had not mourned Marion. If Simon was released, they would not—could not—remain. They would be

211

tainted by suspicion of theft. No one would buy from such a merchant.

He stood by until Felice was fed, then took her from Cristina's arms and placed her in the basket.

He held out his arms. Cristina came into them as if she belonged there. He enfolded her. He knew the answer, but still the words spilled from his lips. "Come to my bed, Cristina. Now. This moment. Just once before you go."

A tremor ran through her body, but she said nothing.

"Just once, Cristina," he whispered by her ear, breathing in the sweet scent of her hair.

Her arms tightened at his waist, and he ached at the soft feel of her against him.

Then, with agonizing slowness, she slid from his arms until they stood connected only by the tips of their fingers. She broke away and picked up Felice. "Nay, my lord, I cannot. I have enough sins on my soul as 'tis."

Cristina did not have to wait long for Simon to be judged. The call came just before noon. She braved the hall, Alice trotting behind her with Felice. Whispers followed them as they made their way to where Lord Durand sat in judgment. She wanted to turn and run away to the deepest part of the forest, pull leaves over herself until she lay hidden in the dark silence.

Two priests, pens scratching across vellum, sat by Lord Durand's side as he rendered decisions on the matters of his manor: a moved field marker, a lost pig, a man who contested damage caused by his mother's cow.

The king wandered about the hall. Occasionally he usurped a case, sitting down and listening intently, and rendering a decision. Lord Durand deferred to the king each time, except in the matter of the cow, and then Lord Durand's words were sharp and the king bowed his head in acquiescence.

Cristina wished she could hear every word, but they spoke for themselves, not the audience. Did Lord Durand wield enough power to sway a king? Cristina did not know if the king was fair. Alice said he was subject to whims and fancies.

She could not think straight. She fastened her gaze on the great paintings that flanked the hearth. The queen and the other courtiers were gathered there to watch the proceedings. Cristina edged through the crowd to be where she could hear better, but felt heat run through her body as she realized she stood but a few feet from several ladies, Nona and Sabina among them. The young man upon whose arm Sabina leaned looked too long and familiarly back at her.

Lady Sabina instructed Lady Nona in loud, condescending tones. "The king will listen to anyone's case. Some folk might offer up to one hundred marks for such a privilege as having a king render their verdict, but he asks nothing."

A shiver ran down Cristina's spine. She desperately wanted Lord Durand to hear Simon's case. If mercy was to be granted, it would not come from such a volatile man as King John.

Simon, his hands bound, ignored her, though he came within a few feet of her as he was led before Lord Durand. His head was high, his manner uncowed.

"Simon le Gros," Durand said. "You are accused of stealing Aelfric's *Nominum Herbarum* from my keep."

"I will speak for Master le Gros," said a tall man in ecclesiastic robes who strode down the center of the hall.

"Father Laurentius!" the king cried. "You are here to plead this man's case? Merchants have highborn lawyers these days!"

The crowd of onlookers laughed. Simon's spine stiffened even more.

The priest bowed. "I'm brought here by Lord Durand, as he believes the merchant thinks himself ill-used. His lordship wished to render unto him all fairness in the law."

Had Lord Durand brought this illustrious personage to aid Simon? Cristina looked down at her hands. How could she—they—ever thank him?

"Begin then, Laurentius," the king said.

Father Laurentius stalked back and forth before the king, his robes flapping about his ankles. "I've spoken at length with Master le Gros and believe he has been most grievously harmed."

The king waved his hand through the air. "Lawyer's words. We have heard them before. All you speak for are grievously used."

"I may have been called forth by Lord Durand, but it is against him I must speak," the priest said, unperturbed by the interruption.

The king stroked his mustache, then turned to where Durand sat. "We'll hear this case, de Marle. If Father Laurentius is to speak against you in some way, we think it best you step aside. And we much enjoy a good joust of wits with Laurentius."

Durand bowed. "Sire, if I may, this case is important to me. It was my book taken, I grant you, but I've a great interest in the outcome—"

"Do you doubt we will fairly render a decision?" the king asked.

Cristina watched a vehement conversation take place between Lord Durand and the king, though she could not hear the words, merely the sharp tones. When the king stopped speaking, Lord Durand bowed his head and then moved his chair back.

What had Lord Durand wanted? Why had the king

ordered him to withdraw? What, sweet Mother of God, was Simon going to say?

"My lord. Sire," the priest began. "It is Simon le Gros's position that Lord Luke contrives to have him hanged."

Silence fell over the hall; then a quick buzz of conversation broke out. Cristina felt dizzy. The noise faded, then settled.

Nay, Simon, nay, she thought desperately. *Do not shame me.*

"In what way?" the king asked.

Lord Durand's jaw clenched so tightly she thought it might crack.

"Lord Luke wishes to have Mistress le Gros for himself and therefore contrives to have Master le Gros hanged, thereby freeing her."

An arm went about her waist. Lady Nona's. "You look very ill, Cristina. Would you like to leave?" the lady whispered.

Cristina shook her head and forced herself to stand straighter and lift her chin. She was not ashamed of anything between herself and Lord Luke. It was difficult, but she ignored the many eyes turned her way.

"We would hear more of this." The king looked about the crowd. "Come forward, Lord Luke, and answer this charge."

Luke walked to the fore and stood by Simon. He, too, looked fiercely angry. Every inch of him was noble from his fine-boned face to his blue tunic trimmed in gold thread. Simon, whose hair hung in dirty hanks and who had straw sticking to his brown surcoat, looked far less than even a prosperous merchant.

The two men bowed to the king at the same time.

"Have you conspired to take this man's wife?" King John asked Lord Luke.

"Nay, sire," Luke said with a shake of his head. "I

215

have no taste for married women." The man with Sabina made a rude noise in his throat.

The priest stalked back and forth between the table and Lord Luke. "Is it not true the Aelfric was taken from *your* coffer?"

"Aye. But many visit the chamber," Luke returned.

"They do? Who, if I may ask?" The priest tapped his finger on the table.

"Some . . . friends."

"Name them." The priest smiled. He had yellow teeth and a long nose.

"Sire," Luke began. "I'll happily do so, but privately."

The king smiled as well. Snickers ran through the spectators. "Write the list down and we shall read it, *privately*."

The agony of watching Lord Luke transcribe his list nearly brought Cristina to her knees. He wrote and paused and wrote, tapped his chin and wrote, scratched his head and looked about the hall. Wrote and wrote, considered and wrote. The hall grew restless. Murmurs started. Lord Durand lifted his gaze from his brother to her.

She held his gaze, but read naught to aid her there. It would not do to hope. Sweat dripped down Simon's cheek.

Someone began to laugh; others joined in. Luke glanced about the hall, then finally stopped writing. He slid the list to the king.

Lady Sabina leaned near her companion and whispered, "His mattress is surely worn to the ropes."

Lady Nona whipped around and disappeared into the crowd. Without her support, Cristina suddenly felt naked of friendship. She was alone in a sea of men and women who cared naught of her fate or Simon's.

The king silently read the list, and his brows arched almost to his hairline. "Lord Luke," the king said. "We wish to have our physician examine you. We are humbled."

The crowd burst into laughter. Luke merely shrugged.

Father Laurentius's face suffused a deep red. "Sire. We beg a word." The priest approached the king's seat. A debate ensued, and finally the king nodded.

The priest moved to where Simon stood, his back stiff and his chin high. "I do not like to make a mockery of these proceedings. This man's life is being considered."

"Proceed, Laurentius. But make your point quickly. This delays a good day's hunting," the king said. Lord Durand's only reaction was a nod to his brother.

The hall hushed and returned to its former sobriety.

"Have you ever seen Master le Gros in your counting room when it was not appropriate that he be there, my lord?" Laurentius asked.

"Nay," Luke said.

"Do you lock the room or the coffer?"

Luke shook his head. "I do not."

"Is a guard posted?"

"Nay. There is naught there but common records I might wish to consult from time to time—and a bed." The crowd snickered. "Those records of great import are moved to another chamber that *is* kept locked and guarded," he continued, as if no interruption had occurred.

The priest nodded. "I see. So this book was of little worth?"

Cristina saw Luke hesitate. "It was of worth to some people."

"And anyone, Lord Durand included, could have come into the counting room and taken the book?"

"Put that way, aye, they could have."

"Sire." The priest waved Luke's list of friends in the

air. "I beg to have Master le Gros freed. As you can surely see, anyone could have taken the book."

But the king shook his head. "Aye, taken it and handed it off to another such as Master le Gros. 'Tis not enough. Bishop Dominic is dead and the book found in his guard's possession. The attack greatly sickened the queen." The king swiveled in his seat to Durand. "Is there more to be said? We understand the bishop's rings have been found."

Was nothing secret in this place? Cristina's hopes sank like a rock tossed in Portsmouth Harbor.

The king smiled. "Lady Sabina informed us."

Lord Durand's expression was stony, and she wondered where the man who had embraced her had gone. This man was cold and hard. He bowed to the king. "Two of the rings were found."

Cristina's stomach danced. How had Lady Sabina known of the rings? The man with Lady Sabina spoke without concern that she could hear his words. "The merchant is a thief, but will likely escape the hangman. One but needs a lawyer these days."

Her stomach turned. Everyone around her believed Simon to be a thief. The tips of Simon's ears reddened.

"The rings were found beneath the merchant's pallet," Durand said.

"Ah," the king said.

Father Laurentius strode to the table. "Sire. Anyone might have placed the rings there. It was most likely done by the man sent to retrieve them. Lord Luke's man, I'll wager."

"My man," Durand said.

"It is as I thought, sire." Father Laurentius folded his arms. " 'Tis the same thing. One brother aids the other."

"This is a serious charge, Laurentius," the king said. "You accuse one of my most trusted barons."

Cristina thought Lord Durand controlled himself

with difficulty. A pulse beat at his temple.

Laurentius continued. "As many enter the merchant's abode as enter Lord Luke's counting room."

The king turned to Simon. "Do you need parchment and pen to make *your* list?"

Simon and Laurentius put their heads together. Then Laurentius demanded the same accoutrements that had been brought to Luke. Simon's hands were not released, and with awkwardness he wrote a few moments on the vellum.

The king read Simon's list. His gaze swept the crowd. "Intriguing," the king said, and Cristina could not imagine whose names were on the list.

"Sire," Lord Durand said, after reading the list passed to him by the king, "it would seem many who had access to my counting room also had access to Simon's abode."

He said nothing more. Lord Durand's lack of further accusation would help Simon greatly, and she knew it was a deliberate act. Was it for her he held his tongue?

The king folded the list. He slipped it into his tunic. Who, Cristina wondered, might be on the list? Then she realized it was not just a list of those who purchased his wares that Simon had given; it was the name or names of *his* lovers, just as Luke's was. Her humiliation was complete.

The king waved Lord Durand to his seat and then rose to face Simon. "There are many doubts surrounding the theft of this book *and* the bishop's death. We've not the time to examine this matter with our usual care. We'll trust in God to give us wisdom. You, Simon le Gros, will be put to the test."

"He wants to hunt, he means," whispered a man standing behind Cristina. She felt the weight of all eyes moving from her to Simon and back. She straightened her spine.

I will not weep, she vowed to herself. *I will not faint.*

219

Laurentius said something to Simon, who gasped, then choked it off. A visible shudder swept his body.

The priest gave a curt nod and then returned to face the king. "Sire, if any man is to be put to the test, it should be Lord Luke, who conspires to have this good merchant hanged."

"Enough," the king barked. "We have decided. The merchant will be tested."

The hall fell silent.

"Let us see this woman so coveted that Lord Luke wishes her husband dead," the king said into the quiet.

All eyes turned to where she stood.

Lady Sabina nudged her with her elbow. "Go," the lady urged her. "Stand by your *husband*."

Sabina's companion took Cristina's arm to lead her to the king. She wrenched from his grasp. "I can find my own way."

Several men nearby snickered, and the man's cheeks flushed an ugly red. The look he gave her at the deliberate snub chilled her. Why had she spoken so sharply? She needed everyone's goodwill. *Everyone's.*

Cristina's knees felt weak. As she went to Simon's side he gave her a look she knew well. She was afraid.

"Sire," she said, and dropped into a deep curtsy.

"Rise, mistress. Are you the wife of this man?" the king asked.

"Aye, sire, I am."

"Are you Lord Luke's mistress?"

"Nay, sire. I am not." She looked up at the king, then at Lord Durand. He met her gaze and she saw something there—pity, mayhap—and knew that Simon's words had branded her as no others could have.

All would henceforth believe the Lord of Skirts had had her.

"As we stated, we can easily settle this," the king

220

said. "And much more swiftly than hearing pretty speeches. We have no time to waste on petty thieves. Put the man to the water test. If he's innocent, so be it. But if 'tis as we hear, that this man not only stole the book, but had his son deliver it hence into the bishop's hands, he is equally guilty of leading his son to crime." A gasp ran through the hall. "Therefore, 'tis our judgment he should lose both hands if such is determined. We have heard enough. Let God decide."

"My liege, I must protest—" the priest began, but the king interrupted him.

"You, a priest, do not believe in placing the question of guilt or innocence in God's hands?"

The priest bowed. "Of course I believe in God's will and judgment, but is there not doubt enough here, sire, that we should not be hasty in condemning this man?"

"We do not condemn him, Father Laurentius. We leave that to God." He strode away, his queen on his arm.

Two sentries reached for Simon. The crowd behind Cristina surged forward, shoving her aside, rushing through the oak doors.

Lord Durand came around the table to where she stood. He placed himself between her and the crowd, but even he was buffeted by the throng. He snatched up her hand when she took a step after Simon. "Stay." Durand said. "You don't need to see this done."

"What's happening? I don't understand." When she fought against his hold, he thrust her into a sentry's hands.

"Simon will be tested, Cristina," Durand said. "Surely you understand the test? He will be thrown into water, and if he survives he is guilty and will lose his hands. If he sinks . . . he is dead."

Her teeth began to chatter. "My lord—"

"You will await me here," he ordered. To the sentry

he said, "You'll see she remains here, or I will have your sword."

Durand reached out and touched her cheek. She moaned softly. There was nothing he could do for her. He strode away.

Alone in the hall save for the sentry, Cristina waited impatiently for some word of Simon's fate. She held no hope of Simon's innocence. That he had contrived to take the book she was sure—and had been since seeing the rings.

She searched her heart and felt, first and foremost, fear. For herself. She also felt guilty. Guilty for her lack of love for Simon.

And she felt angry. She knew that after today, she would spend her life looking after a man who had no means of supporting himself. All who saw him would know by his disfigurement that he was a thief. Or Simon would be dead, and she would find herself alone.

She had lied to Lord Durand. There would be no going home to her father. As a merchant himself, he would not, could not, have a thief in his household. They must go back to a single cart on the road. The thought was chilling. And how would she bear the days till Rose was ready to take Felice to nurse? Even a simple walk through the village would be torment. She must withstand the shame of not just Simon's thievery, but of people believing she was Lord Luke's mistress.

And she would not have even the succor of a child's love to sustain her.

Who had aided Simon? Taken the Aelfric from Lord Durand's chamber and given it to him? Who, along with Simon, had ruined her life?

"Mistress le Gros?"

Cristina rose. One of King John's guards stood before her, a rope in his hand. She could look no higher than the narrow twine. "Aye."

"Put out your hands." She did as he bid. He quickly bound her hands, ignoring the protests of Lord Durand's sentry.

"Why?" It was all she could say. Her voice sounded far away, as if it came from someone else.

The sentry shrugged and tested the rope to be sure it was fast. "The king commands you into custody until you can be tried for theft." At those words, Lord Durand's sentry turned and dashed off, leaving her alone with the king's man.

"Tried?" She stumbled after the guard as he tugged on the rope. Why should she be tried? "There must be some mistake. I don't understand."

The guard said nothing. He pulled her relentlessly toward the steps to the lower levels to the keep.

To the punishment cells.

Chapter Eighteen

"Halt!" Durand strode toward her across the hall, the sentry on his heels. "Where are you taking Mistress le Gros?"

"Below," the king's guard said.

"I'll take charge of her." Durand drew his dagger and sliced through the twine at her wrists.

"Thank you," she managed to stammer as black spots filled her vision. She swayed in place, but forced herself to remain upright. Calm. All would be well now.

"The king will be displeased," the guard said.

"The king will not care where Mistress le Gros is imprisoned, only that she is." Durand took her arm and led her toward the west tower.

Imprisoned. There was no error. She stumbled along, unable to speak.

In silence, they climed the steps to the book chamber. At the door, Durand halted and addressed the king's man who huffed along behing them. "Stand guard if you wish, but remain without unless I command you otherwise."

Cristina forced herself to walk into the chamber. It was flooded with sunlight in mockery of the blackness sweeping over her. She clasped her hands tightly. Her wrists were red from the guard's rope. Heart racing, she offered up a whispered prayer for strength.

With harsh rasp, the key turned and she was alone with him.

"Cristina." Durand said her name almost gently.

"My lord?" She took a step toward him, then hesitated. "Why am I imprisoned?"

He held out his hand. "I must tell you . . . come here."

She stared from his hand to his face. "Is the king finished with Simon?" Her words were barely a whisper in the small chamber.

Still, Lord Durand held out his hand and did not speak. It took all her courage to walk to him and put her hand in his.

He drew it to his mouth and pressed his lips to her fingers. "May God forgive him," he said.

Her heart thumped rapidly. "Please. Tell me."

He pulled her close. She wanted to burrow into his body and hide. For she knew he would tell her something terrible.

"Simon accused you of taking the book for him. He claimed no other aided him."

The room spun for a moment, tipped, and grew dark at the edges. She heard her name, said from afar.

She became aware that Lord Durand had lowered her to the bench. "Cristina. Cristina," he said again. His face wavered above her as if seen through water.

Slowly, his features gained clarity—along with her own sense of what had happened.

She was doomed.

Lord Durand smoothed the hair from her brow. "I've asked Father Laurentius to help you. So all will be well, I promise."

"But Simon has to tell the king the truth. He knows I had nothing to do with it. He must tell the truth. Please . . . make him tell the truth."

He shook his head. "Simon is dead, Cristina."

Durand watched as her body went stiff. Her breathing changed to rapid pants as if she had run a great distance. Her lips went white.

He could do naught but speak quickly. "Simon was cast into the mill pond. I have no need to say he was pulled out alive." He wanted to embrace her, but hesitated. "The king ordered the rest . . . done immediately."

She gave a small moan, and he felt a surge of great anger against her husband.

He forced himself to be gentle with her. "Before judgment was rendered, the king asked Simon again who aided him, and he named you. If God is just, it is only in that Simon did not survive his maiming, Cristina. It happens sometimes."

"Nay. Nay." She covered her face with her hands.

"He seemed to stand the first . . . punishment well. He said naught, even as Aldwin cauterized his wound. Then he had a seizure."

With a gasp, she stared up at him—and through him.

Durand touched her hair, her cheek. "I entreated Simon to speak the truth from the outset. I thought he was about to when . . . I am sure had he lived . . ."

She gripped her knees and gasped over and over. He feared for her. He went down on his knees and took her into his arms. She began to shudder. When he stared into her face, no tears filled her eyes, but he could not help thinking of the dark liquid ones of the hart when she was run to ground and knew the bolt would take her life.

She stared at him with shock etched on every feature. "Do not make excuses for him. He betrayed me."

Durand squeezed her hands. "You need not fear this. I will help you. The king will call you soon, and I've instructed Father Laurentius to be there."

"I thank you," she whispered, covering his hands with hers. "He will not succeed, but I thank you."

He turned his head and pressed a kiss to her palm. He could not bear to think of her maimed. It would not happen.

Slowly she slid her hands from his and tucked them under her arms. "I would like to be alone." She twisted on the bench to face the shuttered window.

Father Laurentius was all he had to offer her.

Her voice was dull when she spoke, and her gaze fixed on the window. "Will I be permitted to see him buried?"

He put out a hand to touch her hair, but changed his mind at the last moment. "Nay. The king has ordered the gibbet."

When she did not respond, he repeated, "I'll send Father Laurentius to speak with you."

Cristina liked Father Laurentius little better now than she had that morning, but he had one quality she much admired: he seemed to have no awe of the king.

"I fear," the priest began, "that you have need of better circumstances than these if we are to speak in comfort." He sat gingerly on the end of the bench near her.

She frowned. "I'll have no need of furniture after the king calls for me."

The priest sniffed. "I'll ask you to be honest with me. From there we shall concoct a tale most appealing to the king."

227

"I have no need of tales," she retorted. "I did not take the book for Simon!" She paced the chamber for a few moments. "Father, I must ask you something of grave importance—as a priest, not a lawyer."

Father Laurentius set aside his haughty attitude for a moment, and she saw a gentleness in him that reassured her. "Sit, child, and ask whatever you desire."

Cristina perched on the bench and folded her hands tightly. "I'm concerned if I should be condemned that I'll die with a certain sin within my heart."

"Is this a confession? I'm not much of a confessor—"

"Nay, I but wish an opinion. I fear the king will put me to the test as he did Simon. I want to know if I would drown if I were innocent of the crime of theft, but still guilty of another."

"Hmmm. Frankly I suspect you of no crime weightier than envy."

She looked up in astonishment. "How perceptive of you. 'Tis envy I am guilty of. I have envied someone's position here and aspired beyond my rank."

"Is that it?" the priest asked. "If that is all, you will sink like a stone."

Acid rose in her throat. "So I am to die today or I will lose a hand or both?"

The priest patted her clenched hands where they lay in her lap. "Nay, child. Not if I can help it. Lord Durand—"

She shot to her feet. "Please do not bring his lordship into this matter."

"I must. He has offered his most grave assurances that you are innocent of the theft of the Aelfric. He is a justice known across the kingdom for his fair and honest dealings. If he had not importuned me, I would not be here."

"How will I thank him?" she mused quietly.

"Who do you think took the book?"

"Truly, Father, I know not. What of the lists Simon and Lord Luke wrote? Could they—"

"I fear they may have held some information the king thought it ill-advised others might see. He kept them, and when I asked to compare them, he said he had burned them."

So, Cristina thought, the king did not care to see justice done. She had only God to help her now. "It must be someone who can enter and leave Lord Luke's counting room with impunity, as well as someone who is of some value to the king, then."

"His laundress is of value to him. Do not see too much in his actions. And take heart that God will punish whoever it is, though we may not." He joined her at the window as a clamor of noise came from the bailey.

"Forgive me, Father, but I cannot mourn my husband as I should," she said. Below, the king's party was leaving for a hunt. How could life move so idly by as if nothing were wrong? Why was the sky not black and crashing with the anger of lightning and injustice?

"I fear Simon is not worthy of your sentiment. Waste no more time on one who offered you naught but public humiliation." The priest touched her shoulder. "Mayhap the king will be merciful."

"I am doomed."

The queen, weary from the hunt, implored the king to postpone the judging of the merchant's wife, that she might enjoy the event without a yawn. Durand's teeth hurt as he clenched his jaw to refrain from a retort that a woman's life was in the balance and should not be weighed against a queen's fatigue. But he said naught when the king agreed to hold the judgment at first light.

Father Laurentius met him on his way to the tower

to see Cristina. He hooked his arm. "Come with me, young man. I seek a private word."

They walked about the bailey, the older man leaning on him with unnecessary weight Durand suspected merely allowed him closer access to his ear. "We must offer the king some alternative to that foolish water test. If one believes in its ability to reliably predict guilt or innocence, this is Mistress le Gros's last night on earth."

"Jesu," Durand muttered.

"But take heart. I believe we can confuse the issue and offer an alternative to the water test or her maiming. Mistress le Gros cannot practice her craft if she is so punished."

"What do you suggest?" Durand asked. "There is little left save arguments and—"

"—combat," the priest finished for him. " 'Tis what I am thinking. We need to ask for the divine intervention of God to fight for her through a champion."

"Who will champion her, Father? She's alone in the world."

"No one is alone in the world. Someone will step forward." Father Laurentius patted his arm. "If not, she is doomed."

Father Laurentius's words chilled Durand more than any winter wind. If only he had left the Aelfric lying at the bottom of the coffer. If he had not used it as an excuse to seek Cristina's attentions, she would be free.

He was as guilty as Simon for involving an innocent woman in this crime, unwittingly or not.

Heat ran through him. His palms were sweaty. He rubbed them on his thighs and stood up abruptly.

The guard Durand had placed in the west tower was William, a trusted, discreet man. "I see one of the king's men is set at the foot of the stairs," Durand said to William with a nod below.

"Aye, my lord, and above," William said with a jerk of his chin in the direction of the ramparts.

"I suppose that means Mistress le Gros will not be fleeing tonight."

William shook his head. "The king must think me incapable of a simple watch." But they both knew the king had set the guard because he did not trust Durand or his men.

"Lock me in," Durand said.

William nodded. If the king's guards were not about, Durand thought, he would simply open the door, give Cristina a heavy purse, send her home to her father— and damn the consequences.

Taking a deep breath, he shut the door behind him and listened for William to do as bidden.

She leaned in the window, head propped on her hands. She did not turn. "I'm not hungry, William."

"But you must eat," Durand said.

"My lord." Her voice was colorless. She left the window and sat on the edge of the bench. Only her fingers betrayed her agitation as she pleated the fabric of her skirt. He went down on one knee by her.

"Do not fear. I will help you." He took up her hand, bent his head, and kissed her palm.

She slipped her fingers into his hair and forced him to look up at her. "I thank you. But there is naught that you can do. Distance yourself."

Her words chilled him.

Her eyes were huge in her face, flecked with gold as the last of the sunlight scattered its gleam across the wooden floor. He could feel the trembling of her body.

"Cristina."

"Distance yourself." Her fingertips lingered on his cheek.

With a groan he wrapped his arms about her and pulled her from the bench, rising, hauling her hard against him. She clung to him, and in the time it took to draw one breath, she touched her mouth to his.

It was a hopeless, helpless kiss.

"All will be well," he said. He kissed her mouth, her cheeks, her eyes, her temples, then buried his face in her hair. Her scent was as sweet as a field of wildflowers, her breath warm upon his throat.

Her breast was swollen, the tip hard when he set his palm against her heart. He pressed gently and brought his mouth to hers. She kissed him back. Frantic, quick touches of lips and tongue.

All the desire he felt for her roared to life.

He gathered her hard against his body. They stumbled back against the shelves. She moaned and closed her eyes. He opened his mouth to her, and she plundered his as if it were the last and only kiss she might be given.

Her buttocks fit perfectly into his palms as he pressed the most sensitive parts of his body to hers.

She shifted on him and gave a soft cry. The sudden touch of her warmth to his sent a jolt of desire through him that almost brought him to his knees.

Her hands swept down his chest to his waist.

His belt hit the floor with a thud. He stripped off his tunic and flung it aside. When he reached for her this time, she leaped into his arms, her kisses on his mouth and face frantic. He thrust his hands into her hair and held her still. For long moments he feasted on her mouth; then he trailed kisses down her throat to her shoulder, sweeping aside the fabric of her gown, pulling apart laces, exposing her swollen breast to his mouth.

She clung to his shoulders. Her breath was sweet on his cheek as she whispered two words at his ear: "Just once."

"Aye," he said, bending his head to drag his teeth across her shoulder. "Just once."

He could wait not a moment longer. Her skirts rode up her smooth legs with one sweep of his hand, as if the summer breezes assisted him.

Her hands quested beneath his linen shirt, and she shoved the remainder of his garments down his hips. She cupped his buttocks as he cupped hers, drawing him hard against her, shifting as he shifted on her.

For long moments he reveled in the taste of her mouth, the feel of her hands on him, the soft brush of her feminine hair across his groin.

Then he wanted more. All of her.

"Cristina," he murmured. How sweet she smelled. He buried his face against her throat and felt the rapid throb of her pulse against his lips.

They stumbled back against the shelves. Rolls of parchment tumbled about them.

With no more words, he lifted her. Her legs came around him. He sought her warmth with his fingertips. A strangled cry escaped her mouth, and he drank it in with his lips and tongue as he touched, soothed, stroked.

She was wet, warm, more than ready for him. Another cry escaped her as she wrapped her arms tightly about his neck and sealed her mouth to his.

He entered her—hard, as deeply as he could, and then held still. He pulled out, thrust in again. Her thighs trembled on his hips.

"Just once," she whispered in acceptance of the joining. Her arms and legs tightened on him along with the hot, silken sheath that enfolded him.

His iron control slipped from his grasp.

With one hand on the shelves to steady himself, one arm beneath her buttocks, he rode the frantic pace of his need.

Sweat broke on his skin.

A quiver within her sent a bolt of sensation from his belly to his feet. She moaned and arched in his arms, nearly throwing herself from his grip. More parchments tumbled from the shelves.

He held her so she could barely move—held her while he moved in deep, hard thrusts with the spill of her liquid heat on him, the scent of her pleasure a heady perfume in the air.

When she met ecstasy, he buried himself as deeply as he could, held himself still, and allowed the intense heaving of her body on his to take him over the abyss.

Finished, drained, they slumped against each other.

Gently he lowered her onto the bench. He straightened his clothes and looked down at her, stretched out on the rough wood, her skirts at her waist. Her thighs glistened wet with his seed.

He felt as if he had fought a battle. Every muscle in his body shuddered.

She stared up at him. Then she cried out and flew off the bench to the window. Her gown off one shoulder, she stood there, her hair in a tangle down her back, like a wild creature set to leap to freedom.

Or oblivion.

In two steps he reached her, but before he could put out his hands to hold her, she buried her face in her arms. Her shoulders shook.

Unsure what to do, he skimmed his hands over her hair. "Cristina?" he said softly.

She lifted her head and turned to him. Tears ran down her face. "That was . . . was . . ." She turned and leaned on the stone again, and her body shook with her weeping.

"Cristina, did I hurt you?" He did not know if he should touch her.

"Nay, my lord," she said through her tears. "You didn't hurt me. I . . . It is just . . ." She looked up at him.

Her dark eyes were huge and shining with her tears. "Thank you, my lord."

Then she broke away from him. Her hands shook as she tried to draw together the front of her gown.

He watched her fumble with the laces and resisted a desire to strip the gown off and see all of her. He wanted to hold her body against his once more, wanted to carry her off to his bed and claim her again and again until the urge left his body.

She picked up his belt. "My lord," she said, and held it out to him. Her gaze never reached beyond his chest.

He looped the belt around his waist.

What words should he offer her? He had taken her without thought of consequences, with no thought of aught but what it might feel to be buried in her warmth.

"Cristina—" he began.

But she cut him off. "Please, I beg of you. Say naught of this. It was . . . beautiful. Do not ruin it with regrets."

"Regrets?" But before he could contradict her, apologize for the wild way in which he had possessed her, William thumped on the door and called his name.

Cristina wheeled toward the sound of the heavy fist. Had the guard heard them? Heat flooded through her.

Then she straightened her spine and her shoulders. "You must go, my lord."

"My lord," William called again.

"We're not finished," Durand promised her. "Open the door," he called to William. The sound of the key turning reminded him of her status and possible fate on the morrow. He touched her shoulder. "I'll come to you tonight."

But she dipped away from him as the door opened. "Nay, my lord. Just once. I meant it. Only once."

"Cristina—"

"My lord," the guard said. "The king has called for you."

Cristina watched Lord Durand hesitate. Then his jaw clenched, and with a stiff nod at her he strode from the chamber.

She looked around to see what the guard must have seen—piles of old parchment rolls scattered about the floor, nothing more. There was no rumpled bed, no couch stained from a pleasured coupling.

What could the guard make of a few scattered records? Or a few muffled sounds? What gossip would run through the castle? Nay, the man was kindly and gentle—not much of a guard, if the truth be known. Mayhap Lord Durand had set him to watch over her for those qualities.

Cristina painstakingly replaced each record on the shelves. She counted to be sure each plank held the same number of rolls.

As she worked she tried to ignore the rippling fear of what her fate would be on the morrow. Her mind shied from thoughts of Simon. He surely lay wrapped in his shroud in the chapel. Or was he already in a gibbet, set at the crossroads?

An anger so raw it sickened her, coupled as it was with regret and grief, rose within her breast. Even in death she was shackled to him with accusations. Wherein lay honor?

Her grief was for what might have been.

She could not ignore the slick heat of Lord Durand's seed on her thighs. Surely she must have been mad. Surely she had lost all reason. Nay. She would not be ashamed of what had happened between them. She had nothing and could not be blamed for reaching out for bodily comfort.

On the morrow, at the least, she would be branded a thief. No honorable man would ever want her again. Therein lay shame.

And no matter Lord Durand's assurances, who would believe her? Father Laurentius had failed Simon and would fail her. Only Simon's accomplice—whoever it was—would find triumph on the morrow.

Tears ran down Cristina's cheeks. Roughly she dashed them away. She did not weep because her life lay in ruins. She wept that there had been but one time with him to call her own, and that one time, she imagined, was now being regretted by Lord Durand as he stood before his king.

Chapter Nineteen

A sumptuous feast lay spread across the table. Finely roasted meats were in evidence: venison, rabbit, and heron. Jellied eels also lay by trays of bread and cheese.

King John picked his teeth. "Tell us more of this woman."

"She's completely blameless," Durand said. He could not eat, and abruptly dismissed the boy who held out a tray of rabbits dressed in sage and marjoram.

His mind was in the west tower. What was Cristina doing at this moment? He had never taken a woman so roughly or quickly. Yet he would not undo one moment of it. It bothered him greatly that she thought he regretted the joining. When could he escape and see her again?

The king leaned close to Durand. "You take an uncommon interest in her fate. Is she Lord Luke's mistress, as her husband claimed, or yours?" A boy poured wine into John's goblet. He traveled with his own dishes and cups. This one was studded with deep red stones.

"Mistress le Gros is not Luke's mistress. She's a simple wet nurse. And she did not take the Aelfric. I gave it to her, and she had no interest in it. She cleaned it and returned it. We both know there were several names on both Simon's and Luke's lists. Why are we not pursuing them?"

John watched him over the rim of his cup. "I have found it is most often those closest who betray. Who better than a wife to do the deed? And we have a dying man's word."

Durand stifled a retort. The king's words cut deeply. "Simon died *unknowing* that he had but moments to live. There is room for doubt."

"Present your doubts on the morrow." The king turned away from him to his queen. It was a dismissal.

Oriel, who looked both ill and anxious, approached the table. "Durand, might I have a word with you?"

Grateful for the opportunity to remove himself ere he said something that would put him in his own dungeon, he rose and excused himself. Oriel led him from the hall into the bailey, chattering rapidly as they went. "She refused to eat, Durand. She will starve."

"Who, Cristina?" He had to almost run to keep up with her.

"Nay." Oriel shot him an inscrutable look. "I speak of Felice, of course. The queen said the babe was not to have any of what she called 'thieving milk,' so we set her to Rose's breast, but she'll not eat."

"Sweet bloody hell," Durand muttered. "The queen decided this?"

"And Lady Nona took the child ere I could object."

"Nona! She interferes." He threw off his fatigue.

"Don't blame Nona. She did only as the queen directed."

He heard Felice before he saw her. The sounds issuing from her chamber might lead one to think the child was being stabbed with a hot dagger. Without further comment, Oriel threw open the door and he stepped inside.

Several maids scattered to the corners of the chamber in various stages of undress. He strode to the hearth.

Rose was a pretty woman, but her face was pinched with anxiety. Her new babe nestled at her breast. Suddenly Felice no longer looked so tiny. Without a word he lifted the screaming Felice from her basket by Rose's feet.

Silence fell immediately. Felice stared up at him, her mouth half-open, her face as red as Oriel's scarlet skirts.

"She knows 'er father," Rose said. "Thank the Blessed Mother."

Or, Durand thought, the child could smell Cristina on his skin and clothes. Without a word he left the chamber. This time Oriel hastened after him.

"I know what you intend, Durand, but will you not anger the queen?" Oriel tugged on his tunic.

He tried, with great effort, to control his anger. "I shall sweet-talk her."

"You?" Oriel frowned. "Pray, forgive me, but you're not known for your soft words."

"I shall learn very quickly."

"Allow me to take the child to Cristina whilst you have your lesson."

He reluctantly gave the babe up. Instantly Felice began her open-mouthed wails.

"Oriel, could you also see that Mistress le Gros has a few amenities and a pallet?"

"I'll see to it; you see to the queen."

* * *

An hour later, a compromise was reached with Queen Isabelle. Cristina could feed the babe. Still, the queen would not allow Felice to remain in Cristina's chamber.

It would be on Durand's head if the babe set to thieving ere she could sup from a spoon, the queen declared, then turned her attentions to Lady Sabina at her side.

Durand gave Sabina a warning glance and deliberately sat near the women so that Sabina might not poison the queen or king against Cristina. She had a caustic tongue.

Finally the king declared he would judge Cristina at dawn and called for a bath. The queen retired with him, and suddenly the hall began to empty.

As men and women laid out their pallets, Durand thought of one who must be sleeping ill upon hers.

Moments later he found himself in the tower. When William opened Cristina's door for him, the chamber lay in darkness save for a wick burning in a dish of scented oil. Durand drew air into his lungs and was immediately aroused. It was the same scent as the soap she used to wash her hair. It lingered about her, and now lingered on his shirt as well.

The shutters were flung open to the night, and a web of mist wreathed the upper tower heights and seemed to enter the chamber and float a few inches above the floor.

She lay on her pallet, facing away from him, garbed only in her shift. He stretched out behind her and touched her shoulder.

"My lord," she whispered, turning to him. "Are you a dream?"

He took her hand and laid it on his chest over his heart. "Does a dream have warm flesh?"

He cupped her face and kissed her lips. This time

241

he would not besiege her. This time he would be gentle and draw out the little time they had together before the dawn. This time he would have her naked against his skin.

Cristina pulled away and leaned up on one hand. She traced his torque with a fingertip. "You are bred to rule."

"Aye. And you to nurture and heal."

"We have naught between us save idle lust."

"My lust is not idle." With that he took her hand and pressed it to his chest again.

She heard no regret in his voice.

His heart thundered against her palm.

She could not see him well in the dim flicker of the flame, and so would have to trust what she could feel—a man whose blood ran as quickly as hers in his veins. She explored with her fingertips from his chest to his throat. His blood pounded there as well, beneath his warm skin.

Just this once more.

Aloud she said, "I knew 'twas you at the door. There is no other who has your scent."

"Or yours," he said. He sat up and helped her pull the shift over her head. Then she was naked before him. He brushed her hair over her shoulders and examined her.

"You are beautiful," he said, and meant it.

His fingertips were warm as he traced the silvery lines of childbirth that marked her breasts, finally coming to the tight peaks waiting anxiously for his touch.

The touch of his hand, his tongue on her warm skin, made her groan.

Quickly he rose and shed his clothing. He drew his dagger and set it close by the pallet. Sadly, she knew he did not feel completely safe here with her.

The single flame made shadows dance on his

body—a strong warrior's body, honed in battle, hardened with time. When he lowered himself over her, fully stretched upon her, she remembered well her dream.

Mayhap she dreamed again. Mayhap she would awake and find a demon nightmare visited upon her. She shuddered.

"I'm hurting you," he said, pulling away.

"Nay!" She wrapped her arms tightly around him. "I was cold."

He enveloped her in warmth, breathing his inner heat upon her shoulder, breast, and throat. A wild ache to be joined, to feel the blade of his desire within her, drove her to near madness.

She learned the shape of his hips and back with long sweeps of her hands. She learned the depth of his passion when he locked his mouth to hers and whispered barely audible words against her lips.

With an urgency building within her, a fire stoked by each touch of his hand, she lifted her hips and silently begged with her body to be joined with him.

He rolled her onto her side, and she found herself staring directly at the gleaming gold that encircled his throat—and set her apart from him.

But not at this moment in time.

Not for this one night.

The shadow of beard painted a harsh line along his jaw. She would see every expression that crossed his face, she vowed silently. She must remember each moment when she was gone.

Or dead.

He spread her open and in one swift movement joined himself to her. It was he who closed his eyes, and she who watched the many expressions of passion cross his face.

Then she could not continue. Her body was afire, her heart seduced. She ducked her head to his shoulder and locked her fingers in his. He drove his hips to meet hers again and again and again.

She felt the quick, hot spurt of his seed deep within her, and every fiber of her body began to tremble.

But pleasure eluded her. She reached for it, but fear of the morrow, knowledge that this was all she would have, kept the prize out of her reach.

He knew it. He, whose chest rose and fell as if he had slain a thousand enemies, knew only that he had found pleasure. He separated himself from her and placed her on her back.

His warm hands cupped her face. He kissed her gently. He stroked each breast, then caressed her belly on a journey lower. No man, save he, had ever touched her in such a way. He nuzzled her warmth, parted her with his fingers and tongue.

A flash of sensation rode through her. She arched and bucked her hips against the hot touch of his mouth, keening a cry of wild pleasure.

He slid quickly up her body and clamped a hand over her mouth. "Hush," he quietly admonished her, and where she was once warm, she felt a rush of cold.

Of course; it would be a mistake to allow anyone to know what they did.

"My lord, may I rise?" she asked after swallowing a few times to contain her rampaging emotions. He opened his arms, and she rolled away from him and off the pallet.

She had to distance herself. Her hands trembled, as did her knees when she poured water into a basin. She lathered a cloth with soap, one she had been making in an effort to capture that intangible scent of his, one so completely wrong now that she had his essence on her skin.

Aware of his scrutiny, she bathed her breasts and thighs.

When she was finished, she drew on her shift and

turned to look at him. He stretched upon the pallet, one leg bent. Fingers of desire clawed at her again. How beautiful he looked, completely exposed to her view, nothing hidden. If they were truly lovers, she would kneel at his side and touch him, learn his body slowly. But they were not lovers. Two joinings did not make love. They merely affirmed lust.

She poured fresh water and took the basin to his side. Quickly she drew a cloth over him, destroying any evidence of their coupling. His body reacted, filling as she touched him. He encircled her wrist and guided her caresses.

What she had tried to hold in check whipped through her. His gray eyes, shrouded in shadow, could only be imagined. And she imagined he watched her as if he were one of the ravens on his banner set to catch prey. Together their hands moved on him.

Her heartbeat rose.

"Cristina. Remove the shift and join me here," he said. "You nurture my desires with your touch."

Though she shook her head, he ignored her. He pulled her astride his hips, tugging her shift to her waist. Settled on his manhood, she could not deny the quickening of her passions. Surely she would expire of such pleasure. Surely he knew it.

An utterly wild need filled her.

He cupped her buttocks and lifted her. But it was she who put a hand to him and guided him to her desire.

Durand drifted to sleep in her arms, but that blissful peace eluded her. She lay there for hours and savored his scent, the hard length of his body, the warmth of his hand tangled in her hair.

When next he woke, he drew her into his arms and, without a word, mounted her quickly. She rode his passions as they flew from his control. At some point he gasped her name again and again.

She said nothing. There was nothing to say.

Dawn had come.

Chapter Twenty

Not more than an hour after Durand had left, a guard fetched her. She went without demur, as she knew there was little anyone could do. Simon had stitched her into her shroud as surely as if he had wielded a real needle and thread.

Though she offered no resistance, the king's man held her roughly and hustled her down the steps and into the hall. A wall of people met her view. Even the upper gallery was lined with spectators, the humbler maids and pages to those who sat near the hearth.

The guard parted the throng by calling out "Make way for the thief," as if she had already been tried and convicted. "Sit," the man ordered her, and thrust her onto a stool by Father Laurentius.

The long table by the hearth held the clerics and Durand. He did not look at her, and she felt chilled.

Did he, somewhere inside, think her guilty? That he might was worse than a thrust from the dagger he had placed in its sheath when he had dressed. That blade, with its raven, and the torque he wore were symbols of who he was.

The marks on her wrists from the ropes that had bound her were symbols of who she was, too.

As she stared at the rough red patches on her skin, anger filled her. How dare Simon involve her in this? How dare this knavish company stand in judgment of her? They who traded beds on a whim, taxed their minions to near starvation, and warred over land, then trampled it wantonly as they hunted?

Not Lord Durand.

She folded her hands in her lap to still their tremor. Lord Durand did not drain the life from his people—nor did Lord Luke, in his stead.

Lady Oriel and Lady Nona came to stand in front of her. They were garbed like twin butterflies in vibrant blues and yellows, as if they had planned to complement each other. Both wore chains of gold about their waists and necks. All the finery did not conceal Oriel's pale face or Lady Nona's delicate beauty.

Oriel kissed her cheeks. Lady Nona was not so familiar, but did touch her shoulder quickly, lightly. They took their places by the hearth with Lord Gilles and his son, who had just entered with Penne. The king was announced. He swept in with his queen on his arm. Cristina knew she would be judged by this man who was said to be as capricious as the summer winds. As if he had touched her, she felt his gaze settle on her.

Father Laurentius hurried toward her from the bailey. His robes flapped around his thin frame, but he smiled gravely and patted her hand. "All will be well, mistress. Take heart."

To show the priest and all who chose to judge her in their own hearts, she straightened her spine and settled her features into what she hoped looked like the countenance of a woman with no guilt or fear.

Several agonizing moments of courtly banter passed as more of King John's party arranged themselves about the hearth area. The queen called for wine and something sweet. Serving boys went about tending to the needs of their masters and mistresses. Did no one care that she waited with a racing heart and sweating palms, her life in the balance?

Lord Durand was every inch the warrior lord as he took a seat by the king. He wore a long tunic more suited to combat than this business. At the neck and sleeves she saw a dark wine linen shirt that somehow reminded her of the colors in his hair when it was touched by the flickers of flame.

He nodded to her, and suddenly she felt an inner peace. He had promised to help her. He was a man of honor. He would keep his word.

The sick churning of her belly subsided.

The king gestured for Father Laurentius to approach. This time there would be no difficulty hearing every word spoken. She was the accused.

To her great surprise—and Lord Durand's, too, if his expression was any window to his thoughts—the king asked Luke to step forward.

Luke went down on one knee and bowed to the king.

John sat in a huge oak chair and leaned on one elbow. The size of the chair did naught to increase his own physical presence. He was a small man compared to Lord Luke. But his splendid robes bespoke his position. He wore several rings, the worth of which would keep ten peasant families all their lives.

Lord Luke also looked splendid, though he was more plainly dressed. He was garbed in russet brown with touches of gold trim. He wore his mantle over one shoulder. It was clasped with a gold pin shaped like a raven—a reminder that he was a de Marle, too.

The king spoke almost gently. "Lord Luke, you take

a most prodigious interest in Mistress le Gros."

She started at her name.

"My interest is that of castellan."

"Come, Luke, we are not blind. The woman is fetching, is she not? And you are most aptly called Lord of Skirts. How is it you have let such a tempting morsel pass you by?"

Durand watched his brother carefully. Hot color filled Luke's cheeks, but he shrugged. "There are so many temptations," Luke said. "And only so many hours."

The hall burst into laughter.

The king smiled. "So," he continued. "You have not *yet* sampled Mistress le Gros?"

Luke shrugged again, but made no answer.

Durand watched Cristina bow her head. It was an indication of her inner turmoil at this open discussion of her as if she could not hear. He wanted to call out to her to sit as before, not cave to one man's accusations.

The queen touched King John's hand. "Lord Luke has neither wealth nor position. He has a pretty face, I grant you, but he has naught to offer a woman of wealth, and so can we not assume he will seek such as this one?"

There was a hint of malice in the queen's tone, and realization hit Durand with a jolt.

The king held an interest in Cristina, and the queen knew it.

King John shook his head. "Are we correct, Lord Luke, that many seek you, highborn and low, for your connection to your brother and any future considerations he might settle on you?"

"Aye, sire. Many seek me for what *Durand* might offer."

Durand saw Lady Nona rise abruptly and slip between Oriel and Penne. She lifted her hem, and it belled around her legs as she darted down the steps to the lower reaches of the castle. What ailed her?

Then he knew. She was humiliated, just as Cristina was at the implications of the king's conversation, now that her name was coupled with that of de Marle. Guilt that he had spent the night in Cristina's arms washed over him. But he thrust it aside. He was not wed to the lady yet and might never make a contract with her. What he had done with Cristina was none of Lady Nona's concern.

The king's caprice in such matters was legendary. But Durand would not undo the night in Cristina's arms for all the wealth and land in Christendom.

"What places have you been alone with Mistress le Gros?" the king asked Luke.

Father Laurentius came to life. He gripped Luke's arm and bade him to be silent. "Sire, Lord Luke is not accused of theft. Mistress le Gros is. She is innocent of everything but a blindness to her husband's perfidious nature. In fact, she was given the book in question by Lord Durand and returned it to him through Lord Luke once she had cleaned it."

Someone in the crowd snickered.

Durand watched Cristina's head snap up. She fixed her gaze on the king with no agitation of her hands, nor telltale blush staining her pale cheeks. He admired her return to courage.

"It is your statement 'through Lord Luke' that we question, Father," the king said. "Can you deny the woman had access to the Aelfric? Can you deny she may have had a second thought about returning such a valuable book when it could fetch up to a thousand pounds?"

"I deny it completely. Mistress le Gros had but to ask Lord Durand and he would have given her the book. Once she had it, she could have sold it to whomever she wished. 'Tis nonsense that she would have stolen it!"

The king tapped his chin in thoughtful contemplation. "If this is the case, Father, then why did Simon not ask his wife to petition Lord Drandu for it? Why would *he* need to steal it?"

"Indeed. Let us ask Mistress le Gros." Father Laurentius turned to her. He bent close to her. "Well?" he asked.

Cristina looked up at the priest and Durand held his breath. What would she say? "I did not tell my husband that Lord Durand gave me the book, as I thought Simon might see something in it beyond kindness. I did not wish to raise his anger. I merely said Lord Durand had given me the Aelfric to clean."

"Did anyone witness this exchange, my child?"

She shook her head. The priest repeated Cristina's answer to the king, and for the first time Durand saw color on her cheeks.

"We see," the king said. The queen distracted him for a moment by leaning and whispering in his ear. "We would speak with Penne Martine," he said to the priest.

Penne approached with a slightly bewildered expression. Durand, too, had no idea why the king wished to speak with him.

"Martine, it is our understanding that you frequent the counting room." The king rose and stood before Penne, his hand outstretched.

Penne bowed over the king's extended hand. "Sire, I am often in the counting room with Luke and others."

"Did you see this woman there, and most particularly alone, at any time near the time to, or before, the theft was noticed?" The king swept out his hand to where Cristina sat.

There was but a moment of hesitation before Penne

spoke. "Aye. I did see her one night alone in the counting room."

"When? And what was she doing there?" the king asked.

Who had supplied the king—nay, the queen—with such information? Durand flicked his glance quickly across the assembled crowd. There were no clues in any faces that he could read.

Penne licked his lips. "I am not sure when . . . a stormy night, I believe. She was doing nothing untoward, sire. She was placing a bottle of sorts upon the table."

"Could she have opened the coffer in which the Aelfric lay before you arrived? Did she remain after you?" The king did not wait for Penne to answer. He forged on with a question to Laurentius. "What was in the bottle, Father?"

When asked the question, Cristina glanced toward Luke. What had Cristina made for Luke? Durand wondered.

"Father," Cristina said, "I am loath to break a confidence."

"You must," the priest said. "Why die for some simple potion you made?"

Cristina's face paled and she visibly swallowed. "I made a love potion."

Mon Dieu, Durand thought as the hall erupted in discord.

The king threw back his head and laughed. "We cannot believe the Lord of Skirts needs a love potion!" The king slapped the arms of his chair.

Luke merely shrugged and looked steadily at the king.

" 'Twas not a usual love potion, sire," Luke said when the hall quieted. "I merely wished that an hour or so of lovemaking might last for three . . . or four."

Silence fell. Durand gave his brother a silent salute.

Trust Luke to fall into something and arise smelling like a rose.

"We are indeed envious. And shall soon be purchasing the same for ourselves," the king said. The many courtiers of his court were laughing along with the king. Roger Godshall whispered something to Sabina, which turned her smile into a frown.

The queen tapped her husband's arm and made a soft comment. The king burst into renewed laughter. "Our most esteemed queen informs me that Luke wears well the appellation of Lord of Skirts, and wishes to know if the potion was effective."

Luke bowed to the queen. "Aye, sire, 'twas most effective."

Durand thought that Cristina would never starve if she survived this. She would be making love potions for the next score of years for every man present.

Father Laurentius cleared his throat. "Is there not sufficient doubt, sire, that this woman must be freed?"

"Notwithstanding our amusement, we have not lost sight of our purpose." The king turned to Durand. "We can see that many had access to the Aelfric. Furthermore, this woman was seen alone in the chamber, despite her very worthy need to be there. Could she not have delivered the potion to Lord Luke at any time? Aye, she could have. Yet she chose a quiet moment when no other was in the chamber. 'Tis a telling circumstance."

Durand quickly interjected. "Aye, sire. And I have seen other women alone there, too." A woman caught his eye. "Lady Sabina, for one."

Cristina felt hope rise within her. If Durand could marshal doubt, she might yet survive. Then her spirits fell. A woman with a father the king called friend would not need to steal.

"Have you succumbed to the Lord of Skirts?" John leaned toward Sabina.

She smiled. "All woman have lost their hearts to him, sire, but not all of us have lost our virtue to him."

"Indeed." The king swept his gaze across the hall and let it come to rest on Cristina. "Rise, mistress."

She did so with difficulty, for she wanted only to melt into the floor. She dropped into a deep curtsy.

"We have a simple solution that will greatly amuse us all," the king said. "We shall allow God to determine guilt and innocence."

"Sire," Durand said sharply, " 'twould be in the best interests in some cases, but Mistress le Gros has duties that she must perform, guilty or innocent. She cannot nurse the infant Felice if she is dead!"

His assumption of her death was an assumption of her innocence. She sent him a silent thanks for his heated support.

"Ah," the king said. "The babe. We have not forgotten the babe, as she most severely tested our ears and taxed our patience last eventide. Our most blessed queen agrees that the child needs her nurse, though we have our doubts as to having a thief nurture such an innocent babe."

Cristina folded her hands in a prayerful and silent plea that God might deliver her from this place and these people.

"There are other tests. We most enjoy the spectacle of single combat, do we not?" the king asked his queen.

The crowd in the hall erupted in a babble of voices. Cristina looked from the king to Durand. What did the king mean? She was to fight for her life? How?

But the king spoke to Father Laurentius, and with the cacophony of sound around her, Cristina heard nothing of what he said. When Father Laurentius nodded, Cristina knew her fate was somehow sealed.

Eventually the noise in the hall settled to whispered murmurs. From the many courtiers, a tall, broad man stepped forward. He looked both old and young—young in the fluid way he moved and old in the cynical cast to his features.

The king rose. "Come, mistress."

She stood at Father Laurentius's side.

"Have you a champion who will fight for you in single combat?" the king asked.

A hush fell over the hall. Not a man or woman moved. So herein lay her fate. "I have not, sire. My husband is dead and my father old in years. My brothers are merchants, not soldiers."

"Then we have no recourse—"

"I will champion Mistress le Gros." Lord Durand rose abruptly to his feet. He walked around the long table and stood before the king. He knelt. "I will champion her," he repeated.

Lady Oriel took a step forward, but was restrained by Penne. Cristina tugged on Father Laurentius's robe. "Please, Father, you cannot allow this."

"Be still," the priest said to her in a hiss.

"Nay, sire, I shall champion her."

All eyes swiveled to where Luke stood. He strode to his brother's side. "It should be me, sire. I have somehow brought this wretched coil to pass."

"This is an amusing turn of events," the king said. "It seems our merchant's wife has no lack of fine champions."

Cristina wanted to scream. The brute who stood by the king was huge, his face scarred. She pulled on the priest's arm.

He rounded on her. "You will say nothing, do you hear? You will be still!"

She recoiled a few steps from his anger. He must have realized he had overstepped, as he patted her arm and muttered, "All is as it should be."

Durand wanted to draw his sword and smite Luke on the head. How dared he muddy the waters! "Sire," he began, "I beg to be allowed to engage your champion—"

"Nay, sire," Luke said. "Select me."

The king crossed his arms over his chest. "We shall set the time of combat for one hour after vespers. Until then, settle between yourselves who will be Mistress le Gros's champion, for we care naught who walks upon the field. Arrive shriven."

With that pronouncement, the king raised his hand. Cristina's guard gripped her arm and hauled her away.

Durand could barely control his anger. He sat through two more judgments on petty matters before he could be released to search out Luke. He found him in his counting room. Lady Nona sat at his side, and Felice was cradled in his arms. They were studying a rolled parchment Luke had stretched across the table. Even the babe looked intently at the parchment, her hand fisted, all her fingers in her mouth, sucking avidly.

"Luke, I have need to speak to you."

Lady Nona rose. "Pray excuse me, my lord."

"Return the child to Mistress le Gros, Lady Nona, if you will," Durand said. He would not explain why.

When the woman was gone, Luke spoke. "Are you here to ask me if three hours is really how long I can keep my cock at attention?"

The jest did nothing to lighten Durand's mood. "You will not champion Cristina."

Luke slowly rolled the parchment and bound it with a leather thong. "Why not?"

Because I used the book to tempt her. Because I— He settled for a half truth. "If I had not given Cristina the book to clean, Simon would not have seen it—"

"What utter rot!" Luke slapped a hand to the table. "This is not about giving Cristina a book. This is about

257

spending last night in her chamber. You're being led by your cock, not your head."

"Where I spend the night is of no concern to you," Durand said stiffly.

Luke did not answer immediately. He took a deep breath, and when he spoke his voice was calm once again.

"Where you spend your nights is of concern to Lady Nona. Have you forgotten she is here to wed you?"

Durand bit off the retort he had planned. He had forgotten Lady Nona, had hardly registered her presence with Luke, save as someone who could take the child away. "I've not signed any contracts with Lady Nona."

"She'll not have you if you so patently champion Cristina!" Luke pointed a finger at him. "I've no prospective bride to impress, no children to mourn me if I misstep with that barbarian John drags about the kingdom."

"You will not win."

Luke's face hardened into angry lines. "I will. I'm the best there is at Ravenswood."

"Save me."

Luke rose. He stood almost as tall. He was younger, mayhap quicker in reflexes. But he did not wish to win as urgently as Durand did. He was not quite as canny.

"Let me repeat," Luke said. "You are doing this for the wrong reasons, and it will kill you. Cristina is naught but another set of large breasts and cushioned thighs—"

"You dare council me?" Anger roared through him. Luke might have lain in Marion's bed, fathered Felice. It should be Luke whom Durand challenged after vespers.

"Someone must!" They were nose-to-nose when the door opened and Penne entered, taking in the situation at a glance. He thrust himself between them, holding them apart with outstretched hands.

"I thought this is what I would find," Penne shouted over them. "Settle. Now." He shoved Luke toward the hearth and glared at Durand. "This is folly. If the whole castle does not think you both share Cristina's bed, I don't know what they think. Will she thank either of you for shredding her reputation? Oriel just came to me to say that Lady Nona found a man scratching at her door when she delivered Felice."

Luke tugged his tunic straight. "He probably just wants the love potion."

"That may be so," Penne said, "but he might also see her as easy game now that you two have offered to die for her! And die you will. Gregory Tillet is undefeated!"

"It does not change anything," Durand said. "I'll meet him and defeat him."

"Are you sure you are not drained of strength from a night of mattress combat?" Luke drawled.

"Cease this." Penne shot a hand out to stay Durand from tearing off Luke's head. "I'm loath to advise you two. I love you both, but I'm sorry, Luke: Durand is the better fighter. Gregory is treacherous, but Durand is ruthless. Step aside."

Luke shook his head and turned to Durand. "Adrian and Robert need you."

Durand felt a pang of conscience at Luke's utterly sincere manner. He let his body relax. He blew out a long breath. "I'm as likely to die in Normandy, Luke. Let it be. I'll champion Cristina, and you'll champion Adrian and Robert if I fall."

"And Felice," Luke and Penne said at the same time.

Chapter Twenty-one

Durand saw only Cristina in his mind's eye as he readied himself for combat. He hoped God would forgive his distraction as he and Tillet knelt in the chapel to be shriven of their sins.

Joseph was helping Durand shrug into his hauberk when Gilles d'Argent entered the armory.

"Joseph," Gilles d'Argent said, "see to the grounds. Walk them and note any spots treacherous to the unwary foot."

"Aye, my lord." Joseph ran from the long stone building without a backward glance.

"I know my own field," Durand snapped.

Gilles took up a sword and inspected the blade. He shook his head and handed it off to the armorer. "Fetch mine from my son Nicholas, will you? He's in the hall."

Durand found himself alone with his friend. Gilles propped his hip on a table and crossed his arms over his chest. Durand waited for him to speak.

"You are determined to this folly?" Gilles asked.

"You think this folly? Do I look the fool?" Anger coursed through Durand.

But Gilles held up a staying hand. "Save your wrath for the field, where it will serve a better purpose. I'm merely here at your brother's behest."

"Luke!" Durand took up the padded cap that would protect his head beneath the mail and helm. He turned it round and round in his hand. "He does not have my skills."

"Agreed, but he has no sons to mourn him either." Gilles plucked Durand's gauntlets from the table. "It only makes sense to send the man with nothing to lose into the field. I agree that you're the better fighter, but that does not mean Luke is not able enough to see it through. I agree with Luke that you have too many responsibilities to throw your life away so easily; let him take the challenge."

Durand held out his hand for his gauntlets. "I cannot, my friend. I carelessly gave Cristina a book that ruined her life, so I must offer her the best chance I can to recover it." He knew he was not making sense, but could not explain himself any better.

He would never tell this man the reasons he had given the book, nor that his trust in Luke was blighted by suspicion.

If one had no trust, one could depend only on oneself.

"I cannot abandon Cristina to John's caprice, Gilles. And you know him well enough to know that he ordered that water test for spite. 'Tis an antiquated piece of business, as well as one only the most blindly religious fanatic believes in anymore. We know some hidden plan's at work here."

"Think you John sees Luke as more malleable to his purposes? More willing to comply with his wishes?"

261

Gilles acted the squire and helped Durand don a gray surcoat bearing a raven in flight on the breast.

"I know it in my bones, but it changes nothing of what I will do here. Most assuredly the merchant died for his sins, but this continued pursuit of Cristina smacks of something else. In the past I have seen John dismiss such questionable business on my advice alone. Why now did he pursue this so?"

And in truth, Durand thought, I owe Cristina, and nothing will change that.

The armorer returned with Gilles's sword. A powerful emotion swept over Durand when the older man took his sword and held it out. "Then have as many advantages as possible," Gilles said.

Durand took the sword. It was the finest of Toledo steel, far finer than any sword Durand had ever held in his hand. He weighed its balance with a few test swipes of the air. His own sword, so summarily dismissed by d'Argent, was well balanced, but this one felt as if it were an extension of his arm.

Any advantage was a blessing.

"I must thank you, Gilles," Durand said, sheathing the fine sword. He bowed to his friend. "I'll not fail."

Gilles and he clasped hands.

"Use the blade well, my friend, but remember: fight with a mind to treachery. Expect it and you'll not be caught unawares."

"Treachery?" Luke walked into the armory, Joseph behind him. Luke was fully garbed for battle, helm under his arm. "Who speaks of treachery?"

"What do you think you're doing?" Durand said in a snarl.

"Saving you from this madness."

Durand thrust his helm into Gilles's arms and drew his sword. Luke dropped his helm and did the same.

"My lord!" cried Joseph.

Gilles stayed the man from dashing forth. "Let them decide it for themselves."

Luke hefted his sword. "Aye. Let us have this out. There is more to this than a simple need to champion your mistress."

"Sire," Durand said with a glance over Luke's shoulder. Luke turned slightly. In moments Durand had knocked his sword from his hand and put him on his back. "You just fell for the simplest of tricks. I've proved my point. You'll not fight this day, do you hear?"

The rain had begun two hours before vespers. The recent heavy horse traffic in the inner bailey had turned it into a quagmire. But men worked to erect pavilions for the spectators as if it were a sunny day and the coming event a fair.

Unable to sit and await the dreaded moment of combat, Cristina had Alice bring her a few herbs and oils from Felice's chamber.

When Oriel came to fetch her, Cristina felt her heart beat out of rhythm.

"What are you doing?" Oriel asked, coming to the mat where Cristina knelt.

With a final stir of the herbs and oils she was blending, Cristina rose. "I'm making a salve for any wounds Lord Durand might sustain. 'Tis dill and century—secured by Alice without Aldwin's knowledge, I imagine—as well as my own bay and almond oil to soothe."

Oriel touched her shoulder. "Could not Aldwin see to it?"

Cristina paused. How to say what she thought of Aldwin without stepping beyond her bounds? "I'm sure Aldwin has his own methods, my lady, but this salve was taught me by my mother, and he may not know it."

The pursing of Oriel's lips and her quick nod told

Cristina the lady understood. In fact, Cristina had said extra prayers over the salve to obviate the fact that the herbs had spent such a long time in Aldwin's hands.

Oriel handed Cristina a heavy mantle. It was of fine green wool lined with fur and suited to protection from a winter storm—or standing in the rain watching men do battle.

"My lady, I cannot take this."

"Nonsense. I have several more." Oriel wrapped a shawl about Cristina's head and lifted the hood of the mantle. "If you catch a chill, you'll not be able to see to my needs. My tassel came undone again."

It was said with a smile, and Cristina knew it would hurt the lady's feelings if she did not accept the mantle. "I thank you," she said softly. "You've not shunned me as others in your position might."

"I have so much to thank you for. And 'twas a potion for Penne that you placed in Luke's counting room that night, as I am sure you must suspect. We decided we should not hide behind 'friends' any longer. Penne didn't know how to request such a thing for himself. So, my sweet Cristina, we would not want you harmed for aiding us."

"My lady," Cristina said. "I would ask you if . . . if—"

A horn sounded outside. Oriel ran to the window and peered out. "Come, say what needs saying. 'Tis time."

"When this night is done . . ." She swallowed. Her mouth was as dry as the Jerusalem desert. "I fear I must leave this place, and I hope you'll express my apology to any who might . . . that is—"

She lost her nerve to ask whether Lady Nona held some antipathy for her. Alice, when she had brought Felice to nurse, had said that gossip of Lord Durand's sojourn in this chamber the previous night had reached that lady's ears.

Alice had spewed a stream of invective at her for succumbing to the same male lust that had killed her lady. Only Cristina's complete silence had finally stopped Alice's tirade. That Alice had wept throughout did naught to still Cristina's apprehensions regarding her status in the castle once this night ended. The trial had tainted her as Luke's possible mistress, and now Durand's presence in her chamber had cast her as his.

She would not be ashamed of her time with Durand. It was an affirmation of life. Nothing else.

Where would she stand at midnight if he triumphed? And he would triumph. Anything else was unthinkable. Her mind shied from thoughts of bloody or festering wounds.

"You'll remain right here at Ravenswood," Oriel said, dismissing Cristina's words with a toss of the head. "This is your home now."

Hope filled her. But then a glimpse of the dark ribbon of the road to the west reminded Cristina the lady was wrong.

Could she go without crumbling? She might acknowledge only that she dreaded the loss of Felice. That alone must account for her tears when she left.

Where would she go? Her father would be ashamed to have her, though accept her he might.

After a final look into the bailey she was ready. "The king will halt this fight before either man is dead, will he not?" she asked. "Alice said 'twas so."

"Oh, aye. John cannot afford to lose such a man as Durand. 'Tis wounds I fear more. More good men have died of them than lived," Oriel said.

Cristina felt a shiver of fear.

Two guards waited at the door to escort her to the bailey. They took her to the largest pavilion, set up in the bailey for the king and his party. She was not to be sheltered there, merely must curtsy to the king and queen and thank them for this opportunity to prove her innocence, Father Laurentius informed her in a quick whisper.

Immediately after she made her obeisance, two of the king's men escorted her to one end of the sparring ground and then took up a post, one on either side of her. All could gaze upon her and speculate on Durand's and Luke's championing of her—and her part in the theft of the Aelfric. Heat filled her, her heart raced, but she looked only at the field and ignored the twist of her insides.

Many men, honing their skills for Normandy, had trampled the green sward to a sticky bog. How could a man maintain his footing in such a place? Real fear at memories of the brigands' attack and the fearful wounds inflicted filled her.

Another horn sounded. The sky was an angry swirl of low clouds as day fled to night's embrace. Smoking torches beneath the pavilions lighted the area with eerie shadows.

Lord Durand and the king's champion stepped onto the field. She saw only *him*, magnificent in his armor, every inch the warrior lord of the immense castle that threw its shadow across the muddy field.

Father Laurentius touched her shoulder. " 'Tis best you know 'twill be a fight to the death unless the king calls a halt, though there's little hope of that."

"Nay," she cried, and grasped the man's hands. "I thought 'twas until one man surrendered."

"Surrendered? My child, how very innocent you are," the priest said. "Men such as these never surrender."

She frantically turned to where the two men stood. "You must stop this," she begged.

"Too late," Laurentius said. "Be at peace. God's will shall triumph."

A powerful trembling began in her legs. She moaned, and one of the guards gave her a sharp look.

Durand's surcoat over his mail was gray and stitched with a raven on the breast. Gregory Tillet wore the king's colors. Somehow the scarlet surcoat reminded her only of blood.

Luke strode out to the combatants and handed his brother a shield emblazoned with a raven striking a serpent. The brothers bowed to one another.

The instant the two men took up their swords, Cristina reached for the priest's hand, but he was gone— gone to the pavilion to sit beside the queen.

Cristina stood alone between the guards.

All had deserted her save the man who stood in the muddy field. He championed her and might die. She toyed with the idea of going to the king and confessing that she *had* stolen the Aelfric, that this horrible nightmare might end.

But to do so would dishonor Lord Durand's gesture.

The two warriors faced the king.

King John raised his hand. "May God's will decide this matter."

The two men bowed and then stepped to the center of the field. The crowd began to shout, their words snatched by the wind and slashing rain.

The king dropped his hand.

The men joined in a crack of shields and swords.

They separated, circled, joined, separated again.

Gregory Tillet yelled, then lifted his sword and brought it down in a smashing blow to Durand's raised shield.

Durand twisted away. His answering blow was swiftly parried.

"God save him," Cristina murmured. She clasped her hands tightly together.

*   *   *

Durand felt Gregory's next blow to his shoulder. It stunned his hand and arm. He raised his blade and met the next, taking it on his sword. Metal slid on metal until they were joined at the crossguards.

"Ye'll have no more whores when I have done with ye," Tillet said in a snarl, jerking away and bringing up his shield.

"Or you," Durand snapped back. Sweat broke on his skin.

The thick mud sucked at their feet. Every motion seemed deceptively slow and languid.

As he raised his sword, Gregory slipped to one knee. But still he managed to evade the blow Durand directed to his exposed neck, and rose again.

They moved and struck, one after the other, alternating blows. The rain fell. It ran into their eyes and turned the mud slick.

Again and again they stumbled or fell. Their limbs grew weighty with mud.

All Durand saw was a blur of grays and browns, with flashes of color. Smoke drifted through the field from dozens of damp torches.

Tillet's sword rose again and again. Quick, glancing blows landed on Durand's legs, which were protected by his heavy mail chausses. His shoulders ached from raising the shield over and over to parry the heavy blade of his adversary.

They alternated supremacy, first one, then the other.

But Durand had not known true combat for several years. He fell back, no longer on the attack, half-blinded by splattered mud.

Tillet pursued him. One small step at a time, Tillet routed him toward the pavilion. He'd be cornered there.

Durand took a deep breath, his lungs on fire. He felt firmer ground under his feet.

He launched himself forward and smashed his shield into Tillet's, but lost his hold on his sword at the same time. It spun away, tantalizingly out of reach.

Tillet rocked on his feet.

It gained Durand a precious moment that allowed him to slip sideways and whirl away from Tillet's sword and the pavilion. Unfortunately it also placed him even farther from his sword.

"Are you ready to give up?" Tillet taunted, stalking toward him with measured steps.

Durand drew the dagger from his belt in answer.

He sidestepped, but many more blows of the kind would take his strength. He fell back again.

Tillet glanced toward the crowd, and Durand leaped close and thrust his dagger past the lowered shield. But Tillet anticipated and took the arm-severing cut on the edge of his blade instead.

For the next few moments Tillet hammered Durand with hard blows. Durand's shield arm grew numb. A particularly heavy blow tore the shield from his hand, taking the gauntlet with it.

Tillet grinned, his teeth showing white in the small gap twixt mail and helm.

Durand dropped low, snatched a handful of mud, and cast it into his taunting face. With a bellow of anger, Tillet raced at Durand. He fell to one knee and dropped his shoulder. In moments Tillet was sailing over Durand's body to fall like a turtle on his back. His shield flew several feet away.

Durand leaped up and whirled around. But Tillet rolled and recovered, rising quickly and leaping at Durand with a blood-curdling war cry.

Durand's dagger met the blade of the king's champion. They locked onto each other's blades, nearly hand against hand.

Durand gripped Tillet's arm, but the mud-slick mail gave him no purchase.

With a muttered curse Durand dropped back, surprising Tillet and throwing him forward. He fell on his side in a wash of mud.

Durand stepped on Tillet's sword.

He grabbed Durand's ankle. They grappled for a moment until Tillet triumphed and tossed Durand onto his back.

The mud sucked at his body, but he floundered to his feet. They stood facing each other, the distance of Tillet's sword blade apart. But there was something wrong with Tillet's hand. It shook with a tremor that told Durand it was gravely injured. Durand kicked the sword from Tillet's hand.

Tillet threw himself on Durand, bearing him to the ground, one knee near his groin. The explosion of pain tore his breath from his chest.

He planted his hands on Tillet's chest and heaved, but to no avail. From all sides men and women shouted. He felt as if he were smothering in pain and mud.

With his last burst of strength, he threw the man off and snatched his dagger from his boot.

How paltry it looked compared to the double-headed ax now lying close by Gregory's feet.

Where had the weapon come from?

Tillet went for the ax. He whirled it on high.

A woman screamed—a long, shrieking cry of agony. Tillet glanced toward it.

Durand did not. He charged in and embraced the man, thrusting his long, thin dagger deep into Tillet's exposed armpit.

He made not a sound as he crumpled. Durand rode the blade and the body to the ground. Warm blood ran over his hand. Tillet stared at him. He moaned. The ax fell from his outstretched hand, red blood mingling with the blue enamel that graced the handle.

Durand staggered to his feet. The crowd whirled a moment. Black spots filled his vision and a roar filled his ears. He swallowed and forced himself to be still until his vision cleared.

The roar continued and he realized it was the crowd—cheering. Luke slogged across the field to him and gripped his arm. "Come. Walk, brother, that no one may see any weakness."

Durand did as bidden, allowing Luke to take some of his weight. He insisted on detouring and picking up Gilles's sword. He sheathed it with a quick thrust, then allowed Luke to lead him before the king.

"It seems God has decided Mistress le Gros's fate," King John said with a hint of anger.

Aye, Durand thought. He rewarded the treacherous man with death—and the sweetly innocent with life.

The crowd surged from the pavilions to the keep. Durand's men surrounded him, and within their protective phalanx he was borne to the armory. There Joseph and William stripped him of his muddy garments and doused him in buckets of cold water. Every muscle in his body ached.

Gilles and Luke watched as his squire rubbed him down with a length of linen, then forced him to eat several thick slabs of bread and honey. The food restored some of his strength.

"Someone threw Tillet that ax," Luke said. "If Cristina had not screamed, Tillet would not have looked away. A fool's mistake."

Durand's body was ice cold. He thought he might collapse, but hoped he could remain on his feet until he thanked Cristina.

"I owe Cristina my life, it seems," Durand managed. He could barely make his lips move.

Gilles shrugged. "Or you owe God. I wish I had seen who tossed the ax, but I was intent on the battle, and when I went later to fetch it, 'twas gone."

"I'll not rest until I get the man for you," Luke said. "Come, Durand," he said. "You'll be expected in the hall."

"Cristina," Durand said. "Where is she?"

"I saw the guards hustling her into the keep, so she's already there," Joseph said, and helped Durand to pull on a linen shirt that felt amazingly warm on his skin. In moments he was garbed appropriately, and with more will than bodily strength allowed his friends and brother to lead him to the hall.

Cristina was not there. He forced himself to walk to the king. "Has Mistress le Gros been released, sire?"

"Oh, aye. Mayhap you would like to accept her thanks? We are sure she will be suitably grateful for the service you have rendered her this day."

Durand bowed. Every muscle in his body screamed as he walked slowly down the center of the hall to the steps leading to the west tower and *her*.

Chapter Twenty-two

No guard stood before the door to the book chamber, and the latch lifted without benefit of key. A brace of wax candles lighted the chamber with a warm glow. It was redolent with heady scents. Cristina stood by the window, the shutters open despite the rain outside. When he closed the door she ran to him and threw herself against his chest.

"Oh, my lord. God bless you."

He grunted and gripped her shoulders. Gently he set her aside. "You'll finish what Tillet began," he said, and laughed at the stricken look on her face.

"You're in pain." She took his hand and inspected it. "Come. I've prepared a salve for your wounds."

"In a moment; first I must thank you. 'Twas your cry that distracted Tillet. It was his undoing."

"My fear got the better of me." She squeezed his hand.

"And saved my life." He touched her cheek with the back of his fingers.

He had meant only to thank her and see that she was truly released. He had meant to do no more than stand at the door and tell her he was glad all was now as it should be.

Instead he followed her across the chamber to the hearth, his hand in hers. "What is this you're cooking?" he asked to avoid all other topics that lay between them—the trial, the king's caprice, his own desire for her.

"The salve. 'Tis best if warm."

Durand used a horn spoon to stir a small pot wrapped in warm cloth. Bringing the spoon to his nose, he drew in a deep breath. "This smells wonderful . . . almost mesmerizing."

She took the bowl from him. "If you will allow me, my lord," she began, "I would tend your wounds." Her eyes were downcast, and he remembered the time she had tended his hand, and the intense arousal he'd felt from her mere touch.

Silence stood between them. The air was filled with more than the seductive scents of her salve. It crackled with heated tension.

"Have you a need to see to the child?" he asked, glancing about.

"She was brought to me ere you arrived."

"Why is she not here then?"

Her face was suddenly blank of expression. "The queen requested that Alice take her away. If Felice grows hungry, Alice will bring her here."

Durand put a hand on her shoulder. "On the morrow I'll see that everything is returned to how it was. But for now . . . I have not the strength."

Cristina covered his hand. All would never be the same. But for now he was barely standing upright. He had defeated death, and now deserved peace.

"Come," she whispered, and led him by the hand to her pallet. She pulled back the furs and removed the stones that were warming its surface, then sat back on her heels.

He looked down at the comforting bedding and, without any thought save the succor it offered, he drew off his mantle, then his tunic and shirt. She helped him with the rest. Finally he lay down on the warmed bedding.

He closed his eyes, stretched his arms over his head, and groaned at the pull of his strained muscles.

Cristina had never seen a man so wonderfully made. The chilly air hardened his nipples, and she felt her own tighten, not from the cold but from arousal. She pulled the shutters closed and picked up the bowl of salve. It lay warm and heavy in her hands as she bore it to the pallet.

As she drew near, she saw angry red welts on his legs, though his chausses had protected him from worse.

"Oh, my lord," she said softly. She set the bowl on the floor and touched his calf where the imprint of the links of mail stood out clearly against his flesh.

"They will be but bruises on the morrow," he said.

But she shook her head, denying his words.

The salve was wonderfully warm when she drew it along his leg. Every muscle in his body tensed. He shivered in anticipation. She noticed and sat back. Wiping her fingers on a strip of linen, she picked up one of the furs from the pallet and made to drape it across his skin.

"Don't," he said, his voice hoarse, and she laid it aside. He met her eyes, and then her gaze swept down his body to his leg. "Your glance is like a hand on my skin."

With the grace of a forest sprite, she perched on

her heels and tipped her head. "Would that I could heal this with a look."

She spread her palm on his bruised leg, and a shudder ran from there to his spine. "Cristina," he whispered.

With a hand so gentle not even his flights of fancy would conjure greater joy, she smoothed the salve across his skin.

This was what he had envisioned, her warm hands ministering to his body as she had once cared for his hands. His fingers curled into fists at the thought. He closed his eyes. Every muscle in his upper body hurt from swinging the sword and lifting the heavy shield. His testicles still ached from Tillet's knee. Yet he craved her touch—everywhere.

"Tell me if I hurt you," she whispered.

He did not answer. He was incapable of words.

She massaged his feet, his calves, and, in long sweeps of her hands, his thighs. His body responded despite the twinges of sensation in his groin.

Every now and then, her hair grazed his skin as she moved by inches up his body. He opened his eyes when she shifted her attentions to his arms.

"How will I ever thank you?" she said by his ear, so softly he almost thought he had dreamed the whisper of a forest sprite.

The silk of her hair brushed over his chest. It was both a delight and an agony.

"Your cry evened the score," he managed. "Think no longer on it."

He looped his arms about her neck and drew her down to his mouth. Her tongue and lips were fever-warm. He entangled his fist in her hair and held her close, but she ducked and evaded his embrace.

She dipped her fingers into the salve, and he put his arms over his head again to allow her to smooth it on his skin. He would be black and blue in a few hours without it.

This time she took even longer to spread the cream on his skin. She traced the shape of the muscles of his biceps and traveled gently along the veins that roped his forearms.

"You're so strong," she said. Her fingers touched his torque. "And this is your symbol of power."

"I'm weak where you're concerned," he returned. In fact, his body ached for release despite his weakness. Each touch, each sweep of her hands on him drew him ever closer to the precipice of his need.

She spread her hands on the insides of his upper arms and drew her fingers down the tender flesh to his shoulders. The massage there drew a gasp from him, yet he did not want her to stop. From his shoulders she ran her hands to his chest. She bent her head and touched her tongue to each of his nipples, her hair floating across his groin.

"I want you so much," he said, thrusting his fingers into her hair. "Just once . . . It is . . . a promise I cannot keep."

Her answer was silent and sent shivers of molten sensations rolling through him. As he had done to her the previous night, she kissed him from his chest to his belly. As he had, she continued, laving him with slow and tender licks and kisses. Her breath heated his manhood, and he drew up his knees in reflex to what would come next—her mouth on him.

"Sweet Cristina," he said in a gasp when she gently touched him with her salve-slick fingertips. Each small movement of her fingers, each touch of her tongue on him, each caress of her breath tugged him closer and closer to the precipice.

Just when he could bear no more, she drew away and stood up. She removed her russet gown and shift, folding them neatly, and he fed his arousal with the sight of her as she moved.

She knelt at his side, blessedly naked. "I don't want to hurt you," she said.

"I cannot imagine any pain more powerful than the pleasure you have wrought with your hands and lips," he said, and reached for her.

His arms were warm and slick with the salve as he drew her astride him. The candles guttered and one went out. The shadows intensified and lent the hard lines of his face a gentler aspect.

The heat of his body made the scent of her salve more pungent. Dill was considered an aphrodisiac, and she feared for a moment that it was that which caused the heat within her and the hardness pressing between her thighs.

Nay, she thought, *I'll not allow it to be the salve that kindles this flame in him. If I'm to have no other night save this, no other to remember when I'm old and alone, I'll not allow it to be one tainted by magic or medicine.*

She licked along the line of his lower lip. He captured her mouth for a kiss while his hands ran down her spine to cup her buttocks. She arched away from him that his mouth might come against her breast.

He kneaded her against his arousal as he kissed her breasts. Each touch of his tongue raised such a heat within her, she thought she might cry out at the pure pleasure of it.

This was not the salve. This was something between them that had existed from the instant they had met. It entwined them more strongly than vine entwined an ancient tree.

It would wither in the sunlight.

When their lips met again he moaned, for as they joined their mouths, they joined their bodies. They moved in concert, his body buried so deeply within her she felt him to her heart. He linked his fingers with hers and stretched their arms overhead, drawing her down on him, kissing her hard, arching his hips to bring himself even more deeply within her.

He tasted of honey and heat.

She could no longer tolerate the ache between her thighs. He gasped when she shifted on him and bore down. With great waves of rapture, she lost all reason and pressed her face to his throat. The hard metal of his torque showered her ecstasy with a chill.

Durand felt the clench of her body on his and continued to arch beneath her. He sought and yet tried to stay the madness so close upon him. Her breasts filled his hands to overflowing as she abruptly rose up on him, the action settling her so firmly on him, his body so deeply within her, he bucked off the pallet in a final, exquisite release.

He lay panting on his back for several moments just watching the sweet rise and fall of her breasts. Then he drew her down to hold her as close as he could, to know each breath she drew. Her hair tangled on his fingers as he stroked his hands through it again and again. Desire cascaded from his groin with each tiny shift of her body.

"I'll see to the care of any child you might bear," he said.

Her body tensed, but she said nothing.

"I'll see you settled in comfort should such be the result of our time together. You and your babe will never want for anything. I'll see it written that should I die in Normandy the result will be the same."

She withdrew. Cold air swept over his sweat-slick body as she stood up. Her hair swayed across her buttocks as she went to the hearth.

He groaned as he sat up. Had he erred in speaking so boldly? "I have bruises on my bruises," he said.

Her hair cloaked her when she knelt to build up the flames.

"Have you nothing to say?" he asked.

She shook her head. It was an effort, but he stood up and went to her. "Allow me to do that," he said.

"I can build a fire, my lord. Any servant can."

He placed a gentle hand on her chin and lifted her face. "You're not my servant. Did I think you one, I would not offer to do the task."

Her dark eyes were warm amber with reflected firelight. Golden streaks filled her hair. "You're so beautiful," he said.

"If I'm not your servant, what am I?"

Her breasts were ivory, tipped with dusky brown. He cupped their fullness in his palms. "You are intoxicating, like fine wine." He touched his lips to hers. "You are healing, your kiss inspiring." They knelt knee-to-knee before the hearth, heated on one side, cold on the other.

She stretched out on the wooden floor, atop a mattress of naught but rushes, and took him in. Arms about his neck, she ignored the cold press of his torque against her cheek and thought only that he had not really answered her.

When the castle stirred to life, and sentries called out one to another as they changed from night watch to day, Cristina left Durand deeply asleep.

She sought Alice and the babe, then looked about for Joseph. It was a difficult task with so many in the keep, and she did not want to draw attention to herself. She knew not her status.

She was free, of course, but that did not mean she was welcome anywhere in the keep. If one went by the icy looks from the maids in Felice's chamber when her care of the babe disturbed their rest, she was no longer welcome there. They probably coveted the Lord of Skirts and resented her as a rival.

Against Alice's advice, she had put Felice in a sling

and taken her off to the privacy of a bench by the stable, away from prying eyes and the light drizzle.

She finally found Joseph cleaning Durand's mail outside the armory. "His lordship must have a soothing bath for his injuries, but I don't know how to accomplish it."

"I'll see to a tub for him, mistress. Should I have it sent to the west tower?"

So everyone knew where Lord Durand was. Cristina looked up at the impregnable stone walls. "Aye. If 'tis not a burden to carry so much water so high."

Joseph gave a laugh. "You'll find that after last night's battle with that barbarian Tillet, my lord's pages will carry stones to the roof for him without complaint."

"He was magnificent, was he not?" she said.

"Aye, mistress. But I've seen him fight before and knew what he was capable of. It did the young ones good to see him, though, as they think him overlearned."

Cristina tiptoed back into the book chamber. Durand had rolled to his stomach and flung off the furs. Despite her ministrations, his welts were beginning the transformation to livid bruises. She moved quietly to where he lay.

In the clear light of day, she saw scars that underlay the bruised flesh on his arms and legs. He had two ropy ones on his thigh and a long patch of skin someone with little skill had stitched, low on his back, near his hip.

Aldwin should be whipped for such poor work. Then she realized Durand had been on crusade. Mayhap this was work done on the battlefield. He was lucky to be alive. The wound was as likely to have killed him as the poor tending afterward. None of the marks detracted from the strong warrior beauty of his body.

An urge to join with him swept over her. She badly wanted to wake him, arouse him, taste him. But she did not.

She could not continue in this vein. His words about caring for any child they conceived together told her what she needed to know. They had but a few moments together and that was all.

She drew the furs over him—for her sake, not his.

The clamorous noise of the boys who delivered the tub, and the many buckets of water they brought to fill it, woke him. His head pounded. Cristina was gone. When the tub was filled, she reappeared, slipping silently around the door.

"Where did you hide?" he asked.

"On the wall walk," she replied, setting Felice on her back next to him on the pallet.

He tickled the babe's chin and watched her try to capture his finger in her fist. Her little brow knitted into a frown, making her appear to be a wizened old woman. The instant she succeeded in her quest, she tried to put his finger in her mouth.

Cristina went to the mat, where several fragrant earthenware bowls sat. She selected one, lifted it to her nose, then went to the tub. He watched as she sprinkled its contents into the bathwater.

"What are you doing?" He sat up and groaned, then forced himself upright. He crawled over Felice, then limped to the tub.

"Certain herbs aid healing and do best in warm water."

"I'm sure Aldwin approves."

She smiled, and it lit her face with a subtle beauty.

He sank into the hot water. Just as it had been each time he had bathed since she had come to Ravenswood, the water felt like fine silk against his skin. The heady vapors filled his head with the fragrance of the forest.

"You conjure such pleasure with your touch," he said. He took her hand and raised it to his lips.

"Nay, any woman who knows her herbs could do the same."

She tugged her hand away and went to the child. He slid down in the warm water, but not so far that he could not see Cristina as she sat, the child within the protective circle of her arms.

Cristina kissed Felice's cheek and traced her tiny ear.

Aye, she thought. *Any woman could make him a fine soap or fill his bath with fragrant and healing herbs.* Most assuredly Lady Nona would next do these honors—as his wife.

"Cristina, come hither and help me."

Urgency filled his voice. She hastily placed Felice on her back and hurried to him. "Is something amiss?" She reached out.

He snatched her hand, tugged, and with a shriek she landed in the tub. "Durand!" she cried when he locked his arm about her waist. "Felice will—"

"Will what?" he asked, then licked up her neck with a tongue so hot it almost burned her skin.

"She . . . she—" Cristina could not think clearly. Her skirts were heavy with water, and she could no more move from his wet embrace than a captured animal could move from a bog.

Felice whimpered a moment, but then settled, sucking vigorously on her fingers, and Cristina felt a giggle bubble up in her throat.

Durand leaned forward and pulled her legs into the tub. "Did you know this is John's tub? Quite large, is it not? He travels with it everywhere."

"The king's tub?" She squealed and tried again to rise. His grip was hard as iron about her waist.

Durand laid his lips against her ear and said, "As he is not in it with us, you can set your fears to rest. In fact, according to Joseph, he sent the tub with his blessings."

There was little Cristina could do but lie back in his arms.

"When was the last time you bathed in a tub?" he asked.

"When I labored to deliver my babe. Lady Marion saw to it."

Durand pulled the wet hair draped over her shoulders to one side. He took her chin and turned her face to his. "I'm pleased Marion saw to your care. She could be generous."

"Aye, she purchased much from Simon, calling him often to the castle. I think she wanted us to prosper." She ducked her head. "How far we have fallen."

"Think no longer of Marion or Simon. Think of the joy of life given you this day." He placed a gentle kiss on her lips.

She shifted in his arms until she was kneeling between his thighs. Propping herself on his chest, she cupped his face and kissed him. Her sodden garments took many moments to remove, but finally she lay in his embrace, wondrously warm and wet.

They took turns soaping the cloth and rubbing it on each other. "Your breasts are—"

"—too large," she finished, spreading her hands over her chest and frowning.

"—worthy of a troubadour's song," he continued. He soaped his hands and rubbed her skin in a leisurely exploration. "If I had some talent, I would compose a tribute to them."

His teasing tone grew suddenly serious. She watched his eyes, silvery in the sunlight, darken. " 'Tis a madness, this need I have to touch you." Beneath her hip, his manhood swelled. Without thought, she shifted on him.

She did as he had and soaped her hands, disdaining the cloth. When she placed her hands on his chest, he tipped his head back and rested it on the edge of the tub. She might never use a cloth for bathing again. The feel of his honed muscles beneath her hands, slicked with the soap, was almost as lovely as when she had rubbed the salve on him. He groaned.

"Am I hurting you?" she asked.

"It will hurt only if you stop," he said with a grin.

She stroked the soap on his nipples with her thumbs, moving over and over them until he snatched her hands and hauled her into his embrace.

He shifted her and tried to pull her astride his hips. The tub was too narrow for what he intended, and they ended with tangled legs, laughing, water sloshing over the tub rim.

But laughter died when he touched her intimately between her thighs. She covered his hand. "You raise such an ache within me," she said softly. Will I ever know such a touch again? she wondered only to herself.

He watched her from beneath his dark, straight brows, his gaze so intent she closed her eyes lest he see within her and know that she had lost her heart and soul to him.

She shivered and trembled. His arm about her waist held her still to his ministrations. Her control slipped. She whispered entreaties to him—entreaties for release—over and over until the heat burst through her.

Durand felt the heavy thudding of her heart against his chest and saw a flush rise on her breasts.

What was she to him? A lover? An ethereal spirit? A woman of courage? Everything a man could desire. How could he keep her?

Chapter Twenty-three

Cristina felt the heat of embarrassment when Joseph brought his lord's clothing. Although she was gowned when the squire arrived, she was sure he knew what they had been about by her wet braid and her blue wool, which a few hours ago had been russet linen.

When Durand ignored his clothing and walked slowly to the pallet, there to stretch out again, she forced herself to look away. She filled a dish with an oil infused with thyme and lit a wick in it. As the scent wafted about the chamber, Durand drifted to sleep.

She took the opportunity to slip from the chamber with Felice on her shoulder and headed for the east tower, where she found Alice spinning. It was time to distance herself from Durand. In fact, a lewd question from one of the king's guards as she crossed the hall told her that whether the people of the keep thought her Durand's mistress or Luke's, this man considered her fair game. Others would, too, if she lingered.

"I were just goin' to ask if'n ye wish me to take the babe," Alice said softly.

"Nay. She's hungry again. 'Tis baffling. One day she's as regular as Father Odo's devotions, and others, as capricious as—"

"Any fine lady," Alice supplied, plying her spindle with dexterous fingers.

Cristina smiled and stretched on a pallet, Felice contentedly curled in the crook of her body. The posture reminded her of how Durand had looked with his daughter, her tiny body within the strength of his.

What was her place at Ravenswood now?

Was she a mistress? Nay. A few fevered moments did not make her one.

Could she talk openly to Durand about seeking a new home? Why had her tongue failed her last eventide when he had mentioned providing for her if she conceived?

What was her place?

She stroked Felice's head and thought of a babe from a man such as Durand—it would be a gift. Then her throat closed. In nine years with Simon, she had failed to produce a living child. Why should it be any different with Lord Durand? It was but God's will, and there was naught she could do to change it.

One thing was as clear as the freshest well water: She could not remain at Ravenswood and watch Durand seal his troth with Lady Nona—or see her brought to bed with his child.

Nona's offer that she go to her manor in Bordeaux was tempting, whether it was offered in kindness or from a desire to see her gone.

She hugged the child. It was as if she were losing another daughter. There was something hollow and empty within her.

At that moment a pounding fist sent Alice scurrying to open the door. One of the king's men stood there.

He walked through the chamber as if he were marching on a battlefield. The scents of rain and the sea came with him.

The old woman held out her arms for the child, but Cristina waved her off. The man stood over her. "You are summoned to the queen," he said.

"Do you know why?" Cristina looked from Alice's seamed face to the blank countenance of the man.

They both shrugged.

Cristina eased Felice from her breast. She tucked the babe into her sling and gestured for the man to lead on.

With a thumping heart, Cristina followed the man to Lord Durand's chamber—now the royal apartment. The queen sat by the hearth, embroidering a delicate linen cap. No maids or ladies attended her.

"Come, sit by me, mistress." The queen indicated a low stool by her side.

Cristina did as bidden.

"This storm prevents the sailing of our galleys to Normandy," the queen said. "But it will end soon and the men will go."

All Cristina could do was nod.

"Our king wishes that our most beloved Nona should marry a strong man who will be able to see to the care and maintenance of her holdings." The queen's eyes were cold when she looked up from her work. "Do you understand how difficult it is for a woman in this world? She is ofttimes the pawn of men."

"Aye, my lady. I understand." Surely the queen was baiting her. Who else, save herself, was better situated to know the lot of a woman?

"Some women find it is more difficult than others," the queen said. "They must take care to align themselves with strength and honor. Lady Nona is an example. Her father is not well, and she will know great wealth and property upon his death. Even now our beloved friend has much from her marriage to Lord Merlainy that might tempt others. It would not do for those great properties of hers to go to one who is not inclined to love and obey our king."

Cristina became acutely aware of what the queen meant. "In what way might I best serve, my lady?" she asked, although she knew the answer.

"One would most wish that you depart."

Cristina stifled a painful gasp. It took several moments for her to find her tongue. She swallowed hard. "I will endeavor to find a place, my lady."

The queen smiled, but again it did not reach her eyes. "It may be difficult for you to leave Ravenswood."

"Aye, my lady." Cristina felt a burning in the center of her chest. "I have come to love this child." She stroked her hand along Felice's back.

"Then you must want the best for her. We are considering a match for her in Aquitaine. If Lady Nona approves, Felice will go to her betrothed's home to be raised there. Do you approve?"

The words were said in a manner Cristina knew would brook no disagreement.

"As it pleases you, my lady." Aquitaine. A lifetime away.

Lord Durand's name would never be mentioned between the queen and her, of course. That he was the true subject of this conversation would never be acknowledged. Durand was to wed Lady Nona and she, Cristina, must be gone so that no impediments to their felicity might exist.

"The king will be pleased with such a match for the child. We will apprise you of the day you must relinquish the child, of course. Until then"—the queen sorted through her silks and chose a new color, holding it against the cloth—"you will remove yourself to the village. You may take Felice for a few days."

When the queen said nothing more, Cristina rose, curtsied, and walked to the door. Her mind was numb with the swift ending of her time at Ravenswood.

"Oh, and mistress," the queen said when she reached the door. "Pack nothing that you did not bring to Ravenswood. I have sent my maids to aid you."

It was a blatant suggestion that she was a thief in need of watching. "You are most gracious," Cristina said with a deep bow.

The walk to Felice's chamber seemed two leagues long. She wove her way blindly through the many who listened to the king's minstrels. A man in a cleric's cassock stepped in front of her. She braced herself for another blow. This man she had seen at the king's side. He was of middling height, middling coloring—an unexceptional appearance.

"Are you the wife of the dead thief?" he asked.

"I am Cristina le Gros," she said. Would she always be known by Simon's sins?

"Might I beg a word?" the cleric asked. His fingers were stained with ink where they clutched a sheaf of parchment.

"I'm to depart—"

"We understand as much. This will not take long." The cleric took her elbow and led her away to one end of the hall. "There is not much privacy here, mistress, but we shall make the best of it."

Cristina felt the scrutiny of many as she stood near the doors to the bailey. "Please make haste, sir." Felice struggled and fussed in her arms. Could the child sense the fears within her breast?

"Our beloved king is most pleased at Lord Durand's triumph. He must hold you in great affection to offer to act as your champion."

"Lord Durand is a man of honor, sir," Cristina said carefully.

"Your husband was not."

To this she had no response.

The cleric signaled a passing boy who carried a tray of wine goblets. "Wine?" he asked, snagging a cup for himself and fumbling with his pages.

She judged it best to take the proffered cup, but did naught but hold it tightly in her hand.

"What are your plans, mistress? Will you return to your family?" The man sipped from his cup. Drops of wine spilled across the front of his cassock.

"I have not made plans yet, sir." A thread of apprehension coursed through her.

"The king maintains a most pleasant household near Winchester that is much in need of your services."

Affecting an air of innocence, Cristina kept her gaze down and said, "They need perfumed soap?"

The cleric gave a short bark of laughter. "Oh, I am sure they have soap aplenty, mistress, but we think there is some special quality to your work that others may merely aspire to."

Cristina could not avoid looking up, nor could she pretend she did not understand. "Be clear, sir."

"Come, mistress, you are not a simpering virgin to cavil over a lucrative offer."

"I have much to occupy me here at Ravenswood." Cristina tried to still the pounding of her heart.

With another burst of laughter, the cleric thrust his empty cup at a passing serving maid, then reached out and touched her wrist. His hand was warm and moist.

He gave her a gentle squeeze. "He of whom we speak would be most generous in his appreciation of your services."

She twisted from his grip. "The babe, sir. Forgive me. I must feed her."

The cleric folded his arms over his documents and leaned his shoulder on the wall. "But of course. Feed the babe. But as you do, think kindly on Winchester."

Cristina hurried to the west tower. It took her but a few moments to return to Durand. The scented oils had done their work. He lay heavily asleep on his stomach beneath a pile of furs.

She knelt by him and considered his face and shoulder, just visible at the edge of the bedding.

Should she wake him and tell him of the strange interview with the king's man? Or of the queen's hasty wish that she depart?

Would he feel a need to rush again to her rescue? Or would her heart be torn when he did nothing—or worse, weighed the advantages of each offer and gave her advice on which to take?

Fear shivered up her spine.

The queen's maids awaited her and might even be reporting to the queen that she tarried in her departure.

She kissed the tips of her fingers and touched them to his shoulder.

He shifted, stirred, murmured, then settled. The sun lit upon the torque at his throat, tipped with ravens. She touched the warm gold, smooth from generations of wear.

Generations of men far above her.

She rose and left the chamber without waking him. When she opened the door to Felice's chamber in the east tower, she saw a wooden box on the table. The queen's maids were locking it.

One of the women was the maid who had entertained her lover, consigning Cristina to wander and end up at the postern gate.

Nay, it was her choice alone that had sent her there.

"What do you want done with all these things?" the woman asked, sweeping a hand out to encompass the many bowls and herbs of Cristina's craft.

She might need them to survive. "I'll crate them up," she said.

"As you wish," the other maid said, and sat down by the hearth on a bench, spreading her ivory skirts about her.

Cristina endured their scrutiny as she worked. Some oils she must leave behind, as she had no bottles for them. Some herbs she knew might be ruined when lying in close proximity to others in the crate. There was little she could do about it.

Her mind would not stay on her task. How could it? Her body still ached from the hours in Lord Durand's embrace.

No wonder Lord Durand had not answered her question. There was no place in his life for her.

She murmured to Felice, so peaceful and watchful in her sling. Her heart ached for Felice's possible fate—passed to a future husband's family to be raised. Would he be a kind man? Was he in the cradle now?

"Hurry, mistress. I am sure Roger Godshall will grow, impatient at the gate," the maid with the lover said.

"Roger Godshall?" Cristina paused in strapping the box closed. She knew that was the name of Sabina's friend—the one she had offended at the trial. "What has he to do with me?"

"He's your escort to the village."

The thought chilled her. "Does Lord Durand know of this?"

One maid snickered. The one with the lover smiled. "He is lord here, is he not?"

With burning eyes, Cristina finished securing the box.

Durand knew of this?

Had he known last night? This morn? Was that why he had not answered her when she had asked what she was to him?

He must want a break that severed their ties with the swiftness of a blade to a man's heart. Only it was her heart cut in two.

She would not think ill of him.

To do so would make him a man she did not know—or wish to.

Cristina pulled on her mantle and cast a quick glance about the chamber. Ladies' gowns and mantles lay in jumbled profusion. The chamber smelled of mingled perfumes.

It was not her chamber—had never been.

She wrapped Felice in the embroidered blankets she had stitched for her daughter who had not survived.

Cristina could not seek out Oriel any more than she could Durand. That gentle lady would read every secret of her heart.

Alice met her at the foot of the steps to the east tower. "Alice, will you tell Lady Oriel I'll be in the village should she have need of anything?"

"Aye. She likes that smelly stuff ye put in 'er pomander. She'll find ye, miss." Then Alice buried her face in her hands and hastened away.

Cristina almost begged the old woman to come with her to the village, but did not. As she crossed the great hall, she felt many eyes upon her. Her skin itched with discomfort. Several maids curtsied to her and smiled. One woman stopped her to kiss Felice. These few civilities warmed her.

Men, the king included, stood by the hearth, maps before them. They were too intent upon their business to note her in any way. But as she walked by, she thought she felt the king's glance upon her. How little she thought of him—a man who could show such public affection for his wife and invite another to be his mistress behind her back—one he thought to be a thief, no less.

For a moment Cristina pitied the queen. Surely the king would make offers to other women, and how many would refuse?

There were no ladies in the great hall, although Cristina glimpsed the bent head of Lady Nona in an alcove.

Lady Nona was a beautiful and kindly woman. She would make Lord Durand a good wife. Although Cristina swallowed several times to still her misery, tears ran down her cheeks. She was thankful when, once she gained the bailey, rain fell in fitful squalls and hid her discomposure.

What had happened to her vow never to weep?

Cristina saw nothing and heard nothing as she walked through the inner bailey to the stable and the waiting men. She passed the empty pavilions with their extinguished torches.

A groom boosted her into a saddle and slapped the palfrey's rump to get her moving. Squalls of rain whipped Cristina's mantle back and dampened her skirt.

Three men rode before her and three behind. Roger Godshall led them. It was far too large an escort to the village. It smacked of the escort of a prisoner to her cell.

As her party rode through Ravenswood's gates, the chapel bells rang. The man directly in front of her looked back.

Cristina did not.

The chapel bells woke Durand. The chamber stood empty, the tub gone—Cristina, too. He had slept the morning through.

He stretched and groaned at the pulling protest of his muscles. Had there been something in the lush vapors of the scented oil to put him to sleep? Or was he just growing old? Soon his hair would be falling out.

He went to the hall on a quest for the largest haunch of venison the cook could provide. John was poring over his maps, his men around him, and Durand decided it would make better sense to attend the king than fill his own belly. He settled for a heel of bread and a slice of cheese, then joined the royal party.

The king acknowledged him with a nod. "We'll sail when Marshall arrives and the weather turns. This messenger from Dartmouth"—the king gestured to a man covered in mud—"assures us all is in readiness there as well."

Durand looked over the map. They would disembark at La Rochelle and drive through Poitou and thence to Anjou, Maine, and finally Normandy. And likely die on the road.

Two of the king's minstrels began to wander the hall, and the king ordered the maps rolled. Drandu searched every face. Someone here had stood aside and allowed an innocent woman to be accused of theft. It was another kind of betrayal, one he needed to avenge.

"Durand, over here." Nicholas d'Argent beckoned him near. Several men-at-arms as well as Gilles's son were sitting and dicing by the hearth.

He straddled a bench and joined them. A boy offered him a goblet of wine. As he lifted the cup, he nearly groaned at the deep ache in his shoulder. Cristina must rub some more of her salve there. His thoughts dwelled a moment on Cristina. He wondered where she was hiding herself. And he knew she was hiding from this company's scrutiny.

As was the habit of men, they examined every aspect of the previous day's combat. He was excused any faults by way of the mud. And triumph always sweetened the tale. The idea amused him. "Surely one of John's jongleurs will immortalize me in song?" he asked the company.

"Nay, they are scratching out something in honor of Luke's cock," one quipped. "They have no time for combat between mere mortals."

Durand could not help laughing along with the men. "How many of you have visited Mistress le Gros for one of her potions that you might be so revered?"

Silence fell. Nicholas cleared his throat. "Surely you know she is gone?"

"Gone?" Durand looked from one face to another, but all eyes slid away save Nicholas's.

"Aye," d'Argent said. "I have it from my groom that the queen ordered her gone early this morn—to the village, I believe."

Durand shot to his feet. He crossed the hall and took the steps to the east tower two at a time. He hammered a fist on Felice's door. A maid opened it a scant inch and peered out.

"Open this door," he demanded, and she gave way.

One of the king's guards scrambled in the bed furs to cover his nakedness. The maid merely walked back to the bed, her hair hiding little of her slender body.

"Where are the babe's things?" Durand asked, not able to mention Cristina, for it was obvious she was not there. The table held no herbs. No bundles of dry-ing flowers hung from string. Even the chamber's scent was that of other women's perfumed bodies.

The maid leaned on the bedpost and ran her hand over the linen draperies in an invitational manner, but answered the question. "Are not all babes with their nurses, my lord?"

With mounting confusion he hastened down the tower steps. How could he not know so basic a thing in his own keep? The usual alcove for stitching ladies held one of his quarries—Lady Nona.

"I understand Mistress le Gros is gone." He tried and failed to keep his voice low and undisturbed.

"You are correct," Nona said, rising and bowing. "The queen gave the order, and it took little to see it done. But she has only gone to the village."

"I see." He realized he was speaking to the wrong woman on this matter.

Lady Nona wore a dark wine-colored gown trimmed with gold. Her hair was loosely held at her nape with wine and gold braided ribbons. Her finery bespoke her station—far above Cristina's.

"My lord," Nona said. "Before you go, might I say that the queen has asked my opinion of a match between Felice and William of Aquitaine and whether Mistress le Gros should accompany Felice to her new home."

Jesu. Cristina and Felice in Aquitaine.

"Although . . ." Here Nona paused and glanced away. "The queen did again bring up the matter of a child's nature being formed through the milk she is fed."

"I see." And he did. Alliances had naught to do with lust. They served one purpose only—securing power. He had married Marion for her connections regardless of how his heart had later been touched by her. "If it pleases you, I have much to do," he said abruptly.

She curtsied and then spoke. "I don't mean to interfere, but if you seek to change the queen's mind about Mistress le Gros, you might do better through the king."

"What does that mean?" He retraced his steps to stand before Lady Nona.

"It means the king has noticed Mistress le Gros."

Durand understood. Lady Nona was trying to tell

him that the queen was motivated by her jealousy, not by care of Felice.

"My lord?" Nona touched his sleeve.

"What?" He had not meant to be rude, but felt impatient to see the queen.

"Allow Mistress le Gros some time to settle herself in the village."

Without a word of parting, he wheeled away.

Cristina had not come to him.

Anger burned through him. At the queen. At Cristina.

Roger Godshall halted the party at the cottage. One of his men helped Cristina dismount, an awkward business with a child in arms. When she moved to the packhorse holding her belongings, Godshall drew his dagger.

It was an elegant weapon, with a handle inlaid with blue enamel. It sliced through the ropes holding her boxes as if they were but embroidery thread.

Her boxes crashed to the ground and split open at her feet.

Felice burst into a wailing cry to match her own. Godshall grinned at her. When Cristina bent toward her boxes, Godshall lifted his dagger. She froze.

"*Mon Dieu*, what have I done?" Godshall asked his friends with a lift of his hands and a wide-eyed grin. They merely smiled, and Cristina realized these were the same men before whom she had embarrassed the spiteful Godshall.

She swallowed. It was too late to wish she'd spoken and acted with more care.

Godshall kicked the contents of her boxes. Wood and clothing scattered. She watched his boots, not his face, nor his blade.

She could not take her eyes from his feet as he crushed her life's work into the muddy puddles in the yard.

Chapter Twenty-four

No matter Durand's intentions of riding into the village after Cristina, the king commanded him and the other barons to Portchester Castle at the head of Portsmouth harbor to inspect the galleys and merchant ships that would transport their force to La Rochelle. The royal castle, about ten miles from Ravenswood, teemed with seaman and soldiers. They, at least, seemed avidly in favor of the offense. Passing through the lengthy bailey of Portchester to the water gate, Durand saw the many masts of John's assembled fleet.

It was best to be here, he decided as he stood with his face to the heavy winds. It allowed some of his anger to wash away.

Durand had never seen so many vessels in one place. The sight of the fleet, composed of both newly made and commandeered merchantmen, reminded him as nothing else could that the matters within his keep were of little weight against those of a king and his kingdom.

Salt air stung Durand's cheeks as he contemplated the caprices of life. Now, when he needed every hour in England to make sense of the coil of his life, God provided the means through unfavorable winds. Were they also responsible for delaying the arrival of William Marshall?

The king's men roamed Portchester's bailey for hours, retiring finally to the hall.

Durand felt little inclination for an indifferent ale. He stood at the water gate and looked out at the ships. Gilles d'Argent came to his side. They watched the angry water slap the stones near their feet and hiss away in a timeless rhythm.

It was prophetic, Durand thought, that d'Argent should seek him out when he most needed an ear.

"My sword did little to aid your efforts, Durand," Gilles said.

" 'Twas the man who wielded it that was inadequate, not the blade." Durand shook his head. "Joseph will return it."

"Keep it," Gilles said. "You may need it another day, and I have others."

Durand bowed in acknowledgment of the fine gift. "The sea gods are discontent," he said. And truly it seemed so in the scudding movement of the green-tinged clouds and whipping winds.

In silent accord, Durand and Gilles walked along the perimeter of the castle walls. "I'm to depart in a few hours for the north."

"To raise more support for John's efforts?"

D'Argent nodded. "Nicholas will go with me."

"Would that I could as well," Durand said lightly, then cleared his throat as he changed the subject. "You wed one of your weavers."

"I wed the woman I *love*," Gilles said, drawing in the

edges of his mantle against the rain that escalated along with the winds. "It matters not what skills she has."

"And you survived a king's wrath." Durand watched a cart lumber by to deliver pigs and geese for the kitchens.

"Richard was not best pleased, but a thousand pounds soon relieved his ire," Gilles said wryly.

"A thousand pounds?" Durand stared at d'Argent.

"Oh, a bride can go for much more when John is concerned in the matter."

"So much?" Durand shook his head. "John already demands a vast amount of me. I can just pay my knight fees."

"You know 'tis John's means of control. He keeps his barons on the edge of penury with fees and taxes. Should you fail to meet your obligations, your lands are forfeit," Gilles said. He crossed his arms on his chest.

"Then to get them back, one must pay again," Durand said. *Or marry where bidden.*

"We are not catching our death in this miserable air that you might seek my advice on your knight fees, are we?" D'Argent smiled, but it did little to relieve the sternness of his dark looks.

"Nay," Durand said, pacing the church steps. "I'm filled with uncertainty. In my hall sits a most comely and well-connected woman—"

"Nona."

"Aye, Nona. She's a pleasant enough woman, but I find I do not think of her from one hour to the next. And in the village is a woman I cannot forget for even one moment."

He shrugged and gave his friend a sheepish grin. "Nona or Cristina? Such are the trials of a well-connected man."

Gilles put out his hands, palms up. He moved them

like a merchant's scales. "Nona and wealth, Aquitaine and Normandy connections. Or Cristina le Gros, accused—but vindicated—thief and herbalist, and probably barren."

Durand straightened. His jaw felt locked. He clenched his fists. "I don't need an heir," he managed. "It seems you have thought on this already."

"Nay, *you* alone think on this. I care not one whit which woman you wed, but I know from previous experience that a *king* will care." Gilles dropped his hands. "I'm merely pointing out what John will think of your choices."

"You did not let a king's thoughts control you."

"Nay. But my king was not named John." Gilles shook his head. "You must do that which sits best here." He prodded Durand in the chest with his finger. "But use this"—he tapped his forehead—"when you do so."

They walked back to the water gate, where their horses were tied.

Durand halted by his mare. "I don't understand why Cristina did not come to me when the queen sent her away."

"Ask her. If I know but one thing about women, it is that they are unaccountable." Gilles shook his head. "You think they'll do one thing, but trust me, they'll do the exact opposite. I've discovered it is best just to ask and then give every indication you think their reasoning right and just."

"And if I don't care for her answer?" Durand swung into the saddle.

Gilles grinned. "I'm not sure that will matter a whit, either."

Durand bid his friend good journey. He envied him the opportunity to escape the king's caprices.

At that thought, the king and a coterie of men rode up. Durand was invited to inspect the royal galley.

With little joy in the task, he joined the king's party being rowed out to board the well-fitted ship that would bear John to France. As was usual with the king, he traveled with every comfort.

Once aboard they toured above and below deck, where the king signed an order to ship all manner of game to La Rochelle, that good hunting would be available when he disembarked.

Durand made another effort to point out the value of treating with Philip. John would not hear.

He sat through a lengthy session with the king on the number of bowmen to accompany them to France and the onerous cost of putting them up in Portsmouth. Eventually Durand found himself alone with the king and seized the opportunity to broach the matter that had been gnawing at him all day.

Nay—from the moment he had joined himself to Cristina.

"Sire, I know 'tis your wish I make a bargain with Nona, but if I might, I have another proposition for your consideration."

King John lifted a brow. "Indeed?"

"Aye. When we are victorious in France, I'll again have possession of Marion's holdings. There will be little need for me to wed Lady Nona. Mayhap there is another who, in an alliance with her, might strengthen your hold in Normandy?"

"What is your reluctance to make this marriage contract?" John asked, leaning closer.

"I would prefer to avoid the shackles of a wife at this time," Durand said carefully.

The king smiled. "Can you not think of the bonds of marriage as aught else than shackles? We find 'tis more a silken cord that binds one."

"If the bride is one such as our queen, then aye, sire, it may be so."

"Did your marriage to Marion so serve you ill that

you would avoid another?" the king persisted.

" 'Tis more that I served Marion ill," Durand said. "It is not the bond I object to, but the one with whom I'll find myself sharing it."

The king's dark, quick eyes met his. "Hmmm." He rose and walked to a table spread with maps, duplicates of those he hourly pored over at Ravenswood. "Take a mistress, if that is your need, and we'll speak to Nona so that she is properly compliant with your needs. We're sure Marion would have understood had she lived."

A small spark of anger sprang to life, but Durand tamped it down. "Marion was not so *compliant* as you suppose."

The king inspected his hand. His jeweled rings glittered in the light of the many candles illuminating his maps. "Marion was a most agreeable woman, was she not? Willing to serve in any humble way she could? Or so it seemed." The air in the small space crackled with tension.

Durand carefully thought on his words before speaking. "Marion best loved to serve you, sire."

A smile kicked up one corner of the king's mouth. "Marion served her king well," he said. "Would that you might do the same."

Durand realized that the previous summer he had summoned together all those whom Marion most favored. Which man had served *her*? And torn his pride to shreds?

Penne, who Marion oft reminded him had been her first choice?

Luke, whose lighthearted manner filled her with amusement?

Or the king?

Marion was beyond his reach. These men were not.

Durand cleared his throat and took an iron grip on his desire to wipe the clever smile from the king's

305

face. He was but a small man after all. Petty in his amusements. "I seek only to serve you, sire."

The king took a seat by him. He slipped a ring from his finger. "Here is a small token to give to Lady Nona. Use it to seal your troth in my service as you both love and serve me."

The ring was cold in Durand's hand. He now had two rings—much as Simon had. Had he any more honor than the thief?

" 'Tis time we spoke of a price for your goodwill, de Marle." John smiled and leaned back in his chair. "Shall we set it at forfeiture of all you—and Nona—hold, should your duty fail you?"

Durand rose. The deck beneath his feet rocked with the escalation of the winds. It symbolized how he felt when dealing with John—it was always an insecure, rocky venture. "Sire." He bowed and turned away, the ring gripped tightly in his palm. On deck, he threw back the edges of his mantle and put his face to the wind. It scoured his cheeks, but he welcomed the burn.

So if he desired Cristina, he could have her as a mistress only, and with Lady Nona's tacit agreement if the king demanded it. When faced with forfeiture, Nona, too, would concede to whatever the king desired.

Forfeiture. As he and Gilles had discussed, it was a common threat of the king's to keep his barony in tow. To jeopardize one's own possessions was one thing; to do so with another's was sinful. Nona was innocent in all of this.

The ride back to Ravenswood was made in silence, Penne and Luke at his side, his men in a trailing line behind him. His brother and friend made no effort to engage him in conversation. When they reached the road to the castle, Durand stopped for a moment to consider the fearsome sight of Simon, nearly unrecog-

nizable. He served as a warning to all who might journey to Ravenswood of the penalty of crime.

Had Cristina seen him? There would be no need to
pass this way to reach the village, but if her escort
was cruel, they might take this way with simple excuses about muddy roads. Who would offer her
strength to endure such a sight?

Durand reined in his horse. "I have business in the
village. Luke, see that all is in readiness for the king's
amusement this night should he tire of Portchester."

Luke frowned. "You cannot think to stay the night
in the village? What excuse do we offer if anyone asks
after you?"

Penne's mare danced, and he circled until he drew
to Durand's other side. Durand was hemmed in. Penne
gripped his arm. "You are making a foolish mistake."

"What mistake is that? And who are you to question
what I'm to do? Have not each of you trespassed
where you should not?"

A blank look of incomprehension overspread
Penne's face. Luke's blotched an ugly red. He opened
his mouth, then shut it.

Durand knew in that moment that he should not
suspect the king—or Penne. The truth was written so
clearly on Luke's face. It was he who had fathered
Felice. An icy cold filled Durand.

Penne glanced from one brother to another, then
looked pointedly toward Durand's men. "This is no
way to conduct ourselves." He placed his horse between the two brothers. "We must return to the keep
and make the most of what little time we have left. We
could be dead on the morrow and should not have
this between us."

Durand edged his horse between the two men and
rode off. His mare kicked up clots of mud, which splattered his mantle's hem and the horse's belly. When
he reached the cottage so recently inhabited by

Simon le Gros, he saw that a thin thread of smoke rose from the chimney.

He tried in vain to sort out the emotions of his discovery.

He had lied to Cristina. When she had asked him what he would do if someone betrayed him, he had said he would run him through.

But he could never raise a sword against Luke.

Luke was tied to him regardless of their love or hate for one another. He could do as John's royal siblings had through the years and cut Luke off without land or monetary consideration. And what reason could he give for such action? Not the truth. That would announce his cuckoldry to all. It would be a very public humiliation.

It was well that Marion was out of his reach.

The cottage, despite the smoking chimney, looked deserted. No groom ran out to tend his mount. Split crates and indistinguishable goods were trampled on the muddy ground before the door.

His ravens, who like most captive birds rarely strayed beyond the food provided them, stalked among the ruined goods as if inspecting them. It was an omen—of what he knew not.

Cristina came to stand at the door, Felice in her arms. The front of her gown, from bodice to hem, was damp. Sweat plastered tendrils of hair to her brow.

She raised her fine dark eyes to his. An instant heat coursed through him.

Luke and Marion . . . they no longer mattered—not this day, nor this hour. One thing was clear to him, though he must keep it to himself.

This woman was all he wanted or needed.

"What are you doing here?" Cristina asked in a tart voice.

"What happened?" Durand swung his leg across the front of his horse and slid from the saddle. The ravens scattered. He went down on his haunches and picked about the ruined boxes.

"A rope split and my boxes fell off the packhorse." There was no welcome in her manner.

He plucked a length of twine from the mire. "This end is cleanly cut, Cristina."

She shrugged. "I must take the babe in by the fire."

"Might I join you?"

"Nay! We're by the road, my lord, and any who pass would see your horse."

"Then I'll stable my horse, Cristina. I imagine I still remember how."

Cristina opened her mouth, then shut it and shrugged. She rested her cheek on Felice's head.

"What's going on here?" He could not help the anger coloring his voice.

Was he really angry at her—or at Luke?

"What, my lord?" Her voice dripped the vinegar of a sour wine. "The queen commanded me. Was I to say her nay? She pointed out quite clearly that Lady Nona was to be mistress of Ravenswood and any other *mistress* was a burden. Surely you know that? You do know all that transpires at Ravenswood, do you not?"

"I think I know more of Philip's court than my own keep." His mount sensed his agitation and danced in place, the heavy hooves clomping near the devastation of her boxes. "And so you took Felice and hastened here?"

Her face softened and she kissed Felice's head. "The queen had me escorted here. So convict me only of protecting myself, my lord. Is there aught more I could have done?"

"You could have come to me," he said gently.

How much was betrayed in those simple words?

His desire for her. Her distance from him.

She dropped her gaze and shook her head. "I thought you approved."

"Approved?" The memories of her body beneath his were too raw and immediate for him to be less than completely honest. He could not deceive her—or himself. The power lay with the king, and some with him, but none lay with her.

Anger died, to be replaced by some other emotion that she had not sought him out and laid her cares at his feet.

"I knew nothing of the queen's scheme." He shifted his attention back to her belongings. "Will you tell me who did this?"

When she did not answer, he pointed to the ruined plants crushed in the yard. "I find myself uncommonly talented in naming these plants. Lavender there. Violets. Roses." Then his gaze swung back to her. "And I am also uncommonly talented in reading the tale in little evidence. This was no accident. Now what happened here?"

Only silence met his query—a very stubborn silence. He knew her well enough now to know she would be silent only to protect someone. In this case he suspected she was protecting him. She probably thought he would dash off with drawn sword and try to exact a punishment. She was right.

He unhooked the heavy purse at his belt and held it out. "Then I shall ferret it out on my own. Replace what is lost and keep what remains for the care of the child."

"For the care of *the* child?" She stepped toward him. Despite the rain, fire snapped in her eyes and words. "For the care of your child! *Your* child. When will you acknowledge her? She may have caused your wife's death, she may be naught but a female, yet she is *your* child. You are responsible for her, and she is precious! Would that I had such a daughter!"

Her words smote him with the force of any weapon

a man might wield. "Go inside, Cristina, ere you become chilled."

Her mouth opened, then closed with a snap. She turned and crossed to the cottage door. He led his mare to the stable and groomed the horse, using the time to contemplate what he must say to her.

Offering the purse had been clumsy.

Durand skirted her muddy belongings and entered the cottage.

She stirred a small cauldron bubbling at the hearth. "What are you cooking?" he asked. He draped his muddy mantle over a bench and placed his gauntlets on the hearth stones to dry.

"I am washing clothes, my lord."

"With such a curious smell, I am thankful 'tis not supper." He grinned, but she did not react to his jest.

Cristina had no humor left. She could not tell him she had naught left but the gown she stood up in. The rest was irreparably stained with the mud of the stable-yard. She had not even a penny to purchase some of the fine lengths of cloth on Simon's shelves to remedy the situation.

That fact made it doubly hard to refuse Durand's purse.

Durand sat on the floor by a thick sheepskin on which Felice lay. "You're the only one to take me to task for my neglect of her." He prodded Felice in the belly with his finger. Her limbs kicked the air. The babe was a living reminder that Marion had sought comfort or love in someone else's arms. But it was time he ceased to blame her for what was none of her doing. "I will leave the purse for *my* daughter's care."

Cristina's dazzling smile amply rewarded him; then she ducked her head and plied the wooden paddle in the wash.

Her gown clung to her body from the heavy, damp

311

heat. He cleared his throat. "Your calling me to account is but one thing I admire in you," he said.

A light blush colored her cheeks. "What have I done, my lord, but state what you already knew?" She used her stick to lift some article of clothing and drop it from the boiling pot to a barrel of cool water.

"You stood by your marriage vows, despite what I imagine was a powerful dislike and sense of shame."

"Dislike?" Cristina wiped the sweat from her brow with the back of her hand. She removed the leather thong holding her hair back. He watched her lift her hair and let the air cool her neck. The action raised her full breasts and drew his gaze to the long line of her neck. The simple action aroused him.

She pulled her hair over one shoulder and said, "I wanted to run at every moment. But he was my sworn husband . . . and my only hope of a family."

"You wanted that so much? A family?" Durand watched her intently.

"I have wanted nothing else. You cannot understand, I am sure, what it is to have no children—to wish and pray for them, but have the prayers go unanswered." She looked down at Felice, and her expression softened. "A child loves you without condition."

"Only a child can love in such a manner," he said gently.

"Aye." She returned to her work.

He changed the painful subject by returning to a count of her strengths. "And you stood without flinching whilst those of lesser honor accused you of theft."

This time she merely shrugged. "What else could I do?"

"Your head was high. You did not allow your spirits to falter. Some men are not so brave."

"Some men would offer to stir this pot," she said with a smile.

He got to his feet and took the stick from her. She worked at rinsing the garment she had removed from the boiling water. Sweat broke on his brow as he swirled his stick through the soapy washwater. "I would not want to do this each day," he said.

"Remember that when you muddy your hem." She pointed at his mantle.

"Aye. I'll give my women a penny each when I return, lest they curse me over their washtubs."

With a soft laugh she pulled the garment from the rinsewater and wrung it out. Then she shook it and draped it over a rope she had strung across the end of the cottage storage area.

Durand recognized the garment from their time together in the west tower. The soft linen shift was so sheer it did little to conceal her sweet form. Now it was blotched with dark stains. He strode to the garment and lifted it, spreading it out that he might see it more clearly. "I was most fond of this shift. What happened?"

" 'Twas in the box that fell from the horse."

"Cristina," Durand said, placing his hands on her shoulders. How small and delicate she was. He almost asked her again who had destroyed her belongings, but realized he could easily discover who had escorted her here. She was protecting him from something. "If you say 'tis how it happened, then 'tis how it happened."

"I want no more trouble." Her eyes entreated him to let it rest.

"And I want you to take Felice and go. Mayhap to Winchester or to one of your family."

Her shoulders went stiff. "Take Felice?"

He gently massaged her shoulders. "Aye. If you remain here, you and Felice will be pawns to the royal pleasure. I want to know that you both are settled whilst I am in France. I know that in your loving hands,

313

Felice will be safe. When you are gone, you will be quickly forgotten by those who might wish you ill." His hands were magic.

"The king will not forget so valuable a child," she said.

"For a while he will," he assured her. "He'll have a kingdom to consider, not a child and her nurse. I'll be better able to direct Felice's future when this foray against Philip is over."

She wanted to shout with laughter. Durand could not know of the king's proposition or he would not be sending her into his snare at Winchester.

Durand soothed the aches and pains of hurts both inside and out. A mad urge to lean back into his arms swept over her.

Cristina stepped away from him instead. "The queen also wishes a say in Felice's future. Now, excuse me, my lord. I-I . . . have something I must do," she said, but did not wait upon his pardon.

She climbed the ladder to the second story. After rummaging in her meager belongings, she found what she wanted. But before she could lift the vial to her lips, Durand appeared on the ladder.

In a lithe leap he was on her, dashing the vial to the floor. "*Jesu!* What are you doing?"

Cristina stared down at the small wet stain on the wooden floor, then looked up at him, a stricken look upon her face.

He gripped her shoulders and shook her. "What was it? Poison?"

She covered her lips with her fingertips and her face paled. "Poison?" She shook her head. "You misunderstand."

"Sweet heaven. Explain it to me then."

"I must see to Felice," she said, and broke out of his embrace. He caught her at the ladder.

He put himself between her and the way down.

"She'll make herself known; doubt it not. Now explain what you were doing." He held out the vial.

Sorrow flitted across her face before she spoke. "I was resisting you."

Chapter Twenty-five

"What?" Durand dropped his hands to his sides. The vial slipped from his fingers to roll away. "You were resisting me?"

Cristina snatched up a length of linen, knelt, and wiped away the wet stain. "Aye, 'tis a simple matter to make a resistance potion. Any good herbalist can do it."

Durand shook his head and paced about the small sleeping space surrounded by stores and goods from cloth to casks of pickled herring. "You were resisting me. *Mon Dieu*. Would that you had made such a potion for me weeks ago."

She sat back on her heels and dropped the cloth, her expression stricken.

"I can still do so, my lord." The words were like thorns on her tongue.

"Nay, resistance is not what I desire." He raked his hands through his hair. "I thought you had poison.

316

That you wanted to end . . . What is the matter with me? You, of all women, do not lack courage."

He extended his hand. Hers was cool and smooth in his. He pulled her to her feet. They stood there, hands clasped. "Do you truly wish to resist me?" he asked softly.

In answer she tugged her hand away and headed for the ladder. He followed her down. Felice lay nestled in her sheepskin, eyes closed, lips moving as if she suckled in her sleep.

"You have not answered me," Durand said when Cristina took up her stick and stirred the laundry with great vigor. "Do you want to resist me?"

She sighed and looked at him over the rising steam. "Verily, you are not the smartest man in Christendom, are you?"

Her insult made him grin. "Lest I completely shame myself, let me guess why you felt a need to drink a resistance potion."

All signs of amusement left his face. Cristina thought him the finest man she had ever seen. Every line of his face, from his stubborn jaw to his noble nose, reminded her that his birth and ancestors destined him for another, worthier woman.

Durand pulled the paddle from her hand and cast it aside. "You took a resistance potion because you are as hopelessly bewitched by me as I am by you. But, in truth, you do not want to resist this thing between us any more than I."

She shook her bowed head.

He folded her into his embrace. The back of her gown was damp beneath his hands. "The king has plans for me, else you would be mine, claimed this instant, part of my body and blood."

How his words touched her with joy and equally with sorrow.

"I understand," she said, the words barely making

317

it past her tongue. "You must act for your sons, as all barons do."

"I did not speak lightly when I said you're to take Felice and go. Besides the king and queen there is someone here who aided Simon, and that person is still unknown. Until I return, I will not rest easy with you here unprotected. I shall have Father Laurentius arrange everything so that your days shall be filled with joy. Never will you want for anything from now until the day you die."

He did not understand. There would be no joy without him. And that thought pierced the shield about her heart.

She squeezed his waist and rubbed her nose on his chest. "We will miss you." How little the words meant when she wanted to cry out at the unfairness of it all.

He tipped up her chin. "I spoke to the king in hopes he might find Lady Nona another husband. He did not look kindly on my wish to be shed of her. In truth there are many who might make a fine match for her, but John will use this as a stick to beat me into submission. Should I refuse to wed Lady Nona, John will seize both her property and mine."

Cristina went to the window and threw open the shutters. The rain had stopped, but the sky was still filled with clouds. The view was not the heady one from the high towers of Ravenswood, but still, it soothed her.

He had no choice but to wed Lady Nona. The fact that he had tried to slip from the king's plans polished some of the raw edge off her pain.

She looked over her shoulder at Felice. She knew it was likely that the babe would wake when it was least propitious, but she wanted this last moment with him.

He went to her and hugged her, but loosely. His heart beat with a slow thud against her cheek.

"We have said this before," she began. "And if I had

drunk the potion, I might not say it now, and yet each time I mean it." Cristina leaned back to see his expression. Her heart raced. "I wish with all my heart that we might . . . That is . . ."

"Just once more," he finished for her, then settled his lips on hers. Every fiber of his being flashed hot when she moved her body against his. He kissed down the damp line of her throat and chest, down her middle until he knelt before her.

He ran his hands up the backs of her legs to her hips as his mouth pressed to the apex of her thighs.

To do just this, on her skin, to breathe her essence, to rub his cheek against the smooth skin of her belly, would be paradise.

She crumpled to the floor, her skirts at her waist. He touched a kiss to the tender flesh on the inside of her knee.

"Durand." His name was sweet on her lips. "Undress for me. I want to feel your body against mine."

He did as bidden and watched her as she also disrobed. He spread his tunic on the floor.

"Now," she whispered, and put out her hand.

But he shook his head in denial of her request. There was something raging within him, something so frantic that if he let it loose, he might harm her.

He took her hand and guided it to his hot flesh. "Touch me," he said. She made a soft, breathy sound in her throat. Her fingers curled about him.

He whispered, conscious of his daughter, who slumbered so close by. "What more can a man wish than to lie with the woman who is all he desires?"

The full, ripe shape of her body drew him with unmerciful need. Her hand was no longer gentle. She urged and inflamed.

"There is no resistance potion strong enough to combat this," he said against the smooth skin of her shoulder. Shocks of sensation cascaded from his belly to his feet. He floated on the edge of madness, saved only when she let him go.

She fisted her hands in his hair and arched to the kiss he placed on her breast, then lower and lower to her inner thigh. Her body bloomed with the scent and heat of passion's thrall.

When his lips moved to the core of her, she gave a sharp exclamation, bitten off before it escalated to more.

He breathed the heady scent of her and licked up the sweet essence that would envelop him and ease his way.

"Durand." She gasped when he moved up her body.

Her nails bit into his arms as he thrust into her heat. For several long moments he held himself still, gazing into her eyes, combing her hair from her brow, examining the precious face that would soon be seen only in his memories. "How can just once be enough?" he asked.

"You rule my heart, my lord," she said. Tears slipped from her eyes. He lapped them with his tongue and then drew their moisture across her trembling lips.

Her heart raced against his hand when he placed his palm to her breast. "As much as I thought I knew of making love . . ." He gasped as her hips lifted beneath him. "Yet until you . . . I knew nothing of being loved," he said.

With an iron will, he held himself in check against a quick end, knowing it would be their last. As slowly as if he measured precious gold, he slid in and then out of her. Her hands roamed his back, buttocks, hips, shoulders, and hair. She whispered his name again and again along with indistinguishable sounds of suppressed passion.

"Hold nothing from me, Cristina."

He thought his heart might cease its beat when she

pulled his head near and whispered to him. "I love you," she said so softly he thought he might have dreamed it.

Then she gasped, her thighs tightening on his hips. She had found her pleasure. Still, he waited. He fought a need to move, to give in to it, until each pulse of her body had stilled.

When she settled beneath him, he rose over her. Outside the window, a thrum of raven's wings beat time to the pulse of his release.

Chapter Twenty-six

Cristina woke to the inky shadows of early morn. Opening the shutters, she saw that stars filled the sky outside. It was clear. A fine day for sailing.

The open window allowed an eddy of air to sweep out the scent of boiled clothing. Returning to where Durand lay on their piled clothing, she placed Felice between them and fed her. He woke and smiled. Gently he skimmed his fingertips across the babe's cheek to her breast and back again.

She reached out and linked her fingers with his.

"Could you be a mistress?" he asked.

She knew why he asked. A noble woman ofttimes tolerated her husband's concubines.

She shook her head. "I could never share you. When I was tied to Simon, I could pretend what I felt for you was just desire, though you filled my thoughts day and night, but now . . . Nay, I could never share you. I am possessive of my love. It pains me that you could so easily do so—"

He rose on his elbow and interrupted her. "Nothing about this is easy. Most especially this parting." He then rubbed his hand over his face. "Neither of us would be content with such an arrangement, but I had to ask."

Felice stirred between them at the rising voices over her.

"Is that what all men do when passion claws, Durand? Take a mistress?" She wished that she could see his face clearly.

"I have never taken a mistress, for in truth, I thought I had all I desired at Ravenswood." He leaned over and kissed her. "Now I still have all I desire right here, yet out of reach."

His kisses were gentle, but filled her with a longing she knew would go unfulfilled.

"I'm sorry, Cristina, that I made such a ruin of your life."

She gripped his hand. "None of this is your fault!"

"Aye, I must admit that I brought you the Aelfric to tempt you. I may not have realized it when I fetched it, but the result was the same."

She smoothed her fingers along his furrowed brows. "I was tempted ere you brought the book, and Simon, I fear, was tempted by riches and women long before we came to Ravenswood. He chose to steal the book. Please do not leave me with regrets."

He enfolded her in his arms, the babe between them, and kissed them both. "If I can regain Marion's properties then I have no need to wed, and might yet convince the king of such."

Cristina said nothing. She knew in her heart that even if he regained the properties, he would never be hers. If the king agreed to release him from marriage to Nona, still he would not then allow him to align himself to a penniless woman.

"Had I no children, I would give all I possess to Luke and have him marry Nona!"

The trees became outlined against the brightening sky. "You must go, Durand. Now. Ere your men seek you."

Her words worked a devastating magic. He stood up. She could just distinguish the beautiful lines of his body as he drew on his clothing.

There were no words to capture what lay in her heart. And if there were, she did not know them. Instead, when he knelt by her and stroked his fingers along her cheek, she turned her head and kissed his palm.

"Bar the door when I leave and expect some of my men to arrive shortly; I'll not have you here alone. And look for Father Laurentius—he'll have charge of your care," he reminded her.

Awkwardly he bent down and kissed the sleeping babe's head, then cupped Cristina's cheek. "I have desired you from the first moment I saw you, but I think I fell in love watching you care for Felice."

Then he was gone.

As she lay there, the whitewashed ceiling overhead blurred with her tears. Outside, his horse snorted and shook with a harsh jangle of harness when led from the stable. She hastily rose to her feet and ran to the window, Felice in her arms, to catch a final glimpse of him as he rode off.

Durand mounted and turned his horse to face the cottage. As if he could see her in the shadows, he lifted his gloved hand.

Low mist lay across the ground. Morning stars filled the sky. The wind was fresh and would blow the fog away. He would sail to Normandy, and she would never see him again.

"Go with God," she whispered when he was lost in the dawn mist.

Durand shifted in the saddle as he pushed the horse to a quicker pace. Every muscle of his body still ached from combat, exacerbated by a night on a hard wooden floor. He watched the dawn blush conceal the stars. How clear the day would be.

How clear everything seemed in such air.

He must somehow have Cristina as his wife. He wanted to watch her move about a chamber in the light of a fire. He wanted to call her to him and see her face light with pleasure.

He wanted to know that such a woman valued him.

There must be an answer to this coil. He had all of his time in Normandy to think of a way out of marriage to Nona. What if her father could be persuaded the match was an ill-conceived venture? He could don a reputation as a drunken lout so that no father would have him. . . . Nay, many a father in search of a wealthy connection would give away a daughter no matter the man's reputation.

He cantered straight to the chapel. Dismounting, he threw open the door and stood there, hands on hips. He saw Father Laurentius, head close with Father Odo. With great impatience he waited for the two holy men to notice him.

Laurentius saw him first. "Thank God, my lord. The king was quite piqued to find you 'missing' last night. He wants you joined with Nona ere you leave for France." The priest hurried toward him, his already austere features pinched with anxiety.

A fire ignited in Durand's chest. "Now? What in all of God's kingdom is served by that?"

"Your cooperation, I'm sure, my lord. Last night John said he was sailing today whether William Marshall was back or not, and three barons balked over the decision. Now come. Let us wake the lady and see to the business. I do dearly wish to get back to Winchester."

"I need a moment," Durand said, extricating his arm from Laurentius's sharp grip.

He walked to the fore of the chapel and sank to his knees. The two priests would never disturb a man at prayer. Clasping his hands, he set his mind to a scheme to prevent this hasty wedding.

When he finally arose, the two priests waved anxiously for him to go. "Come, come, we must see to the wedding," Laurentius said.

Durand shook them off. "Delay in some way." He strode to the chapel doors.

"But my lord! Where shall we say you are?" Father Odo called.

"Tallying up my bridal gifts," he replied as he stepped from the chapel into the clear, fine day.

Nona's delicate features were pinched with anxiety. She stood in the counting room, Luke by her side. Her hair was down, her rich blue gown in disarray. It was obvious she had been given as little time to compose herself before the wedding as he.

"Leave us, Luke," Durand said. When would he ever look upon his brother without cold anger coursing through him?

"Durand," Luke began, "there is something I must tell you."

"Luke, if you don't leave within the next few moments, I'll tear your head from your shoulders, spit it, and roast it."

Lady Nona gasped. Her hand went to her throat. Luke said nothing. His face flushed to the roots of his hair. "As you wish," he finally said. He bowed to Nona and walked stiffly to the door.

"Set a guard," Durand ordered.

"As you wish," his brother repeated coldly, and left.

"Sit, my lady." Durand gestured to the hearth bench. "Father Laurentius informs me the king wants our wedding to take place ere we sail today."

She nodded. Her fingers were tightly woven together. "My lord, I—"

He interrupted her. "I don't care what you think of what I'm about to say, but I ask simply that you hear me out."

"I will hear you, my lord, but then I ask that you hear me."

"Certainly." He nodded. "You come from an illustrious family, and any man would be flattered to be aligned with it. But I find I have enough ancestors and alliances already, and, having so recently suffered the loss of a wife, I don't yet wish to wed."

"I beg your pardon?" Lady Nona's mouth dropped open.

"However, as much as I do not wish to wed, the king has demanded the forfeiture of all you own, and all I own, should we refuse this match. 'Tis my belief that he'll care much less about it if he's victorious in Normandy. Therefore I ask that you cooperate in a scheme to put off the wedding until we return."

Durand watched Nona open her mouth and close it several times. She must feel like unwanted baggage.

"What scheme is that, my lord?" she finally managed. "I have no wish to be consigned to the king's dungeons or a convent for reluctant brides."

"This is not a time for levity," Durand said sharply. "I ask that we postpone the wedding. Should John still insist when we return, then I'll honor the bargain."

"Thank you, my lord."

Durand thought he detected a touch of vinegar in her tone. If she was insulted that he did not treasure the match, that was unfortunate, but unavoidable.

"The scheme is this—you will become gravely ill, so

327

ill you cannot possibly wed. Your illness will be a catching one, and you'll remain ill until our return."

An incredulous look overspread her face. "What if the campaign takes months?"

Durand frowned. "Then rally and sink a few times. Surely you can devise something suitable?"

"How will I effect this illness, my lord? Aldwin might see through the scheme."

"Refuse Aldwin. Ask for Mistress le Gros instead."

Nona rose stiffly to her feet. "Mistress le Gros? Is that what this is about? I much admire the lady, but I'll not tolerate your mistresses. Is that clear?"

He stood up as well. "If you are not wed to me, you will not have to tolerate anything. And *I* will not tolerate any discussion of Mistress le Gros; is that clear?" He fisted his hands on his hips. "Now what was it you needed to tell me?"

"Nothing, my lord," Nona said, subsiding to the bench.

"Nothing."

The king's face suffused to a dusky purple as he stormed before the hearth. The hall was crowded with men awaiting the king's pleasure and the tides. His fingers curled like claws. "Nona is ill? Near to death?"

Durand muttered a hasty prayer for forgiveness for his lies, then said, " 'Tis more a question of her spreading her illness to you, sire, at this most vital time."

Father Laurentius added the weight of his support now that the weight of his purse had doubled. "I have seen this before, sire. Once it gets among us, we will all be fighting for seats in the jakes. No one will be fit to sit a saddle."

"No more!" the king shouted. He roamed the hearth

area. He had been ranting over every petty annoyance since dawn, according to Laurentius.

Roger Godshall joined the king and murmured at his ear as he paced back and forth. Durand knew Godshall had wreaked the havoc on Cristina's possessions. It had taken but one question of a trusted groom. He silently added Godshall to his list of those who deserved retribution for Cristina's pain.

Finally the king halted. "We are seriously vexed," the king said. Godshall stood with him. The king pointed at Durand. "You had better pray Lady Nona rallies ere we return or you will greatly regret it."

He next swung his attention to a trio of men who stood near, barons who had balked at this Normandy invasion. "You'll each offer a son as surety of your service."

Offer? Durand knew it was just the king's way of saying the men would give up their sons as hostages. Should the fathers prove disloyal, the sons would suffer for it.

Durand watched one man, Guy Wallingford, step bravely forward. There was a tremor in his voice when he spoke. "Please, sire—"

"Silence," the king shouted. "You will offer a son. Anything else can only mean you do not love your king."

Wallingford bowed and retreated to the group. They had all seen the king in a rage before and knew they had little influence to halt it.

"And you," the king said, swinging back to Durand. "Where were you last eventide when we wanted you?"

Before Durand could answer, the king continued. "You, too, shall offer a son. Nay, two sons, as you are of twice the importance of these leeching dogs."

Two sons.

An icy finger touched Durand's soul.

"Get to Portchester—now," the king ordered.

* * *

Nothing would prevent this hapless venture, Durand thought as he rode into the inner bailey of Portchester Castle with the king and his entourage. But there on the keep steps stood one who might. William Marshall—a man revered and honored by three kings.

"William, you don't appear ready to make this journey," the king said when the customary civilities were rendered.

"I cannot go, sire," Marshall said.

A hush fell over the groups of men. Save the carters moving goods to Portchester's water gate, no one spoke.

"Explain yourself." The king fisted one hand on his sword hilt.

Durand imagined that Marshall felt as beleaguered as any other man who must deal with this capricious king.

Marshall sighed. "You sent me to attempt peace with Philip. Whilst there I found I had no choice but to swear liege homage to him. I cannot take arms against him."

Durand watched the king's face darken. His fingers curled on his reins. Liege homage meant Marshall was John's man while in England and Philip's while in France. He could take up the sword against neither of them. It was a move that left the king without the arms of the greatest warrior England had known.

"You protected your properties! Not our interests!" the king raged. Durand thought the king would draw his sword and smite the old warrior.

"Nay, sire. I did as you directed—made peace with Philip."

"To your benefit! Not ours!"

"For all our benefits." Marshall swept a hand out to encompass the other barons. The barons with hostage children moved fractionally toward Marshall.

The king's face turned almost purple. He sat tall in the saddle, his body stiff, and addressed them all. "Are you with me or with Marshall?" John's voice was low and deceptively calm.

Durand felt as if he were being drawn and quartered. He forced himself to think only of Adrian and Robert. With silent watchfulness, he remained where he was, at the king's side. Penne and Luke trotted to where he waited. Then all the king's bachelors aligned themselves behind the king.

The king did not turn to Durand or his brother or friend. He turned to Godshall and his cronies. "What is your belief? Is Marshall in company against me?"

The young men who found their way by the king's favor concurred with him. Alone, however, they had not the means to defeat King Philip in either men or machinery.

Durand had no need to think on his words should he need to choose between William Marshall or the king.

He was never asked.

William Marshall stood immovably with the other barons against the king's departure.

Abruptly the king wheeled his horse and rode off through Portchester's bailey toward the water gate. His young men followed him.

"Where do we stand now?" Penne asked.

"Right here," Durand said. "He is likely to return in a few minutes, and we will need to be ready to embark. But without the support of the great William Marshall, this effort is doomed."

And I am doomed to pursue it for my sons' sakes.

"I'm back to Ravenswood," Luke said.

Durand found himself alone in Portchester's hall, awaiting the king's pleasure. Hours passed. When the tide turned, a king's guard rode up to where he and his own men waited.

"The king is for Winchester. He'll remain there until he decides what to do with William Marshall."

Durand wearily shook his head.

"Should we go to Winchester?" Penne asked.

"Nay. The king has to return here to embark," Durand said.

"We could return to Ravenswood and sleep in our own beds," Penne said.

"And have John return to discover I'm not awaiting his pleasure?" Durand asked. "Nay, I'll not put my sons at such risk." And in truth, he no longer cared where he slept.

Durand placed his pallet in a small chamber off Portchester's hall. He lay awake. No matter how many arguments he gave himself against it, he came back again and again to the same thoughts—to take Cristina and Felice and go after his sons. It meant the forfeiture of all he had, and might put a price on his head. But he could not allow his sons to be used in such a manner.

Someone pounded on his chamber door. He struggled heavily to his feet, exhausted from combat and lack of sleep.

Penne threw himself into Durand's arms. Behind him, torches flickered in their iron brackets and cast his friend's face in demonic shadow.

"What is it?" Durand tried in vain to break from Penne's fierce embrace. "Come. What is it?"

Penne took a shuddering breath and stepped back. He retained his hold on Durand's arms. "A messenger came. Adrian . . . Robert."

Whatever Durand had expected to hear, it was not his sons' names. "Penne." He shook his friend. "Make sense!"

"The king ordered Guy Wallingford's son hanged."

"Sweet *Jesu*," Durand whispered, staggering back as if struck.

Penne could only nod. "The messenger said Guy was deep in his cups, as was the king. They argued over William Marshall's pledge to Philip." Penne gulped. "And the king . . . h-he flew into a rage. When Guy did not back down, the king . . . he ordered Guy's son hanged."

Durand fell onto a bench. His stomach churned. "De Warre fostered Guy's son, did he not?"

"Aye. The king will do whatever he needs to see his plans carried out. You cannot say one word against him, do you understand? Nothing. Hold your thoughts to yourself."

Durand looked up at Penne. "I can keep my council." His mouth was dry. He licked his lips.

"Aye, most times, but when you're angry . . . John will return on the morrow. He'll demand you display your loyalty; I know it. Make no false steps, else Adrian and Robert—"

"—will be hanged," Durand finished for Penne.

Chapter Twenty-seven

Cristina raked out the herb garden behind the cottage and rescued a few vegetables for a pottage with which to feed the men Durand had sent to guard her. She sat on the bench in the sun and watched the road. Would Durand ride by? Or was he gone to Normandy with the morning tide?

A clatter of horses made her rise. The queen and her ladies, Sabina among them, rode into her yard. Durand's men went forward to greet their queen. Cristina dropped Isabelle a deep curtsy.

"You're still here?" Lady Sabina looked down her sharp nose.

"I'm making plans," Cristina answered carefully. Father Laurentius had come with the guards and detailed a plan that would keep her well cared for all her days. Laurentius had said it was merely a safeguard should she not be able to sell her soaps and sweet scents. It helped to know Lord Durand would never let her starve.

"And you still have Felice, I see." Lady Sabina lifted a gloved hand and pointed to the sling Cristina wore.

Cristina dipped a small curtsy in answer.

"You'll take the child to Rose, the baker's sister. Then you'll depart this place. You try the queen's patience."

There was no expression on the queen's young face. Her ladies smirked or outwardly smiled. Sabina, garbed as finely as the queen in a gray gown stitched with silver thread, patted her palfrey's neck and gave Cristina a tight smile.

"If 'tis the queen's will," Cristina said.

The queen inclined her head, then lifted her hand, and the party cantered down the road toward Portsmouth.

For several long moments Cristina could not breathe. She was aware of the warmth of Felice's body against hers and of the cool breezes on her cheek.

This, then, was how it would end.

Rose took a sleeping Felice from her arms and placed her in the basket. The woman's small cottage in the village was warm and scented with roasting partridge, spitted over the hearth. Rose's babe lay on a pallet in the corner. Her husband sat at a table, a delighted expression on his face. Lord Durand's child represented a great increase in their income, in addition to which, the queen had sent the family a fat purse.

"She'll like it 'ere just fine. You watch; she'll settle soon enough," Rose said.

Cristina fought her tears and held out her shawl. "This surely carries my scent. Keep her in the sling, which is familiar, and I'm sure when she is hungry enough, and tired—"

335

"Leave 'er to me," Rose said, rising and embracing Cristina. "My man and I'll do just fine by 'er."

"Parsley will encourage your milk," she instructed. Then, when there was no more to be said, and she could not insult Rose by repeating herself yet again, she gave Felice a final kiss and squeeze and tore herself away.

The long walk back to the cottage seemed to last forever. She hardly noticed her surroundings. Durand's men bowed to her as if she were a fine lady, but she barely registered their presence.

The hearth fire was low, and after she built it up she sat there and stared into the flames. She was, for the first time in her life, completely alone. She had no one to care for . . . and no one to care for her.

She almost did not hear the tap at her door, and felt little energy to speak to anyone. It was surely just another man seeking the potion she had made for Luke.

"Lady Oriel," Cristina said when the door revealed her visitor.

"May I?" Oriel asked.

With a listless nod, Cristina stepped back and allowed Oriel to sweep forward into the cottage.

"Have you heard?" Oriel asked, wrapping an arm about Cristina's waist.

"My lady?"

"Durand's sons are made hostage with de Warre. He can make no false steps or the boys will be hanged."

"Hanged?" Cristina staggered in Oriel's embrace. "Hanged?"

Oriel burst into tears. "We thought 'twas just another of John's threats, but he has ordered Guy Wallingford's son hanged as an example." She looked at the window. "It must be done by now," she said softly.

They stood there in silence for a brief moment; then

Oriel began to tremble. "I don't want to remain alone whilst Penne is gone. I'm sick each morning."

"Oh, my lady. Are you with child? Did the potion work?"

" 'Tis more like the other, Cristina, the sweet moment. I know it here." She touched her breast. " 'Twas after the bishop's attack. Penne was so—" Her ashen cheeks colored.

Cristina hugged Oriel and kissed her cheeks. "I'm so glad for you. I did believe in such a moment. And now you have proved it. Penne will be so pleased." She led Oriel to a bench. "But how are you alone at this time? What of Lady Nona? Can she be no comfort to you?"

"She's very ill—some fever or other. 'Tis why I've come. She'll not see Aldwin and insists on having you at her side. She was too ill to wed Durand before they departed for Portchester Castle."

"Wed? So soon?" Cristina whispered. She stared at Oriel. She felt suddenly ill herself.

"It did not happen, as Nona was so ill."

"When did the men sail?" Cristina asked.

"They have not yet gone. The king argued with William Marshall. Marshall would not accompany the king, and John called for all to take his side. So many of the barons aligned with Marshall that the king was furious. He took hostages, and Guy persisted in his support of Marshall and . . . Oh, that poor boy."

Cristina led Oriel to the hearth. She poured her a cup of ale. "Drink this, my lady." Next she went to a small cask and measured out some fennel and sweet violet—left from Simon's wares. She put it in a small pomander and handed it to Oriel. "Breathe this, my lady; 'twill ease your discomfort."

Oriel raised the pomander to her nose. "What will Durand do?"

Cristina's hands were ice-cold. She tucked them beneath her arms. "Oh, my lady . . ." Moments later Cristina collapsed into Oriel's embrace. "What *will* Durand do?"

Cristina knew the queen might take umbrage at her presence at Ravenswood, but Oriel had insisted she tend Nona.

They skirted the great hall, entering through the main doors, but quickly taking the way of servants to storerooms below. From there Oriel led her to Luke's counting room, where Nona lay on a pallet.

Nona's color was good for one so ill she could not wed a great lord.

Cristina touched Nona's brow. She held her hand. The women said little. Durand stood between them as surely as if he were there in the flesh.

"What ails you?" Cristina asked.

"I have a very catching fever and must visit the chamber pot every few moments."

The room was scented with sweet herbs, strewn by her own hands only a few days before. "You're not so afflicted you can make it to the jakes each time?" she asked.

"I stay here. 'Tis a catching illness. Oriel was so kind to fetch you, though she endangers herself."

"Hmmm." Cristina sat by Nona's side. There was a tray on the table with the remnants of a substantial meal.

Oriel perched anxiously on a stool. "Do you wish privacy? Shall I go?"

Cristina nodded. "I think Lady Nona and I should be alone."

When Oriel was gone, Cristina confronted the lady. "You look plump as a well-fed stoat. Why do you not tell me the truth? I have come at some risk, as the queen holds me in displeasure, and don't wish to play games."

Lady Nona sheepishly stared at her hands. "Lord Durand felt a need to postpone our nuptials. As I'm not so anxious to marry yet, I agreed to a small deception. You'll tend me, will you not? Or else Aldwin might suspect something. I've told the queen I cannot abide a man to touch me. And *she* will not come near, as I am catching."

"Anyone who enters this chamber will know you're not ill. This chamber is scented like a lady's bower."

Nona studied her, then leaned back on her many cushions. "Have you something to change that?"

"Oh, just leave the chamber pot full now and then."

Lady Nona wrinkled her nose.

"Borrow Lady Oriel's pomander, if need be." Cristina paced the chamber. The question spilled from her lips ere she could stop it. "You don't wish to wed Lord Durand?"

Nona shrugged. "I'll do as bidden by the king—as will Durand. But we don't wish to wed in haste at the king's caprice."

They would do as bidden by the king. . . .

"I cannot promise to tend you as you wish. The queen has taken Felice from my care and wishes to see me gone." Cristina went about the chamber arranging a basin and towels, drawing the chamber pot near the bed, and building up the fire as one would for an invalid.

"I'm sorry," Nona said. "Isabelle is very young, and the king has noticed you. She's just jealous, you know. Don't think of me again. See to yourself."

Cristina nodded. And she desperately hoped the king's attention would serve her well. "I'll send you a few herbs, but then, my lady, I'll be gone from here."

Nona pleated her skirt with her fingers. "You'll not wait for the men to sail?"

Cristina shook her head. "Nay, I have no part in this business. I wish I still had the key to Lady Marion's

339

garden. It would be quicker to get what you need there than from the village."

"Oh, I know where to find the key." Nona jumped up from her pallet and dashed to the coffer that had once held the Aelfric. She tossed Durand's Aristophanes onto the table and rummaged about. She withdrew a small chest and flipped open the lid. "Surely 'tis one of these?" She held out the box.

Cristina thought it very telling that Nona knew where Luke kept his keys. She found the one to the garden and then lifted the Aristophanes from the table. She smoothed her fingers along the gilded cover and remembered the time Lord Durand had offered her his books to read. Gently she replaced it in the coffer.

Quickly, lest one of the queen's men or ladies saw her, she hastened to the garden. There she used an empty sack from Durand's storeroom to gather herbs to cause a harmless purging when Nona felt it necessary.

Other plants she gathered were to remain her secret. As she gathered, she prayed for the power of the greenery and God's mercy on her tasks. With a last look at the lush space, she locked the gate and went to the chapel. There she learned from Father Odo that she need not send a message to Winchester for Father Laurentius. The priest was still at Ravenswood. The queen found gentle Father Odo's masses ill-suited to her tastes and had commmanded the illustrious Laurentius to serve her needs. It seemed that everyone must bow to the royal wishes.

Father Laurentius stared at her. "You wish me to arrange an escort for you to the king at Winchester?"

Cristina curtsied and nodded. "Aye. He made a proposition to me through one of his clerics, and I have reconsidered it."

The priest leaned on the scarred wooden table in the cottage. "I must say I'm greatly disappointed in you."

Many would say the same words in the next few days. She must harden herself to the criticism. She shrugged and attempted to look and behave as Lady Sabina would in the same situation. That lady cared naught for a priest's opinion.

"Is not Lord Durand's offer lucrative enough? It will not cease upon his disinterest, I assure you," the priest said carefully.

"I thank you for your concern, but it is important to me that I get to the king. This night if possible."

"You understand that Lord Durand will be most enraged at this turn of events. He might withdraw his offer. Even now he does not know you are no longer his daughter's nurse."

She would never forget she was no longer Felice's nurse. Her breasts ached to be emptied. Her heart ached as if she had again lost a daughter.

"Will you arrange my escort to Winchester?" she asked again.

"Oh, aye. Lord Durand said to grant your every wish."

Cristina waited patiently in a small chamber to be summoned before the king. The room, off a larger bedchamber in the king's hunting lodge outside Winchester, was bare save for several benches for petitioners. The lodge was filled with men. The few serving women about were greatly beleaguered by groping hands.

Cristina had almost turned and run when she saw Roger Godshall among them. But a page's terse order for her to follow had drawn her on.

What she was about to do frightened her. But in truth, once thought of, the idea would torture her till it was done. She could think of no way to set the idea aside and live with her conscience.

Just as it made sense to send the man with nothing to lose onto the battlefield, so it made sense that the woman with nothing to lose should sacrifice herself for the one with everything at stake.

Felice was lost to her, as was Durand, and everyone thought her a whore already. She had naught left to lose.

The same page summoned her before King John after little more than a quarter hour's wait. He sat in a deep chair by a long table strewn with maps and documents.

"Mistress le Gros," the king said. "You are as fickle as the wind that will carry my ships to Normandy."

"Sire," Cristina began, a hitch in her voice. " 'Tis but the nature of woman to change her mind."

"A quality that twists mortal man in knots, mistress."

"I would not wish to cause you any discomfort," she continued carefully, mindful of the royal rage Oriel had described.

Her hesitation was quickly interpreted by the king. "Say whatever you wish within these walls."

The room, paneled in fine English oak and lighted by wide windows with real glass, was as long as the lodge itself. A high screen at one end shielded the necessaries, she assumed. Below, men reveled and minstrels sang. There was little of the king's anger and disappointment on display.

"If I understood your most kind and benevolent offer properly, sire, you wanted me to share your bed."

"You are blunt." He raised his eyebrows.

"I don't want to waste your precious time."

His eyebrows lifted. "Then explain yourself."

"I don't know my worth, sire, but I would like to discuss—"

"Remuneration?" the king supplied.

"You are most understanding."

"And what price do you set? Twenty marks? Fifty?" The king smiled. A cask inlaid with ivory sat near him. The air was scented with precious sandalwood.

Cristina took a deep breath. "Lord Durand's sons."

The king's mouth opened then closed, much like that of a fish in Portsmouth harbor. "Lord Durand's sons? How so?"

"I want to exchange myself for them."

"Exchange? You for them?"

"Aye, sire. I want to offer myself as surety to Lord Durand's good behavior. That is what sons are for, are they not?"

"Again, mistress, you are very blunt." His brows drew together, and she feared she had made a grievous error.

"I'm no longer so happily situated, sire. So, as I was concerned that—"

"—Lord Durand might say or do something that would cause him difficulties . . ."

She nodded. "I thought to better my own circumstances whilst aiding him in some way. He is oft quick with his words and regretful later." She hoped Durand would never hear her portrayal of him.

"Ah, now we are at the heart of the matter. You wish to better your circumstances."

She had calculated correctly. The wish to better herself he understood. "And with . . . with Lady Nona so ill and his wedding postponed, I believe Lord Durand might find it more difficult than usual to hold his temper."

"Indeed." The king rose and walked to where she stood. He lifted her hair from her shoulders and skimmed a finger along her throat. "You are lovely. You might still be young enough to steal a heart or two."

She shivered beneath his touch.

"So in exchange for the volatile de Marle's sons, you

would await your king's pleasure at de Warre's castle?" he made it a question. "It may be a very long wait if winds remain favorable."

"I would be ever at your service, sire," she said, a shiver of fear and illness coursing through her belly. "I would be at your pleasure whenever you might need me."

He snapped his fingers, and a cleric scurried from behind a screen. She had not known someone was in the chamber, and her skin flushed hot that this man, the same one who had approached her at Ravenswood, had heard her sell herself to the king—in exchange for two children, but still, she had sold herself.

The king and cleric moved away from her. Their murmured conversation as the cleric scratched out a parchment directing de Warre was inaudible to her, but she did not really care.

The missive was sealed with the king's ring, along with her fate. The king's promise was tied and wrapped in oiled cloth.

Another flick of the king's hand and the cleric scurried back behind his screen. The king held out the parchment, but when Cristina reached for it, he shifted it out of her reach. "When you take this, mistress, you are ours. Never forget it."

Cristina nodded, unable to speak. He truly was as capricious as gossip painted him. One day he thought her a thief of little value and the next he thought her worthy to share his bed.

He dropped the parchment into her palm. "Carry it hence to de Warre yourself and see the deed done."

She dropped into a deep curtsy and kissed his hand.

"Oh, one more matter," the king called. "Practice your craft on yourself, mistress, as a sweetly perfumed woman is at the apex of a man's pleasure."

Chapter Twenty-eight

As a boy, Durand had come to just this spot over-looking the harbor to seek comfort from either his father's anger or his mother's sharp tongue. Now, as he looked over the many ships lying at anchor, await-ing John's decision to invade Normandy, he sought that comfort.

It did not come. He was not a child who might have his innocent wishes granted. John's decision to hang Guy Wallingford's son told him all he needed of the man he followed.

In service to King Richard he had witnessed much of cruelty. But the hanging of an innocent boy because a man was in a drunken rage was not to be borne.

Regardless of his later fate, Durand determined to leave when darkness fell and snatch his sons from de Warre's hands. This, he knew, was an action that also left his mother vulnerable. But she had made her own way for more than a score of years and must continue to do so.

Retrieving his sons with Cristina and Felice in tow would take all his powers of imagination.

Luke rode up behind him. He left his horse to crop the grass and came to Durand's side. "I thought I might find you here."

Even his quarrel with Luke seemed somehow unimportant against the lives of his sons. "I'm leaving," Durand answered.

"Oh? Where are you off to? Winchester, to try to talk sense into John? Without Marshall and his army this offensive is off, is it not?"

"Nay, I'll not be going to Winchester." Durand turned to his brother. "There's little hope of your retaining Ravenswood after what I'm about to do, but should John not seize it, I want you to have it."

"So," Luke said. He leaned against an outcropping of rock. "You will hie yourself off to de Warre's stronghold and lay siege to it by yourself."

"If necessary." Durand nodded. "And Mother will need to look to herself if Philip wants to bring pressure to bear in that direction."

"She's like a cat. She'll land on her feet; she always has."

Durand acknowledged the truth of Luke's words, though he knew his conscience would prick him.

"Being your brother is a trial," Luke snapped. His horse lifted its head at his sharp tone. "We both know you'll be killed, Ravenswood will be forfeit, your sons in de Warre's care forever—or worse, hanged."

"Enough," Durand said. "You have no right to criticize what I do. You who have no—"

"No what?" Luke stood very straight and met Durand's hard glare. "Let us have it out between us here. Here, where no one will witness our words, if that is what holds you from speaking."

"Aye. Who might hear is what holds my tongue." Durand could not stay the words from spilling from his mouth. "Your face, your evasive glance, betray you daily. Each touch of your hand to her declares your guilt."

Luke bowed his head. "We fought it, but—"

"Did you? Not hard enough, it appears." Durand swung from his brother to the harbor. "What does it matter? I'll claim her no matter her circumstances. I've no other choice, for, in truth, she has laid claim to a part of my heart."

"Your heart? You are cold as ice! You may lust after a woman, but you have nothing to offer a—"

Durand swung around. "Lust? A woman? What are you talking about?"

"Nona. You cannot love her. Your every word is sharp-edged, or you ignore her completely!" Luke fisted his hands on his hips.

"Nona? I'm speaking of Felice." Durand stared at his brother.

"F-Felice? I don't understand. What has Felice to do with you and Nona?"

"Nothing. But I don't wish to speak of Nona." Durand approached his brother. "Do you deny you are Felice's father?"

"Felice's father?" Luke shook his head. "Are you mad? You—" he broke off, his mouth agape. Luke stumbled back against the rock. "You question Felice's parentage?"

Durand could not bear the gently spoken question. And it was too late to withdraw the accusation. "I don't question her parentage. I *know* her parentage. She is Marion's without doubt, but not mine—equally without doubt."

With the admission, some part of the festering wound was lanced. He went to his horse and hid some of his emotion in tightening his girth and checking his stirrups.

"Sweet *Jesu*." Luke stormed to where he stood. "You believe Marion and I . . . that we . . ." He snatched up his reins. "You think I have so little care of you I would trespass on your wife?"

Durand looked away. "Aye. I trust no one."

"Then I pity you." Luke leaped into the saddle. In moments he was gone.

A roiling confusion filled Durand. If Luke's guilt was over Nona, then his attentions to Felice were merely those of an uncle—and similar to how he had always treated Robert and Adrian. It was an ugly parting. And he didn't expect ever to return.

Father Laurentius entered Ravenswood's armory behind Durand. He nodded stiffly to the priest as he belted on the sword given him by Gilles d'Argent. He placed several daggers into a leather roll, which he then tied up and stuffed into a saddlebag. In another he placed bread and cheese, a sack of coins, the two rings from the king, and the Aelfric.

"I have some news you may wish to hear," the priest said.

"I've no time for gossip." Durand pulled on his mantle and secured it with a gold pin incised with ravens in flight. Every part of his garb bore ravens, from his daggers to his surcoat. He wanted de Warre to have no doubts who came to claim his sons.

Durand hefted his shield and helm and strode from the armory to where Marauder waited. The priest trailed after him. Next to the destrier was a gentle mare, also saddled.

" 'Tis not gossip. I must tell you that against my advice, Mistress le Gros took herself to Winchester this morn."

"Cristina went to Winchester?" Durand paused in

the act of strapping the bags to his saddle. He had been about to collect her from the village. "Why?"

"It seems John had made an offer to her and she decided to take him up on it."

Durand stared at the priest. "John? What kind of offer?"

"Please, we are well aware of what kind of offer our king would extend to a woman such as Mistress le Gros."

"Make sense." Durand restrained himself from shaking the aged priest.

"You see." Laurentius moved closer and dropped his voice to a whisper so that those who moved about the inner bailey might not hear his words. "There's a very sweet young clerk in John's service who oft shares gossip with me—for a small remuneration, of course, but nothing harmful, mind you."

"Get on with it!" Durand bit out.

"Well, this young man told me Mistress le Gros traded herself for your sons." Laurentius dusted his hands together. "There, I have said it all. My conscience is clear."

Durand snatched Laurentius by the cassock. "What in God's holy name are you saying?"

"Contain yourself, my lord!" Laurentius said in a hiss. "Eyes are upon us."

Durand dropped the priest as if his hand burned. He lowered his voice. "Explain the meaning of this tale."

"Your mistress became the king's mistress in promise of the release of your sons. She is, at this moment, traveling to de Warre's castle."

Durand ran past the priest and leaped into his saddle. He jerked the reins and in moments was through the inner bailey. At the outer gates he reined Marauder in. Luke and Penne waited there, fully armed. It struck him with the force of a blow; despite his harsh words with Luke, his brother was prepared to risk his life and livelihood on his behalf. Penne, too. Durand was humbled.

"De Warre has Cristina as well," Durand just managed. Without another word the men turned and followed him across the bridge and onto the road.

The sky was black with clouds as de Warre's castle came into view. It was more a fortified manor house than a castle, but still its high palisades and gates looked impregnable to Cristina.

Sheets of rain filled the ruts in the road to overflowing. The enclosed wagon in which she sat slowed to a near crawl. Water dripped through the small opening that offered a bit of air to the wagon's occupants along with the limited view.

Each step of the horse toward the manor house on the horizon was a step closer to her new life. De Warre's property lay on the road halfway between Winchester and Marlborough. The castle itself was said to sit on a lake crafted by fairies and inhabited by dragons. She stroked the seal on the king's missive.

Durand's sons would be safe.

He would not want her once she had lain with the king.

He would be wed to Nona and lost to her no matter her circumstances.

She had made her choice. Verily, there was truth in Aristophanes' words. There was nothing so shameless as a woman. She would not be ashamed.

Nona led her horse and Oriel's into the sheltering arms of a stout English oak. Rain streamed from their mantles and steam rose from their mounts. She turned to Oriel. "This was beyond foolish, was it not?"

"We could not let them go off on their own!" Oriel offered up a silent prayer that her child would not suffer from this headlong dash after Penne and Luke.

Nona sighed. "Nay, we could not. But I would trade two of my manors for a warm fire just now."

The women huddled closer together.

"Father Laurentius is sure this is where they are going." Oriel bit her lip. "Thank God your maid told you of the king's intentions. If she were not enamored of Laurentius's groom, we would never have discovered it." Oriel cleared her throat. "Durand must love Cristina very much to go after her this way."

Nona pulled her hood closer about her head. "You must acknowledge he is also going after his sons."

Oriel nodded. "Aye, but don't forget, she, too, must greatly love Durand to exchange herself for two boys she has never met." They walked their horses back onto the roadbed when the rain abated. "Could you wed Durand now?" Oriel ventured. "Knowing he loves Cristina?"

"The question is whether Durand will have Cristina once he learns what she has done. Such folly." Nona's words were matter-of-fact.

Oriel persisted. "But will you want Durand?"

Nona considered the sky. "I'll wed a de Marle; doubt it not."

"I wish Penne loved me half so much," Oriel said wistfully.

"He adores you! Now stop sniveling and let us get along!"

Nona kicked her horse into a canter and took to the road.

Edward de Warre was a balding man of about two score years. He was missing his left arm, which explained why he was not called upon to make the journey to Normandy. He held out his right hand. Cristina offered him the missive.

He broke the seal with his thumb and shook out the

parchment. "Latin?" de Warre said with a sneer. "For what purpose does the king write me in Latin?" He barked an order, and in a few moments a priest arrived.

The young man scanned the king's missive. "This is most private in nature, my lord."

The two men went to the hearth, where several ranks of candles cast a brilliant light on a table.

Cristina shivered in apprehension. She was not invited to the light nor to the warmth of the fire, but if she had been, it would mean standing near de Warre. He murdered children. Just being in his presence frightened her.

The priest used his finger to mark his place as he read aloud. Cristina couldn't hear the king's words, and didn't need to. De Warre lifted his head and smiled at her when the priest finished.

"Come, Cristina; come join me." He beckoned her closer.

De Warre helped her remove her mantle and pulled a roomy oak chair carved with his arms toward the fire for her ease. She sat gingerly on the edge. "Will the boys be returning in my cart?"

De Warre shook his head. "I'll provide a better conveyance when the rain lets up."

"Then might I meet them and ascertain they're in good health?" She spread her damp skirts to the fire's warmth.

"But of course." He nodded to the priest, who bowed and departed into the shadows at the end of the narrow hall. "After you have met them, we'll see you are placed in a chamber suitable for the king's pleasure." He gave her a hard smile. "He comes here from time to time and much likes his pleasures ready and waiting."

The cold of the storm outside settled within her, and she suspected she would never be warm again.

* * *

Durand knelt on a small rise and watched de Warre's gates. He pounded the ground with his fist. "We're too late. That cart carried her in; I'm sure of it."

Luke and Penne, stretched at his side, agreed.

"Aye," Luke said. " 'Tis one of the king's conveyances. Why not ride down there now and demand entrance? De Warre is not expecting us, and we can snatch the boys and Cristina before he raises an alarm."

"That was my first intention, but the rain has washed some sense into me." Durand glanced up at the angry gray sky, then to the walled castle. He might never see his boys or Cristina again. "I'll not put their lives in jeopardy with a foolish plan. We will wait to see if de Warre releases my sons now that he has Cristina."

Cristina had given herself for his sons. He owed her a debt not payable in this lifetime.

Together they watched and waited for three hours. The gates remained closed. A powerful need to act swept over Durand.

"I'm going after them." Durand leaped to his feet, but Luke and Penne restrained him. "De Warre cannot muster many men," Durand argued. "The most able are in Portsmouth ready for the offensive." Durand tore from their grip. "I'll not wait any longer."

"Mayhap de Warre will release them on the morrow, when the weather improves. Come, let us wait a bit longer." Penne cajoled him back to their vantage point.

But Durand knew de Warre would never release his sons.

"The king will hang us all together, I imagine, when he learns we're gone." Luke adjusted his mantle closer about his neck. Penne cleared his throat. "This damnable rain set us back but a few miles, else we would have had Cristina on the road and been back to Ravenswood ere John discovered we were gone," Penne noted.

"The boys would still have been hostages," Durand pointed out. He dug in his saddlebag and drew out the Aelfric that had caused so much difficulty in their lives.

"What need have you of that?" Luke asked.

Durand turned the book about in his hand to be sure the oiled cloth in which it was wrapped protected it still. "It was the source of all this trouble. I thought, as it is so valuable, it might serve as a bribe."

Penne shook his head. "To a heathen such as de Warre? Never."

Durand's sons were brought to her in the hall within an hour of her arrival. Adrian, at ten and five, showed all the markings of a handsome man. Save his vivid blue eyes, he was enough like his father to bring a huge lump to Cristina's throat.

Robert was still a gangly, awkward boy of ten and two, and resembled his mother with his softer blue eyes and light, golden brown hair. His features were still childlike, and Cristina could not imagine what had shaped de Warre that he could intend to so mercilessly hang someone so innocent.

The boys did not bow to her, but she was not a fine lady to be insulted by their omission. Nay, she was now a king's mistress and deserved no such respect.

"Thank you," she said to de Warre when they were escorted to a table far from hers.

"They're quite well, as you can see." De Warre's hand was hot where he pressed it to her back as he led her to a table at the fore of his hall.

"When do they leave?" Cristina asked again. The many who sat at the tables were curious about her, their gazes following her every step. They were de

Warre's men or other young boys being trained as knights. Their glances were as wary as those of Durand's sons.

De Warre lifted his hand, and one of the servants hurried away. "We shall have some music to celebrate your arrival," de Warre said. "My minstrels are not as talented as the king's, but you'll not be disappointed, I think."

"When will the boys leave?" she persisted.

"Mayhap you would give me your opinion on the entertainments I have planned for John's arrival on the morrow."

"On the morrow?" She dropped her goblet, and the wine spilled across the table to drip to the stone floor.

De Warre snapped his fingers. A serving boy rushed forward to clean up the mess. "Aye. 'Twas in the king's message. I was to prepare for him. I've been waiting for such an honor since he last visited, and can now put into action some fine plans. You shall certainly add something sweet to end the entertainment."

The king was coming on the morrow? What had become of his plans to sail to Normandy? Then she heard the drumming of rain on the roof overhead. It must be the weather, she thought. She had expected to have several months before the king claimed her.

"When will the boys leave?" she asked again.

De Warre rubbed her hand. "In a few days. They'll want to see the king and enjoy the festivities, will they not?"

Cristina suddenly understood. The boys would never leave. And now she was another hostage to Durand's cooperation. She forced herself to contain her fears of betrayal. De Warre must not know what she was thinking.

"What's the nature of your entertainment?" Cristina asked hastily.

De Warre leaned forward with avid enthusiasm. "A

mock battle to honor John's prowess in war. He shall be greatly pleased."

Or heartily annoyed, since his own war plans were in abeyance, she thought.

"And when John is pleased, he likes something sweet at the end of an evening. *That* part of the plan eluded me, but here you are, and now all is complete." He pressed her hand and smiled.

Luke kept watch on the road while Penne and Durand argued over a means of breaching de Warre's gates. He opened his eyes wider and shook his head. He must be dreaming.

"Penne. Durand. Look!" He pointed to the road.

"Oriel," Penne cried.

Durand abandoned his vantage point overlooking the castle and strode to the small hillock on which could be seen the greater part of the road. "*Jesu!* And who's that with her?"

The men mounted up and angled their way through the trees to the road. Durand hissed a warning. "Wait in the trees until they draw near lest there be some trickery in the offing."

The women appeared to be completely alone. Nona and Oriel both screamed when the men emerged like phantoms from the wood.

Penne snatched Oriel's reins from her hands and, without ceremony or word, hauled her horse along behind him into the safety of the trees.

Nona waited in the road—alone. Neither Luke nor Durand claimed her. She turned her horse and followed Oriel. Within moments the five of them found themselves back in the hollow where the men had lain.

"Explain yourself!" Penne demanded the instant Oriel's feet hit the dirt, but gave his wife not one moment to speak. "You, who are with child, risk your health! For what?"

"How did you guess?" Oriel threw herself into his arms. She clung to his neck and kissed his cheek.

"A husband knows," he said. His arms went around her, and with a sheepish look in his friends' direction, he patted her back.

Nona rolled her eyes. "Let me explain, my lords. We knew you were going after Cristina and thought you might need our help."

Luke tucked his gloves into his belt and threw his mantle over one shoulder. "You, lady, are mistaken. We need no help from you. When you are rested, you will return to Ravenswood ere some harm befalls you."

Durand watched Nona's face set into stubborn lines. She was just what Luke needed. "What made you think you could aid us, my lady?" Durand asked her. "And what will John think when you're no longer too ill to wed, but well enough to dash about the country?"

"Oh, my maid is putting it about that Oriel has caught my illness, and I left orders that only my maid may tend me. My chamber will be avoided as though we have the plague."

Durand acknowledged the sense of that with a slight bow, but doubted the ruse would stand up for more than a day or two.

Nona continued as she tugged off her gloves. "This maid of mine makes love to Laurentius's groom. It seems he heard some gossip that the king has no intention of exchanging Cristina for your sons."

Durand felt no surprise, only an inner chill.

"So," Nona said, taking a seat on a fallen branch, "we're here to help you."

Luke snorted in derision. Penne was too busy kissing his wife to pay them any mind.

Nona lifted her chin and impaled Luke with a haughty stare. "And women can ofttimes go where men cannot."

Durand stared down at the silent fortress. The gates were shut. The rain had diminished to a light mist.

Durand nodded. "I believe, Lady Nona, you are the answer to our prayers. Thankful I am you've arrived, for I was about to despair of ever seeing my sons—or Cristina—again."

An hour later, Durand had outlined a plan for the women to enter de Warre's castle and determine the whereabouts of the postern gate. Once they had the information, they were to open it, if possible, or leave immediately.

Oriel hooked her arm through her husband's and tried to reassure him. "We'll not be harmed, my love. De Warre knows us not. We'll be just Nona and Oriel, sisters lost on the way to the Abbey at Ludgershall, seeking shelter for the night. We'll certainly be warmer there than out here. You men must trust us."

Durand rose hastily and left them.

"What did I say?" Oriel asked the company.

"Nothing amiss. 'Tis just that you have asked the impossible. Durand trusts no one," Luke said bitterly.

Cristina sat at de Warre's side for the evening meal. She did not need to see shackles on Durand's sons to know they—and she—were prisoners. Did Adrian and Robert understand that their status had changed from fostered sons to hostage ones? Two large men accompanied the boys to the hall and sat on either side of them as they ate.

She had her own guard in de Warre, who touched her arm each time she shifted in her seat. His constant references to the king's pleasure turned her stomach. The row of charred partridges before her did naught to tempt her appetite either.

"Might I seek my bed? I'm exhausted from the journey." She smiled her warmest smile at her host.

De Warre plucked up her hand and kissed the back. Her skin crawled as if a serpent slithered up her hand. "As you wish." He directed a sullen girl to take her to her chamber.

Once out of de Warre's sight, Cristina cast off her fatigue. "Can you show me to the jakes? And, if I may say, you have very pretty skin. I have a fine cream that would bring out the rose bloom on your cheeks."

The girl flushed and smiled tentatively. By the time they had walked to the jakes, they were the best of friends. Cristina's next request, that she be shown about the castle, was quickly granted.

As the serving girl shared the castle secrets, Cristina shared her mother's directions for removing freckles and adding shine to hair.

"We need to put some of our anger behind us," Luke said to Durand as they watched the women make their way to the castle. Penne, who stood a bit aside, gnawed his thumb in anxiety for his wife's safety.

"How?" Durand strode to his brother and stood inches from him. "How do I put aside a betrayal?"

"No one *here* betrayed you." Luke did not back away. His words were heated. "I'm not Felice's father any more than Penne is."

"How can I know that?" Durand was tired of the whole business. It sapped energy that was better set to rescuing the woman he loved.

"You *do* know that! You know me! Has a lifetime of brotherhood meant nothing?" Luke gripped his sleeve.

Trust the history you have with a person. Durand heard Cristina's words as if she were there at his side. Grief that he might never hear her again swept over him.

"Cristina said much the same thing." He placed his hand on his dagger. His fingertips traced the raven's head. "She also said sometimes one must make a leap of faith."

"Marion and I kept each other company whilst you were gone, but I never touched her. I have never lain with a married woman—ever. Their husbands have swords." He gave a lopsided smile.

Durand could not respond to the levity.

"And Penne"—Luke pointed to where their friend was chewing his thumb bloody over his wife—"he can see no farther than Oriel's fingertips."

"Then who fathered Felice?" Just saying the words aloud further lanced the wound. "Am I left with only the king as suspect?"

"Marion had no love of John," Luke said, but Durand watched his gaze slide away.

"What do you know?" Durand demanded.

With a sigh, Luke answered. "I know only that Marion much loved to flirt. She was lonely, and lonely women sometimes stray."

Nona and Oriel reached the gate, ending Luke and Durand's discourse. In moments, as Nona had predicted, the gate opened and they rode inside.

Luke put out his hand. "Know this. I pledge myself to your service at any time or any place, save this—I want Nona. And we'll take Felice from your care, if that is what you wish."

How had he doubted his brother?

"You're welcome to Nona." Durand clasped his brother's hand. "But Felice is mine."

Chapter Twenty-nine

Cristina paced within the silence of the king's richly appointed apartment. Might he ride through the night as de Warre hinted? She shuddered. Quickly she looked through the few herbs she had brought. If she was careful and clever, she might postpone the consummation of her folly.

But first she relieved the engorgement of her breasts. As the milk flowed, so did her tears. Had Felice accepted Rose yet? She dearly wished for Felice's happiness, but had to stifle jealous desires that the babe miss her.

Next she pummeled a few leaves into a paste. They would blend well with water and raise a rash within a few hours.

Finally Cristina lay on her pallet in the anteroom to the king's chamber. Her bed was thinly stuffed with straw. John's was draped in silk, tied with gold cord, his mattress stuffed with goosedown. She prayed she would never know its softness.

A tentative scratching at the door set her heart to drumming in her chest. But it was only the serving girl, Maud, who'd shown her about the castle.

"Miss," Maud said, "there's two in the hall that looks like fine ladies, but they're cold and might need a bit o' yer care."

Cristina nearly fainted when she saw who sat in abject misery in the corner of the hall, their mantles soaked, their hems bedraggled. She strode quickly to them ere the men who still lingered at their ale and dice might accost her.

"Come," she whispered with scarcely a look at them. She hastened down a gallery, then out into the kitchen gardens.

Luckily Oriel and Nona followed without demur.

The women walked in the light rain among the rows of vegetables, safe from even the cook's gaze at this late hour.

"What possessed you to come here?" Cristina demanded.

"We had to deliver a message to the men," Nona said.

"What men?" Cristina asked, but knew the answer.

"Durand, Penne, and Luke. They came to rescue the boys and you, of course," Oriel finished in a rush.

Nona took Cristina's arm. "The king does not intend to exchange the boys. You, too, are now hostage to his whims."

Cristina bowed her head. "I am a fool. What must Durand think of me?"

"Oh, I imagine he will rail a bit, but in truth he loves you too much for one of his truly splendid tirades." Oriel gave her a quick hug. "Now we must find the postern gate and let them in."

"Impossible," Cristina said. "The king and his men

are due here on the morrow. You cannot expect to use the gate."

"On the morrow? What should we do?" Nona asked Oriel.

But it was Cristina who answered. "*You* will do nothing. Seek your beds and leave at dawn. When the king arrives I'll demand he keep to the bargain we struck."

Nona shook her head. "Now that is folly! We must find another way, Cristina. Durand's sons depend upon us all."

"Let me think on it." Cristina walked about the garden and pondered her fate and that of Durand's sons. She knelt and plucked a few leaves of mint and nibbled their edges. The scent cleared her head. "I have it, ladies." She smiled. " 'Tis like this mint."

Oriel and Nona looked blankly at her.

Cristina explained. "The mint appears harmless, but if left unchecked it will take over a garden. 'Tis the appearance of harmlessness we need. And who appears harmless? Why, women, of course."

Nona cocked her head. "Explain, please."

"Here is my plan. I know 'twill work," Cristina continued, pacing before her friends. "On the morrow, at dusk, de Warre has planned a mock battle to entertain King John. Surely there will be great confusion and men dashing all about. Even if 'tis orderly, the king's attentions will be on the battle. Could not a few extra soldiers join in? A few extra soldiers who have gained entrance as harmless women? And I know a way to obtain suitable garb for our men."

Nona clapped her hands, then slapped them over her mouth in regret of the noise she had made.

"I'll send a serving girl to you with all that the men will need. But please go early in the morn and remain hidden. If the king sees you he'll know something is amiss," Cristina warned.

Nona took her hands. "We'll do as you say, but keep

safe, Cristina. Durand loves you very much and is as much out on that hill for you as for his sons."

"You will wed him knowing . . ." Cristina could not finish.

"I will wed but one de Marle. And he is not Durand."

With that Oriel hooked Nona's arm and hurried her into the shadows. Cristina stared after them. Nona loved Luke? She did not want Durand? Joy filled her, then slipped away. If their plans failed, the king would have his way.

Durand waited impatiently for the women to return as dawn broke over de Warre's castle. The day was gray and looked as likely to rain as not. When the women emerged from the castle gates, he felt a moment of elation. Soon he would have those most precious to him in his arms.

But the news Nona and Oriel brought sent him into momentary despair. They would not be able to use the postern gate. A king's arrival always heightened defenses.

"Don't look so long-faced," Nona said, tugging open the straps on her saddlebags and pulling out a tied bundle. "Oriel and I have brought you the means of entering de Warre's castle without suspicion."

Durand laughed when he saw what she held.

An hour later, Nona stared at the men with a finger on her chin. "You make most unattractive women— save Luke, and he looks like a tart, not one of the king's laundresses."

Durand checked their weapons, concealed in what he hoped would be mistaken for the common baggage of women. He gathered his heavy skirts into his arms so that he might mount Nona's palfrey. "I do wish whoever wore this last had bathed more often."

Oriel tugged Penne's headcovering lower on his

forehead, then skimmed the back of her fingers on his cheek. "You are all quite nicely smooth-cheeked now, but you, Durand, will not look so in a few hours." Penne kissed her fingertips and climbed clumsily into the saddle.

Luke hesitated a moment before mounting his mare, his eyes on his brother.

Durand spoke first. How clear all seemed to him now after a night of vigil over de Warre's fortress. The walls of doubt within him were of his own making.

"I do trust you, Luke. And you, Penne. I must beg your forgiveness for doubting you. 'Tis my nature and not easily controlled. But henceforth I vow to try. Now." He nodded in Nona's direction. "Kiss her quickly and let us be gone."

Luke held out his arms. Nona glanced at Durand, then turned to Luke. She stepped into his embrace, and Durand knew she had been there before. Her unkempt look the other morn now needed no explanation. He sighed. There was much he did not know . . . or had ignored.

The women were condemned to await the outcome from the hollow. They were not capable of controlling Durand's or Penne's warhorses, so escape by horseback was impossible should they be discovered. Luke had brought his favorite mare instead of a destrier, and so with that mount, and the women's palfreys, the men had made their way to the castle gates.

Durand had a terrible moment as the guards inspected them, but found easy entrance when they said they were the king's laundresses come to see to his linens ere he arrived.

Laundresses were not paid the same attention as were servants. The men were left to their own devices, which allowed them to carry their baggage themselves and thus conceal their weapons and mail within a convenient distance of de Warre's lakeside battle.

Men and women servants ran to and fro in preparation for the king's arrival. On the shore of de Warre's lake, small fishing boats were lined up and painted to look like the galleys of war.

As directed by Nona, the men, heads down, hastened to a place a warrior would not likely go—the kitchens.

Cristina sat in the corner, stirring something in a bubbling pot. Durand walked to her side and leaned over to sniff the mixture. "It smells like a summer garden," he said in a whisper.

" 'Tis a soothing cream for the chapped hands of de Warre's laundresses," she said with no sign she knew who he was, but her hand began to shake. "I'm making it in exchange for your garb."

"Take us somewhere private."

With a nod Cristina directed a small girl to stir the lotion. "Pour it out when 'tis cooled." She pointed to a row of clay pots.

Cristina led them from the kitchens to a ramshackle building behind an abandoned dovecote. She dug in a pile of old straw and drew out a sack. Within was a mix of mantles and tunics in both John's and Philip's colors. "You will need mail, helms, swords—"

Durand snatched her into his arms. She answered his kiss with the intense passion and love in her heart. Tears ran down her cheeks. "I so feared you would despise me," she whispered, lest Penne and Luke, who hovered in the shadows, hear her.

Durand squeezed her tightly and kissed her brow. "Why did you do it?" His words were gentle, not angry.

She stared up into his silvery gray eyes and touched the hard, cold torque beneath his women's garb. "I could not have you—"

She did not finish. He stopped her words with his lips.

Luke hissed like a cat with a mouse, breaking their embrace in an instant. Her heart pounded.

"You need not worry about our weaponry," Durand said, his voice suddenly rough. "Our horses were heavily laden with baggage, as 'tis fitting for vain women. We have what we need."

The men stripped their gowns and, as Cristina kept watch by the entrance, donned the garb of John's soldiers.

When they were ready, she held out a mantle to Durand and helped him pin it closed.

"If you are able," he said, "tell my sons I'm coming."

"They have guards," she said. "But I'll try."

He touched her cheek. "Where will I find you?"

"Don't worry about me," she said lightly. "I'll keep my eyes on your sons, and when you effect their rescue, I'll follow."

"I'll not leave it to providence." He wrapped his arms about her.

"You will," she insisted, squeezing his waist. "I may not be able to leave the king's side. You must take your sons when you have the chance and go!"

"I'll not leave without you."

Each touch of his lips chipped away at her resolve. But he must leave when the chance arose. "What is this?" She turned his attentions, placing her hand over something lumpy he had concealed beneath his clothing just above his heavy leather belt.

He covered her fingers with his. "The Aelfric. It might serve as a bribe, and after all the trouble it has caused, I'll not let it out of my sight."

"We must go," Luke insisted, pushing past them to peer from the entrance.

Durand kissed her. Quickly. Hard. "I love you."

"And I you." She held him close, sure it would be the last time.

"Durand, now!" Penne urged.

Durand cupped her face. "If you don't break away from here by this time on the morrow, I *will* be back for you!"

There was no mistaking the fanfare of an arriving king. The midday meal had ended an hour before, and Cristina wished she had indulged in the roast boar and savory cheeses. Her stomach ached with emptiness and fear. Would the king come directly to his chamber or give de Warre an audience?

She slipped into the king's tub. If need be, she would sit there all day until he came to his chamber. It must appear that she had used this selfsame water. She shivered in the cold water, as she could not afford to waste the hot water buckets steaming by the hearth.

Her heart thundered in her chest. "I will bear it," she said to herself. "I will." But her knees were weak.

Boots and men's voices could be heard on the steps, John's among them. Cristina called out to the serving girl, who mended a deliberately torn shift in the other room. "Maud, come help me add more hot water to this tub; the king comes."

Maud ran into the room. "I'll do it, miss," she said. In moments the tub was steaming. Durand must never know her plan. If he did, he would surely have one of his splendid tirades.

Her body trembling, she shook her wet hair to lie in a tumble about her shoulders, then stirred the seductive paste of herbs and oils into the hot water. "The king will greatly enjoy this scent," she said to the maid.

"Aye, miss," Maud said just as the king opened the door.

He froze in the doorway. Cristina dropped into as

respectful a curtsy as she could and still remain fully covered by the length of linen the maid discreetly held before her.

"Be gone!" he ordered Maud and his own manservant, who stood behind him.

Cristina trembled. Her wet hair and the drops of water on her shoulders would point to her having just bathed. "Sire!" She feigned a blushing-maiden stance. "Forgive me. I was just indulging in a bath."

"Please, Cristina." The king bowed as if to his queen. "Our bath is your bath." He walked toward her. Only the tub and a drying cloth stood between her and dishonor. His heated gaze raked her scantily covered breasts and hips.

"The water is still hot, sire," she said, frightened by the tremor in her voice.

He drew his fingers through the scented water. " 'Tis as the women say: you are mistress of all that grows."

" 'Tis naught but simple lavender and oil of bay." With a sweep of her hand, she indicated a beautiful silver bowl on a nearby table. Other, more important ingredients had no odor.

"Come." He beckoned her near. Her relief that he only expected her aid in disrobing almost buckled her knees. She acted the maid while fighting to keep her wrap of linen in a decorous position. When he settled with a sigh into the warm, seductive water, she crossed her fingers and prayed the king would not blame the bath for the rash he would surely have in several hours. She prayed he would see her unblemished skin and exonerate her for what he was soon to experience.

Set near to hand was also a salve for use as a last resort should the bath oil fail. The salve would raise a nasty, blistered surface wherever it was rubbed. She intended to slather it between her thighs if necessary to keep the king at bay.

As John reclined with his eyes closed, she took the opportunity to pull on a shift.

"Come tend me, Cristina," he said, rousing himself from a near doze. She did as any good wife would—scrubbed his back and washed his hair. The instant she was finished she surreptitiously washed her hands in clean water and rubbed them with an ointment of betony and comfrey.

When he rose from the tub and donned a fur-lined bed robe, she stifled the unkind thought that if kings wished to remain imposing beings, they should never allow their enemies to see them at their bath.

John invited her to a seat by the fire. There, on the table, she had set out a sampling of delicate temptations. John poured them each a goblet of wine. Before she could raise it to her lips, he began to scratch. By the time he had finished his honey cakes, he was raking his skin with vigor.

It was far too early!

"Sire, is something wrong?" she asked.

He scratched at his neck. "This damnable robe. It must be jumping with fleas." With a stronger oath, he flung it off.

Cristina averted her gaze from the rash overspreading his entire body.

"I have a salve that is particularly effective against fleas," she offered.

"Fetch it," he said from within a long linen shirt he pulled over his head.

When she returned with an innocuous salve, his manservant was in attendance. The man plucked the salve from her hands and hissed a warning that she get out. The royal lust was not so strong as the royal rash.

Cristina fled to the antechamber and donned a soft

ivory underdress and russet gown embroidered with
scarlet and gold thread. It was far finer than any she
had heretofore worn, and a gift from the king. She
quickly plaited her hair, then darted from the chamber lest the king change his mind and call for her.

She hid among the laundresses. They were in a twit-
ter that the king variously blamed his rash on their
work or a dirty mattress.

At dusk Cristina crept from the washing shed to a
scene of confusion. Within the small bailey, men
formed up into two armies, some garbed as John's
soldiers, some as Philip's. She scanned each face for
Durand's, but saw no one she knew.

The weather had deteriorated. The sky was as dark
a gray as Durand's eyes. A light rain tapered to a drizzle that wreathed the battlements of de Warre's castle
in a soft haze.

When de Warre found her, he gripped her by the
arm. "Get to the royal pavilion and soothe his temper,
else you'll find yourself on your back serving my men
instead of the king."

She jerked from his grasp and walked the long distance to the shore of the lake. Torches lined the pebble beach. The boats, anchored on a small island at
the center of the lake, were no longer visible, as the
haze enveloped the water.

Those who would act the English were out there,
Durand among them, playing John's army, ready to
embark. Their landing site was a clearly marked patch
of land set out with flags before the king's pavilion.
Within the designated area, men garbed in Philip's
colors waited. Dotted about the field so men could
seek some form of shelter during the melee were
wooden structures painted like castles. Cristina also
surmised that they represented territory to be taken
back from Philip.

She took a place behind the king. The spectators

were all men of the king's party or de Warre's. Several she recognized from Ravenswood. They gave her curious glances. Several acknowledged her with a bow.

Cristina watched the king. He scratched incessantly at his neck and hands. Angry red marks stood out against his skin. He snapped at all who spoke to him. Surely a man of such canniness must soon suspect the bath?

Then she froze. Making her way to the king's pavilion was Lady Sabina.

What was Sabina doing here? Truly, Cristina thought, the woman was a festering thorn in her side.

Cristina turned slightly away. She did not need the lady's notice. It had never occurred to Cristina that the king had brought more than just his men. Sabina climbed the two steps of the pavilion as if she were John's queen, then sat by his side.

Drums sounded. All turned toward the lake. Decorated to look like the galleys of war, the boats coalesced, one by one, from the wall of fog. Torches flamed at the bows, their smoke rising to wreath the masts.

The soldiers bore only weapons of wood to denote the nature of the melee to come. It was entertainment, not death, that the royal guest would watch.

And he would want something sweet after. . . .

Her heartbeat rose in time to the ever-escalating thud of the drums.

De Warre climbed up on a high platform to laud his king and offer an introduction to the festivities. With a sudden insight that turned her stomach, she realized de Warre stood on a platform whose use could only be for hanging.

As he spoke, the wind rose and flapped his empty sleeve. The heavy fog in the near dark and the emerging boats, crowded with men, stole her breath. It was like watching a real invasion.

She looked about for Durand's sons and saw them standing off to one side with other fostered boys. Their two brutish companions flanked them.

The boats seemed to come from a mystical place as they each slid ever closer. They touched the shore.

The English representatives leaped from their boats with all speed and clashed with the waiting "French."

Recognizing Durand, Penne, and Luke would be impossible. Instead she locked her gaze on the dark and light heads of his sons that she might see the very moment Durand took them.

It might be the last time she ever saw him.

She clasped her hands tightly to still their trembling.

The battle was all too real in appearance. Blood flowed as enthusiastic men plied their mock weapons. Several men fell and were summarily trampled.

The king and other men called encouragement while bets flew between the spectators on the pavilion. Surely they must know only King John's men would win?

John was, himself, upon his feet. He scratched and shouted, cheering when one of his men felled one of Philip's.

Behind him, Cristina saw Lady Sabina talking to a man garbed in the king's colors. There was something of the familiar in his stance and size, but his helm and mail also made him as anonymous as Durand and his friends.

Returning her gaze to Durand's sons, she almost cried aloud. For there was Durand—no other fought quite like him. She recognized the way he moved, the way he swept his sword across the blade of his opponent. Gold at his throat gleamed a moment in the torchlight. He engaged a swordsman of Philip's army.

Suddenly Adrian leaped to his feet and cried out something unintelligible.

Had he recognized his father? Cristina's heart raced. She rose. Durand would take his sons now—or never.

"What is it?" the man next to her asked. His grip on her arm told her he was as much a guard as were the brutes flanking Durand's sons.

"This mummery sickens me," she said, subsiding to her seat.

Adrian stood on tiptoe, his hand on Robert's arm, pointing into the melee. The warriors before him sparred back and forth, but Durand no longer made much effort. Cristina realized Durand fought Penne, who was garbed in French costume.

Where was Luke?

The drum pounded a mesmerizing beat. The melee shifted from one field to another. The figures moved within and without the swirls of haze.

Another party fought close to the boys. One moment they were spectators, and in the next, the center of the conflict.

Heart in her throat, she shot to her feet. Her guard gripped her wrist. Durand shoved his sons toward a man in English garb—Luke.

When the boys and Luke were lost in the fog, Durand turned and rushed for the pavilion. Just as he skirted the corner, Sabina turned and looked straight at him. So did her companion. He rested his foot upon the step. It was then that it burst upon Cristina. Here was one of the brigands. She recognized his spurs, enameled with blue. Her throat closed. She had seen other enameling just like it.

On Roger Godshall's blade.

With a stifled gasp, she stood up. Godshall shifted his attention toward her, his eyes dark holes in the shadows of his helm.

At that moment Sabina saw Durand. "Durand!" she cried, and pointed.

The king turned at the name and missed the spectacular firing of the mock castles. Across the battlefield flickered clumps of flame, as if someone had fired hayricks in a farmer's field.

The flames painted Durand in a red-gold glow as he mounted the pavilion steps, discovered and uncowed.

"Seize him," Godshall ordered the king's companions.

Two men reached for Durand, but he lifted the tip of his sword . . . not the mock ones of the battle, but the fine blade given him by Gilles d'Argent.

"Hold," the king ordered. He looked from Durand to Godshall, then to Sabina. "You make trouble wherever you go, Sabina."

"Sire?" The lady placed a hand to her heart.

But a rousing cheer in the melee turned the king's attention. "Take him," he ordered his guards. He swept out a hand in Durand's direction.

"Sire," Cristina said. "Please, this man—" She pointed to Godshall.

Godshall thrust himself between Cristina and the king. "Whores should know their place," he said with a sneer.

But John frowned and put up a staying hand. "You take too much upon you, Godshall. We would hear what Mistress le Gros has to say."

Cristina realized she was the favored woman of the moment and must seize it. She swayed in place, one hand at her throat. "I-I know this man."

"Aye. Roger Godshall. You saw him often enough at Ravenswood," the king said.

She wanted to seek the strength of Durand's embrace, but a favorite of the king did not show affection to other men.

"Nay, sire, I mean I know he's one of the brigands who slew the bishop's men."

"Lying whore," Sabina sneered.

Cristina stood straighter. "Sire. This man, wearing these spurs and wielding a dagger with the same blue enamel, fought Lord Durand and others against the bishop's party."

"Explain yourself," the king demanded of Godshall.

"She lies. As Sabina said, whores lie." Godshall spat on the floor.

The king's face flushed. Godshall had gone too far.

Durand dropped to one knee before the king. "Sire, the ax thrown to your champion was likewise enameled. I shall never forget it." He lifted his head, but his gaze and words were for Sabina. "Can you, sire, consider that if Godshall slew the bishop's men it could only be to obtain the Aelfric? And how could he know of it or know its value unless someone close—Sabina—told him?"

Sabina gasped. "W-w-why would I do such a thing?"

Durand answered her. "Your father's holdings suffer. You were told there would be no alliance with Ravenswood."

Cristina suddenly realized that if Sabina was involved in the theft of the Aelfric, the king's friendship with Sabina's father had protected her until now. Cristina's hopes sank.

Durand rose and took a step closer to Sabina. "And who met privately with Simon in my chapel? 'Twas not a lover's tryst I witnessed, was it? 'Twas you handing off my Aelfric. You and Simon sold it to the bishop, did you not? Where's the last of the bishop's rings? In Portsmouth harbor, lest it incriminate you? Or hidden somewhere to be turned to coin when all of this is forgotten?"

Sabina's face turned as pale as her ivory skirts. Her

head trembled on her neck. "What nonsense. Why risk all for a simple ring?"

Cristina spoke into the silence following her words. "Aye, the ring was too small a reward for all you risked. Did you send Godshall to take the book back from the bishop to sell to another greedy abbey?"

The king slashed the air with his hand, then clawed at the red marks on his neck. His voice was cold. "Sabina, your father may be an honored friend, but I can no longer protect you."

And Cristina realized why the king had destroyed Luke and Simon's lists. Sabina's name must have been on both.

Godshall shoved Cristina aside. "Sire, you cannot listen to them! She's a whore, and de Marle defied your orders!"

Durand turned to the king. "I ask for justice."

The king shrugged, then turned to his men. "Take them. We will judge this on the morrow."

Sabina stumbled away from the two men who reached for her. She turned and lithely leaped from the pavilion and ran.

Godshall made to follow, but Durand stepped in front of him.

Then Godshall cried out as if in pain. They all turned to look over the battlefield and saw what he had seen.

Sabina, in her flight, had dodged through the fighting men, but run too close to a burning castle. Her skirts flamed.

"Sabina!" Godshall struggled violently in his captors' arms.

Cristina watched in horror as Sabina turned and twisted, slapping her skirts. Men fought on around her.

Durand ran to the pavilion steps, but two more of the king's men blocked his way. They too wore very real swords, which they pointed at his chest.

"Sire, save her," Godshall begged with a violent twist, breaking from one man's hold.

"Let the witch burn," King John said. Cristina felt ill.

"Jesu," Durand swore.

Cristina whispered a prayer. Within but a moment, Sabina had floundered into the lake. She stumbled. Fell. Struggled to rise and fell again. This time she did not rise.

Godshall shrieked Sabina's name, then collapsed to his knees.

"It seems you are wrong, Lord Durand. Her soul must have been pure." John turned to where Godshall sagged between his guards. "It must have been you, then, who took the Aelfric from Lord Durand."

Godshall's head snapped up. He surged to his feet. "Nay. I demand you release me!" he cried.

"You demand!" the king shouted. "We demand! You obey!"

No one moved. Cristina's throat dried. She could not look at the still, silent lake.

Godshall moaned and tore away from his captors. He drew his dagger and charged the king.

Durand stepped before John, and as Godshall attacked was borne to the ground beneath him.

Cristina screamed. The king's men fell upon Godshall and snatched him away. She dropped on her knees beside Durand.

Godshall's blade was buried in his stomach.

Chapter Thirty

The king knelt at her side. He helped her pull off Durand's helm and coif as Durand struggled for air.

A young boy's reed-thin voice wailed his father's name. Penne and Luke escorted Adrian and Robert to their father's side. Robert burst into tears and fell on his knees at his father's side. Adrian, more aloof, but white-faced, stood off to one side.

"Cristina. My sons," Durand said in a gasp.

Cristina shoved both king and son aside. "Give him space. He needs air."

Durand licked his lips and put his hands to the blade handle protruding from his middle. " 'Tis the Aelfric." To a moan from his son, he jerked the blade out.

Cristina did not know whether to laugh or cry. She knew there was only one way to show Durand's worried sons that he would be fine. She helped Durand open his tunic and pull out the herbal. No blood stained the book or Durand's middle.

She handed the book to Robert. The deep cut in the wooden cover showed where Godshall's blade had embedded itself. Luke and Penne, along with the king, helped Durand to his feet.

"You'll have a bellyache for a few days," the king said. As Cristina watched, the king put off his concern and donned his royal demeanor. "Bring him here." He pointed to Godshall.

Torches smoked. Fog wreathed the shore and obscured the smoldering ruins of the mock ships and castles. There was no sign of Sabina.

"We have seen much this day, Godshall. You are accused in the attack upon Bishop Dominic's party. How say you?"

Godshall was a dead man. Cristina saw the man's knowledge of it on his face. He had tried to kill a king.

The man straightened his spine. "Aye. Sabina took the Aelfric for Simon le Gros. He told us he earned just two rings, one for her and one for him, the lying dog." He struggled in his guard's arms. "The fool told us the true value of the book, and she thought 'twould be worth taking back and selling again. Churches are fat." He slipped to his knees. "I had not the wealth to have her." He began to sob. "But I loved her."

"Then you must join her," the king said. With a quick jerk of the royal hand, Godshall was dragged away.

"Now, de Marle. Let us deal with your sins against us."

Penne and Luke ranged themselves at Durand's side. His sons moved closer, too, their faces pale in the dying flames.

"By rights, you should forfeit your life and the lives of your children."

Cristina put her hand in Durand's. He squeezed it.

"But we recognize the deed done this day in our service. We recognize, too, the injustice visited upon Mistress le Gros."

With that he swept back his mantle and scratched at the back of his neck. "Go free, Durand de Marle, and take with you whomever you please." With a nod, he included Luke, Penne, and the boys. "But go without title or land, and never enter England or France again. What say you?"

Durand went down on one knee. "I ask nothing, sire, but safe conduct for my family."

"Granted."

Edward de Warre rushed forward and made a deep bow. "Sire, I beg of you, do not allow this man to go. He'll foment trouble among your barons. You're too kind. Too easy."

The king turned to the crowd that had gathered. "Too easy?" he asked the people. "Is banishment easy?"

De Warre impaled Durand with a hard look. "He came in secret to remove his sons, whom we held as surety to his good favor. For that alone he deserves death."

"Aye," the king acknowledged with a nod, "but we recognize his bravery in saving his king's life. As we know he has loved and served us well, we send him hence with safe conduct."

Cristina trembled. She knew King John was not known for a generous gesture. She clung to Durand's hand for strength as de Warre protested anew.

"Sire," de Warre interrupted. "I fear—"

The king began to laugh. "What fear have we of this man? He has no influence, no power. He is lord of nothing. Lord of naught but the mist."

Durand's sons rode behind Luke and Penne. Cristina rode in the shelter of Durand's arms. When they reached the crossroads, Cristina could bear it no longer. "Stop, Durand."

He drew Marauder to a halt. The rest of the party also drew up. She shimmied from Durand's arms and dropped to the ground.

"I can go no farther." She smoothed her skirts down.

The horses ringed her. Adrian and Robert, who knew her not, watched her with avid curiosity. Durand threw his leg over the front of the saddle and dismounted.

"Let me guess," Durand said. "You feared in some way we might leave without Felice."

She burst into tears. "I cannot go without her."

Durand smiled. "And I never planned to do so." He held her tightly. "Trust me. We'll make a camp here for the night."

The men helped the women to dismount. They led the horses into the depths of the woods, keeping the little stream on their right. The light grew purple and green the deeper into the forest they walked. The fog muffled their steps.

They found a small hollow with a sheltering canopy of branches. It would serve for the night, but Oriel needed the warmth of an abbey house, at least. Durand thanked God he had a heavy purse to see her comfortable until they were far from John's reach and retribution should he renege on his generosity.

With great awkwardness, Durand introduced Cristina to his sons. They bowed to her, but Adrian watched her with wariness, and Robert with open confusion.

"Luke," Durand said, "you have no need to be a part of my punishment. Go back and offer your services to the king. Mayhap one day he will reward you with Ravenswood." He then turned to Nona. "You, too, have no need to suffer from this. John does not yet know you aided me. Return with me when I get Felice and make some excuse for your absence."

"I go with you," Luke said. "Ravenswood is naught but stone and wood—replaceable."

Penne lowered himself to the ground on a mantle he had spread out for Oriel. "Don't tell me to leave. I knew what I risked by aiding you. We're content to make a new start somewhere else, are we not, Oriel? And without William Marshall, John will never triumph over Philip."

Durand put his arm about Robert's shoulders. The boy leaned against him. "Are you sure, Penne? You'll soon have your own child to see to."

Oriel drew Penne's hand to her waist. "We're sure. I was so sure he would die in Normandy. Now—" She broke off and buried her face against Penne's neck.

"Then I want you to wait here. I'll be back in a few hours." He set his son aside with a quick ruffle of his hair. Then he walked to where Cristina stood alone. He kissed her fingers. In moments he had mounted up.

"Go with God," Cristina whispered as he disappeared into the shadows. She sat on a fallen log and watched the boys. They skirted around her, finally perching near Luke and Penne. The men and boys recounted the events of the mock battle, the shock of Godshall's attack on the king. Their words became a drone. Fear and fatigue put her to sleep.

The snort of a horse and the jangle of harness woke her. Leaping to her feet, she dashed blindly into the trees. It was him, a bundle in his arms. She grabbed Durand's reins.

"Are you looking for this baggage?" he asked, smiling down at her. He bent near to place Felice, wrapped in thick blankets, into her outstretched arms. She whirled away and sank to the ground on her knees.

Durand dismounted and knelt at her side. He

watched Cristina pull open her gown. He touched the backs of his fingers to her cheek. "I love you," he said.

Cristina pressed against his hand. "She will be mine, will she not? I mean, I could act as her mother. I could—"

"Hush," he said, laying a finger to her lips. "As my wife, you will be mother to my children. And she is mine."

She lay her head on his shoulder and he embraced them both.

When Felice was fed, Durand lifted his daughter into his arms. "I wondered if you could still feed her."

She put her arm about his waist. "I worried about it day and night, but I chewed parsley to keep my milk, so you see, everything has worked as it should. Was Rose much disturbed when you took her?"

Durand laughed. "Oh, Rose was more startled than concerned. Felice was shrieking her head off, and I merely lifted her up and she stopped instantly. I gave Rose a very courtly bow and left."

"Oh, my," Cristina said. "Rose will miss the extra pennies."

"By the expression on her husband's face, he'll not miss the noise."

Durand and Cristina entered the clearing. Nona was preparing a simple meal of bread and cheese from her saddlebags. Food might become a difficulty, Durand thought.

He sent his sons to fish in the little stream. When they were out of earshot, he called for his friends' attention.

"Luke knows what I am to say, but as I rode back to this place with Felice in my arms, I thought I must tell everyone of this child here, for she represents much to me—betrayal, love, lust, and even forgiveness.

"When the king and I visited Ravenswood last summer, Marion and I fought over her flirtations. We slept apart. And thus I am not Felice's father. Who it is has tortured me in many ways. Not the least of which is knowing I had failed my wife. Pride would not allow me rest. I had to know Felice's sire."

No one spoke. Only Nona's and Penne's faces registered surprise.

Durand lifted Felice and kissed her cheek. "But Cristina showed me that if not in blood, still this babe is mine to care for, and before you all, I claim her as mine, daughter in name, and now close to my heart."

He put out his hand to Cristina. "When we find a priest, I will wed the woman I love and give Felice a mother. Will you take my brother as your husband?" he asked Nona.

She bit her lip. "I don't know if I can wed the Lord of Skirts," she said softly.

Luke shot to his feet. "Lord of Skirts! I'm sick of that appellation. I'm guilty of naught more than coveting Lady Nona when I knew she was for Durand," he swore to the company. "I've done naught to be ashamed of, and when I wed—*if* I wed—I will be the most faithful of husbands!"

"What of your list of lovers?" Nona rose just as swiftly. "A list so long 'twas a source of great amusement—"

"That was Durand's doing." Luke swept a hand out to his brother. "He could not see Cristina suffer and sought to raise some doubt as to Simon's guilt that he might save *her*. If you listened well, you heard the king ask me who visited the counting room. I collect the Ravenswood rents, you know. I see every man, woman, and child of the manor in that room!"

Nona stared at him but a moment, then threw her arms about his neck with a soft cry of joy. She kissed Luke's cheek, and, along with a promise of eternal love, she also extracted a promise that he put off using Cristina's rank hair preparation no matter how bald he might become.

"Well, I'm sadly disillusioned," Penne said with a laugh. "How the famed lord has fallen. Now there will be no one left at Ravenswood to flatter the ladies and soothe their troubled spirits."

The words struck Cristina as if it were she who had taken Godshall's dagger to her middle and not Durand. She thought of how Simon's son, Hugh, had reminded her of Felice. She thought of how her husband had inquired so of Lady Marion as she lay dying. She remembered well how often Lady Marion had called Simon to the keep when first they had come to Ravenswood.

Cristina looked at Oriel, who dropped her gaze and bit her lip. "It was Simon, was it not, Oriel? He flattered Lady Marion and soothed her troubled spirits, did he not?" She found it did not hurt as she expected. Nor was it quite so great a surprise. "Come, admit it, Oriel; they are beyond our touch and want only our forgiveness."

Durand looked down at Felice. "You think—"

"I said nothing for Cristina's sake, Durand," Oriel said. "I thought 'twas just another of Marion's passing fancies that would disappear like the morning dew once you returned. Only you did not . . . and when she found herself with child . . ."

"Say no more," Durand said. "She knew well my anger." Cristina saw regret upon his face.

"I'm sorry, Durand, Cristina," Oriel said softly. "I think she might have loved Simon in her own way. And forgive me; I did little to discourage her, for I was already very jealous of her and thought she would turn her attentions to Penne." She put her head on her husband's shoulder.

Durand shook his head. "Forgiveness has never been one of my strengths, but this time I find it simple.

And I must put this behind me. I have sons to care for, and now a daughter." He held out his hand to Cristina. "You taught me many things, trust and forgiveness among them."

Several hours later, when his children were sleeping, Durand placed Felice in Oriel's arms. "Practice your mothering skills," he said.

He drew a mantle from his saddlebag and tossed it over his arm. He then took Cristina's hand and led her into the purple and black shadows of the woods.

They walked for what seemed over a league to her. When he stopped, it was in a tiny clearing. Moonlight washed the small glade bright as day. It gilded the gold on his mantle. When he swept out a hand in invitation, she went to him.

He stripped quickly and dropped to the mantle. Every fiber of his body went taut with anticipation as he watched her unlace her gown. With sudden modesty she turned away. Her gown fell to the ground. The soft linen underdress joined it.

She set her hair free to tumble down her back. When she turned, his breath caught, and it had naught to do with the injuries to his body. "I dreamed of this here, in this place," he whispered, offering his hand to her so that she might come and lie at his side. "It made me curse the dawn for sweeping the dream away."

She linked fingers with him. Going down on one knee, she touched her mouth to his pulse. There were no more words between them as she licked along his inner arm. His blood ran hot.

Ready, nearly shaking with want, he pulled her astride him. But he could not contain the need to conquer and possess. He rolled her beneath him, rising on his hands and staring down at her. And it was he who was conquered as she whispered his name. It was he who was possessed when she arched and met his every move, her fingers molding each muscle of his back and hips.

In a rush of sensation, at the height of her release, he gave himself to her.

The air cooled. She knew they must dress and return to the others.

He stroked Cristina's hair from her cheek. "I have neither castle nor finery to offer you. I have only myself and my children. Will you be my wife?"

"Oh, aye!" she whispered. She put her arms about his neck and kissed him hard. "I know I'll never want for anything in your care."

Breaking from his arms, she spun around the glade, twirling, her hair belling out from her shoulders.

She reveled in the freedom, the caress of the cool air, the sight of him, naked and painted with moonlight. She danced into his embrace. His arms were strong, his body warm against hers.

"It seems right and proper to love you here," he said.

"How so?" She looked up into his silver eyes.

"You are so much a creature of the forest."

He kissed her throat, her cheek, her lips, and she knew she needed him as surely as she wanted him. "And it seems right and proper to tell you I love you," she whispered, "in this, the place where first I saw you."

Epilogue

Wales
Winter 1205

Cristina stood on the top of a hill and looked over the untamed land Durand had claimed. Months before, their company had ridden into Wales, hungry and exhausted. A ruined keep, its ramparts lined with ravens, had emerged from the rising morning fog.

About its walls, about twenty peasants ignored the crumbling of their great house and lived their simple lives. Their baron, long dead without issue, had not risen from his grave to haunt their party when they had moved into his keep.

Nor had the peasants done aught but go about their chores. They had taken one look at Durand's torque and another at the birds on the ramparts and accepted him to a man.

Now, as she stood on the hill, she acknowledged

that all had not gone completely smoothly. Adrian missed the life and mother he so well remembered. But in balance Robert was fascinated by Felice and carried her everywhere. Luckily Robert also had a facility for languages that quickly allowed him to act as translator between his father and the peasants.

Nona grew fat and happy along with Oriel. The ancient priest from the nearby church had joined Nona and Luke on the same day he had joined Cristina to Durand.

Each day she thanked God for her new family. Each night she basked in the warmth of Durand's embrace.

Sheets of fog stretched in layers of white and gray over the valley floor. She must imagine the lush greens that were unlike any she had ever seen in her many travels. She would travel no more. Her heart was here.

A man emerged from the mist. He wore an unadorned tunic as green and dark and rich as the hills and forest surrounding them. And she knew that when the sun broke from the clouds, it would touch his hair with a thousand shades from black to red.

When he reached her, she put out her hands.

"I should have known I'd find you here." He lifted her basket and they walked together down the hill. "I'm off in an hour," Durand said, putting an arm around her waist. "With luck, the abbey over the mountain will give us a fair price for the Aelfric, despite the hole in it."

"And if they don't, there are other abbeys," she said. "We have each other, this place, and peace. We'll manage."

He kissed a smudge on her nose. "Never underestimate the power of peace. I'm taking Adrian and Robert with me."

The mists enclosed them as they drew closer to the old keep.

"With the promise of Nona's and Oriel's babes on the way, we have everything," she said. "And smell this." She plucked a wild rose from her basket. "It may be the last. 'Tis a gift of nature, and now, when I give it to you, 'tis a symbol of my love."

He took the flower and considered it. "You have given me so much. And I have naught to give you." Then he grinned and tucked the rose into his tunic. "Mayhap there is something I have."

He reached up and pulled the torque from around his throat. He settled it about hers and it lay there, warm from his skin, heavy in meaning.

"Durand . . . why?" She touched the torque with her fingers and looked up into his smiling gray eyes.

" 'Tis simple, Cristina. You rule my heart."

VIRTUAL WARRIOR

ANN LAWRENCE

Where does reality end and fantasy begin? With a computerized game that leads to another world? At the fingertips of a bedraggled old man who claims he can perform magic? Or in the amber gaze of an ice princess in dire need of rescuing? As the four moons of Tolemac rise upon a harsh land vastly different from his own, hard-headed pragmatist Neil Scott discovers a life worth struggling for, principles worth fighting for. But only one woman can convince him that love is worth dying for, that he must make the leap of faith to become a virtual warrior.

Virtual Desire

Ann Lawrence

His silver-blond hair blows back from his magnificent face. His black leather breeches hug every inch of his well-muscled thighs. He is every woman's fantasy; he is the virtual reality game hero Vad. And Gwen Marlowe finds him snoring away in her video game shop.

She knows he must be a wacky wargamer out to win the Tolemac warrior look-alike contest. But the passion he ignites in her is all too real. Swept into his world of ice fields and formidable fortresses, Gwen realizes Vad is not playing games. On a quest to clear his name and secure peace in his land, he and Gwen must forge a bond strong enough to straddle two worlds. A union built not on virtual desire, but on true love.

___52393-0 $6.99 US/$8.99 CAN

Dorchester Publishing Co., Inc.
P.O. Box 6640
Wayne, PA 19087-8640

Please add $2.50 for shipping and handling for the first book and $.75 for each book thereafter. NY, NYC, and PA residents, please add appropriate sales tax. No cash, stamps, or C.O.D.s. All orders shipped within 6 weeks via postal service book rate. Canadian orders require $2.00 extra postage and must be paid in U.S. dollars through a U.S. banking facility.

Name_____
Address_____
City_____State_____Zip_____
I have enclosed $_____ in payment for the checked book(s).
Payment <u>must</u> accompany all orders. ❑ Please send a free catalog.
CHECK OUT OUR WEBSITE! www.dorchesterpub.com

Lord of The Keep

Ann Lawrence

He has but to raise a brow and all accede to his wishes; Gilles d'Argent alone rules Hawkwatch Castle. The formidable baron considers love to be a jongleur's game—till he meets the beguiling Emma. With hair spun of gold and eyes filled with intelligence, she binds him to her. Her innocence stolen away in the blush of youth, Emma Aethelwin no longer believes in love. Reconciled to her life as a penniless weaver, she little expects to snare the attention of Gilles d'Argent. At first Emma denies the tenderness of the warrior's words and the passion he stirs within her. But as desire weaves a tangible web around them, the resulting pattern tells a tale of love, and she dares to dream that she can be the lady of his heart as he is the master of hers.

___52351-5 $5.99 US/$6.99 CAN

Dorchester Publishing Co., Inc.
P.O. Box 6640
Wayne, PA 19087-8640

Virtual Heaven
Ann Lawrence

The warrior looms over her. His leather jerkin, open to his waist, reveals a bounty of chest muscles and a corrugation of abdominals. Maggie O'Brien's gaze jumps from his belt buckle to his jewel-encrusted boot knife, avoiding the obvious indications of a man well-endowed. Too bad he is just a poster advertising a virtual reality game. Maggie has always thought such male perfection can exist only in fantasies like *Tolemac Wars*. But then the game takes on a life of its own, and she finds herself face-to-face with her perfect hero. Now it will be up to her to save his life when danger threatens, to gentle his warrior's heart, to forge a new reality they both can share.

___52307-8 $6.99 US/$8.99 CAN

Dorchester Publishing Co., Inc.
P.O. Box 6640
Wayne, PA 19087-8640

Please add $2.50 for shipping and handling for the first book and $.75 for each book thereafter. NY, NYC, and PA residents, please add appropriate sales tax. No cash, stamps, or C.O.D.s. All orders shipped within 6 weeks via postal service book rate. Canadian orders require $2.00 extra postage and must be paid in U.S. dollars through a U.S. banking facility.

Name_____
Address_____
City_____State_____Zip_____
I have enclosed $_____ in payment for the checked book(s).
Payment <u>must</u> accompany all orders. ❏ Please send a free catalog.
CHECK OUT OUR WEBSITE! www.dorchesterpub.com

THE HOLDING
CLAUDIA DAIN

It is done. She is his wife. Wife of a knight so silent and stealthy, they call him "The Fog." Everything Lady Cathryn of Greneforde owns—castle, lands and people—is now safe in his hands. But there is one barrier yet to be breached. . . . There is a secret at Greneforde Castle, a secret embodied in its seemingly obedient mistress and silent servants. Betrayal, William fears, awaits him on his wedding night. But he has vowed to take possession of the holding his king has granted him. To do so he must know his wife completely, take her in the most elemental and intimate holding of all.

__4858-2 $5.50 US/$6.50 CAN

They are pirates—lawless, merciless, hungry. Only one way offers hope of escaping death, and worse, at their hands. Their captain must claim her for his own, risk his command, his ship, his very life, to take her. And so she puts her soul into a seduction like no other—a virgin, playing the whore in a desperate bid for survival. As the blazing sun descends into the wide blue sea, she is alone, gazing into the eyes of the man who must lay his heart at her feet. . . .

Lair of the Wolf

Also includes the fourth installment of *Lair of the Wolf*, a serialized romance set in medieval Wales. Be sure to look for future chapters of this exciting story featured in Leisure books and written by the industry's top authors.

___4692-X $5.50 US/$6.50 CAN

the Black Knight
Connie Mason

He rides into Chirk Castle on his pure black destrier. Clad in black from his gleaming helm to the tips of his toes, he is all battle-honed muscle and rippling tendons. In his stark black armor he looks lethal and sinister, every bit as dangerous as his name implies. He is a man renowned for his courage and strength, for his prowess with women, for his ruthless skill in combat. But when he sees Raven of Chirk, with her long, chestnut tresses and womanly curves, he can barely contain his embroiled emotions. For it was her betrayal twelve years before that turned him from chivalrous youth to hardened knight. It is she who has made him vow to trust no woman—to take women only for his pleasure. But only she can unleash the passion in his body, the goodness in his soul, and the love in his heart.

___4622-9 $6.99 US/$8.99 CAN

The Pirate Prince

CONNIE MASON

She is a jewel among women, brighter than the moon and stars. Her lips are lush and pink, made for kissing . . . and more erotic purposes. She's a pirate's prize, yet he cannot so much as touch her.

Destined for the harem of a Turkish potentate, Willow wonders whether she should rejoice or despair when her ship is beset by a sinfully handsome pirate. She is a helpless pawn in a power play between two brothers. She certainly had no intention of becoming the sex slave of a sultan; and no matter how much he tempts her, she will teach her captor a thing or two before she gives her heart to . . . *The Pirate Prince.*